DARK
SIREN

E-Book ISBN: 978-0-6453899-2-0

Paperback ISBN: 978-0-6453899-3-7

Cover design by: Maria Spada

Formatting by: Cassandra B. Andreucci with Atticus

Published by: Drucci Publishing

TRIGGER WARNINGS

THIS BOOK CONTAINS THE FOLLOWING,
BUT IS NOT LIMITED TO:

EXPLICIT SEX SCENES
VIOLENCE, BLOOD & MURDER
DEPICTIONS OF DOMESTIC & CHILD ABUSE
ALLUSIONS TO CHILD SEXUAL ABUSE
DEPICTIONS OF A TOXIC RELATIONSHIP
HARASSMENT, BULLYING & BODY SHAMING (NOT BY THE
MAIN COUPLE)
DRUG USE
BLASPHEMY
KINK-RELATED ACTIVITIES, INCLUDING BUT NOT LIMITED TO
IMPACT PLAY, USE OF KNIVES & BONDAGE.

PLEASE READ THIS NOVEL WITH CAUTION

FOR ALL THE PEOPLE WHO THINK THEY NEED TO BE FIXED.

YOU NEVER DID.

— *C*

ONE

— Q —
♠

DEL

MY HANDS TREMBLE AS I try to apply mascara to my lashes. I can't cry, not now.

He's going to be so *pissed*.

I close my eyes and take deep breaths, calming my racing heart and frazzled brain. I need to get it together long enough to get through today, then I can sort everything out tomorrow.

When I open my eyes, my focus is on finishing my make-up and changing into the dress Mum picked out for church. At least it has long sleeves and a high neckline, so it'll hide the bruises.

I pull the slimming black slip on before stepping into the dark purple dress. The zip on the back gets caught at my waist and refuses to budge.

"Fuck."

"Mind your language, Delphine."

My heart stutters, panic flooding my system. "S-sorry, sir."

I drop my hands from my dress and clasp them together in front of me. He usually gets his belt out for foul language. As long as I don't cry and ruin my make-up, we won't be late, and he won't have to punish me again.

His big hands slide up the sides of my hips, and up to the zipper stuck at my waist. He finishes zipping the dress, his hand trailing across my shoulder and down my arm. He grips my elbow surprisingly softly and turns me to face him.

I don't dare to lift my gaze—one beating is enough for today. His finger tilts my head up, forcing me to look at him, but his eyes linger on my neck.

"Where is your rosary?"

Double *fuck*. "On the counter behind me. I didn't want to get it wet in the shower."

My reasoning pleases him, especially since he was the one that punished me last time I got it wet. He steps forward, plastering his body to mine and pushing me into the counter behind me as I hear the soft clatter of the wooden beads being picked up.

He doesn't step back as he places the beads over my head, pulling my thick, waist-length black hair out from under the necklace and letting it fall down my back.

His fingers trace the beads on my exposed flesh.

"You're so beautiful, Kitty," he says reverently.

"Thank you, sir," I barely whisper, keeping my eyes lowered and giving him a small smile, fighting to keep down the bile rising in my throat at his touch.

"So beautiful, but such a disappointment."

My eyes flick to his, terror slicing up my insides. He knows. He fucking *knows*. How the fuck does he already know?

His lingering touch tightens around my neck.

I sit up, sweat drenched and choking, my hands frantically trying to pull phantom hands off my neck. Nothing but smooth skin.

I try to slow my shuddering breaths—a nightmare, just another nightmare. Those stupid memories like to taunt me at this time of year, like fucking clockwork.

Once I have my breathing under control and my heart isn't trying to break my ribs, I feel around in the darkness for my phone, squinting at the screen. Four in the morning.

Groaning, I pull myself out of bed and to the bathroom—there's no point in going back to bed now. I take longer than necessary in the scorching-hot shower, washing away the echoes of this particular nightmare, then exit the steam haven and rummage through my wardrobe for a clean uniform.

I pull on the grey tartan skirt, white shirt, grey tie, the dark crimson wool pullover and knee high white sock before heading downstairs.

One of the chefs is already in the kitchen dicing up vegetables. He greets me with a polite smile as I step around him to the carafe of freshly brewed espresso next to the stove. If coffee is already made, then—

"You're up early," Dr. Sakura says as he enters the kitchen with a mug in hand, from the direction of the library.

"Couldn't sleep," I mumble as I finish filling my own mug and then turning to refill his.

His hooded brown eyes are warm with knowing as he nods.

"Did you have a call out?" I ask, adding sugar and milk into my coffee, and preparing another cup.

"Emergency surgery, I just got back."

Shuffling footsteps echo in the foyer, drawing both our attention as Claudine, Dr. Sakura's wife enters the kitchen.

"You're back," she says to her husband with a soft smile. She crosses over to him and plants a soft kiss on his lips before turning to me. "And you're already up. Nightmares again?"

I nod, keeping my attention on the coffee I'm making.

"Maybe we should set up an appointment with the psychiatrist, again?" she asks, stepping closer to me.

"Yeah. I'll call them today." I murmur as I add a *lot* of sugar to the cup and slip out of the kitchen with both mugs in hand before Claudine tries to coax me into talking about it. I climb the stairs to the second floor and head to Scarlett's room.

Her bathroom light emits a soft warm glow from the slightly open door as I slip into the larger room and pick my way through the discarded clothes on the floor to the bedside table. Scarlett is in her usual position, curled up in the centre of the large bed cocooned under two thick blankets, completely oblivious to me putting the mugs down and climbing into the bed next to her.

I grip her shoulder softly and shake her. "Wake up, Scar."

All I get is nonsensical grumbles before she settles back into her blankets. I pull my phone out, connect to Scar's sound system, and blast some grunge music. Scar jolts up in bed and whacks me in the arm.

"Turn it off," she whines, trying to wrestle the phone out of my hand.

I chuckle, easily rolling away from her clumsy attempt. "Get your ass in the shower; we're getting breakfast before school."

I pull the blanket completely off her bed as I escape her room with my mug of coffee. If I wasn't Scar's best friend, she would have clawed my eyes out by now—she's *not* a morning person.

I return to my room to dry my damp hair, tie it into a low bun, and put on my shoes and blazer, then grab my bag and head for the foyer. It doesn't take long for Scar to tear down the stairs in a huff.

"It's six-thirty," she complains as she ties her honey blonde hair into a long ponytail. "Why are we leaving goddamn early?"

"You can nap in the car."

We climb into the sports car Claudine lets me borrow, and Scar blasts one of her more energetic music playlists as we leave the Sakura property, opening her window despite the chilled May weather.

No matter how cold it gets, as long as it's not raining, we always have the car windows down so 'the rest of Melbourne can listen to quality music', as Scarlett likes to say. It also helps with her claustrophobia.

We go to our favourite breakfast spot, ordering our usual breakfasts—cream cheese topped bagels, extra crispy bacon and fresh carrot, apple and mint juices—and sit in the back of the eclectic cafe next to their fireplace. I pull out a textbook and finish off some homework as Scar puts make-up on since I dragged her out of the house before she had the chance.

Scar once told me that make-up made her feel more protected in a world she never felt safe in, even though I wish she didn't cover the beautiful smattering of freckles across her face.

"What did you end up getting Raph for his birthday?" Scar asks as our food arrives at our table.

"It's so hard to shop for a man who has everything."

Scar smirks. "You know you could just—"

"If you say a lap dance, I will hurt you."

Her big brown doe eyes glitter with mischief. "I was going to say you can just fuck him."

"*Scarlett*," I chastise.

She arches a manicured brow. "You know you want to."

"He's my boss."

She picks up her juice. "He's insanely hot. *And* he's into you."

I sigh, snatching up my own drink. "I'm not fucking my boss. Plus, he's like ten years older than me."

"Just call him '*Daddy*' while you ride him."

"Jesus Christ, woman," I laugh, as we clink glasses and dig into our food.

I didn't call the psych like I said I would. I tried to twice, but I don't need to traumatise her again with my history, despite that being her job. It's just this time of year, I'll be fine in a month, just like the last two years.

The lack of sleep catches up to me in my last class as I doze off in chemistry, *again*. A sharp jabbing pain lances through my ribs as I jolt awake.

I clear my throat, my heart thundering as I shuffle around my books, my ears picking up the slight hum of Mrs. Thornton's voice as she goes over the formula of some chemical.

Why the fuck did I torture myself with chemistry during my last year of high school? Scar nudges her notebook closer to me so I can see her notes, and I scribble them into my book.

I just need to finish the school year brain, please and thank you.

The shrill noise of the bell startles me, and chaos ensues. Scar and I gather our things and slip past Mrs. T before she pulls me up for sleeping in her class. As we leave the science building, we slow our pace towards the lockers. I inhale the cool air as we weave in and out of the students rushing to leave campus.

"Are you even listening to me?" Scarlett asks.

"Definitely not," I sigh, resulting in a smack on the arm.

"I said, how are we getting to Silvia's party tomorrow night?"

I cringe as I get to my locker. "Do not tell me you said yes."

"I may have," Scarlett mumbles.

I groan. "Fucking hell, Scar."

Silvia has had it in for me since I was the new kid two years ago. Some say it's because Scar ditched her for me. Some say it's because Silvia was just born to be a nuisance.

"It'll be fine," Scar reassures me as she shoves things into her bag and closes her locker. "Half of Melbourne is going to this party. She will have enough distraction to keep her off your back."

I shut my locker and hoist my bag onto my shoulder. "I'm not going, Scar."

"Fine. I'll go on my own, but don't blame me when I end up all over Flynn again, telling him about the—"

"Jesus Christ, *fine*." She might be my best friend, but the bitch loves to blackmail me into doing dumbass shit. "If I start a brawl, it's your fault."

She loops her arm in mine, leading us to the carpark. "Luckily, my mum loves you, and she's a beast of a lawyer."

We get to the car, shooing off boys ogling the sports car as we slide into the car and I start the engine.

"We also need to talk about your birthday," Scar says as she selects a rock playlist.

I turn to her with a sigh. "That's six months away, and it's my nineteenth, so we're doing nothing."

"Come on," Scarlett whines, turning her pout full force on me, "we didn't do anything last year. And I'll be eighteen so we can go out."

"I don't want to make a big fuss about it." We've been having this same argument since my birthday last year.

She folds her arms over her chest. "Listen, you might be older, but I am the wiser one of the two of us, and I say it'll benefit our personal development that we celebrate you."

I roll my eyes, pulling out my sunglasses from the centre console. "Just because you're able to punch a teacher in the face and get away with it doesn't make you the wiser one."

"I would never. I'm an angel."

"Yeah, yeah, *Angel Face*," I mutter as I put both our windows down and pull out of the car park. "The answer is still no."

"You can't say no to me, Del," Scar declares before cranking up the music.

We get a lot of stares as I pull out of the lot onto the bustling city streets, singing along to the heavy bass pop music.

Scarlett turns the music down as we hit the tree-lined streets of the suburbs. "What time is dinner at Raph's tonight?"

"Luisa said six-thirty." I turn into Scarlett's street, slowing over the speed bumps. Raph's mum Luisa and Claudine have been friends since high school, and over the years of going to a couple of Luisa's gatherings, we know not to be late.

"I guess a nap is out of the question," Scar grumbles.

I chuckle as we pull into Scar's driveway, waiting for the front gates to open. This entire property takes my breath away every time I see it. Nestled in one of the most expensive neighbourhoods, the Sakura mansion just *oozes* money.

A gravelled, winding driveway leads to the grand two-story white mansion with huge arched windows that look out over the vibrant green lawns and perfectly manicured landscape.

The Sakuras have enough money to last them many lifetimes.

I park the car next to the three other expensive cars in front of the house and follow Scarlett inside, heading straight to the kitchen.

"Hi, girls," Claudine calls from the foyer, her heels clicking on the marble floors, most likely coming from her office.

Despite being in her mid-fifties, Claudine doesn't look a day over forty. Her warm ochre skin glows as she floats in, her sharp suit fitted perfectly to her plump body. Fierce, deep brown eyes soften when she spots us—I've seen those beautiful eyes intimidate the worst of the worst. Her rich, dark brown braids are down for a change, instead of her usual massive, twisted bun on the top of her head.

"Hey, Mum," Scar greets as they exchange kisses on the cheek.

"How was your day?" I ask Claudine as I grab out a plate of pre-cut fruit.

"Busy as usual," she sighs as she turns on the kettle before turning back to us. "Did you call the psychiatrist's office?"

I give her the most convincing smile I can muster. "Yeah."

Luckily, she's too distracted to see through my lies as she checks her watch. "Dinner is at six-thirty, and we can't—"

"Be late," Scar and I say in unison.

TWO

DEL

AFTER CLEARING THE FRUIT plate with Scar, and being shooed off by Claudine, I'm standing in front of my wardrobe contemplating what to wear.

It's only a birthday dinner for Raph at his parent's place; it's not like all of high society will be attending. Unexpected nerves flutter in my gut—I've been working for Raph three or four days a week for almost two years in his restaurant. Why am I suddenly concerned about what I wear?

He's into you.

Fucking Scarlett.

I shove those ridiculous feelings away and decide on dark wash blue jeans and a band t-shirt, paired with a thick, grey cardigan. I pull my black and cobalt blue hair out of its bun and curl it with my straightener.

The shoulder length hair is much easier to manage than the long, thick tresses I used to have. I finish styling quickly, and then apply a light dusting of powder over my face, a sweep of mascara to my lashes and gloss to my lips before shoving my feet into combat boots, grabbing my phone and heading to Scar's room.

Even dressed down, Scar looks exceptional. She's paired a loose periwinkle knit jumper with black skinny jeans and heeled ankle boots.

She catches my eye in the mirror as she powders her face. "You put make-up on."

"So have you, Angel Face."

"You never put make-up on unless you're at work, *or*—"

"Get your mind out of the gutter."

She scoffs, returning to powdering her face. "Never."

Scar grabs her phone, and we meet her parents in the foyer.

"You two look beautiful," Claudine comments, the question in her tone.

I pinch Scar's arm before she says something, resulting in her laughing and batting at my hand, further piquing Claudine's suspicion.

Thankfully, Claudine says nothing as we all walk out of the house and climb into Dr. Sakura's flashy sedan. The drive to Raph's parents' place is a short trip, since they live in the same neighbourhood. Luisa and Mario, Raph's dad, are in the open doorway as we park next to a row of expensive cars in their driveway.

"*Ciao a tutti,*" Luisa calls. She approaches Claudine with her arms out, pulling her into a tight hug, then repeating the hug with Scar and Dr. Sakura.

I suck in a breath as she pulls me into a hug, fighting the urge to step away too soon. I plaster a polite smile on my face as she pulls away, my skin crawling at the contact, and breathe again when she releases me and ushers us to the front door.

Mario's grey-hazel eyes shine as he kisses both cheeks of everyone until he gets to me, and grasps my hands. "*Ciao bella.*"

"Hey, Chef."

He leads us into their stunning modern home, down a wide hallway and into a huge open plan living, dining and kitchen area.

Raph stands by sliding glass doors on his phone—his grey suit fits his tall, muscular body to perfection, and his chestnut brown hair is artfully tousled. He looks good, as he usually does.

"Raphael, put the phone down, *per favore*," Luisa scolds as she picks up a bottle of red wine from the kitchen bench.

Raph looks up, his grey-hazel eyes locking onto me immediately and his beautiful, warm smile beaming. *He's into you.* Fucking *Scar.*

"Everyone sit," Mario says, motioning to their huge round table set up for only seven people.

"Sophia isn't coming?" Scar asks, her tone innocent, but her meddling clear as day to me.

Raph's eyes darken slightly, but his smile never fades. "Not tonight, no."

"Hmm, that's too bad," Scar comments, the glint in her eyes devious.

Scar passes my gift bag to Claudine, pulls me to a seat at the table, and then grabs Raph's arm and pulls him to the seat next to mine.

"Mario said sit," she commands, with a brow raised.

"She's meddling again, I see," Raph murmurs as he pulls out my chair.

I glare at her as I sit down. "She doesn't know how to stay out of other people's business."

I pull out my phone and stab out a message to Scar, who's beaming on the other side of Raph.

> I hate you right now.

SCAR

> No, you don't. I expect a heartfelt speech at your wedding.

I roll my eyes and put my phone away as Mario takes the seat to my left, and Dr. Sakura takes the one next to Scar. Luisa and Claudine carry over bowls of food as they fill the other two chairs next to their husbands.

Conversation flows across the table as we all dig into Mario's home-made wine and Luisa's exceptional cooking. Luisa and Claudine have been friends since high school, so the Sakuras and the Dragones have always been close.

The Dragones were so welcoming from the moment I first met them a couple years ago, when I began living with the Sakuras. Mario insisted I work in his restaurant, *Seduzione*, and Raph was always so patient with my initial cluelessness even though their restaurant is one of the most exclusive in the city.

"Have you found a new head waiter yet?" Claudine asks.

Raph clears his throat, angling toward me. "I was hoping Del might take on the role."

I feel every set of eyes on me. I put down my cutlery and snatch up my sparkling water. "Stella has been there for five years. She's more qualified."

"I asked, and she proceeded to tell me she's pregnant again, and intends to leave just before she gives birth," Raph counters.

My head whips up to him at the surprising news. His smile is soft, *hopeful*. I force out a breath, I'm not succumbing to his perfect face.

"Florentina, then."

"Notoriously unreliable."

"Then give it to Queenie."

Raph's smile deepens. "You know she doesn't want it."

"Sophia?"

He smirks. "Absolutely not."

God damn it. I sigh. "*Fine.*"

"*Brava!*" Mario bellows, holding his wine out for a cheers and the whole table clink their drinks together.

"Speaking of Sophia," Claudine comments, "where is she tonight?"

"Prior engagements," Raph says before taking a sip of his wine.

"On your birthday?" Claudine pushes.

"I told him she was no good," Luisa huffs. "Why don't you date someone like Del?"

I forcibly swallow my mouthful of water.

"Ma..." Raph sighs.

"What? She's a good girl. And so beautiful. Unlike—"

"Luisa," Mario chides. "*Lascia stare.*"

She clicks her tongue, waving him off. "Fine, fine."

She thankfully drops the subject and launches into another conversation about charities with Claudine. I excuse myself from the table for the bathroom, but instead, slip out the front door.

I walk around to the side of the house and through to Mario's impressive vegetable garden. I stop in front of the large section of herbs, enjoying the earthy scents around me and the chilled soft breeze. I wasn't expecting tonight to include a promotion or Luisa and Scar trying to play matchmaker. My hand drifts up to my neck, searching for the beads I used to never take off, finding nothing but smooth skin.

"You know my dad will murder you if you touch his herbs."

I smile. "Chef would never. He likes me more than you."

Raph laughs stepping up next to me. "That is very true."

"Luisa apparently likes me as well," I comment.

He winces. "I'm sorry about that."

"It's fine. At least she's not sneaky like Scar is trying to be."

"I don't know which method of manipulation I prefer."

"Neither would be great," I mutter, turning back to the herb patch.

"Very true," Raph concludes.

We're both silent for a few moments, enjoying the quiet. "So, where is Sophia tonight?"

Raph sighs, looking up at the sky. "Out with her friends, some sort of event she couldn't miss."

"You really should stop dating aspiring models," I comment.

"You're probably right."

"Del?" I hear Scar call from the entrance of the garden.

I turn to find her skipping down the row toward us. "Am I interrupting something?"

"Just admiring Mario's affinity for herbs."

"Sure," she drawls, eyeing Raph, and then hooking her arm in mine. "Dad has a call out so we have to go."

"See you tomorrow at work?" Raph asks.

"Nope," Scar answers, "we're going to a party."

Raph's about to say something, but his phone starts to ring. He pulls it out of his inner jacket and frowns at the screen. "Have fun at your party."

He answers the phone as Scar pulls me out of the garden and towards the car.

"So?" she asks. "Are we picking baby names?"

"Shut up," I laugh, opening the car door.

THREE

DEL

I PULL DOWN THE hem of this skirt for the umpteenth time as I look in the full-length mirror.

Most women on the heavier side like me wouldn't wear something like this, but they don't have a friend like Scar.

"Can you stop fussing, Del? You look amazing," Scar grumbles over the music.

She insisted I wear this fitted plaid skirt, which my mother would curse me for with the amount of thigh showing.

I must admit, it's super cute paired with sheer black stockings, a black band t-shirt and black combat boots. Scarlett twists the end of the t-shirt, knotting it at my waist.

"Yeah, no," I say, immediately undoing the knot, smoothing the t-shirt down so it hangs to the top of my hips. "I'll wear this skirt, but the t-shirt stays loose."

"You're no fun," Scarlett huffs.

She pulls her long, honey-blonde hair into a high ponytail and admires her tight, lilac mini dress in the mirror. Her perfect ivory skin shimmers from her body oil and her legs look killer in the gold heels—those will end up off and in her hands by the end of tonight, for sure.

"Why am I going to this party again?" I ask as I pull half of my hair into a high ponytail, fluffing out my natural waves.

"Because I want to go, and you go where I go."

"You're a pain in my ass, Angel Face." I apply another coat of mascara on my lashes, the dark shadow that Scar applied accentuating my green eyes.

"You love me," Scar says as she shoos me away from the mirror, fussing with the gold glitter around her brown eyes, and applying more gloss to her plump lips.

Scar crosses to her wardrobe and pulls out a bottle of tequila. "Shots!"

I groan. "You're bad for my liver."

"It's cute that you think you have a choice."

I roll my eyes as she takes a mouthful of tequila without so much as a flinch. After a couple of force-fed mouthfuls, bickering over jewellery and both of us pulling on jackets, we order a car service and take the short ride to Silvia's mansion.

The place has turned into a raver's dream—spinning, colourful lights, a smoke machine, and people everywhere.

Scar and I find the bar immediately, and both of us are drunk enough now that we're dancing in the sea of people like nobody's watching, even though I'm pretty sure there are *many* people watching.

My brain is swirling, but I feel lighter, like the demons that torture me daily have been chased off by vibrant, radiant lights and copious amounts of alcohol.

Over the thumping of the music, I hear my name being called, and suddenly a pair of slim arms clutch me from behind.

"Del, you came," Silvia shouts, as I pry her arms off me and turn toward her. "How are you, babe?"

Babe? What is this chick playing at? I give her a practiced smile. "I'm good. Great party."

"I'm so glad you're having a good time," she beams, her blue eyes shining with something akin to sincerity. Silvia seems genuine, but she's always scheming.

"Del!" Scar shouts from across the room, waving me over.

I look at Silvia and her two friends. "See you around."

"No," Silvia whines, wrapping her arms around one of mine, "let's hang out. I feel like we never see each other."

That's because I avoid her as much as I can. I force a smile and pull her along with me, making my way towards Scar, who's wrapped around Flynn, her ex, in the doorway of a darkened room.

"Scarlett Sakura," I hiss, shaking Silvia off me and pulling Scar away from Flynn.

"Hey." Flynn stands straighter, looking down at me.

"You don't want to fuck with me tonight, puppy."

Flynn snorts, looking at his buddies surrounding us. "Just because you're a big bitch doesn't make you scary."

"Your insults are old, pup," I call over my shoulder as I pull a giggling Scar down the hall.

"You didn't have to rescue me from puppy dog Flynn," she drawls, flinging an arm around my waist.

"Looked like you were about to fuck him in front of everyone." I test a door handle on my left, and thankfully, it's a bathroom. I push her into the room and lock the door behind us.

"I had everything under control," she slurs as she hikes up her dress with no shame and tugs her panties down, then sits down on the toilet.

"Oh, yeah, as he was trying to shove his tongue down your throat."

Scar scoffs, finishing her business and fixing her clothing. "I was trying to steal his stash, and I was close, too."

"For someone with the nickname Angel Face," I say, watching her wash her hands, "you sure know how to break every cardinal sin."

Scar rolls her eyes. "Please don't start with the religious shit."

Soft tapping on the door draws my attention. "Scar, Del, are you in there?"

I roll my eyes and pull the door open to her sugary sweet smile and fight a wince; she's so fucking fake that it hurts my face to return a smile.

"Everything okay?" she asks, looking between me and Scar.

"Peachy," I grit out.

Scar wraps an arm through Silvia's, both talking about shoes as we get back to the darkened room. Inside, we find some of our classmates playing a card game.

"It's 'Strip or Drink,'" the one shirtless guy calls over to us. "You three want to join?"

Silvia and Scarlett look back at me expectantly. I sigh. "Deal us in."

The girls, currently at the table just in their underwear, take the advantage and stumble out of the room in a fit of giggles as a few more guys join in. The original shirtless guy explains that we're playing Texas Hold'em, and we can either give up an item of clothing or drink if we lose.

The first few rounds, all the losers decide to drink, myself included, but as the group gets more intoxicated, the clothes come off. It starts with Silvia's shoes, followed by Scarlett's heels, and then the shirt of one guy. A few more rounds, I have kept my clothes, except for my shoes and jacket, but everyone else is at least shirtless, if not without pants as well. I finally lose a round, and I can't stomach any more shots of tequila.

"Top or bottom?" I slur.

Silvia rests a small hand on my forearm. "Oh, sweetie, you don't have to."

"What?"

"You don't have to take anything off. We understand."

I frown. "Understand what exactly?"

"That someone your size would—"

"Do you have to be a bitch all the fucking time?" I ask.

"I'm just trying to make you comfortable, babe. You don't have to be so sensitive," Silvia accuses. "I was just trying to save you from the humiliation of all these people laughing at you."

Before I throw this twig of a girl across the table, I stand, collecting my boots and back away from the table. Scar tries to collect her things to follow as I storm out.

"Del, wait," I hear her shout over the music, but I keep charging through the sea of bodies toward the front door. A small hand grips my arm as I'm about to leave; I swing around, ready to slap the person, but it's Scarlett.

"Where are you going?" she asks.

"Anywhere but here."

"Del, please." She bats those big brown eyes at me, which I normally give in to.

"Unless you want me to get arrested, I'm taking my ass out of here." I fish my phone out of the pocket of my jacket that she's holding and tuck it into my bra. "I'll call you when our ride gets here."

I make it out of the house and suck in the crisp autumn air, feeling a little less angry. One day Silvia's going to regret the things she says, and I hope I don't end up in jail. I fish out my phone as I walk down the driveway, swaying slightly on my feet—I'm a little more buzzed than I'd like to be right now.

Scarlett and I promised Claudine we'd come home together, and since there's no fucking chance I'm going back into the party, I don't want to go far. The only place nearby I know that's open is the church.

Oh well, might as well go confess my sins.

FOUR

Q
♠

DEL

AFTER WALKING A FEW blocks, my adrenaline has worn off and I'm now shivering from the cold—I should have taken my damn jacket. I stumble up the stairs of St. John's Church and push the heavy doors open into the warm sanctuary.

Lifting a hand I can barely feel, I cross myself with holy water and slide into one of the back pews. The small, warm lights on the elaborate chandeliers that line the centre aisle swirl slightly as I admire the cathedral's architecture and detailed artwork on the ceiling.

The church was a welcoming, safe place to me when my grandmother took me every Sunday as a child—a place to 'feel God's eternal love', she would say.

Maybe I did for a time, but that was until—

I try to shake myself out of thinking about *that*. Soft murmurs draw my attention as I see three elderly women sitting together in the middle pews with their eyes closed and rosary beads clutched in their hands as they pray. Memories of doing the same on bruised knees and tear-stained cheeks flood my head. *His* face, that cruel face, flashes in my mind. I can almost feel his hot breath on my neck.

My stomach churns, my throat burning. I need to get out of here before I throw up tequila all over the marble floors. I stumble out of the pew and turn, slamming into a huge, hard body.

"Careful, sweetheart," a deep, rumbling voice whispers.

A heady scent hits my senses full force—It's spicy but with a hint of sweet citrus and musk. I'm looking at a broad chest dressed in a white shirt, black tie and black suit jacket. I tilt my head up, meeting cerulean blue eyes.

Holy hell.

I'm paralysed by the clarity of the colour; I've never seen such a pure blue. They're beautiful. A sharp, wicked mouth distracts me from those vortex eyes as they curve into a panty-soaking half smile.

Fuck, this man is almost too attractive, with his strong jaw covered in a few days' growth and high cheeks highlighting those striking, almond-shaped eyes.

I register that his thick arms are locked firm around my waist, and his warm, hard body is flush against mine. I clear my throat, stepping out of this stranger's arms.

Christ, he's intimidatingly tall, and has this aura around him that screams danger.

He's fucking temptation in the flesh.

Why is he in a church in the middle of the night?

My eyes roam over his black hair, swept back in a neat style, a few greys peppering the short sides. And that neck—thick corded muscles, and smooth bronze skin. My teeth ache at the thought of marking that neck.

I feel the flush blaze over my face as I try to get the image of this stranger bending me over a pew and fucking me senseless out of my head. I shouldn't want to desecrate this holy place, but...

"Are you okay?" he asks, his eyes burning into mine. This delicious specimen has rendered me speechless. He smiles again and I clench my thighs together. "You look like you were trying to get out of here pretty fast."

"I'm perfectly fine."

He steps forward, closing the space between us. "Liar."

I narrow my eyes. "What gives you the right to call me a liar? You don't know me."

His long fingers trace my jaw, down my throat, falling away at my collarbone. My skin tingles at the contact.

Why am I letting a stranger touch me? Where are my survival instincts? This man could be a murderer.

I try to take a step back, but my hip hits the edge of the pew. Before I can fall, the mystery man wraps an arm around me again, pressing my body into his.

His eyes flash as I slip my hand between us, running my hand up his thigh to his crotch resting against my stomach, brushing against—

"Are you hard in a church right now?"

He smiles, pressing himself further into my hand. "I wasn't expecting to find sin in the flesh when I walked in, but here you are."

"I didn't think the Devil could enter a holy place."

He chuckles. "I like the pain, sweetheart."

How am I so ridiculously wet right now, and he hasn't even touched me anywhere other than my waist? Why am I touching his cock? I clear my throat, remove my hand, and try to step away from the wicked temptation wrapped around me, but he locks his arms.

"What's your name?" he asks.

"What's *yours*?"

"Enzo," he announces.

"Del."

He arches a thick, manicured black brow.

"Delphine," I admit.

"*Delphine*," he breathes like he's tasting my name on his tongue.

My stomach clenches. My name sounds good from those lips; I'm sure they taste even better.

I place my hands on his broad chest and push back, Enzo finally lets me go. I start down the centre aisle slowly, never giving him my back, needing the distance.

"Why are you here?" I ask, curiosity getting the better of me. I need to leave before I do something really stupid like lick this man's throat.

"Why are *you*?" he counters, following my retreat leisurely, like he knows I won't escape. Am I trying to?

"Can't a pious woman worship in the early hours of the morning?" I ask, making it to the front of the church and veering toward the alcove on the side of the church. I know there's an exit there.

"*Pious?* In that outfit? I doubt your Lord would approve." He continues to follow me, almost like a predator playing with his food.

"Is there a reason you're following me?" I ask.

"Is there a reason you're running?"

"Ever heard of stranger danger?"

He chuckles, the sound dripping in heat. "Do you touch every person inappropriately when you meet them?"

I halt in my escape. "You had your hands all over me first."

Enzo takes a step closer, his eyes dancing with challenge. "Did I?"

Why am I even talking to this man? I blow out a breath and turn on my heel, entering the alcove and coming face-to-face with a statue of a saint and an explosion of candles. Shit, there's supposed to be an exit here.

Heavy footsteps echo in the dark space, and the hairs on the back of my neck stand to attention as a large body looms behind me.

"If you're looking for the side door, you're on the wrong side of the church, sweetheart," Enzo murmurs softly, close to my ear.

Warnings ring through my head—this man is *dangerous.* I need to leave. But...

"I have to go, before I do something I shouldn't," I whisper, looking up at the statue in front of me.

"What sins are troubling you?" Enzo asks, his fingers trailing down my spine. I lean into his touch like a damn fool.

"You," I croak.

"Me?"

"Yeah," I breathe, "you're a temptation I don't need."

"Mm," he rumbles, his hand sliding down to my hip, and slipping under my t-shirt. His hand is warm on my skin. "Are you sure?"

"Damn sure," I grind out, jerking forward, trying to get away from his scorching touch.

Instead of letting me go, Enzo spins me to face him, his eyes blazing as he tilts his lips closer to mine. "Such blasphemous words from a *pious* woman."

Why am I not running for my fucking life? Or screaming for help from the old ladies? My eyes flick over to where they were sitting, but they're gone.

"Only me and you now." His voice is hypnotic. Low, rumbling, almost soothing. This man is *consuming*.

"Let me go." Even to my ears, my voice has no conviction at all.

Enzo's hand moves from my waist to my ass, grabbing it possessively and pulling me flush against him. "Ask me again, and I will."

Do I actually want him to let go? Maybe. But...

My eyes flick to his mouth, then back to his cerulean depths.

"Fuck it," I hiss, my body trembling as I press my mouth to his.

His tongue darts out across the seam of my lips, demanding entrance. I oblige and his tongue claims its prize, stroking and dancing with mine. My hands trail down his chest to his belt, and I hook my fingers into his waistband. Enzo growls, trapping my bottom lip with his teeth.

I try to tug it free, but he bites down harder. Oh, so we're playing this game. I pull his waist towards me sharply; it unbalances him, and he releases my lip.

"That's mine," I whisper, opening my eyes and my breath catches.

His eyes burn with intensity, his expression hard. "It won't be for long."

Tingles burst through my whole body as he grasps my elbow and hauls me to the confessional's dark wooden door and pushes it open, dragging me into the tight space and closing the door behind him.

Heavy purple drapes cover all the walls, except for one, which has a sliding compartment for the priest to take confession. The only furniture in the room is a comfortable-looking chair and a small table with a lamp that radiates soft light.

Enzo pushes me up against the wall, my shoulders smarting at the contact, as he pins me with his hips, his erection pressing into my stomach. His eyes glow with the promise of so many filthy things that I almost whimper as I pull his mouth back to mine.

He explores my mouth with his tongue as he takes both of my wrists, locking them together above my head with one of his hands. His other hand slides down my body to the hem of my skirt, pushing the fabric up to my hip, exposing my ass to the smooth wall.

Enzo pulls away from my mouth and jerks me to the left, pressing my front into the wall, his hand still holding my wrists above me.

"You have a glorious ass," he breathes as he splays his hand over one cheek reverently. "I'd love to mark up this pretty skin."

I push back into his hand, my breathing laboured. He needs to touch me more before I combust. Enzo's hand traces the lace panties along my ass cheek, following it lower, hooking a finger into my stockings, the flimsy fabric tearing with ease. His fingers continue their exploring, slipping into my panties, stroking my dripping core. My legs tremble. The only thing keeping me up right now is his hold on my wrists.

"*Christ*," he groans as his finger circles over my clit, making me jerk at the contact.

"Don't set a fire by saying the Lord's name in vain," I pant.

"The place can fucking burn," he growls into my ear.

His finger slides down and teases the entrance, but goes no further. I push my hips back, forcing his finger into me, and my eyes roll closed.

"Fuck," I groan, bouncing back and forth, my body clenching hard around his finger already.

He pulls his hand free, forcing a whimper from me as he shoves his coated finger into my mouth. My arousal sings across my taste buds as I swirl my tongue around the length.

"What would your Lord say about your wicked ways now?" Enzo croons into my ear as he fucks my mouth with his finger, adding another as he releases my wrists.

His free hand goes back to my ass, pulling off my panties and ruined stockings. His fingers pull out of my mouth and grips my jaw tight as he turns me around, crushing his mouth to mine. My hands slip under his jacket, and push it off his shoulders, letting it drop to the floor. Enzo steps back, over the discarded clothing, pulling me with him, and sinks into the chair, forcing me to straddle his lap.

My hands land on his belt and undo it, along with the button and zipper of his pants, pulling out his shirt. Enzo lifts his hips slightly, assisting me with his pants, and freeing his cock. I pull away from his mouth and glance down.

Fuck, that's the most beautiful cock I've ever seen. Long, thick, and slightly curved. I run my short nails softly from base to tip, delighting in the shudders under me.

"I advise against teasing me, sweetheart," Enzo warns.

"Or what?" I challenge. I swear I have a death wish.

Enzo's answer is to lift me from the back of my thighs, forcing me to collapse against his chest. The fact he can lift my overweight ass is amazing and downright fucking exhilarating. He positions me above him, then drops me onto his entire length. My back arches, the searing pain of the stretch and fullness sends waves of heat through my veins.

Fuck. I clench tight around his cock and Enzo's head falls forward, muffling his groans between my breasts.

He lifts me again, almost all the way off his cock, and then releases me again. I grip both his huge shoulders, whimpering at the pleasure, the pain, the ecstasy pulsing through me. I roll my hips forward, the friction on my clit making me pant.

"Do that again," Enzo demands, his tongue licking my throat as his fingers dig into my ass. I roll forward and we both moan.

A click of a door echoes in the small space, and we both freeze. A shuffle of feet moves toward us and the thud of someone sitting down on a chair on the other side of the dividing wall. I lean back and crack the slider open ajar.

A deep voice instructs softly. "We will start with the Sign of the Cross."

Sweet fucking Jesus. I look at Enzo—a devastating smile curves across his lips.

Shall we play?

"Yes Father," I respond breathlessly to the priest, crossing myself. Enzo does the same, the sick delight burning in those cerulean pools.

"I am Father Michael. You are safe in this confessional. You may open the divider."

Enzo flexes his hips up and I gasp. "I don't want to taint you with the sight of a sinner, Father," I choke.

"Confess your sins so you shall rid the burden of shame."

Like confession will help. I'm committing a plethora of sins at this very moment. I'm *definitely* going to Hell.

"Please, give me a moment, Father."

"Take your time."

I roll my hips as I lean further back and pull my t-shirt over my head, leaving me in a bra and my bunched-up skirt. Enzo's eyes devour my body, his hands sliding over my skin as I pull my phone out of my bra strap and put it next to the lamp.

"I'm ready," I declare to both the priest and Enzo.

The Devil beneath me smiles, clutches my ass, and drags me up his length devastatingly slow, almost to the tip again, and then drags me down as he thrusts, the sensation overwhelming. I stifle the groan, which comes out as a pained sound.

"Have you done this before?" Father Michael asks.

"Yes," I rasp, answering the question and the sensation.

"May the Lord be in our hearts to help you make a good confession," Father Michael begins. Enzo moves again and I bite down on my bottom lip.

"Forgive me, Father, for I have sinned. It's been months since my last confession. Ah…" I breathe as Enzo meets my falls with swift thrusts, an orgasm building with ferocity at the combined movements.

"Tell me your sins," Father Michael prompts.

'Faster,' I mouth and tip my head back. Enzo presses his face in between my breasts as he locks his arms around my waist.

"I took the Lord's name in vain," I pant, gripping Enzo's shoulders as he thrusts harder and deeper. "And I've lied so many times." My body burns with sensation, the muscles around Enzo's cock quiver and pulse as my breathing turns into short pants.

"I've had sinful thoughts about men outside the confines of marriage," I choke as Enzo slips his hand between us and finds my clit, stroking it in time with his punishing thrusts. How this priest doesn't know this is happening is beyond comprehension.

"And... And I've missed Sunday service for a while now," I groan. Enzo lifts his head, a lazy smile playing across those wicked lips. He thrusts hard again, finger circling my clit and I whimper. I'm on the edge of oblivion and I can't stop it.

"It's okay, continue with your confession," Father Michael probes.

"Jesus save me," I blurt out. My hand claps against my mouth as I explode around Enzo, my legs trembling hard.

"If it is too much to tell me, tell the Lord. Pray the Rosary and four Our Fathers. Now, please recite the Contrition."

"Lord Jesus, Son of God, have mercy on me, a sinner," I pant, trying to catch my breath.

Father Michael says the Prayer of Absolution, but I can't hear him over the thundering beat of my heart in my ears and my rasping breaths.

I look down at Enzo with hooded eyes. His self-satisfied grin and the evil glint in his eyes send chills down my spine. This session is not over, it seems.

"... I absolve you from your sins, in the name of the Father, and of the Son, and of the Holy Spirit. Amen. You are forgiven," Father Michael concludes.

Enzo jerks upwards again. My eyes roll closed, and I clench around him. "Thank you, Father."

"I look forward to seeing you again on Sunday," Father Michael comments before the poor priest leaves the confessional with a click of the door closing.

Enzo chuckles darkly. "My turn."

His arm tightens around my waist as he begins a fast, brutal rhythm. Sharp pain registers a moment later, and I open my eyes to Enzo's teeth clamped down on my breast. He releases the skin and runs his tongue over the grooves of his mark.

"Fuck," I breathe as he does it to the other breast, the pain mixing with the ecstasy, my body barrelling towards another orgasm faster than expected.

My racing heart beats erratically as Enzo's thrusts become feral. One hand grips my hair by the roots, his mouth swallowing my moans as I come again, harder than before. He buries himself deep, groaning into my mouth as I feel him spill into me.

I collapse on his chest, my body spent, hot, and sated. Enzo's hand strokes up my mostly naked back absently, his heavy breathing slowing down. I feel... safe in his arms. The last time I felt like this was a long time ago, and that turned out to be a nightmare.

I sit up. "What time is it?"

Enzo lifts his arm to inspect his flashy watch. Someone is obviously wealthy. "It's just hitting three in the morning."

"Shit," I grumble, lifting off Enzo's lap, groaning at the sensitivity.

"What's wrong, sweetheart?" Enzo purrs. Can he not be so tempting?

"I have to go," I say, pulling my t-shirt on, scooping up my phone, and looking for my panties in the dim light. I find the black lace beside the partition wall and scoop them up.

Before I can put them on, they're snatched out of my hand. I turn to a put-together Enzo, amusement shining in those cerulean irises.

"These are mine," he declares, stuffing the lace in his pants pocket and picking up his jacket from the floor.

"You know, stealing is a sin."

"I'm the King of Sin. I don't give a shit."

My eyes roll as I adjust my skirt, but my body is on fire at his words. I wish he'd do a lot more sinful things to me. Perhaps in another lifetime. I shake the filthy thoughts away and step out of the confessional.

There are two newcomers to the church; two men in dark suits standing at the front pew with hard expressions. Have they been here the whole time? Ignoring the warning tingling in the back of my neck, I stride to the front of the church and cross myself. I just fucked a stranger in a church with a priest next to me, but best not to be completely disrespectful to the Lord.

A tug on my wrist stops me as I turn to leave. Enzo pulls me closer to him. "Where do you have to be in such a hurry?"

"Somewhere that isn't here."

"Where exactly?" Enzo says low, demanding, as he pulls on his jacket. Damn, he's fine in a suit.

I step closer, tugging at the knot of his tie. It comes loose and I unhook the top button of his shirt as I loop the soft fabric around my neck. "I'm going home, Enzo."

His eyes darken at the sound of his name. Those eyes are pools of clarity that I want to fall into and run from.

The warning tingles again. *Dangerous.*

"Stealing is a sin, remember?" Enzo purrs.

I smirk, stepping backwards away from the entourage of suited men, caressing his tie.

"Thanks for the ride," I say with a wink, then turn and walk away.

Chapter 5

Thanks for the ride?

Delphine backs away with a smirk and a wink, *and* my fucking tie. She turns on her heel and struts away, that perfect ass swaying, beckoning me to follow. I take two steps forward before Peter grips my arm.

"Boss, Creed will be here any minute."

I turn, staring down at the idiot. "Touch me again and lose a hand."

He holds his hands out and steps back. If he didn't have good connections to the biker gangs, I would kill this fucker. I run a hand through my hair and try to settle my wired body.

Who is this siren?

Delphine. Just her name stirs a side of me that doesn't need to be tempted.

She was young. Fucking hell, I hope she was at least eighteen. I shouldn't have fucked her. She could have been a hooker. No, she looked too ... *pure.* But the terror in those clear green eyes was so potent, so *broken*, as she tried to bolt like demons were chasing her. Which is partially true. My blood sings at the memories of stalking through the church, trapping her in a dark corner, with no escape.

She's stunning prey. Maybe I should...

The rumble of Harleys stops me from abandoning this meeting.

Creed strolls in with two of his men, his usual cocky smile lighting his face. "You sure know how to pick a meeting place."

"You have five minutes."

Creed chuckles. "Did I pull you away from something? Or *someone?*"

He's stopping me from chasing my siren. *No.* Not mine—she's just a random girl in a church. That's it.

"I should be at a benefit right now that my family is hosting, so get on with it."

Creed sighs, running his tattooed hands through his hair. "Product didn't show up today."

"Excuse me?"

"We went to the drop, and they showed up with nothing."

This is the second fucking time. "How are your levels of product?"

"We're good for now," Creed's man says. "But we'll be running low if we don't get more soon."

I button my suit jacket, pulling out my phone. "Leave it with me."

Creed's eyes harden. "We might have to try—"

"I'll get you more product," I cut him off, knowing what he's about to suggest. "Peter will give you the new contact information if you need to contact me again."

Lucas and I exit the side door to the car. He pulls up next to the motorbikes at the front of the church and Peter gets in before we head back into the city.

Lucas parks in the underground car park of *Luxuria* and the three of us take the service elevator up to the ballroom.

I take a moment to compose myself, plastering on the businessman persona more palatable for Melbourne's high society.

I slip into the benefit through a back door and act as if I never left, mingling with the crowd and dazzling benefactors for the new bullshit venture Vivienne is trying to launch under the Herrington name.

Life would have been a lot easier if my father died *after* he divorced her. He was calculating to the grave and left nothing to Vivienne in his will. He also knew it would be damaging to the Herrington reputation if I tossed her out on her ass, so I'm stuck with the vulture until another high society asshole is shopping for a trophy wife.

Laughter nearby catches my attention, and I turn to see Matteo talking with socialites. I approach the gaggle of gossiping busybodies, catching Matteo's eye, tilting my head slightly toward the exit.

Before we can make our excuses to leave, a thin arm wraps around mine and a sickeningly sweet scent gets stuck in my throat.

"Enzo," Vivienne purrs, pushing her breasts into my arm.

I force myself not to throw her off me and give her a small smile. "Yes?"

"You've misplaced your tie," she observes, her tiny hand stroking down the buttons of my shirt.

One woman reaches for Vivienne's elbow, giving it a sympathetic squeeze. "Condolences for your loss."

"Thank you," she says, dropping her hand from my chest, gripping my forearm. "It has been hard on all of us."

Another woman approaches our small group, her eyes alight with scandal. "Did you hear? Clara is back in Melbourne."

"For good?" Matteo asks, taking a sip of his drink.

The woman nods, her eyes flicking to me for a moment before returning to Vivienne. "Her mum is sick, so she's moving back."

"Also with Sienna's—"

"If you'll excuse Matteo and I," I say, interrupting Vivienne as I cover her hand on my forearm and pull it off me firmly. "We have some business we need to attend to."

Blood rushes in my ears as I walk away from the women before I have to listen to any more of their fake bullshit.

I'm surprised Clara stayed away this long. My wife's former best friend is the star of Melbourne high society; I'm sure she's missed the spotlight.

"What did Creed say?" Matteo murmurs low as we weave through the crowd, heading toward the exit.

"He fucked us again," I grumble, keeping my face stoic.

"Bastard." Matteo breathes. "I'll set up a meeting."

Matteo veers off on his phone as I slip out of the ballroom. Lucas is already at the elevator, holding the door open. I nod my thanks as we slip in and I hit the penthouse button, swiping my keycard. The businessman mask slips off and I allow the darkness to coat me once again.

"Clara is back," I inform Lucas.

"I'm aware."

I narrow my gaze at my head of security. "And you didn't think that was something you should tell me?"

Amusement glows in his otherwise stoic face. "You were preoccupied."

I frown.

Lucas smirks. "You were in confession."

Delphine.

"Did you want me to look into it?" Lucas asks, stepping to the door as the lift stops.

My cock aches at the reminder of our rendezvous. "Find out who she is."

Lucas acknowledges my request with a nod and he steps out, checking the small hallway and then indicates it's safe.

My phone buzzes with a message from Matteo confirming the meeting as I make it to my bedroom, my hand automatically going to my neck for my tie, and finding nothing. I sigh, closing my eyes and tipping my head back.

The tension with my importer is affecting business, and I really don't want to deal with this bullshit. Creed thinks I should look into new connections for the product we need, and at this rate I probably will have to, no matter the consequences.

I head for my bathroom, turn on the shower, and strip out of my suit. As I pull off my jacket, a hint of strawberries tickles my nose. Siren. I bring the lapel of my jacket to my nose and inhale. Burning frankincense clings to the fabric; old memories of swinging thuribles and swinging fists almost make me drop the jacket in disgust.

Delphine's sweet, ripe, strawberry scent cuts through those memories, replacing them with flashes of sultry, clear green eyes, with black shadow smeared all around them.

I drop the jacket before I stand here and inhale her scent all night, removing the rest of my clothes and stepping into the hot spray.

How would those eyes change when I brought her to the edge of orgasm but never gave her the satisfaction of release? I bet they'd *burn*.

And those lush pink lips—I'm sure they'd look incredible around my cock.

The image makes me hard. I wrap my hand around my cock, wishing it was Delphine's hot mouth, taking every inch. Slowly. Until she's gagging. And those fiery eyes looking up at me with tears streaming down her face while she's on her knees. There are so many ways I can make her cry. Fuck.

I groan, one hand on the tiled wall, the other sliding up and down my cock with a firm grip as water beats down my back.

I want more of the wicked siren—the sound she makes when I fill her to the hilt, those little grinding motions that almost make me black out. I want her under me, begging me to never stop, coming over and over. I want her cries and her tears when I mark that perfect, light golden skin with my touch. The thought of cane welts over Delphine's perfect ass sends me over the edge, and I shudder, coming hard.

As I clean myself off, I ignore the demon under my skin, who's whispering that just one taste of Delphine won't be enough. That dark part of me won't be satisfied until he finds that stain of darkness on her soul again and owns all of it.

SIX

DEL

MY WHOLE BODY IS buzzing as I walk back to Silvia's house—what did I just do? I can be reckless, but that was something else.

Scar is *definitely* going to have some thoughts about this. My legs tremble in exertion as I quicken my steps; that drunkard is probably passed out on a bathroom floor or calling the cops right now.

I tuck Enzo's tie under my shirt as I walk up Silvia's driveway, the music still pulsing through the walls as I approach the house. I just need to get Scar out, order a car service, and then I can pass out.

The front door opens and Scar bursts out, stumbling towards the bushes with her hand over her mouth.

She almost falls headfirst as she pukes into a bush. I hold in laughter at her misery as someone looms in the doorway.

"Delphine?" That voice—a deep, soft lilt. The hairs on the back of my neck stand up.

"What are you doing here?" Of all people, I wouldn't think I'd run into *Isaac*.

He flashes a smile. "It's so good to see you."

Another round of Scar's vomiting pulls both of our attention. Isaac darts over and pulls Scar's ponytail out of the way, rubbing small circles on her shoulder with his other hand. Silvia appears at the door. Her eyes are glazed over, her cheeks flushed.

"Scarlett, sweetie," she slurs, "you should have just gotten naked instead of taking that last shot." She laughs with her gaggle of fake friends as she uses the doorframe to keep herself upright.

"You shouldn't be forcing people to do things they don't want to," I bite out, drawing the attention of everyone in the doorway.

Silvia's lips curve up. "Unlike you, people want to see Scarlett naked."

One moment Scar is puking her guts up, the next she's trying to launch herself at Silvia. The only thing stopping her is Isaac holding her back.

"Say one more thing about Del, and I will fucking end you, Silvia," she shouts as she struggles against Isaac's hold.

I should be the one outraged, clocking Silvia in the face for her comments, but after what just happened in the church, I shake with laughter. If only she knew. The slightly hysterical sound stops Scar's thrashing and once again draws everyone's attention.

"I'm sorry," I say between laughter. "The effort you go through to bring me down is just so *adorable.* " I step closer to Silvia, my eyes boring into hers. "You don't think I've heard every single one of your insults before? I get it. You're disgusted by my presence, or maybe threatened."

Silvia barks out a laugh. "You think I'm threatened by *you?* You must be delusional."

"Silvia," Isaac chastises as he steps up next to her, "that's enough."

Scar stays on her feet as she makes it to my side and wraps her arm around mine. I point between Isaac and Silvia. "You two make an interesting couple."

Both of them look at me in utter disgust at the notion.

"Someone just told me they're siblings," Scar hisses.

Isaac's expression confirms the connection. I knew Isaac had another sibling. But I never made the connection that it was *Silvia.*

I scoff. "Interesting."

"*Interesting?* Our father is a broken man because of *your* mother," Silvia spits.

"Okay?" Why is that my fucking problem? "Are you telling me your stupid obsession with annoying me to death is some weird revenge plot because my mother's a whore?"

"She ruined him!" Silvia shrieks as Isaac holds her back from launching at me. "My parents got divorced because of *her!*"

"Please, spare my ears from your whiny complaints. Take your grievances to the woman who gave birth to me. It's got nothing to do with me."

Silvia shouts unintelligible words as I steer Scar away from the house, wrestling to get my phone out of my bra. I order a car service to meet us a few houses away while dragging the half-conscious Scar along, making her sit on a low fence at the right spot to wait for the ride.

"Delphine." Isaac's tall body comes jogging down the street toward us.

"Run back to your family. You're not needed here."

He stops a couple of metres away, barely out of breath. "You are family."

I scoff. "We barely share the same genes."

"Del," he coos, taking a step forward, "I just want to talk to you."

"And I don't want to hear anything that comes out of your fucking mouth."

"I'm not the same person I was back then," he argues, stepping forward again.

"There's nothing you can do to change what has already happened."

He's silent for a few tense moments. "Mum told me you moved out."

I laugh, shaking my head. "That was two and a half years ago."

His eyes dim with guilt. "I didn't... I haven't—"

"You haven't given a shit to keep up."

He winces slightly at my words. "And you changed your hair."

"Yeah."

"I like it."

"I don't care." I cross my arms over my chest, looking down at my phone, checking the wait time for the car service.

"You're not wearing your rosary."

My head whips up. "Why are you asking me all these questions? You lost the right to know anything about me when you left."

Isaac reaches out, his hand landing on my shoulder. "Please, Del. I'm your brother, I just—"

I push him away, recoiling from his touch. "Touch me again and watch what happens."

Something like sadness or regret flashes in his eyes before his head tips down and he sighs to the ground. "At least let me take you home."

"I've got it covered," I say waving my phone in front of him.

He looks up, eyes no longer sad but fierce. "You can't trust those car share drivers. They're more dangerous than you think."

I bark out a laugh. "And I should trust you?"

"I'm a federal officer, so yes."

"You're a cop?"

He nods. "That's where I've been, training and working."

"Mum must be *so* proud," rolls off my tongue sarcastically before I can stop myself.

Isaac chuckles. "She's actually pissed off that I didn't go into corporate law like my dad."

My phone buzzes with a notification, and headlights glow up the street. "That's our ride." I turn to the passed-out Scar and hoist her up, enticing a groan from her as I wrap my arm around her waist. "Good chat."

Isaac looks like he wants to help me, but he's wise enough not to interfere. "I really hope we can talk properly soon."

I push Scar into the car and turn back to Isaac. "Let's hope I never see you again."

"That's your tell."

I frown, looking up at Isaac. "My what?"

His light brown eyes shine as he smiles softly. "Your tell. You play with your rosary when you have a bad hand."

My hand releases the beads immediately—I didn't even realise I was doing it. I look at my cards again, and then at what Isaac called "the flop". He taught me all about the different combinations to win, but I have none of them. I blow out a frustrated breath and push the cards toward the centre of the coffee table, bringing my knees to my chest.

"I'm never going to be good at this," I grumble, watching Isaac collect all of the cards.

"It takes practice, Del," he reassures as he splits the deck and does that cool shuffling technique with his thumbs, like in the movies.

"How are you so good at it? You're seventeen. Isn't this an adult's game?"

Isaac chuckles. "I practice with my older friends." He starts to gather the poker chips and distribute them evenly between us.

"Poker isn't really about having the right cards, it's about learning to read people."

"I didn't have anything in my hand."

"But your opponents don't know that. That's when you try to trick them into thinking you have a better hand. It's called bluffing."

I frown. "I don't get it."

Isaac sighs, his brows furrowing together like they do when he's concentrating. It's the exact expression Mum does when she's reading. Isaac puts the deck down, his eyes returning to mine, his gaze careful. "You know when... when we can tell *he's* in one of his moods? And we're on our best behaviour, even though we don't want to be? That's like bluffing."

I know all too well what it's like to pretend with *him*—to bluff.

My hand drifts back to the dark wooden beads around my neck, toying with the cross at the end.

"I hope he doesn't come back," I whisper. The bruises on my hips and thighs throb. He's due back tomorrow from his business trip. I swallow the bile creeping up my throat.

"I know," Isaac murmurs, reaching over and grabbing my tiny hand in his. "One day, we'll be away from him."

I pray to God every day for that to come true. I look up at his face. "Can you take me with you? When it's time?"

His eyes darken, determination etched across his face. "I'd never leave you behind."

I nod, pulling my hand away, and sitting up straight. "Let's go again."

Isaac and I play another couple of rounds, and I practice my bluffing even though Isaac still wins every time.

The door slams open as Isaac is dealing out another hand. My heart pounds against my chest, my whole body freezing in place.

He's not supposed to be back yet.

You'll receive my punishment and God's if you let your brother corrupt you with his poisonous nonsense, Delphine.

He's going to be so angry at Isaac and *me* for not following his rules.

Scarlett groans and leaps out of the bed, stumbling to my bathroom. She's saved me from the worst part of that particular memory. Seeing Isaac again is not going to make these nightmares go away anytime soon.

"Do *not* puke on the floor," I warn as the sounds of her heaving echoes through the room. A moment later, the toilet flushes, the sink turns on and off and the bed shifts. Scar snuggles closer to me and flings an arm around my waist as she always does when she's not feeling well.

"Tell me what happened last night," she states.

"What part?"

"All of it."

"Are you sure you want to know?"

I wince as she swats my breast, right over one of the bite marks Enzo left. "Tell me."

I sigh. "We drank a lot. Silvia was being a complete bitch. Isaac showed up—"

"Oh fuck, I remember someone telling me they were siblings last night." Scar tightens her arm around me, forcing me to turn and face her. "I guess you found out?"

"Yeah." I haven't told Scar the exact details of my past, but she knows I don't speak to my brother, and try not to speak to any of my other family.

"Did you kick him in the balls?" Scar huffs as she untangles herself from me and turns.

I laugh. "No, he was there when I got back, and we left almost immediately since you almost passed out in your own vomit."

Scar scrambles up in the bed, letting in more cool air. "Back up? When you came *back*? Where did you go?"

"Were you really that drunk that you don't remember anything?"

She smacks me on the arm again with expectant eyes. I sit in bed, my head pounding, and other parts of me tender as I tell her about the strip poker situation. "And then I went to church."

Scar mouth pops open. "Of all places, you ended up in a *church*?"

I shrug. "My mother always said to turn to God in my hours of need."

Scar rolls her eyes. "Your mum and God. A match made in heaven."

"She likes to think so," I mumble, adjusting the pillows behind me.

"What did you even do there?" Scar asks as she slides out of the bed and stretches.

"Confessed my sins." While committing them at the same time. I pull the blanket higher as a flush burns over my face and chest.

Scar wanders into my bathroom, rifling through my drawers, probably looking for a hairbrush like she usually is. "Why are we awake at six-thirty on a Saturday?"

"Because you woke me up with your puking."

I see her smile in the mirror. "Let's annoy someone for food."

After taking a long shower and getting into tracksuit pants and a t-shirt, Scar and I venture downstairs to the kitchen, where both Claudine and Dr. Sakura are sitting at the breakfast table with laptops in front of them.

"Morning," Scar sings as she kisses both her parents on the cheek and claims a spot next to her dad.

"You're oddly perky this morning," Claudine comments without taking her eyes off the screen.

"She got all her puking done already," I say as I slide into the seat next to Claudine.

Dr. Sakura sighs, closing his laptop and facing Scar, pushing his glasses higher up his nose. "What did I tell you about excessive drinking at such a young age?"

"Yeah, yeah," Scar breathes, "liver and kidney damage, blah-blah."

Claudine shakes her head and smiles as she closes her laptop and takes both to the kitchen island as the chef drops plates of food in front of us and fruit in the centre of the table.

"How are you doing after last night?" Dr. Sakura asks across from me.

"I didn't drink as much as this one," I nod towards Scar who pokes her tongue out at me, "so I'm fine."

Dr. Sakura goes on a lecture about the effect of alcohol and child development as we all eat. Claudine Sakura is the best defence lawyer in the country, and her husband is one of the leading doctors in adolescent health.

I remember the day I met both of them like it was yesterday. Dr. Sakura was the treating doctor when I walked into the hospital almost three years ago. He was so easy to talk to with his soft voice and kind brown eyes. Once he knew the reasons I was there, he called his wife, and they both changed my life for the better, like they have done for so many other kids.

The Sakura's don't have any biological children, but they have three adopted children, Scarlett being one of them, and two ex-foster kids who are now adults that they also consider their own. They took me in when I was four months shy of sixteen, and I have been living with them ever since.

They're both incredibly generous and caring to me even though I was never one of their foster or adopted kids, and they've allowed me to continue living here now that I'm not a minor.

After an educational breakfast and a promise to be home for dinner, Scar and I retreat to our rooms. I change into shorts, then spend most of the day catching up on homework and napping, but the delicious tenderness from last night keeps pulling my attention.

Every time I doze off, I dream of Enzo—his imposing frame looming over me and the feel of his soft suit under my fingertips. I wish I had more time to have those large hands all over my skin. And his scent—fresh like sweet grapefruit, but cut with something heady, like black pepper and sandalwood. There was something else about his scent, something I can't quite put a name on. It's dark, sweet almost; it sends tingles across my skin.

Cerulean eyes flash through my mind; I think they'll haunt me for a long time.

I shake myself from the filthy daydreams and turn up the house music blasting through my sound system. I will never see Enzo again—last night was just a fun thing to blurt out to my retirement home nurse when I'm ancient.

As I'm finishing a crazy amount of math homework, Scarlett barges into my room with the same textbook in her hand and a confused frown on her face.

She takes a seat on my unmade bed as I turn down the music. "Why is half the work figuring out what the question is actually asking?"

"I'm sure it's because mathematicians are demons in human form and like to torture people for fun." We work through the ambiguously written questions she's stuck on and pack away our books.

"What did Isaac say to you last night?" she asks as we both lie across my bed.

I sigh. "He had the audacity to call me family and claim to want to talk to me about God knows what."

"Doesn't he live in another state?"

"That's what I thought, but apparently he's back, and a fed."

Scar's head whips over at me. "He's a *cop*?"

"Yeah. It's funny that he thinks he can show up nine years later like nothing happened and wants to mend fences or whatever." Isaac left when he was eighteen and I haven't seen or spoken to him until last night.

Scar sits up and crosses her legs. "If he wanted to patch things up so badly, why was his first stop Silvia's place?"

I nod. "He's full of shit."

"I remember what Silvia said about you out the front of her house," Scar announces, rage igniting those brown eyes. "I should have punched the bitch."

I laugh, scooting over and laying my head in her lap. "As much as I would love to see that, you can't get arrested if you want to go to a good university."

"Gross," Scar whines, running her hands through my hair, "you sound like my mother."

We both laugh then fall into silence, my eyes falling shut, enjoying the soft touches on my scalp.

It's hard for me to allow someone to touch me, which is why last night was such a surprise. I don't like hugging Claudine, and she saved my life, yet I let Enzo, a complete stranger, and a *man*, touch me in ways that used to make me hurl my guts up.

Scar above me clears her throat, pulling me out of my reverie. "Del, please explain those *very* specific bruises on your thighs."

I open my eyes and see the oval shadow on both upper thighs she's referring to. I don't bruise easily, so Enzo's grip was harder than I thought.

"You know me, super clumsy. I ran into the corner of a pew last night."

"Mhmm," Scar hums, "turn over, show me the back."

When I don't move, she tugs on my hair. I reluctantly flip face down, out of Scar's lap, as she crawls down the bed and pokes a sore spot on my thigh, drawing a hiss out of me.

"These look an awful lot like handprints," she says, poking another bruise.

"Will you cut it out?"

"Not until you tell me about them."

I roll over and sit up, meeting her suspicious gaze. "Fine, I met someone at the church last night."

Scar smacks me in the shoulder. "Why the *fuck* didn't you lead with that earlier? Tell me everything, and if you leave anything out, I will injure you."

"You should see someone for these violent tendencies," I complain as I rub my arm and launch into a watered-down version of last night with Enzo. I definitely don't mention the priest.

Scar's eyes are wide; I don't think she's blinked in a few minutes. "So, you don't know his name?"

"Nope," I lie. "It's not important, anyway. I'm never going to see him again."

Scar scoffs. "The man has henchmen. I'm sure he could track you down if he really wanted to."

"He won't find anything if he tries, your mum did a fantastic job of making me disappear." When I moved in with the Sakuras, Claudine used her legal and not so legal channels to completely separate me from my previous self. If you try to find anything about me, you'll find Del Blaire: orphan. If someone asked around, they'd run into a few non-disclosure agreements.

I shrug. "I was just a convenient opportunity."

"Don't make me smack you again," she warns. "You're way more than that, Del. You're the most amazing person I've ever met, and I've met a lot of people."

"Thank you, but that isn't true in the slightest." I'm just a stray her parents allowed into their home; another soul damaged beyond repair.

Frustration lines Scar's beautiful face. "We're going to have to agree to disagree on this one."

"So, you and Flynn last night," I say, changing the subject.

Both of our phones buzz and we pick them up from the side table. The entrance gate's intercom system connects to our phones and rings when someone presses the button. Scar opens the camera feed to show none other than Isaac sitting behind the wheel of a black sedan.

"I don't live here," I say immediately.

Scar nods and taps the microphone button. "Sakura residence, this is Scarlett."

"Uh, hi, this is Isaac Bennett. I don't know if you remember, but we met last night?"

"I remember. What are you doing at my house?"

Isaac clears his throat. "I have a jacket belonging to Delphine." Shit, I didn't have my jacket on when we left last night.

"*Del* doesn't live here."

"I know, but you know her, so I was hoping you'd be able to get it to her."

Scar looks at me, and I nod.

"Drive up and park next to the other cars. I'll meet you in the foyer." Scar presses the gate release button on the screen and pockets the phone. "You can eavesdrop from the landing."

We both leave my room and head for the foyer. The Sakura house has a curving grand staircase in the foyer that leads to the second floor. The entire space is open and bright with a massive, ornate chandelier that's the major feature of the space. The benefit of the space being open is that I can sit in the seating area upstairs and still hear what's happening downstairs, but hidden from the people below.

I slide into a plush armchair as I hear Scar open the front door and a set of heavy footsteps clip on the marble floors.

"Sorry to disturb you on your Saturday," Isaac's voice echoes through the space.

"How did you know where I lived?" Scar asks.

"I know your mother; we've met once or twice."

"Sure," Scar mumbles, "thanks for bringing the jacket. I'll pass it along to Del."

"Do you know where she's staying?" Isaac asks softly.

"Why would I tell you if I did?"

"I'm her brother. I just want to know she's okay."

I hear Scar scoff. "In the time I've known Del, she's only mentioned you once, and she said she never wanted to see you again."

Isaac sighs. "I understand where she's coming from, but I want to patch things up between us."

"Look," Scar bites, "Del has gone through enough. She doesn't need you turning up and demanding an audience. Just cut your losses; she obviously doesn't want a relationship with you. Thanks again for the jacket. Now please get out of my house."

"I won't stop trying to be her brother. She needs a family."

"Don't worry, she's got a family," Scar states as the front door opens. "It just doesn't include you."

SEVEN

— Q ♠ —

DEL

T HE TRAM JOSTLES THROUGH the city as I watch the buildings pass by, drowning out the chatter of the passengers with country music crooning through my headphones. We jolt to a stop and three police officers climb on at the front of the tram, passengers nearby making room for them.

It's been a week since I ran into Isaac, and thankfully, he hasn't tried to contact me. Maybe he heeded Scar's warning and decided it wasn't worth the effort to pursue a 'relationship.' The damage has been done, and there's no turning back.

Seduzione is one of the most prestigious Italian restaurants in Melbourne. Nestled on the promenade along the docks, it's the perfect spot for multi-billion dollar deals to be discussed and socialites to wine and dine while enjoying the view of yachts cruising in and out of the harbour. However, it's a horrible spot to find parking that doesn't cost you a kidney.

I get off at my stop and set off towards work, finding Florentina juggling a few boxes at the back door, so I hustle over and open it for her.

"*Grazie*," she says as we walk through the back hall past Raph's office. Florentina turns into a storeroom, and I continue into the busy kitchen. I greet all the cooks and kitchen hands, then head over to Mario by the stove.

"Good morning," I sing, planting a kiss on his cheek as he stirs an enormous pot of pasta sauce.

"*Buongiorno bella*, I thought you weren't working today."

"I swapped with Stella."

Mario pulls the wooden spoon out of the sauce and wipes his hand on the towel tucked into his apron. His kind, grey-hazel eyes glow with concern. "She takes advantage of you too much."

"It's okay, Chef. I was happy to help."

We have a brief conversation about the lunch menu before I hustle out of the kitchen and onto the floor.

The restaurant itself is small, the main floor only having twenty-five dining tables, a bar which stretches along one wall, and a small, plush lounge area at the front of the restaurant, making it highly exclusive. The mezzanine above has only one grand table and a separate bar, used for the most important clients.

I spot Raph on the phone at the host desk as I cross the restaurant towards the bar. While Mario owns the place, Raph runs all the logistics. Queenie, our hostess, polishes glassware with one of the bartenders.

"Did you hear?" Queenie whispers, stopping me at the door to the break room. "Sophia is gone."

"What do you mean, gone?" I ask.

"He broke up with her last night. Apparently she ran out of his office crying."

"Interesting," I comment, slipping into the break room. At least with Sophia out of the picture, none of us will have to pick up the slack—she wasn't great at her job.

The room is comfortable, with a couch and armchair on one side, lockers and two bathrooms on the other, and a table with four chairs in the middle of the room. I approach my locker, peeling off my crew-neck jumper, and pull out my apron.

I take my make-up case into the bathroom and adjust my uniform. The elbow-length, black shirt has '*Seduzione*' embroidered in gold on the left breast pocket, and the black skirt is tight and knee length. I change from my sneakers to thick black stockings and flats, then apply a sweep of mascara, face powder and lip balm before tying my apron around my waist, putting all my items away and leaving the break room.

I cross to the host desk where Raphael is typing away at the computer.

"A little birdy told me that we had a resignation yesterday?" I ask as I pull my hair into a low bun.

Raph smirks, his eyes not leaving the screen. "Queenie needs to stop spreading gossip, but she's not wrong."

"Do you want to talk about it?" I tease.

He chuckles, pulling an ordering tablet out from under the host desk and passing it to me. "I'm good."

Lunch is busy until we close at three. I put the ordering tablet back on charge at the host desk before escaping into the break room. I take off my apron, pull on my jumper, and check my phone. There are a few messages on there from Scar complaining about life and one from my mother.

ELEANOR

> Are you coming to Bridgette's baptism next weekend?

My stomach twists. She expects me to go to the baptism of my half-sister, whom I have never met, like an obedient daughter, even though I haven't considered myself her daughter for a while.

I type out a short reply.

> I have work.

A reply comes through almost immediately.

ELEANOR

> Please, Delphine, William and I want the whole family there. It's important to us.

If I go, I know shit will probably go down. If I don't go, there will also be problems. I'm fucked if I do and fucked if I don't. Damn it.

> Send me the details. I'll try my best.

She knows that means I'll turn up.

Florentina pops her head into the break room and we head to the staff lunch room off the kitchen. In between every lunch and dinner shift, the entire staff has a meal together.

Mario sits at the head of the table, with the seat on his right reserved for Raph, and the rest of the team fill the empty seats. The space is buzzing with various conversations as Florentina and I find seats at the end of the long table.

Raph joins us shortly after carrying a tablet and a small gift bag.

"Good afternoon everyone, thanks for your great work this afternoon." He walks down the table, directly to me, dropping the gift bag in front of me. "It's probably no surprise to anyone, but Del is now our head waiter."

A round of applause rumbles through the room as Raph heads for his seat next to Mario. "And yes, we've had a resignation on our wait team. I will try to fill the position as soon as I can."

"Try not to date this one, yeah?" Queenie comments across from me.

Raph rolls his eyes and launches into the menus for the evening, rostering, and a rundown on any compliments or issues that need to be addressed.

Once business is completed, we all dig into the feast, which is spectacular as usual. The room is noisy with chatter and laughter as I'm coaxed into having another piece of Mario's signature lasagna.

Florentina demands I open the gift bag, which contains a new uniform, as the head waiter's uniform is different, a bottle of champagne, and an envelope with a cash bonus. I'll be giving that back as soon as I can.

After clearing all the lunch dishes and dropping them off in the kitchen, we all go our separate ways for the last couple hours of our break. Queenie, Florentina, and I go out for some retail therapy—Raph handed over the company credit card since the new uniform requires me to wear heels and I need completely different underwear, since the sports bra I currently have on won't work.

When we get back to the restaurant, I lock myself in one bathroom with my new purchases, my makeup bag, and the new uniform.

I add a bit more powder to my face, a blush-coloured lipstick, and a sweep of shadow to my eyes. I take my hair out and shake out my waves, twisting and pinning the front parts away from my face, and leaving the rest down.

I change into a plunge bra and the matching high-waisted panties. I needed sheer black tights, but the store I went to only had thigh highs, so I put on the garter belt I purchased and fasten the stockings to the latches.

Finally, I pick up the uniform; it's a black wrap dress with the restaurant's name and my own, embroidered on the left breast in silver, elbow-length sleeves, and a shorter hem than my usual work skirt.

I pull on the dress and tie it tight around my waist, then gape in the mirror. The fabric is thick and soft, and tighter than something

I'd choose for myself, but the silhouette the dress creates is... amazing. But the top of it is obscenely open.

Gathering all my items, I step out of the bathroom; Queenie is on her laptop at the table and Florentina is on the couch reading a book.

"Please tell me one of you has a safety pin."

Both of them look up and their mouths gape open.

Queenie whistles low. "God damn, Del, you look hot."

"Let me remind you that you have a wife," Florentina chastises as she stands, "and Del is eighteen, practically a minor."

I laugh as I put my things away and Florentina finds a safety pin in her handbag. We work together to pin the cross section of the dress so it's less revealing, and the pin is concealed.

I have about an hour before we start service, so I throw on my crewneck jumper and take out my homework, sitting next to Queenie on the table. I put my headphones over my ears and blast music, drowning out the world with heavy metal.

It feels like a blink in time when Queenie taps my shoulder, jolting me out of my little chemistry world. I put my things away, take off my jumper and put on the moderately heeled black pumps I purchased and grab my phone.

Raph is at the bar with the sous chef as I leave the break room. They stop talking and stare after me as I walk over to the host desk and look at the reservation list for tonight. There are quite a few regulars coming in, as well as a booking upstairs on the mezzanine floor.

The mezzanine is a private dining area that only Raph books very important clients into, and as his head waiter, and also since Sophia is gone, I'll be the one hosting those clients.

I climb the stairs next to the host desk up to the mezzanine where Ty, the upstairs bartender, is already behind the bar counting stock. He's always been a more reserved member of the *Seduzione* team, but he hears and sees everything.

"I see Raph picked his favourite to lead the team," he muses, continuing to count bottles in the fridge. "I wonder if you'll be his new Sophia?"

"That type of arrangement won't happen between us," I quip as I lean against the entrance of the bar.

Ty looks up, taking in my ensemble, and chuckles. "Oh, yeah, sure. With you looking like that, he definitely *won't* try."

I roll my eyes. "I'm not even his type." Everyone knows his weakness is for bubbly, wraith-thin blondes.

Ty shakes his head. "You have no idea what you're talking about."

"Talking in riddles today, are we?"

"Sowing the seeds of chaos is the highest form of entertainment."

"Stop meddling, Ty."

That wicked glint in his brown eyes shines brighter. "Never."

Instead of smacking the back of Ty's head, I turn to the large round table in the centre of the space. The decor is the opposite to the downstairs' airy and light dockside atmosphere.

Dark wood floors, and walls of deep, midnight blue create an ominous mood. A large, ornate, copper chandelier above the twelve-person table that emits enough light to see each other but allows the shadows to hide the room's more questionable secrets.

Apart from the table and the bar that sits along the furthest wall from the stairs, there are two small sleek couches and two matching armchairs cluster around the front of the space, facing the wall of glass showing the docks and city beyond.

I check that every surface is clean, and I set up the table for five guests, moving the spare chairs into a small storeroom at the back of the bar.

Once the preparation is done, I offer to help Ty, but he's ready to go, so we wait.

"Stop fidgeting," Ty says, amusement lacing his tone.

"I'm not used to being idle," I murmur, forcing my hands to the sides of my body so I stop picking at my nails.

"Up here, everything is done with purpose."

"More riddles," I breathe, picking up a glass and filling it with water.

Raph appears at the top of the stairs as I take a sip of the cool liquid, trying to calm my overheated body. Why am I so nervous? This is just a normal day, a normal shift, just a different part of the restaurant.

He crosses over to the host podium opposite the stairs, and takes off his suit jacket. Dread sours my stomach, my hand snaking up to my neck; he's never without his suit jacket, unless he's pissed.

I force my hand down and head to the podium. "Raph?"

"How long have we known each other?" he asks absently, staring down at his phone.

"Almost two years."

He looks at me. "So, I can trust you?"

"Yes," I say without hesitation.

Raph stares at me for a few moments, and then the tension in the room pops as he nods. "What you hear and see tonight can't be repeated."

I nod. "Okay."

"I'm serious, Del. The people coming in tonight are..." He sighs, running his hand through his hair. "The shit you're about to learn about me is heavy."

"Your secrets are safe with me," I say as reassuringly as possible. I have no idea what secrets I'm promising to keep, but Raph and his family have been good to me.

It couldn't be that bad, right?

But why do I feel like I've stepped into something that's about to swallow me whole?

I take Raph's jacket from the podium and hold it open to him. He smiles, before turning around and slipping his arms through the sleeves. I smooth out the shoulders and turn him around, straightening his collar and checking his cufflinks.

"I made the right choice, choosing you," he says vaguely before heading back downstairs. Does he mean for this position? Or something else?

He's into you.

Absolutely not. Scar is just reading this whole thing wrong.

Murmurs of downstairs diners settle my nerves slightly. I'm still in my home city, with a shitty family and amazing friends. This dinner is probably just some shady meeting with a politician that Raph is trying to bribe for something to do with expansion or whatever restaurateurs do.

I pull out my phone and check my make-up with the camera for the sixth time, and then turn on the tablet on the podium. The reservation for the mezzanine is highlighted, which means they're here.

Heavy footsteps and soft conversation echo up the stairs, so I put on a soft, polite smile that I save for work.

Raph and a shorter blonde man—Jace, Raph's business partner, if I remember correctly—climb the stairs. Raph's face looks polite and invested in what Jace is saying, but I can see the calculating glint in his eyes. Hello, Raphael, the businessman. I know for a fact that he has one of the best poker faces I've ever seen.

Raph and Jace both acknowledge me with a nod before heading over to the bar, still deep in conversation.

More footsteps come up the stairs, so I turn my attention back to the newcomers.

Two men in pristine suits march up the stairs, both with the same hard expressions. They both narrow their eyes at me as they take spots on either side of the staircase.

I swear you can pick a security team in a crowd just by that expression.

I try not to roll my eyes at their attitude as I give them a tight smile and turn back to the couple climbing the stairs.

My heart batters against my ribcage and I fight to hold my face neutral.

Enzo.

EIGHT

— Q ♠ —

DEL

I FORCE AIR IN and out of my lungs before I pass out as the Devil himself appears at the top of the stairs.

He seems bigger than I remember; his shoulders broad and solid, the dark charcoal grey suit fitted in absolute perfection.

He's wearing a tie that matches his suit over a soft blue shirt, but the sliver of that tempting neck peeking out still tempts me to mark it.

His pants, sweet Jesus, hug his huge thighs like a sin. He's even more terrifyingly beautiful now that I'm sober.

I'm transfixed, and he hasn't even turned those haunting eyes on me yet.

He's looking down at his companion as he lands on the mezzanine, and I tear my gaze from him to the short woman next to him.

She's breathtaking, with her long, caramel brown hair, hourglass shape, and obviously expensive dress. Her dark eyes gaze adoringly up to Enzo like he's God himself as she wraps her small arm around his huge bicep.

Fuck, is this his wife?

My eyes flick to Enzo and I almost miss the grimace at her touch before his perfect face smooths back into comfortable indifference. So maybe not his wife then?

His eyes turn to me, and I brace myself. For what? I'm not sure.

Whatever I expected, I didn't expect him to look at me like I was nobody. I swallow the surprising disappointment and smile a little brighter.

"Welcome to *Seduzione*," I say, looking at both Enzo and his guest as I step out from behind the podium. "If you require anything, please don't hesitate to ask."

The woman gives me a saccharine smile, which screams fake. "Thanks, hon."

Hon? This chick is going to grate on my nerves all night; I just know it.

I walk the pair over to the bar, stepping to the end, blending into the background like a good waiter should. Enzo orders a bourbon from Ty and a cocktail for the woman as Jace engages in a conversation with her.

Raph steps up to my side, his hand slipping to the curve of my back, the touch surprising me, taking my attention away from Enzo. His smile warms his face and *almost* dazzles me.

Raph leans closer, his warm breath tickling my ear. "I forgot to say earlier that you look incredible."

"Thank you," I whisper, a flush heating my cheeks.

His eyes hold me, his jaw clenching like he wants to say something.

"What?" I ask, but he doesn't answer me, instead pulling away from me and approaching Enzo.

"Lorenzo," Raph says, holding out his hand.

"Dragone," Enzo acknowledges Raph by his last name, accepting his handshake.

"Where's Matteo?" Raph asks.

"He'll be arriving any minute," Enzo states, picking up his drink and steering the woman by the elbow to the table.

They take seats next to each other, Jace sitting next to the woman, both having a polite conversation as Enzo pulls out his phone.

I take a settling breath, approaching the table, placing tonight's menu on the plates, starting with the empty seats, and moving around, approaching Jace.

He thanks me before I step between the woman and Enzo, place a menu down in front of her, and then step to Enzo's right side.

I don't want to disturb him, so I barely lean forward and drop the menu on his plate.

A large, warm hand slides up the back of my leg, curving into my inner thigh as it creeps higher.

I squeeze my legs together hard as Enzo's fingers reach the lace tops of my stockings.

So, he *does* remember me. Satisfaction blooms in my chest.

His hand clutches my thigh hard, painfully, and I fight the whimper lodged in my throat.

"Sparkling or still water?" I ask, my voice just audible.

Those damn eyes lift to me and my thighs tremble. The cerulean fire glowing in them is hot and bright.

"Sparkling, please," he says, his rumbling tone sending sparks through my whole body.

"Me too," the woman says. This could be his *wife*.

Enzo blinks at the sound of her voice, and like that, the fire is gone, glorious indifference cooling his features.

He pulls his hand away discreetly, allowing me to step back. I pull my attention to Jace, who also agrees to sparkling water, and then I cross back to the bar. My hands tremble slightly, and my heart is galloping.

I could handle this dinner if he dismissed me completely, but with that touch?

Wife. I shake the train of thought and switch back into work mode, opening a large bottle of sparkling water, returning to the table, and filling all the glasses. As I reach the bar again, the sound of someone bounding up the stairs snags my attention.

The man, barely puffing at the top of the stairs, must be related to Enzo. He has the same sharp jaw, tall frame, and neat, black hair, but he's not as large as Enzo and seems a lot younger.

I cross over to him with the usual soft smile on my face. "Welcome to *Seduzione.*"

The new guy's smile lights up his entire face. He steps forward and pulls me toward him, the fast move unbalancing me, so I fall against his chest.

"You spoil me, Raph," the man drawls, his arm tightening around my waist. His eyes are a dark blue compared to Enzo's vibrant cerulean.

"Matteo." The single name off Enzo's tongue in such a deadly tone makes my body tense in fear and my panties wet.

Matteo sighs, looking up toward Enzo. "You're no fun, bro."

His brother, that makes sense. Matteo releases me carefully, considerate since he practically snatched me into his arms a moment ago, and then crosses over and takes the seat next to Enzo.

I smooth down the front of my dress and cross to the discreet dumbwaiter door at the back of the room, once again blending into the shadows. If no one man-handles me again tonight, that will be an appreciated miracle.

Raph, who has been at the bar talking to Ty, strolls over to the table, taking up the last spot. "Dinner, and then business."

As I suspected, the woman, whose name I keep forgetting, is the most demanding witch I have ever served. She asks for changes on every item on the *set* menu, driving me and the kitchen insane.

The little angry notes with her dishes that the chefs leave in the dumbwaiter have me holding back laughter, but the notes have kept the tension at bay as I focus on my job and not on Enzo.

It helps that Enzo's back is to me most of the time, but I still notice the stiffness in his shoulders whenever the woman does something obnoxious. He's obviously not happy she's here.

At least my fear of being a homewrecker has been answered from the conversations I've overheard—apparently this woman is his father's widow. I'm pretty sure she's not even thirty. I'm not one to judge since I think Enzo is double my age.

The dumbwaiter lift clinks into place, and I pull up the door to five plates of dessert, one different from the others because the witch asked for something else entirely. I carry three plates over and serve them, then take over Enzo's and the witch's desserts.

"This isn't what I asked for," the witch whines as I put down *exactly* what she requested.

"Enough, Vivienne," Enzo murmurs low enough for only the two of us to hear above the lively conversation happening around the table.

The woman, *Vivienne*, shrinks at the warning in his tone, but pure, wicked satisfaction warms my chest as I step to Enzo's right side and place his dessert down. The slightest brush of his fingers on the side of my thigh zings through my skin. We're playing a secret game that only we know about.

"Any other drinks for the table?" I murmur softly to the group.

I concentrate incredibly hard on the orders thrown at me as Enzo's finger traces up my leg again, higher and higher, tingles crawling across my skin. I step back to the bar and put the order in, my breathing rough, and a flush heating my chest and face.

The party doesn't take long to finish their food and I clear the table of their plates.

"Let's move this conversation somewhere more comfortable," Raph says as I'm stacking the dirty dishes into the dumbwaiter. The party stands, all of them buttoning their suit jackets and collecting their drinks.

Vivienne is swaying on her feet, and Matteo sighs. "Time for you to go home now, Viv."

She scoffs. "Like hell I will."

Matteo motions to one of Enzo's henchmen and he immediately steps forward, placing a hand on her elbow. She struggles in his hold, but a harsh look from Enzo makes her obey and leave quickly.

All the men apart from Raph move to the couches. The tension in the room changes to something different. It feels dark, dangerous.

Raph waits by the bar as I approach. "Ty, you can go. Del can finish up in the bar."

"Sure thing, boss," Ty says immediately, grabbing his things and leaving like he was ready to run the moment he could.

Raph takes a slow breath, his eyes closing for a split moment, before he opens them again, and he looks... different. Harsher. He picks up his drink and walks over to the men who are lounging in the chairs.

They might look comfortable on the surface, but the shifting of eyes and controlled breathing looks like they're waiting for a weapon to be pulled. What is this?

"The shipment will be ready within the week," Raph announces, his tone cool and business-like.

"You're slacking, Dragone," Enzo drawls, swirling the bourbon in his glass. "You've been late on delivery twice now."

"There was a disruption in manufacturing and imports, but we've amended that problem. We have new connections in both areas."

"Do you at least have samples?" Matteo asks.

Raph nods at Jace, who pulls out a plain envelope from the breast pocket of his jacket and hands it to him. Raph pulls out something small and slides it over the low table between him and Matteo.

Matteo picks up the item and holds it up, shaking it. It's a tiny ziplock bag of white powder. Raph is a cocaine dealer? I let the information sink in as I watch Matteo open the bag, dip a finger in and then into his mouth.

He blinks a few times and then smiles. "This is better than the last shipment."

"I know," is all Raph says. He's not the dealer, but the supplier.

Enzo's face hasn't changed from indifferent contemplation. The room is silent, and I'm holding my breath, not knowing what is about to happen. He finally takes a sip of his drink and looks at Raph. "I'm taking an extra five percent."

"Excuse me?" Jace asks.

Enzo glares at him. "You want to run your drugs through my businesses, then be on time with delivery." Enzo's eyes are back on Raph. "This time it's only five percent; next time I take half of your profits."

"It won't happen again," Raph says.

"You have a week," Enzo states, standing from his seat and walking toward me at the bar. "And I want to meet your new import partner."

He leans his forearms on the marble top, rolling his glass between both hands, as Matteo mumbles something about signing paperwork. Raph offers his office as somewhere more secure to finalise things and the three men leave, leaving Enzo and me alone with one remaining security guy by the stairs.

"Would you like another drink?" I ask, trying to fill the tense silence.

Enzo looks up at me and that blazing fire back in his eyes. "Raphael should not have left us alone."

NINE

ENZO

"**H**E'LL BE WATCHING THE cameras," Delphine murmurs softly as she turns, reaching up to the top shelf bourbon.

The hem of her skirt lifts, reminding me that she's wearing lace-top stockings under that scrap of fabric.

I wonder if she'll let me take them off with my teeth.

She's only *eighteen*. And still in fucking high school. I'm twice her goddamn age.

Lucas couldn't find much else about her. She's an orphan—abandoned at a hospital when she was born and got lost in the foster system. He thought it was suspiciously odd that he couldn't find anything about her time in the system.

She has no bank accounts in her name, her licence address is an abandoned block in the middle of nowhere. She doesn't even have an internet presence. Raphael must have her off his books, because there's no record of her working here.

Who is this siren?

That question has been frustrating me the whole week. Is she hiding from someone? She works for the Dragones, is she in the life? Is she an informant?

The lack of information should steer me clear of her. Her fucking *age* should keep me away—she's *barely* into adulthood.

But seeing her again, that defiance simmering in those clear green eyes; I want to see her on her knees, begging me for her life.

"Does his feed have audio?" I ask, watching as she takes a clean glass and freely pours a perfect bourbon.

"I don't think so." She places the fresh drink in front of me and then steps back with the bottle, leaning against the back bench, setting the bottle down next to her. I have a perfect view of all of her—those ample breasts, supple body, and those thick thighs wrapped in stockings that I had my hands on earlier. I want them draped over my shoulders as I—

"What do you want?" she demands, her clear green eyes brim with cool irritation, like grass after a frost.

"Listen to me carefully," I murmur low, leaning forward slightly over the bar. Despite the distance, she leans back, her hand momentarily reaching up to her throat, like she's searching for a necklace, but then forces the hand down. Interesting. "Nobody walks away from me without consequences, Delphine."

Her brow raises, her tongue running across her teeth as she considers me. She's brave, and reckless, to be standing here so defiantly after everything she witnessed tonight. "Should I be scared, *Lorenzo?*"

I smile, the motion anything but nice. "So, you want to play, sweetheart?"

"You say that like I won't be able to win." Dangerous, dangerous response.

I stand straighter, picking up my glass. "You shouldn't challenge me, because I *will* win."

She sighs, picking the bourbon bottle again and stretching up to put it away. "I'm not a participant in whatever you think is happening."

"Have you been dreaming about me?" I ask before I can stop myself. Has she completely dismissed me in the past week?

Delphine spins back, those frosty eyes locking onto me. "Have you been dreaming of *me*?"

"I can't get you out of my head." She's there every night in my dreams, taunting the darker part of me that wants to consume her.

Her breathing changes, picking up slightly, and she grips the bench behind her tighter. *This* is the game. If she gets to goad me in my dreams, and rob me of peace in the waking hours, then she deserves the torment I'm going to deal out.

"I keep remembering those whimpers you made when I fucked you," I continue. "And the way you took my cock like a greedy little whore."

She smirks. "You should see what I can do with my tongue." She steps forward, heat flashing through her defiant gaze. "I'll have you begging."

I grip my glass hard, surprised it hasn't shattered in my hand. "Don't say things you can't back up, sweetheart."

"Can't handle a little tease, Enzo? You're not very good at this game."

"Say that to me when I've wrung out so many orgasms that you're sobbing, begging me to stop, and only then I'll bury my tongue into that dripping cunt and force you to come again."

She's practically panting, her arms trembling slightly. And those eyes, no longer frosty but bright emerald. I give her a shit-eating grin and take a sip of my drink.

Delphine clears her throat and stands up straight. "Too bad that devil tongue won't get anywhere near me."

"Oh really?"

She laughs softly, the sound sinking into my bones. "You think I'm that easy?"

"You fucked me in a church after knowing me for less than five minutes."

"That was a one-off. You'll have to try much harder next time."

"I'm going to carve deep into your soul, sweetheart, and pull out your darkest fantasies."

That defiant burn simmers in Delphine's eyes as she smiles. "You're going to have to catch me first."

The dark part of me pushes forward at the challenge, demanding I take what we want.

I watch her walk the length of the bar, my body not moving a muscle—she's lucky there are cameras, or she'd be bent over the table and fucked until she forgot her own name.

She pulls out her phone from under the bench and then steps out from the security of the bar.

I watch every step and every intake of breath as she heads towards the staircase. Is her heart beating rapidly?

I follow a few steps behind her, watching her body sway, desperately wanting to pin her against a wall and taste her. No, not taste, *consume*.

As she hits the bottom of the stairs, Matteo, Jace and Raph approach from the back of the restaurant.

I step up behind Delphine, close enough that I can feel warmth radiating off her. This is the closest I've been to her all night, and I inhale deeply. Ripe strawberries and burning frankincense. I have the absurd urge to press her against me, so her scent lingers on my clothes again.

"Is it sorted?" I ask Matteo, keeping my hands at my side.

Matteo nods, his attention on his phone. Delphine takes a soft, shaky breath and crosses to the door, that fake cheery waitress smile plastered across her face. Any fire or frost leaves her clear green eyes—I hate it.

Matteo walks out without a second glance, and so do Lucas and Dragone's man, Jace. Raphael walks toward Delphine and wraps an arm around her waist. Surprise flashes through her eyes before settling back to blank politeness.

"Pleasure doing business, Dragone," I grit out as I exit the restaurant.

"Lorenzo," Raphael says with a nod, holding out his hand. I shake it once before turning and walking away.

Delphine forgot to mention that she's already claimed. And by Dragone, no less. Raw, ugly anger skitters over my skin.

"Do you need a lift home?" I hear Dragone ask softly.

I can't help but stop and turn, waiting for Delphine's response. Maybe it was just a show on Raphael's part, maybe they're not...

"Yes, please," she says with a shy smile.

Fuck.

TEN

— Q ♣ —

DEL

I STEP AWAY FROM Raph, my skin crawling from his unexpected touch, walking back into the restaurant toward the staff room. I'm wired and my hands are shaky from the interaction with Enzo—the things he said, the things *I* said.

I let out a breath as I put my crewneck over my dress, grab my bag from my locker and meet Raph at his office. We make our way to the back exit and walk over to the private parking spot that Raph rents in the building behind *Seduzione*—parking around here is a nightmare, so I tend to get public transport.

"I have so many questions," I blurt out as we enter the elevator of the car park.

"I expected that." Raph sighs as he leads me out to his grey sports car. I slide onto the beige interior, my brain filtering through all the information I learned tonight, as Raph gets into the driver's side and backs out of the space.

"Does your dad know?" I ask as I adjust the temperature controls.

"It's a *family* business, so yes." There's something about his clipped tone, like he's encouraging me to listen to what's *not* being said.

"Family crime business. Sure, like the—" Oh shit. My head whips to Raph. The mafia? Surely not.

Raph's eyes flick to mine, and he nods at my silent question before looking back to the road.

I laugh, the sound a little hysterical. "Of all people I end up working for, it's ..." I can't bring myself to say it out loud. I knew Enzo was dangerous when I met him, but I didn't think I was a magnet for all the criminals in Melbourne.

"Is it you or Mario in charge?" I can't imagine sweet old Mario being a ruthless mob boss.

"Dad is still the head of the family, but I'm in charge of all operations."

"I find it really hard to picture the Chef dealing illicit—"

"*Import*," Raph corrects. "We import the products, and Lorenzo's family sells them."

I don't even know what to say, what to think.

"It's a lot to take in," Raph murmurs softly, "and I'm sorry I've dragged you into this, but there's no one else I'd trust to keep this to themselves."

"Why me?"

"When Sophia joined our team, what do you think she wanted?"

"A job."

Raph laughs sardonically. "I wish, but no. She saw the money, the influence, and wanted it."

I turn my body towards Raph. "Did she know?"

"Absolutely not, but when money is involved, people always have an angle."

"I never even thought about it."

"And that's why I trust you, because you have no ulterior motives."

"How long have you been in the import business?"

"Three generations," Raph mutters, his eyes flicking to mine before returning to the road.

"How do you know them? Your business partners."

Raph sighs, raking his hand through his hair. "Mario and their late father go way back."

"How does it work?"

"It's best you don't know the specifics," he says as he turns into my street. "But you need to know the Herrington family is dangerous."

Says the mobster. Raph stops in front of the gate of the Sakura property when I register what he said. "*Herrington?*"

"The one and only," Raph grits out.

Everyone in this city has heard of the Herrington family. They're renowned for their vast conglomerate, mainly in hospitality and construction. They own a large portion of the buildings and businesses in the city.

Raph switches the car off and grasps my knee. "Promise me you'll stay away from them."

I shuffle in my seat, trying to dislodge Raph's touch. "What?"

"I saw the way Matteo touched you," he says, his face bitter. "He's not someone you should associate with."

I can't help but laugh. If only he knew which Herrington brother was the real threat to my safety. "Don't worry, I can look after myself."

Hot, panting breath warms my ear as he crushes me under his heavy body.

"Thank you, Kitty," he huffs, kissing the skin under my ear. My ribs ache at the force of holding back the sobs. I need him to sneak out now like he usually does so I can be alone.

"*Kitty*," he grunts, his head lifting from my neck, his angry eyes on mine. "I said, thank you."

"You're welcome, sir," I whisper, thanking God that the sobs are at bay. I can cry when he leaves.

He finally rolls his huge body off me, my thighs burning in exhaustion as I roll to my side, tucking my knees into my chest and gripping onto my rosary for dear life. It's nearly over, he'll leave soon.

His rough hand skims down my spine, the touch reverent. "You have such pretty skin, Delphine."

"Thank you, sir," I respond, silently urging him to leave. Once is enough today.

His hand continues to stroke my back, making me shiver, twisting my gut in tight knots. The bed dips closer to me, his body heat radiating into my back as his hand slips around my waist, his hand stretching over my stomach.

"So soft," he murmurs into my ear. His hand twists, clutching my thigh, pushing it away from my chest and hooking it over his. Not again...

I jolt awake, my head pounding and sweat coating my skin. I take a few moments to clear my head and calm my heart rate before dragging myself out of bed. It's around dawn, judging from the silvery blue light glowing through the windows, as I turn the water on in the shower to just below scorching.

I leave the lights off in the bathroom, not wanting to deal with the brightness right now as I strip down and walk under the huge downpour of hot water. The stinging of the water's hard pressure releases the hold of the memories wanting to drag me back into that pain inferno from which they slithered out.

Memories are assholes. The happy ones are messy, vague black and white reels in the periphery. But the nightmares? They run on repeat in brilliant technicolour at the forefront of your mind in precise detail when you let your guard down.

I take my time washing my entire body twice over, rebuilding those walls in my mind and preparing myself for today.

I've been fine all week, concentrating on school and going to work, and not about the absolute shit-show this baptism will most likely be. Especially because I know all the people I don't want to see will be there.

I rinse out the hair treatment and step out of the shower, wrapping myself in a towel, and drying my hair with another. The light is now a soft grey as I sit on the floor in front of the full-length mirror on the door of my wardrobe.

The dark hollows around my eyes accentuate the green irises in all the wrong ways. My skin has light pink scars from picking at my face over the years, a nervous habit I picked up after I stopped wearing rosary beads, but at least it's not textured.

I apply moisturiser all over my face and get to work on my make-up. I keep it minimal, evening out my skin tone, filling in my brows, coating my long lashes with mascara and applying a tinted gloss to my dry lips.

Now that I look less disturbing, I leave my hair to air dry as I get up, put on underwear and a bra, and then contemplate an outfit when Scar swings the door open.

"Good morning," she sings as she closes the door behind her and flops onto my bed. "You're looking gorgeous today."

"Uhuh," I grumble, pulling out a long-sleeved t-shirt and a calf-length flowing skirt from my wardrobe.

"Are you sure you don't want me to go with you?" she asks me for the hundredth time this week.

"As much fun as that would be," I muse, tucking the dark grey top into the black skirt, "I can handle this one on my own."

"But think of your mum fainting when we make out *in* the church."

I laugh. "You're terrible, Scar."

"You love it."

"I do, but I promise, I'm fine." I pull on shorts under my skirt and take out my beat-up black leather jacket, flinging it on the bed next to Scar. My mum hates this jacket, so naturally it's my favourite thing to wear when I'm forced to be in her presence.

I pull on socks and zip up my buckle-covered biker boots as Scar braids my hair into two boxer braids, with a few strands hanging loose at the front. The night I moved in here, Scar found me with kitchen scissors cutting off all my waist-long hair.

He always liked my long, wavy black hair, and threatened violence if I ever dyed it, so that first night we also bought supplies and dyed the ends of my hair cobalt blue as a big fuck-you to my past life.

"Thanks, Angel Face," I say, tracing the braids softly with the tips of my fingers and standing up from the floor.

"I think we should change the colour," Scar contemplates. "Maybe green or red."

I laugh. "Let's do it tonight; surprise me with the colour."

Scar's face lights up and she bounds out of the room. I pick up the car keys, my phone, the baptism present I picked up and leave the Sakura property before I decide not to go.

I make the short drive to the St. John's church and park in a side street. The place is teeming with people. Of course, my mother and William are making a big fucking spectacle over this event with all their stupid society friends.

I roll my shoulders back, straightening my posture as I walk through the throng of glamour and glitz, every judgemental gaze landing on me.

The storm cloud of my mother's life is here, and I dare any of these dickheads to make a single comment, because I'm ready to strike like lightning.

I enter the church, cross myself with the holy water and make my way down the centre aisle towards the people I am forced to call relatives.

Sometimes I forget that my mother is a beautiful woman. Today her straight, rich brown hair falls in a glossy sheet between her shoulder blades, away from the soft angles of her face; her light brown eyes and smile scream kindness. She's small, thin, and always perky, but that pretty shell holds a selfish, sour heart.

Next to her is William, her fourth husband, holding a small baby dressed in white. William is tall, but average looking with his blonde hair, blue eyes, and thin body—he's definitely batting way out of his league with my mother.

But of course, she didn't marry him for his looks, but for his bank account.

Bridgette is cute for a baby. She has wisps of light brown curls and fat cheeks; her blue eyes are the same as her father's, but she has the same round eye shape as our mother.

My eyes finally land on Isaac and my heart squeezes. Isaac is basically our mother's replica, with his neat brown hair, light brown eyes, and handsome face, but he's much taller. We both get our height from our respective fathers.

Ice shards slice through my lungs as I lock down memories trying to surface. I breathe slowly, stopping a few steps away from the four of them. The moment my mother's eyes fall on me, I can see the shadow of disapproval in their depths.

"Delphine, I'm so glad you made it." Her tone is polite but clipped.

"Mum, William, Isaac," I force out as a greeting. I hold out the small gift bag. "This is for Bridgette."

"Hold it until the reception; we have a gift table there," my mother says.

"I'm only here for the church ceremony." No way I'm putting myself in a situation where any of these people can corner me.

As she's about to berate me, my mother's eyes flick behind me and a blinding smile lights up her face.

"Vivienne, darling," she croons, as she steps past me. I turn and almost bolt. It's the little witch from the dinner last weekend.

"Eleanor, you look amazing," she says as they embrace—the display is polite but formal. These people don't have a genuine emotion in their cold bodies.

"You're looking good yourself," my mother says, her eyes travelling over Vivienne. "How are you holding up?"

"I miss my poor Joseph." Vivienne's tone falters. "But it gets a little easier every day." The inauthenticity of these people grinds on my patience, but I just need to get through this ceremony and then I can escape these people.

My mother sweeps her arms toward me. "You know William. This is my daughter, Delphine, my son, Isaac, and our little angel, Bridgette."

My heart stills. Shit.

"Oh, you are as beautiful as your mother," Vivienne says to me. From the shiny eyes and surprised expression, she obviously doesn't remember me from last week's dinner.

I loosen my breath and give her the blank smile I use at work. "Thank you."

My mother and Vivienne wander over to William and Bridgette, releasing me from the spotlight. I shove the gift bag in Isaac's unsuspecting hands and then take a seat in the third pew from the front—I don't need the lecture if I sit any further back.

I admire the architecture of the ornate ceilings and how the late autumn sunlight shines through the stained-glass windows as the sounds of chatter increase from people filing in and filling the pews.

Someone steps into my pew from the other side in my peripheral, shuffling closer and taking a seat next to me.

"We need to stop meeting in this church."

ELEVEN

— Q ♠ —

DEL

ENZO AGAIN.

"Mr. *Herrington*," I say, turning to face him.

"So, you know who I am." A smile plays across his face. "But I don't know who *you* are."

"You know, it's kind of odd that your name is Lorenzo. Shouldn't you be James Herrington the Third or something obnoxious like that? I'd expect the prestigious *Herringtons* to have names they pass down to their men."

His smile deepens, but I don't miss something darker flashing in his eyes. "Our mother had a love for Italian Renaissance painters."

I nod, getting the feeling asking questions about his mother would be dangerous territory. "I didn't expect to see you here."

"It's a surprise to see you here, as well. Much like the first time we met in this church."

Heat blooms on my cheeks, my eyes immediately sweeping over to the confessional. I clear my throat, turning my attention back to the front of the church.

Enzo leans closer in my peripheral, his citrus and spice scent stirring around me. "Should we go confess our sins?"

"You haven't caught me yet, Enzo," I whisper, watching as Vivienne shuffles to the front pew, sitting next to one of Enzo's henchmen from the other night.

"It's only a matter of time, sweetheart," he murmurs into my ear as the conversations around us hush.

"Your hubris knows no bounds," I say as I stand with the congregation.

"We're going to run into each other again in these circles," Enzo points out as the choir fills the church with angelic hymns.

"I'm not part of this snake pit." The priest walks down the centre aisle, an altar boy swinging a thurible in front of him, the smoke stinging my nostrils.

"Why *are* you here?" Enzo whispers.

"I really wish I wasn't," I mumble, directing my attention to the priest talking to my mother and William, but I can't really hear the words.

My head is swimming, my vision narrowing. I try to breathe slowly, but my throat feels like it's closing as Isaac and one of William's older daughters step up to the priest's other side.

My chest burns, tears stinging my eyes. I need to breathe, just *breathe* ...

A warm hand slides onto my thigh, gripping it firmly. The touch pulls me out of the wormhole in my head, and I grab onto Enzo's hand like a lifeline. The air pops, my brain stops buzzing, and I can hear and see again.

I take a deep, shuddering breath, gripping Enzo's hand tight as the ceremony drags along like I didn't just almost pass out.

I manage to go through all the motions I'm supposed to, Enzo's touch never leaving me as the priest pours the holy water on Bridgette's head.

Freedom taunts me; just a few more prayers, and I can get the fuck out of here.

My mother steps up to the podium, tapping the microphone twice. "I just wanted to thank everyone who came to this special event today. William and I appreciate it immensely." Her eyes find me in the crowd. "Especially to my children, Isaac and Delphine, who stepped away from their important studies and jobs to make this day extra special."

A polite smile etches on my face, hiding the anger bubbling under my skin. She's provoking me, daring me to leave now when all these people will expect me to be at the reception. Fucking hell. She steps down from the podium as the priest begins the last prayers.

"You're an Anderson?" Enzo murmurs softly to me, his hand slipping out of my lap.

"Definitely not," I whisper.

"Then who *are* you?" he asks. The question makes me turn to him. Enzo's eyes search my face. His facial hair is longer than the last time I saw him, and I have the sudden urge to run my fingers over his jaw.

"I'm nobody."

"That's not true," he says as his eyes hold mine.

It's my turn to frown. He doesn't know anything about me, or the complete nothingness that fills the missing pieces of my broken soul.

The ringing of the altar boy's bells snags my attention away from Enzo as the choir starts another hymn, the priest walking off the dais, slipping past a wooden door through the arch to the left. Chatter erupts through the church, filling the space with white noise.

"Why are you here?" I ask Enzo.

"Vivienne needed an escort," he says, "and Matteo doesn't do churches."

"Surely one of your henchmen would be enough?"

He frowns. "Vivienne tends to make a spectacle of herself when she's left unattended at one of these things."

As if summoned, the witch appears at the end of our pew with a bright smile on her face. "Lorenzo, I see you've met Eleanor's daughter, Delphine."

"It's Del," I say.

My mother and William approach from behind Vivienne, followed by Isaac holding Bridgette.

"Are you sure you can't make it to the reception, Delphine?" My full name being thrown around is going to make my ears bleed.

"I can stop by," I force through clenched teeth.

My mother's face shines, turning my stomach. She knows she's won. "Fantastic! You can ride with us."

"I drove here; just send me the address."

Confusion flashes in her eyes. "You're too young to drive."

I genuinely smile for the first time today. "I've turned eighteen since the last time I saw you."

The surprised looks of Vivienne and others warm my heart as I turn on my heel and stalk out of the church.

I don't slow down until I'm in the street where I parked the car and gulp in air, trying to calm my racing heart as I close my eyes. Why can't my mother just pretend I don't exist, instead of dragging me into these stupid games?

"She blamed baby-brain on why she forgot your birthday," Enzo's deep voice rumbles behind me.

"She's flawless at excuses," I say, opening my eyes and continuing toward the car, not sparing a glance back.

"Delphine," Enzo calls.

"Please, don't call me that."

As I get to the car and unlock the door, a warm hand wraps around my elbow and I'm shoved into the closed passenger door. Strong fingers grab my chin, tipping my head back, forcing me to stare into cerulean flames.

"Why the fuck are you ignoring me?" Enzo growls.

"Who do you think you are to *demand* my attention?"

He releases my chin, his hand gripping the side of my neck just under my ear, his thumb tracing the front of my throat. "Obviously you didn't catch on last weekend that I'm not someone to fuck with."

I chuckle, ignoring my heart skittering at his touch. "It's cute that you think I care."

Enzo's eyes darken, and then he slams his mouth to mine. The move startles me, my lips opening to him so he thrusts his tongue into my mouth. My body relaxes for the first time in days, my racing thoughts easing further as I stroke his tongue with mine.

From the moment we met, Enzo has never triggered the usual panic that seizes me when someone touches me, something I never thought would happen. But can I really trust this feeling of security?

Enzo's free hand slides down my arm, his mouth still dominating mine, as he pulls the car key out of my hand.

I pull back. "I would have thought car theft was beneath you."

Enzo releases my throat as he chuckles. "Get in the car, sweetheart."

I slide away from the passenger door and Enzo opens it, waiting for me to climb in. Curious to know where this is going, I slip into the car. Enzo closes the door, crosses to the driver's side as I fasten my seatbelt and climbs in, starting the engine.

"Where are we going?" I ask.

"To the reception," he says simply as he reverses and swings out of the parking spot.

"How disappointing," I murmur, pulling my phone out and fiddling with the car's music controls, picking a heavy metal playlist.

"It won't be a disappointment, trust me," Enzo says as he turns the music up to an ear-piercing level and drives past the church at an alarming speed.

Laughter bubbles out of my chest as I see the disapproving faces of the dwindling crowd flying past and settle in for the ride.

We don't talk throughout the drive into the city, letting the music's heavy sounds fill the silence. I turn the music down as we turn into the lavish driveway of *Luxuria*, one of the Herrington Family's high-end hotels. Enzo climbs out of the driver's seat as a valet attendant opens my door.

I thank him as I get out and walk toward Enzo, who gives another valet attendant the car key and then disappears through the hotel doors.

Okay?

The other attendant gives me a ticket, and I walk through the glass doors into the huge foyer.

Everything is clean, from the polished marble floors to the sleek white front desk. A few people lounge on the low couches and armchairs clustered in the middle of the space and there are businessmen and women with small suitcases waiting to be served by the desk attendants.

A simple white board with the words 'BRIDGETTE'S BAPTISM' in bold letters sits near the elevators at the back of the foyer. As I get closer, it informs me the reception is in the ballroom on the third floor, so I take an elevator.

Two security guards stop me at the door, asking for my name.

"Del or Delphine Blaire," I tell them.

One of them flips through a clipboard and shakes his head. What?

"Delphine," my mother calls, approaching us. "I was worried you got lost." She points to the second page over the guard's shoulder. "Here, Delphine Garcia."

The audacity of this woman. Does she live to twist the knife in every time we meet? I haven't been known by *that* last name since the day I left, and I never will again. The other security guard unhooks the rope, allowing me access, and my mother wraps her bony arm around mine.

"So, you drive now?" she muses.

I laugh, pulling my arm from her grip. "We don't have to do this."

"Do what?" she says, feigning confusion.

"You don't have to pretend I exist. I'm perfectly happy being an orphan."

She gapes. "I am your mother. I lo—"

"We know *none* of what you're about to say is remotely true." I walk away before she can say anything else and enter a set of double doors.

The ballroom has massive sparkling chandeliers dotting the roof, the lighting dim.

A sea of pale pink and white covered round tables are set throughout the space, with an open area in front of a stage where a band is playing soft music.

All this money spent for a six-month-old who won't remember or care about any of this in the future—typical behaviour for these upper-class assholes.

A small table on my left has a seating chart, which I scan. Delphine *Garcia* is sitting at a table with the Andersons, but Del Blaire is going to sit at the table with an empty seat on the other side of the ballroom.

I weave in and out of the tables, finding the table with people I don't know, and slide into the seat, smiling.

"Hi, everyone," I say to no one in particular as I wave down a waiter and order a Tom Collins.

Gin is definitely the answer today.

Not that I can drink much, but I need to take the edge off.

When my drink arrives, I thank the waiter and settle into my seat, watching the power plays happening around me.

There are a lot of important people here—politicians and celebrities. If you know what to look for, you can see the careful gestures and hear the precise words. I don't know how they play this game day after day; it looks exhausting.

I can feel eyes on me, and hear my name said occasionally, which is grating on my nerves. This is why I didn't want to come to this thing—I don't want to be thrown in with these sharks, I just want to be forgotten.

A hush goes over the crowd when Vivienne, Matteo and Enzo walk in, going straight to my mother's table.

Vivienne exchanges another one of those weird polite hugs with my mother and then strikes up a conversation with her as Matteo shakes Isaac's hand.

I can't help but look at Enzo. He's magnetic; his presence steals your attention and doesn't let go. He exudes danger, and I want to burn myself on that infernal flame.

I drag my eyes away from him. I need to shake this sick fascination I have with this devilish man. And, *no*, I don't want to see him naked.

I polish off my drink and pick at the food set out in front of me, questioning whether my mother poisoned my plate just for the spectacle.

As I pick up my fresh drink, the familiar sensation of someone watching me tingles on the back of my neck.

"I hope you're not thinking about drinking and then driving?" Enzo murmurs into my ear.

"I've moved on to soda water," I say, holding my drink up to my shoulder. Enzo leans forward, and I see him in my periphery wrapping his lips around the straw. He takes a small sip of drink before he pulls back.

"Good girl," Enzo whispers into the other ear. *I don't want him to whisper filthier things into my ear.*

"I'm curious," Enzo murmurs, "about your time in foster care, Miss *Blaire*."

"So you did look into me," I say softly, trying not to panic. He didn't find anything. It's fine.

"Delphine Evelyn Blaire," he rumbles into my ear. "Orphan—abandoned at three days old."

"That's me."

His warm finger trails down my neck. "Why are you lying to me, little siren?"

I fight the shivers, the urge to run coursing through my veins. "I looked into you too."

"And what did you find?" he whispers.

"Lorenzo, no middle name I could find, Herrington. Thirty-six year old CEO of Herrington Global."

"And?"

"Your father recently died, leaving you the entire Herrington dynasty, so you have a *lot* of money. Mostly from property and investments. But people don't know your *other* form of income." I pick up my glass and take a drink. "Speaking of, shouldn't you be networking, or breaking someone's kneecaps, or whatever you do at these things?"

No, Del, you aren't interested in the crime lord side of him.

"Why would I do any of those things when I can be here playing with you?" I've piqued the interest of the Devil, and that's a dangerous fucking game.

"I'm not into this particular game, Mr. Herrington." I shouldn't be into *any* game with Enzo.

His breath is hot against my neck as he chuckles softly. His spiced grapefruit and sandalwood scent swirls around me. Why does he have to smell so damn *good?*

"Pick someone," he rumbles, dragging my focus back to the present. I'm surprised that no one has been paying attention to us since he's a Herrington and I seem to be a topic of gossip.

"For what?" I whisper.

"Pick someone you want me to hurt."

I sit further back in my chair, feeling the warmth of his body against mine. "Is this the type of game you *really* want to play?"

"I'd rather be fucking you until you're screaming my name." Enzo's tongue runs a hot path up my neck and then he nips my ear, sending shooting pain through the earlobe. My thighs squeeze together tight. "But let's start with a little foreplay."

His finger traces across my shoulder and down my arm, his big hand grabbing mine and pulling me from the chair. We weave through the crowd, and I notice they turn their attention away from us, like they don't want to draw the attention of the Devil among t hem.

I like to think that I'm smart, that I walk on the safer side of life, but that would be a lie. Pure darkness rolls off Enzo in a thunderous wave. It has the potential to cause absolute fucking destruction, and I want to drown in it.

TWELVE

DEL

ENZO AND I WALK directly up to the Andersons and the other Herringtons.

Matteo's blue eyes sparkle in recognition. "Raphael's girl."

My mother turns, her eyes dropping to where Enzo has wrapped an arm around my waist, questions brewing in her stare.

"Delphine," Enzo corrects, his hand squeezing my hip, bringing me closer to his side.

"Just Del," I insist.

"Raphael?" Vivienne asks. "You know Raphael Dragone?"

"She was working at his restaurant last weekend," Matteo explains. "Perhaps you were a little too liberal with the cocktails to remember."

I bite down the smile forming at the anger simmering in Vivienne's dark eyes.

"What brings you here, Del?" Matteo asks.

"She's my sister," Isaac blurts out next to Matteo.

"You're a Bennett?"

"Oh no," I answer Matteo with a saccharine grin. "I'm the child from Eleanor's second marriage."

"And how do *you* two know each other?" My mother interjects, her tone too bright, which means she's livid.

"We met at church," Enzo says.

He's not wrong.

"If I knew there was such interesting company, I might actually go," Matteo comments, his smile predatory.

I feel Enzo go very still next to me, so I turn to William. "How do the Andersons know the Herringtons?"

"We're in business together," William says, bouncing Bridgette in his arms.

"Yes," my mother says, cutting off William's next words. "Our company looks after the cyber security for many of the companies under Herrington Global." *Our company*, like my mother actually contributes anything to it.

As the group begins to talk about business, Enzo seems to loosen slightly next to me. The conversation about money becomes white noise as my eyes scan the room.

People finally get the courage to approach Enzo, also talking business, and I think I need to order another drink, or five, if I'm going to have to listen to this drivel all night.

Enzo draws my attention back when his hand slides from my hip to splay over my ass cheek, the possessive squeeze like a brand.

"Found anyone yet?" Enzo says so softly that no one near us notices; he's referring to our earlier conversation about busting kneecaps.

"I have a list," I murmur.

"We could start from the top."

"Tempting," I muse, looking up into his simmering blue depths.

"I have to conduct some *other* business. Care to join me?"

I blink in surprise at the invite. "Are you sure?"

"There may be violence."

"I hope so," I say without thinking. The opportunity to be thrust into the underworld at the Devil's side makes my body ache in the most devious way.

Enzo's eyes burn brighter. "Wicked siren."

He turns back to the group, who have been oblivious to our exchange. "If you'll excuse us."

Everyone except Matteo has a mix of confusion and curiosity flash across their faces as Enzo steers me away toward the staff door near the stage. As we step into a hallway, the music is muffled when the door closes behind us.

"I can't wait for the endless questions coming my way for that departure," I comment as we approach another door at the end of the hallway.

"William is smart enough to not ask questions about his boss' personal life."

"My mother won't play by those rules." I point out as he opens the door. The same two men stand by an elevator wearing their usual dark suits.

"Henchman one and two," I say in greeting.

"Lucas," henchman one says, pointing at himself. He was there the night I met Enzo and at the restaurant. He's tall, has stern dark brown eyes and has a buzz cut, which gives him an intimidating edge.

Lucas points to henchman two, who's blonde and not much taller than me. "Peter."

Peter smiles at me, and I force myself not to cringe. He's attractive, but there's something about him that sets my flight instincts on edge.

"Are our guests here yet?" Enzo asks Lucas, drawing my attention away from Peter.

"They're halfway through their game," Lucas confirms, pressing the elevator button. The doors slide open almost immediately and the four of us step in, Lucas pressing the sixth-floor button.

"Did they bring security?" Enzo asks.

"The usual did," Peter answers.

"Weapons were checked in at the door," Lucas adds.

"Excellent," Enzo says as he squeezes my waist. I look up at his amused face. "Have you played any type of poker before?"

"I've played a game or two, but it's been a while." Any chance we could, Isaac and I snuck away to play poker in secret from *him*. I liked the pretty patterns on the cards, and the colourful chips. It was the only time I wasn't constantly living on the edge, wondering when he was going to...

"Good," Enzo says, pulling me from spiralling too far into that particular train of thought as the doors slide open. Lucas and Peter step out first and then motion for us to follow.

We're in a short service hallway with nothing in it except for two doors on either side, one with a sign that says 'stairs'. We go through the other door into a dark reception area. A stunning woman stands at a black desk with a beaming smile as she sweeps her hand over toward the heavy curtains on the left.

"Welcome back, Mr. Herrington," she says, her eyes glued on him, not even acknowledging my existence.

Enzo nods once in response as Lucas and Peter pull the curtains, scanning the area and then nodding at us to enter. The room we enter has the same decor: dark carpeted floors, dark walls, low lighting, but the atmosphere is tense. A large, circular poker table is in the centre of the room, with four men around it and a card dealer.

As we approach the only two empty seats, I recognise one man straight away. He's some state official that was recently accused of being lax with approving things that are not exactly up to code. I guess being at a poker table with someone like Enzo would make sense for someone with his reputation.

Enzo pulls out one of the black leather chairs and offers it to me. I sit, expecting Enzo to take the one next to me, but he leans on the back of mine, his fingers playing with the end of one of my braids.

As every pair of eyes land on me, I meet each one of them with an unrelenting gaze.

The guy sitting next to the state official is quite attractive, with tattoos covering every inch of visible skin from the chin down. The light reflects off multiple rings on his tattooed hand as he plays with one of the rings of his snake-bite lip piercings. His light honey-brown eyes burn with mischief—if anyone is going to start trouble, it's definitely going to be him.

He's wearing a black t-shirt over his broad, muscled body, and a leather cut with a distinctive patch on the left side. I don't linger on the black wings stitched into the leather, knowing it's the logo for allegedly the most violent motorcycle gang in the country, The Savage Wings. This guy is probably their president if he's here.

Enzo releases my hair, and points to my right, drawing my attention to the man next to me. "This is the Surgeon."

I've seen this doctor before at the Sakura residence. He's a heart surgeon accused of murdering four patients in the last three years and gotten away with it.

I force my eyes away from him as Enzo continues the introductions. "And this is the Politician, the Mechanic, and the Barrister."

The Barrister is also someone I've never seen before, but being around this table, he's probably the lawyer of Melbourne's underworld. He looks like your typical lawyer—neat blonde hair, clean-shaven face, and grey eyes that take in everything he sees.

The code names are for anonymity but also represent their depravity. I wonder if Enzo has a code name.

"This is the Siren," Enzo murmurs above me. It should terrify me, gaining the attention of the city's most notorious villains, but with the Devil on my side, it's *exhilarating.*

His arm wraps across my chest, just under my chin. "What's the play?"

"Texas Hold'em. Three hundred, six hundred game," the Mechanic says, sliding his cards toward the dealer. "Where's the Dragon and the Blade?"

"They won't be attending," Enzo says as a brick of hundred-dollar notes and two bricks of fifty-dollar notes land on the table in front of me. "Our buy-in is fifty thousand."

I keep my face neutral as the dealer scoops up the cash and slides over stacks of colourful chips. Fifty *thousand.* I know the Herrington's are drowning in money, but Jesus Christ. Enzo must be crazy to trust me to play with his money. His arm uncurls around me, and both hands clutch the armrests, his chin resting on my shoulder.

"Try not to blow through all of my money at once," he whispers into my ear.

"I can't guarantee that." I turn my face toward him, our lips touching. "Remind me how to play."

Enzo captures my bottom lip between his teeth, biting down before releasing it and then explains the game happening in front of me. He points out the different ways to bet and reminds me of the hands that win. I watch a few more rounds before I tell the dealer I'm ready to play.

The dealer puck is with the Surgeon next to me, so I put in the small blind, and the Barrister slides over the big blind as the dealer throws over cards.

The Mechanic folds his hand immediately, blowing out a frustrated breath as scrapes he fingers through his dark brown hair.

"How's business, Executive?" the Politician asks as he checks his cards and folds them as well.

"There were slight delays with shipment," Enzo murmurs at my shoulder. "But the Dragon has tied up loose ends."

So, Raphael is part of the dark committee, his code name making sense as his last name translates to 'dragon'.

The Surgeon checks his cards, and raises to a thousand, turning to me with a smirk. I've only seen him a couple times when I lurked in the shadows at some of Claudine's fundraisers, but I've always gotten bad vibes from him. He probably thinks he's attractive, but the dark greasy hair and over-whitened teeth just make him look creepy.

I don't even look at my cards as I call his raise. Soft laughter rumbles around the room, the Barrister also calling.

"The Siren's come to play," the Mechanic comments as he leans back and crosses his arms. I smirk, and then finally look at my cards. A pair of Kings, a strong hand. The dealer deals three cards into the centre of the table, one of them being another King, giving me a triple.

"Three thousand," I say, throwing out the chips. The Barrister folds, leaving me and the Surgeon.

The cocky grin plastered across his face makes me want to punch him. "Raise to five thousand."

"Call."

I watch the Surgeon as the dealer flips the next card. His eyes widen a fraction and I see him swallow before his cockiness returns. I turn to the cards; it's a two, the lowest card in poker. I check, but the Surgeon bets five hundred, so I call his bet. The next card thrown is a four, and I check again.

"Two thousand," the Surgeon says, throwing out the chips, looking at me like he's expecting me to fold. I throw out the chips to call and sit back.

The Surgeon flips his cards confidently, showing his double Tens on the table. "Better luck next time, love."

I flip over my cards, staring hard at the Surgeon. "Don't ever call me 'love' again."

"Oh shit," the Mechanic chuckles. "This is going to be fun."

THIRTEEN

ENZO

ANGER DARKENS THE SURGEON'S eyes as he glares at Delphine before turning his attention back to the dealer.

"I'm impressed," I murmur into Delphine's ear. Strawberries and frankincense fill my senses when I'm this close.

"Be prepared to have your mind blown," she whispers, stacking her winnings.

"If only you were blowing other body parts."

"Later," she purrs as she looks at her new hand and folds immediately. The games go quick, Delphine making calculated moves and betting smart. She seems to have good instincts for the other player's tells as well. She's observant, my siren.

No. Not mine. But ...

"Sir," Lucas murmurs behind me, pulling my attention from the poker table. He holds out my phone.

I walk to the far end of the ballroom, leaving Peter to watch Delphine.

My phone lights up with Dragone's name as I slink into the shadows.

"Do you have the package?" I ask as I answer.

"Handing it to the courier now."

"And the meet with your new partner?"

Dragone sighs. "Still working on it."

"He has two weeks before I find another importing company."

"Why are you suddenly so invested in the way I handle business?"

"Because you've dropped the ball, and I won't have it disrupt *my* side of business."

Dragone laughs. "You know our business arrangement is under blood oath, you can't get out of it without consequences."

I smile. "You're close to breaking your end of the bargain, so it won't be me that is causing problems."

Low voices murmur in the background of Dragone's line and he bites out a confirmation. "I'll contact you with the meet details. And tell your brother to stay away from my employees." The line cuts out.

Matteo needs to stay away from—

"Executive, you'll want to come watch this," the Barrister calls from the poker table.

I take a steadying breath as I walk back over to Delphine, pocketing my phone. My hand glides over the soft skin of the side of her neck as I take in the play.

Delphine seems to be nursing about forty grand and the Surgeon is down to the dregs of his borrowed funds. There's a

Five, Six, Seven, and an Ace in the flop and a lot of chips in the pot.

One of the Surgeon's cards is flipped over and it's an Ace; Delphine has a Six flipped over, making the Surgeon's Ace pair a lot higher.

I chuckle. "What an interesting play."

My hand traces down Delphine's arms as I lean forward, placing my hands on each arm of the chair, my chin just brushing the top of Delphine's head.

Sienna suddenly crosses my mind. Delphine's taller, around five foot seven compared to her five foot three. And her strawberry and frankincense scent is soft, *pleasing*, and doesn't make my stomach roll like Sienna's floral one. Thinking about that perfume gives me a fucking migraine.

One thing's for certain, I can't even fathom Sienna sitting here playing poker with the worst people in the country. But the Siren seems almost comfortable surrounded by darkness.

I snap back into the game. Frustration simmers in the Surgeon's eyes as he shoves all his chips towards the middle. "All in."

"I'll call that bet," she says immediately, stacking the right chips and pushing them forward.

The dealer sets one card aside, and then flips the last card. A Nine. The Surgeon flips his other card and slams it on the table, it's an Ace, giving him a triple.

"You should have heeded my warning," he huffs.

Delphine tilts her face toward me, those clear green eyes swirling with mirth. "Care to do the honours, *Executive?*"

I turn the card, an Eight, and a round of expletives erupts around the table. Clever, brilliant little siren. My hand brackets her neck and I kiss her.

My whole body turns to fire as she strokes her tongue along mine, a low groan slipping out of me. Delphine's body trembles slightly as my hand tightens slightly around her neck. How can someone taste this ... addictive?

"I'm leaving," the Surgeon says, rudely interrupting us. "What fucking bullshit."

I pull my mouth away just enough to look up toward the Surgeon. "We have business to discuss, so sit back down."

I look at Delphine, those eyes now liquid emeralds and her cheeks flushed. Fucking stunning. I plant a hard kiss on her lips before pulling back and standing, straightening my cufflinks.

The Surgeon scoffs, collecting his phone and pocketing it, but Lucas shoves him back down by the shoulders.

"What is this about?" he asks as he struggles against Lucas' hold.

"You're five hundred thousand dollars in debt to me, Surgeon," I say, circling slowly around the table behind the Barrister. Delphine stacks her chips absently, her eyes following me as I pass the Mechanic.

"I said I'd win it back and pay you," the Surgeon says, his voice cracking slightly as he stops struggling.

"What makes your word reliable?" I ask, passing behind the dealer. "You just lost another fifty thousand, mostly to my Siren."

"You said you'd give me a month, Herrington." The panic is slipping through.

"We don't use names here," the Barrister chastises.

"What did I tell you, Surgeon?" I sigh, passing the Politician, ignoring the Surgeon's plea.

I stop between the Politician and the Surgeon, looking down with both hands in my pants pockets. The Surgeon breathes heavily, his eyes wide on mine.

He knows he's trapped prey, waiting for the predator to strike.

I tilt my head slightly. "I told you that if you went too far, that I would take what matters to you most."

"Please," the Surgeon begs, "leave my daughter out of this."

I laugh, the sound anything but joyful. I grip the back of the Surgeon's chair, leaning forward as he shrinks back. "She's not the most important thing in your life, have another guess."

"S-she is, I—" A whimper escapes the Surgeon as I strike him hard across the face.

"Don't lie to yourself." I grab a fistful of his greasy hair, wrenching his face back, angling it toward mine. Half of his face is pink and his lip is split, leaking blood down his chin. "Think harder, what matters to you *most*."

As the Surgeon stutters, completely dumbfounded, my eyes flick up to Delphine. Her eyes are transfixed on the scene next to her, burning with wild flame, like she's enjoying the show.

Lust sears my nerve endings—I want to forget this whole debt and bend Delphine over the poker table. Show everyone who's claimed her.

I shift on the spot, forcing my mind to focus on the task at hand and not on my aching cock as I hold out my empty hand toward

Peter. The cool hilt of a combat blade presses into my hand, and the Surgeon's eyes bulge out of his face, panic coating the air around him.

His wild eyes turn to Delphine. "Please, stop this."

I slam the knife into his hand, pinning it to the poker table—how *dare* he speak to my siren. His shriek of pain rings in my ears as I twist the knife. The Surgeon's hand spasms and blood pools on the poker table, soaking into the felt top.

"Who said you could beg?" I ask calmly as I yank out the knife.

The Surgeon's sobs make the Mechanic chuckle. "I hope you were ready to retire," he says, his hands locked at the back of his head as he watches the blood pooling on the table.

"You know," Delphine murmurs softly, drawing everyone's attention. She gives me the sweetest smile. "Surgery requires both hands."

If my cock could be any harder, it would be. The dark part of my soul preens, delighting in the wickedness. "You're right, my sweet Siren."

Lucas grips the Surgeon's other forearm, forcing his right hand onto the table. I don't waste any time as I slam the knife into the other hand, twist it, and then wrench it out and hand the bloodied knife back to Peter.

"Now," I breathe as the receptionist appears, handing a small white towel to me, "you know the repercussions if you mention this place to anyone once you leave my hotel."

"M-my hands," the Surgeon weeps. "I can't—"

"Don't fret, Surgeon," I drawl, handing the now blood-stained towel back to the receptionist. "I'll get someone to take you to the emergency. I'm not a total monster."

Peter pulls the Surgeon from his chair as Delphine pushes her chips to the dealer, exchanging them for cash.

"Almost doubling your money," I croon as she stacks the bricks of cash. "Not bad for your first time at the elite table."

"I doubled *your* money," she points out, leaving the money in a neat pile.

I chuckle, shaking my head as she stands. "The money you won is yours."

Her rosy mouth pops open. "Excuse me?"

I trace her jaw, stopping at her chin and sliding my thumb into her open mouth. "I want to fuck this mouth."

She bites down hard without breaking eye contact, before sucking my thumb in more, swirling her tongue around the teeth marks and dragging her mouth to the tip, releasing it with a *pop*.

Fuck.

I let go of her face and grab her hand, pulling her towards the security office.

"Where are we going?" she asks breathlessly.

I open a black door in the back of the space into a small, dark office, locking it behind us.

The only light in the room is coming from the screens rolling security footage on the left wall, which illuminates the desk and the chair, the only furniture apart from a couple of filing cabinets on the right wall.

I spin Delphine towards me and capture her lips with mine. They taste like sweet sin, and I want to know if the rest of her tastes the same. I step forward, forcing her further into the room until her thighs hit the desk. I reach under her leather jacket, trying to push it off her shoulders.

She pulls away from me, her hand on my chest as she leans back, looking up at me. I frown, forcing myself to breathe slow.

"What are we doing?" she asks softly.

"Like I said, I want to fuck your mouth."

She searches my face, her expression conflicted. Does she not want this?

"Enzo," she breathes, her green eyes resigned. "I can't do this right now."

What is she saying? "What do you want, sweetheart?"

"I—" Hesitation and something like panic flashes in her eyes. She clears her throat. "I need to go."

My grip tightens around her. "Is it *him?*" It has to be.

She frowns. "What?"

"Are you running back to him? Raphael?"

She narrows her eyes. "Raph is my boss, why would you ..." She stops, and scoffs. "A lift home and a friendly smile makes you believe I'm fucking my boss?"

"It wasn't just a *smile,* Delphine. He looks at you like he owns you."

"He doesn't." She pushes at my chest, trying to get away from me.

I don't believe her. Raph wouldn't let a beautiful woman like her be alone for long. I untangle from her, readjusting my suit jacket. "See Peter for your money."

She pulls her jacket around tight, avoiding my eyes. "It's your money."

"Delphine—"

"Goodbye, Enzo," she blurts out as she slips around me and escapes the office.

FOURTEEN

Q
♠

DEL

ENZO LET ME GO, so why am I still thinking about him?

As I'm walking with Scarlett to our last class of the day, cursed chemistry, a sudden onset of dread tingles at the bottom of my spine.

I slow my pace, taking a steady breath as the sensation creeps up my back. Scarlett notices the change in my stride, and veers us into a dark alcove out of the main thoroughfare.

Even with all that happened last weekend at the poker table and the baptism, I was graced with a reprieve from my nightmares, but apparently the panic attack I managed to avoid last week is coming now with vengeance.

"Back against the wall, and close your eyes," Scar instructs, taking my books as I do what she says.

My mind is spinning and the sobs I'm trying to hold in are burning in my chest. I screw my eyes shut as I take faster breaths in, my body trembling uncontrollably.

Phantom rosary beads digging into my throat choke me as I claw at my neck, pulling my school tie loose. Breathe. I need to *breathe*.

"Del," Scar's soft, soothing voice cuts through the pounding in my ears. "Tell me what day it is."

"Friday," I croak, tears now streaming down my face. My lungs are frozen. I'm going to suffocate.

Scar's gentle touch slides down my arm. "What's the weather like?"

Air. I focus on inhaling the crisp air, finally getting a lungful of desperately needed oxygen. "Cold, it … it's supposed to rain later."

"Describe the wall you're touching," Scar instructs calmly.

I feel the cold, rough stone under my palms, and listen to the hum of chatter going past us beyond the alcove. My spiralling mind starts to settle, and the tingling stops in my spine.

"What am I doing?" I whisper as my eyes flutter open to concerned brown eyes and a soft smile.

"What do you mean?" Scar asks.

I wipe away the tears from my face and fix my tie. "With everything—work, school, life. What the fuck am I doing?"

"You're doing what you're supposed to be doing," Scar reassures, handing back my books.

I chuckle, the sound empty. So I'm supposed to be running from nightmares, and obsessing over one of the most dangerous men in the city?

I clear my throat. "Thank you." Scar picked up the signs of my panic attacks pretty early into our friendship, and knows exactly what to do.

"You know I'm always here for you." Scar hooks her arms in mine and we rush to Mrs. T's classroom, just making it before the last bell, her usual disappointed frown greeting us.

Scar and I settle into our seats by the windows, my eyes catching Silvia's sneer at the back of the room. We've both been avoiding each other since her party, but I know this tense cease fire between us is going to go off eventually.

Scarlett and I work together to get all the class work done since the Sakuras are hosting some hospital benefit tomorrow night which will take over the entire house.

As the bell rings and I'm stacking all my things, Flynn and two of his buddies perch on the desk in front of me.

"How's it going?" Flynn asks.

"What do you want, pup?"

His hands fly up in defence. "I'm just checking in, I know AA can be a tough program to go through."

I rise slowly from my seat. "Excuse me?"

"Flynn," Mrs. T barks behind him. "Take your friends and go." She watches the group go, and then turns back to me. "A word, Del."

"Del has work," Scar says, grabbing my elbow, "and she needs to take me home beforehand, so we have to go."

"It'll only take a few minutes," Mrs. T assures with a small smile.

I sigh, she won't let it go if I don't talk to her now. I turn to Scar. "I'll meet you at the lockers."

She nods, eyeing Mrs. T as she goes, leaving just the two of us.

"Del," she begins, "as school counsellor, I know of your situation." She wouldn't know the true story, just the version Claudine and I gave the school. "But it has come to my attention that your coping mechanisms have taken a dark turn, and you're having substance abuse issues."

"Oh really?"

"I wanted to ask you first, before I made a judgement call." She reaches for my forearm and I step away from the contact and she drops her hand.

"Who gave you this information?" I'm pretty sure I know already.

"A fellow student," Mrs. T says vaguely.

I bark out a laugh. "You can tell *Silvia* that her meddling in my life will get her nowhere."

"I never said—"

"I'm aware that I'm still a high school student, but don't forget that I'm eighteen and the consumption of alcohol is legal for me," I say, stepping around Mrs. T. "And the amount I consume is of no concern, so maybe you should be focusing on more pressing matters like the *underage* drinking that plagues the student body, or fixing the underdeveloped sex education program. You have *no* idea how many of the final years have chlamydia right now."

I don't wait for her response as I stalk out of her classroom towards my locker.

I really shouldn't care about the opinions of anyone else in this place, but this kind of rumour puts a spotlight on me, and now every move will be questioned by a god damn teacher. I didn't need Silvia to add another fucking thing to my plate.

Scar is waiting for me with my bag out as I stomp over and throw my things into the open locker and slam the door. I pull my bag onto my shoulder and look for the car keys in the front pocket.

"Who do we have to beat up?" she asks.

"Who do you think?" I grumble, finding the key and setting off toward the parking lot.

"Silvia has no idea who she's fucking with." Scar huffs.

I smirk. "It's idiotic of her to piss you off with your taste for violence, Angel Face."

I get to work late, still annoyed by the earlier school drama. Raph doesn't question my tardiness, and just informs me that I'm needed for a mezzanine meeting in fifteen minutes, so I should hurry.

I change into my uniform, this time with a black camisole underneath to cover some of my cleavage, and race up the stairs, meeting Ty's amused expression.

"It's all good, princess, I did your prep," he says as he wipes the bar top.

"Never call me 'princess' again," I say, trying to catch my breath as I cross to the bar. "And, thank you."

"What's it like to be in the inner circle?" Ty asks.

"Which inner circle?"

"*The* inner circle." Ty hoists himself onto the back bench. "You got to witness a private meeting between the Dragones and the Herringtons."

"Okay?" Where is he going with this?

His eyes shine. "Come on, Del, spill the details. What happened after I left?"

"I'm so confused right now."

"Don't play dumb. The Herringtons are one of the most powerful families in Australia, and they *own* this city."

"I'm aware of who they are."

"Then you must have heard some good shit when they were here." Ty hops down from the bar and approaches me slowly. "Come on, Del, we're friends."

I laugh, shaking my head. "Ty, *friend*, when rich people start talking about how they're about to make more money, I zone out."

Ty pouts, turning and pulling out a clean glass. "How disappointing."

"Why are you so curious?" I ask.

Before I can coax out an answer, familiar laughter filters up from the staircase. I smooth down the front of my dress as I cross to the host podium with a polite smile plastered across my face.

Jace appears first, followed by Raph, Matteo, carrying a small box, and Peter. They're all in sharp suits, hiding the darkness that lurks underneath.

"Good evening," I greet, all sets of eyes on me as they go directly to the table, except for Peter standing at the staircase with a grin on his face, his eyes lingering a little too long on my chest.

I ignore him and follow the rest of the men to the table, taking their drink and food orders, then returning to the bar to put in the order.

"How's the construction of the new restaurant coming along?" Matteo asks.

"We're ahead of schedule," Jace responds. "Your men are highly efficient."

Matteo smirks, tracing the edge of the box he walked in with. "I know."

Are they talking about an actual restaurant or the *other* business? I place all their drinks on a tray and take it over, placing them with the correct owner. Matteo lifts his face to me with a beaming smile. "It's lovely to see you again, Del."

I nod once. "Mr. Herrington."

"You left so abruptly last weekend that I didn't get the chance to speak with you."

I see Raph lean forward ever so slightly next to Matteo. It seems that Matteo likes to play games like his brother.

"I had other matters to attend to."

"Mm," Matteo hums, his eyes burning in amusement. "Yes, *other* matters."

I bite my tongue as I step away with my tray and return to the bar. Ty's eyes are wild with curiosity as he sidles up next to me.

"You're in with the Herringtons outside of *Seduzione*?" he whispers.

"Not at all," I mumble as I cross over to the dumbwaiter, wanting to dissolve into the background and not get interrogated anymore.

Thankfully, I get a reprieve as the food arrives and the conversation at the table is mundane and trivial. As the party decides against dessert but agrees to a nightcap, Raph once again dismisses Ty early, leaving me to tend the bar.

I prepare the drinks as Matteo brings over the box with a shit-eating grin on his face as he sets it on the bar. Raph and Jace join him and I hand out the drinks.

"Are you coming to the poker tournament in a month's time?" Matteo asks Raph.

"Most likely," he says, before taking a sip of his drink.

Matteo turns his attention to me and his grin widens. "Bring Del with you."

Raph's eyes harden. "I don't think—"

"I insist," Matteo purrs, returning his attention back to Raph. "From what I've heard, Del is quite the poker player."

"If it's hosted by the Herringtons," I snipe out, drawing everyone's attention, "your buy-in is probably stupidly high. My waiter's wage wouldn't cover it."

Matteo runs his hands over the box on the bar. "That's where *my* gift comes in."

His gift? The glint in his eye is mischievous, and I know *exactly* what's in that box, and it's *not* from this particular Herrington.

Fucking. Enzo.

I curl my trembling hands into tight fists as I keep the rage off my face. He wants Raph to think I'm being pursued by Matteo in order for Raph to know that I'm not an option. And it's working. Controlling, possessive bastard.

If he wants to play, then we'll fucking *play*.

"That's so kind of you, *Matty*," I say lightly, smiling at Matteo's eyes narrowing at the nickname.

"Most of my friends call me Matteo, Teo, or Herrington. *Special* friends call me Sir," he says with a wink.

I roll my eyes, ignoring his comment. "I'll attend your poker event. That's if it's okay with Raph?"

Raph's assessing eyes run over me, then Matteo, and finally he nods. "I guess we'll both see you then."

Matteo's phone rings in his pocket, and he fishes it out, answering the call and walking to the other side of the room.

"Did you need a ride home tonight, Del?" Raph asks, drawing my attention.

"I have it sorted, thank you," I say, ignoring his questioning gaze as I start to clean up the mostly spotless bar.

"Boss," Jace murmurs, showing his phone screen to Raph. "You might want to look at this."

"Shit," Raph whispers as he snatches the phone, scrolling and reading the contents.

"Everything okay?"

"Yeah," Raph responds without his eyes leaving the phone, "but I have to handle a few things. Can you walk Matteo out and lock up?"

"Of course," I say as he puts keys on the bar top and walks off with Jace close on his heels.

Matteo finishes his call and stalks back to the bar, his usual jovial demeanour dimmed. He pushes the box closer to me, the smile he has doesn't quite reach his eyes. "He was impressed with your *poker* skills."

"What's going on?" I ask, crossing my arms.

"Just your average mob bullshit," Matteo shrugs. "Nothing to worry about."

"Matteo."

"Oh, so it's *Matteo* again?"

I roll my eyes. "Where's your brother right now?"

"Preoccupied," he answers.

"By?"

"The mob bullshit."

I shove the box back towards Matteo. "Tell *Lorenzo* I don't need his money."

"He wanted me to—"

"Anything he wants to say to me, he can say himself." I pick up the keys, stalking the length of the bar and towards the stairs.

Matteo steps into my path with the damn box, almost knocking me over. His eyes are hard, his jaw set. "Take the money, there's an invitation in there, too, and go straight home."

"Why do the Herrington men think—"

"*Please*, Del," Matteo cuts me off. "It's not safe out there tonight. Go home."

I take the box without argument and nod, then lead Matteo and Peter downstairs, settling their bill and locking the restaurant doors.

I turn off all the lights as I head for the staff room, stripping out of my dress, leaving the camisole on and pulling on jeans, a hooded sweatshirt and sneakers before heading for Raph's office. I knock a few times before opening the door, but the room is dark. I guess I'll hold on to his keys until tomorrow.

I slip into the kitchen with the box and use a steak knife to cut through the black wrapping. Two bricks of fifty and hundred dollar bills sit neatly in the box.

I pull out the crisp, white envelope with *Luxuria's* logo on the front, and open it. Inside, I find a small embossed black piece of thick paper with a date and time on it, and nothing else. I put it back in the envelope and pull out a piece of paper, unfolding the note.

> *As I told you, this money is yours.*
> *Bring the invite for the poker tournament.*
> *I'll pick you up tomorrow after work for dinner.*
> *—Enzo*

I stuff the note, the envelope and the cash into my bag, discarding the box, then storm out of the restaurant, lock up, and head toward the tram stop.

If Enzo thinks I'm going to do things his way, then he's very wrong.

FIFTEEN

DEL

I **GET OFF THE** tram and walk the short distance to *Luxuria*. For almost midnight on a Friday, the hotel lobby is eerily quiet as I approach the lone desk attendant.

She smiles as I approach, but I can see the slight judgement in her eyes as she takes in my outfit. "Good evening. Welcome to *Luxuria*."

"Hi."

"Are you after a room?" she asks, typing away at the computer next to her.

"No, I'm looking for Mr. Herrington."

She pauses her typing and a small frown creases her brows. "I'm sorry, madam, but we can't disclose any information about our guests."

"We both know Mr. Herrington isn't a guest here. I need to know where I can find him."

The attendant sweeps her arm to the door. "I'm going to ask you to leave, ma'am, before I get security to escort you out."

I look at her name badge. "Listen, *Rose*, you're doing a great job, but I need to speak to your boss right now, so please point me towards his office."

Rose picks up the phone and presses a button, then waits a beat. "There's a visitor for Mr. Herrington." She listens to the person on the other line, nods, and then hangs up, a pristine smile plastered on her face. "Someone will be down shortly."

I turn my back to her, and a few moments later Lucas comes stalking out of an elevator, his face stormy until he recognises me.

"Miss Blaire, you shouldn't be here."

"I need to speak to Enzo."

"He's busy right now."

"I don't care."

"You're as bad as him," Lucas mumbles as he steps to the desk. "This is Miss Blaire, Mr. Herrington's personal guest." Rose lowers her gaze at Lucas' tone. Lucas turns back to me. "Do you have your licence on you?"

I nod, fishing it out of my bag and handing it over. Rose takes it eagerly, scanning it on a machine behind her and then gives it back with a smile.

"Ensure that your team is familiar with Miss Blaire, and if she ever needs anything, accommodate her request without question," Lucas instructs.

"Yes, sir," Rose responds, tapping furiously at her computer. "It won't happen again."

I look up at Lucas. "Is he here?"

"Yes."

"I need to see him."

"He's preoccupied right now."

I cross my arms and turn back to Rose with a smile. "Rose, do you know how I would get to Mr. Herrington's office?"

Rose's wide eyes shift between me and Lucas. "Y-yes, his office is in his private suite on the top floor."

I hold out my hand. "May I have a key?"

"Del," Lucas warns, "you shouldn't push him today."

I push my hand closer to Rose, prompting her to pull out a black key card and put it on a reader. "Then he shouldn't be a controlling prick."

Rose places the key card in my palm and I head for the elevators. I get into an empty one, scan the keycard, and press the top floor button. The elevator jerks up quickly, making my ears pop, and a few seconds later they open into a short, dark hallway.

I cross to the large double doors, scan the key card at the handle, and push into the suite.

The place is massive and open, with dark decor and low lighting. This high up, the view of the city is stunning whichever way you look, the lights of the buildings glittering and blinking in various colours.

I walk further into the space, noting the chef's kitchen and the world's largest couch stretching across the space in front of a sleek, glass fireplace. Everything in here is huge, and dominating, just like its owner.

I make a guess and steer towards the hallway behind the fireplace, pulling out the bricks of cash and Enzo's letter from my bag as I go. I can hear Enzo's deep, muffled voice beyond the door at the end of the hall.

I don't knock as I open the door to a neat office and an angry-looking Enzo. He has rolled the sleeves of his white shirt to his elbows, and loosened his tie, the top buttons of his shirt undone. He pauses his pacing in front of the floor-to-ceiling windows with his phone to his ear.

If I thought he was angry before, the look he gives me promises death.

"I'll call you back," he barks to the phone, and he bashes the screen with his thumb, his furious cerulean eyes never leaving mine.

"What the *fuck* are you doing here?" he demands, his voice low.

I stalk forward, slamming the money and envelope on the black, glossy desk with a loud slap. "Reminding you I'm not a dog that you can summon at your own convenience."

Enzo chuckles low and menacing. "Well, that's not exactly true. You're here, aren't you?"

I pick up a brick of cash and throw it at Enzo before I know what I'm doing. He dodges the stack and it hits the window, the green notes raining to the floor as the band breaks. I snatch up the next brick, but Enzo moves fast around the desk and grips my wrist and jaw, halting my assault.

"Are you out of your fucking mind?" he growls.

"You're a fucking bastard," I grind out, his grip on my jaw restricting movement.

"Matteo told you to go straight home."

"And you thought you could buy me like I'm property."

"I told you last weekend, that's *your* money."

I poke a finger into his hard chest. "And I told *you,* that it wasn't."

Enzo closes his eyes in irritation and releases me from his hold, taking a step back. "You're driving me crazy."

"Then forget about me," I blurt out.

His eyes snap back to me. "You think I haven't tried?"

"Try harder," I bite back, putting the cash down and rubbing my wrist.

"What did I tell you the other night?" Enzo asks, stepping forward. I take a step back, keeping our distance. "I love a challenge. And you, sweetheart, are a *very* intriguing challenge."

"I'm not a conquest, I'm a person."

"A person with secrets," he says, taking another step forward. I retreat again. "Delphine Blaire, the orphan, is a carefully cultivated lie, and I want to know *why*."

He stalks forward again, and I back up, my hip hitting a chair. My bag falls from my shoulder and lands on the floor. "There's nothing else to know."

He moves again. "Do you work for the Dragones?"

I blink in surprise. "No."

"Are you a sneaky little informant, sweetheart?"

The darkness seeping off Enzo is terrifying. My heart pounds in my ears, making me dizzy. I shouldn't have come here.

"No," I breathe.

Enzo moves fast, slamming my back into a bookshelf and trapping me under him. "Why should I believe you? Isaac Bennett, your brother, is a federal police officer. Are you reporting what you find out to him, Delphine?"

"I haven't spoken to him in eight years." I try to keep my breathing even, my voice steady, so I don't provoke him. I need to get out of here.

"Why is there no record of Eleanor having another child between him and Bridgette?" His voice rumbles through my body, his scent thick around me, igniting something *deep* in me. How do I still want to fuck him when he's probably about to kill me? Maybe I *should* call that fucking psychiatrist.

I close my eyes, so close to begging God for salvation. But I know he doesn't listen.

No. I can't give up now. I open my eyes, meeting the eyes of the Devil with my own hard stare. "I told you already. I'm nobody."

He grips a handful of hair, wrenching my head back and straining my neck, pain radiating into my head. "Why are you still lying to me?"

"I'm not," I grit out, refusing to wilt. "I'm not an informant, or a Dragone spy. If you kill me here, no one will fucking care."

The *snick* of a switchblade echoes through the room. I know that distinct sound because Isaac sent me one for my thirteenth birthday, and I flipped that thing so many times until it was taken from me. Enzo slides the flat of the cool steel across the exposed skin at the collar of my top.

"It would be so fun to break you, to taint you with darkness so I could drag you down to Hell with me." The blade drags up my exposed neck and he presses the blade tip just under my jaw, just enough to feel the sting of it breaking the skin. "But you're already broken, aren't you, sweetheart?"

My eyes never leave his as I close my hand over the blade, feeling the bite of the sharp edges cutting my palm. "You have no idea."

Laughter vibrates out of his chest as he pulls the knife out of my grasp, the double-edged blade slicing through my palm and finger. His hand releases my hair and slides down my neck, following along the path of the blood oozing slowly down my skin. His touch drags out memories of other hands around my neck, and I can't help but shiver.

"Do you know how hard it was to get your sweet voice out of my head?" Enzo asks, continuing to stroke my neck, his eyes fixated on the movement. "I could hear your taunting challenge whispering in the back of my head."

I breathe out a laugh. "You think this is part of our little game?"

"Looks to me like I've caught you."

"Enzo," I purr, my uninjured hand sliding up his chest and over his jaw, the stubble sending tingles through my fingertips. "Your hands on me mean nothing. Do you think I'm going to submit to you?"

Enzo's grip returns to my hair, sending sparks down my spine. "I expect it."

"Prepare to be disappointed."

Cold anger flashes in his eyes.

"Do you want to hurt me, Enzo?" I ask.

"Yes," is all he says.

I hear the promise, the warning in that simple word. *Yes.*

"What would make you hurt me?"

"Disobedience," he croons, releasing my hair as his eyes track the blade up my throat. "Dishonesty. Disloyalty. Deliberately putting yourself in harm's way."

I scoff. "You'd hurt me for getting hurt? That makes no sense."

"When you make stupid decisions like tonight, then it makes perfect sense."

"Are you going to hurt me now?"

"I already have," he says. I remember my cut up hand dripping warm, sticky blood onto the wood floors, and the blood drying on my neck. "Shouldn't you be running now?"

"You think intimidation and some pain would chase me off? I'm broken, remember?"

Enzo's eyes flicks down to my neck once more before he steps back and storms around his desk, disappearing through a door next to the bookshelves on the opposite wall, and comes back with a hand towel, sitting down on his leather desk chair.

"I wouldn't have expected you to be squeamish about blood," I say, closing my fist, ignoring the throbbing pain.

"Show it to me," he demands.

"Come on, Enzo," I say, moving closer. "Don't you want to play with me anymore?"

"Sweetheart," he purrs, turning his chair toward me as I approach his side. "I want to play with you until this game of ours becomes your only reality."

"What if I didn't want that?"

"Then you'd be lying to both of us."

"Would I?"

"Show me your palm," Enzo instructs.

"Answer my question."

The way he stares up at me is answer enough, the *hunger* darkening those cerulean pools has my thighs clenching together.

"What if I want to hurt *you*?" I ask, holding his intense stare.

His lips lift on one side. "You can try, sweetheart."

"You don't think I can?"

He smiles, ignoring me. "Show me your palm."

"No."

He wrenches my hand toward him, forcing me to settle between his thighs, as he twists my palm up. I keep my fist closed tightly, the wound throbbing harder.

"Delphine—"

"Don't call me that."

"I'll call you whatever the fuck I want. Now show it to me."

"There's no need for stitches," I mutter as I open my palm to him. He inspects it intently, his grip never relenting. I tug against his hold but he doesn't let go as he presses the hand towel into the wound, stands and leads me through the side door into a small bathroom.

I tug my arm again, and this time he lets go. I push up the sleeve of my jumper, turning on the tap, the water almost instantly lukewarm. I clean out the cut on my palm. Soon enough, the bleeding stops, at which point I pat dry the wound with a fresh hand towel and clean the blood off my neck.

I glance up at Enzo's hard face in the mirror. "Why is everyone so jumpy today?"

"Just business issues, nothing—"

"If you say 'nothing to worry about', I will punch you." I discard the towel into the basin and turn to Enzo. "I don't like being kept in the dark. Tell me."

"Your *boyfriend* didn't tell you?"

I roll my eyes. "I've told you already, Raphael is my boss and nothing else."

Enzo steps forward and staring down into my eyes. "Prove it."

I've never met a man who has made me want to tear out his throat and fuck his brains out at the same time. "How would you like me to do that?"

Enzo smiles that stupid half smile. "That's for you to work out."

Fine. I grab his wrist, pulling him back to the desk chair and nudge his chest. "Sit."

He hesitates for a second before sitting down, amusement playing across his face. The amusement disappears as he watches me sink to my knees in front of him and slide my hands to his belt.

I undo the belt on my own, unbutton and unzip his pants and have his half hard cock out without breaking eye contact.

I wrap my uninjured hand around the base, rest my injured one on his thigh, and lean forward, still staring into those cerulean flames as I run my tongue up the curved length, swirling around the tip. Enzo's eyes shutter, darting down to watch my tongue repeat the motion, but as I get to the tip this time, I close my lips around it and suck hard.

Enzo's eyes close as his head falls back. "*Fuck*."

I continue my exploration with my tongue and suck just the tip, already addicted to the taste. Enzo's laboured breathing is music to my ears as I continue my tease. He's getting frustrated, judging by the way his hips lift, trying to sink more of his cock into my mouth.

I pull my mouth completely off him, and suddenly his hand sinks into my hair. I flick my eyes up to his and my thighs tremble at the feral sneer.

"You shouldn't tease me, sweetheart," Enzo pants. "I have very little patience."

I wet my lips with my tongue. "Learn to enjoy torture, then."

Before he responds, I sink my mouth around his cock until my throat is contracting around the tip. The moan from Enzo's lips and the firmer grip in my hair makes my core ache and my panties even wetter than they already are. I stay in that position until my eyes water and I need to come up for air, then deliberately drag my mouth up slowly all the way to the tip.

"Much too clean," I mumble as I let saliva coat the tip of Enzo's cock, and dribble down my chin, making the shaft slick, and look up at him through damp lashes.

His entire face is feral, his eyes a cerulean inferno.

"Grip my thighs with both hands," Enzo instructs, and I follow his instruction immediately, squeezing both hard.

His grip on my hair tightens again as his other hand rolls a black and red tendril between his fingers. "You changed the colour."

What a random thing to notice at this particular time. I hum my agreement, dropping my eyes.

"Look at me," he demands, and my eyes flick back up immediately at his harsh tone. His thumb brushes over my wet lips. "You'll look at me as I fuck this pretty mouth of yours."

I nod, struggling to breathe, let alone trying to find words. I'm supposed to be in control here, but I don't fucking care when he's looking at me like that—like he wants to destroy me and worship me simultaneously.

I shift slightly back and raise a brow as I open my mouth wide, my tongue lying flat. Enzo's cock jumps, tapping against my tongue.

"Tap my thigh when you need to breathe," Enzo says before he pushes my head down, his cock cutting off my air flow.

I hold this position for a few seconds before the urge to breathe makes me gag, filling my mouth with more saliva. I tap the side of Enzo's thigh twice and he releases the pressure, sliding my mouth up his shaft, giving me a few seconds to recover before his hips thrust up, filling my mouth again.

Using the grip in my hair and thrusting his hips, Enzo fucks my mouth so hard that tears stream down my face and saliva continuously drips, coating the short hairs at the base of his cock, his balls, my chin, everything.

It's dirty, and rough, and *hot*.

My body aches to be filled and my panties are soaked as his thrusts get harder and more erratic.

Enzo shoves my head down, the quick move making me choke. "Eyes on me."

I look up through damp lashes into his feral gaze. "You better not waste a drop."

In a few quick thrusts he comes on a strangled groan, his release quickly filling my mouth, but I manage to swallow it all down as his cock pulses on my tongue.

Enzo finally releases his grip on my hair, and I drag my tongue along the underside of his shaft, sliding him out of my mouth.

I wipe the tears from my cheeks and the saliva from my chin before Enzo grips my forearms and lifts me, pulling my body flush against his chest as our lips collide.

He groans, his tongue sliding over mine, tasting his own release. "You taste fucking perfect with me coating your tongue."

I sink my hands into his hair and pull back. "Are you convinced?" I pant.

His eyes sparkle. "For now."

For *now*? I release his hair and push off his chest. I'm done with this bullshit. "Fuck this."

"Delphine—"

My hand flies across his cheek, the slap stronger that I thought possible. "Don't call me that, *Lorenzo*."

Enzo chuckles, the sound dripping with poison, as he fixes up his clothing. "I'll give you that one, sweetheart." His eyes bore into mine as he stands, and I back up. "But the next time you decide to inflict violence, be ready to run."

"You'll be lucky to ever see me again."

"Your threats don't faze me." He prowls forward, backing me up into a bookcase again. "You want to be here as much as I want you."

"If you're never going to trust me, then I don't want to be a part of this."

"I need to know you're going to do as I say when—"

"You don't own me, Enzo."

Enzo smirks. "The moment you agreed to fuck me in that church was the moment you became mine. It was just a matter of time before I found you again."

"You have issues," I huff.

"I never did," he says, tracing my jaw, "until you."

I cross my arms over my chest. "I have two conditions."

"You think you can negotiate?"

"One," I ignore his question, "complete transparency. I don't want to be kept in the dark about *anything*."

Enzo nods. "I can agree to that."

"And two, don't question my relationship with Raphael *ever* again."

His eyes narrow. "If he, or anyone else, touches you—"

"Like you just touched me?"

"Sweetheart," Enzo warns, fitting his body against mine. "I can touch you however I like, but if someone else does, in *any* way, there will be dire consequences."

"For me, or for them?"

"For both of you," he says as his hand tucks my hair behind my ear. "So *behave*."

"You don't want anyone else to play with your new toy?"

"No one touches what's mine."

I sigh. "You keep forgetting that you don't own me."

"Give me your phone." His eyes challenge me to fight him as we hold each other's stare, both of us refusing to yield. This is another one of his games, but I can't bring myself to refuse to play.

I roll my eyes as I slip around him and head for my bag on the floor, pulling out my phone and placing it in Enzo's waiting palm.

"This is my number," he says, tapping on the screen a few times and then hands it back. "Don't do something idiotic like blocking it."

"You're so boring," I mutter, locking the screen and picking up my bag. "This has been interesting, but I have to go."

Enzo picks up his phone from his desk and taps on the screen. "Lucas will be downstairs with a car to take you home."

I nod and turn to leave, but pause, looking back. "What happened tonight that has everyone on edge?"

"Someone hit one of the storage facilities," Enzo says as he sits back in his chair. "Taking out my men and Dragone's as well."

"Do you know who did it?" I ask.

"Not yet," Enzo mutters, pulling open a drawer and taking out a laptop.

I head for the door.

"Sweetheart," he calls, his tone making me pause and turn. "Answer when I call."

"We'll see," I say, exiting the office.

SIXTEEN

— Q ♠ —

DEL

I MAKE LUCAS DROP me off at St. John's Church despite his protests, and he waits until I'm in a car service before he drives off. The driver drops me off at the Sakura gate, and I enjoy the silence as I make the trek up the driveway.

The house is quiet and dark as I lock the front door behind me and climb the stairs, exhausted. I slip into my room and drop my bag on my desk, put my phone on charge at my bedside table before heading for the shower. I take my time under the hot spray, washing the day off my skin.

What has my life become? Laughter bubbles up from my chest, and I close my eyes. I work for a mob family, and I'm pretty sure I've just agreed to become a crime lord's play thing. The laughter rakes through my chest harder, shaking my shoulders. I'm pretty sure this isn't what Scar was thinking when she said I was doing what I'm supposed to be doing in my life.

As the water starts to sting, I get out, dry off, then pull on a loose t-shirt and sleep shorts and pull back the thick blanket. I almost jump out of my skin when I find a small body in my bed.

Scar is curled up on her side in the centre of the mattress, sound asleep. The woman could sleep through the apocalypse. I slide in next to her, covering both of us with the blanket and curl my arm around her waist.

"You're late," she grumbles sleepily, snuggling closer.

"I had a stop to make after work," I whisper, exhaustion tugging at my consciousness.

"Church guy with the henchmen?"

"Yeah," I breathe. "He found me."

The cutlery clatters on the plates as *he* slams both hands down on the dining table and stands. Today started out so well. The weather was perfect, sun shining, blue skies and white, puffy clouds. We've just come back from Isaac's high school graduation, everyone surprisingly happy and calm, unlike most days.

But then Isaac told Mum that he's taking a year off before he goes into university, and *he* is not happy about that.

"Don't even think about it," he bellows, pointing his finger in Isaac's face. "You'll be starting your studies in February and you *will* be working for me."

"I don't have to do anything you fucking say," Isaac shouts back, standing from his seat.

"You do if you want to live in this house."

"Then I'm out of here," Isaac seethes, pushing his chair out, knocking it to the floor and stomping out of the dining room.

"Isaac," Mum calls out, and then turns back to *him*. "Now look at what you've done."

I flinch as he backhands Mum across the face so hard that she crumbles to the floor. "Don't fucking talk to me like that, you stupid bitch, and get that little fuck under control."

Mum cradles her pink cheek, angry tears shining in her eyes. "You're a fucking bastard," she whispers as she scrambles out of the room after Isaac.

He's breathing hard, his fury thick in the room. He reaches over and clutches my bicep, wrenching me out of my seat and dragging me toward his office. Luckily, I didn't get a chance to eat much—who knows what punishment I'm going to bear today.

He shoves me inside the office and locks the door behind us. He grabs the back of my neck, pulling on the wooden rosary beads tight against my throat, as he turns me to face him, and forces me to look at his face.

"If you ever pull any of the shit your mother and brother do, you will end up in a body bag. Do you understand me?"

"Yes, sir," I croak, trying to stop myself from choking. He'll just pull the beads harder if I do. He delights in the sound of my pain.

The rage in his eyes simmers down, and he suddenly pulls me in for a bone-crushing hug. "Please don't make me hurt you like that, Delphine. God forgive me, I will if I have to."

"I won't, sir," I whisper, clenching my fists at my sides. "I promise I'll be good."

He pulls me over to the armchair, sinks into the black leather, and pushes me to my knees on the floor between his legs. He caresses the rosary beads he gifted me, playing with the cross on the end.

"I wish your mother and brother were good to me and their Lord like you are, Kitty," he comments, and then unbuckles his belt, guiding my hands to the button of his pants.

I wrench myself awake and bolt for the bathroom. My throat burns as I empty my stomach into the toilet, sweat sliding over my skin. I can hear his heavy breathing like he's right next to me, feel those stupid fucking beads around my neck.

I don't know what I did to the universe, but it's decided that my past can no longer be avoided. I'm not ready—the pieces of me that were broken through those years are still mortal wounds, but it seems like my nightmares are going to demand more suffering.

A small, soft hand rubs gentle circles between my shoulder blades as another wave of dry heaving seizes my body.

Scar continues the soothing rhythm with her hands and hums a calm melody, easing some of the tension in my mind. Scar has the most beautiful singing voice; she can bring people to tears with the angelic sound.

My breathing finally calms and the heaving stops. My head pounds as I flush the contents of my stomach and stand on trembling legs. I turn to Scar, who passes me a hand towel.

"The nightmares are *this* bad again?" she whispers.

I nod, wiping the sweat from my face.

"I'll rustle up breakfast," she says. "See you downstairs in a few."

I nod again, watching her leave. She never pushes to know what my nightmares are about, and I'm thankful for that every time. Over the years, we've both tried to tell each other things about our past, but every time we've both not been able to.

She knows I have nightmares about the past, and I have panic attacks. I know she can't be in tight spaces or complete darkness.

I strip out of my damp clothes and rinse off the terror in the shower before dressing in track pants and a t-shirt. I check my hand and neck wounds, both scabbed over nicely, before grabbing my phone and heading to the kitchen.

Scarlett is sitting at the kitchen island, talking to the chef with a place set next to her. I slide onto the bar stool and food immediately appears in front of me. All my favourites: extra crispy bacon, toast, avocado with chunks of feta cheese and a small bowl packed full of pomegranate seeds.

I smile, leaning over and planting a kiss on Scar's cheek before digging into the food.

No one tries to talk to me as I sit back and listen to conversations about tonight's menu for the benefit. I really wish I could curl up in bed, listen to music and pretend I don't exist, but I promised the Sakuras I would stay long enough for the big surprise announcement they're making tonight.

Claudine glides into the kitchen as Scarlett and I are almost done with breakfast, kissing both of us on the cheek before setting up her laptop on the breakfast table, the chef taking over a plate of fruit and coffee.

My phone buzzes on the counter as I'm handing over my empty plate. Enzo's name flashes in my notifications.

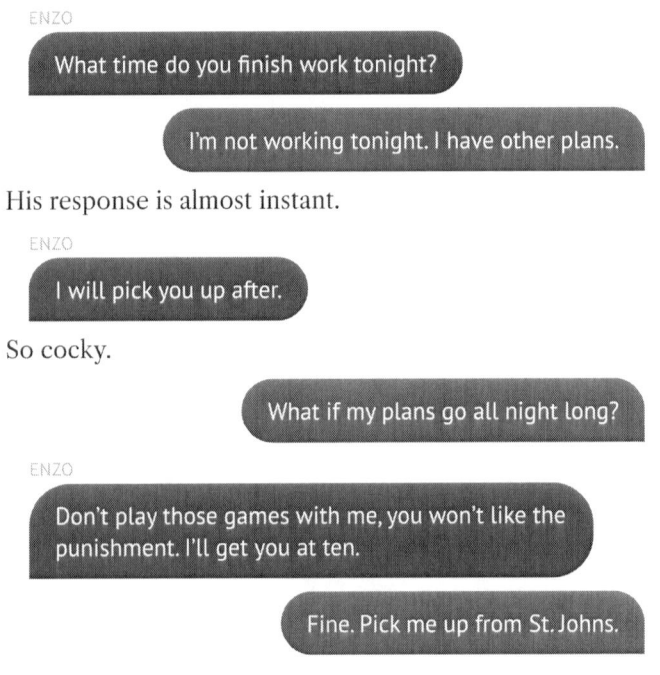

ENZO
What time do you finish work tonight?

I'm not working tonight. I have other plans.

His response is almost instant.

ENZO
I will pick you up after.

So cocky.

What if my plans go all night long?

ENZO
Don't play those games with me, you won't like the punishment. I'll get you at ten.

Fine. Pick me up from St. Johns.

ENZO

I'm almost certain you don't live at that church.

I smirk.

I didn't tell you I was a nun? Weird.

ENZO

I'll find out eventually, sweetheart.

Only if he tortures it out of me.

I'll be at the church by eleven.

♠

"Why do they make it so hard to get into a dress?" I grumble as I struggle with the zip in front of the mirror.

Scar giggles, batting my hands away. "They make them so much easier to get off."

"Get your mind out of the gutter," I laugh, readjusting the elbow-length sleeves as she manages to close the zipper.

Scarlett insisted I wear a floor-length gown, much to my annoyance, but I hate to admit that I love the soft, flowing skirt.

The red of the fabric is so dark that it looks almost black, and the soft glittering threads woven through catch the light when I move, but it's subtle enough that it doesn't draw too much attention.

The neckline sweeps low, but not too low to worry about anything inappropriate falling out, though the structure and tightness of the bodice keeps everything in place, anyway.

I step back so Scar can use the mirror. Her dress is strapless, emerald green, and fits her body tight, creating soft feminine curves and then flows out from her knees to the floor.

We both spent a couple hours in make-up chairs getting done up by professionals, and I'm glad they fashioned my hair into an intricate bun, because I will probably be hot after the many drinks I plan to consume.

"Do I really have to wear heels?" I ask Scar, turning from the mirror. "No one's going to see my feet under all this fabric."

"Shut up and put them on," she huffs, grabbing the heels from the floor and pushing them into my hands before turning back to the mirror.

I sit on the edge of her bed, slipping on the moderately high heels, knowing that my feet will hate me in less than an hour.

I help Scar into her matching emerald green, strappy heels, and then we both grab our phones and head for the foyer. As we descend the stairs arm in arm, there are guests already moving through the foyer, disappearing further into the house toward the ballroom at the back of the house.

The security guard at the bottom of the staircase lifts the velvet rope for us, his hard expression never changing as Claudine and Dr. Sakura greet guests at the door after invitations are scanned by the event coordinators.

They both look good dressed in their gala attire, but they look even better because they're genuinely happy, unlike most people in high society.

Claudine does a double take as Scar and I approach her side. "Girls, you both look amazing."

"Thanks, Mum," Scarlett says, squeezing her arm.

"Thank you, Claudine," I say as a newcomer draws my attention at the door.

"Dr. Richards," Dr. Sakura says in a greeting, stepping forward.

The Surgeon with his greasy black hair steps up to Dr. Sakura, both of his hands wrapped in black bandages.

"Benjiro," he says as a greeting, using Dr. Sakura's first name.

"So it's true?" Claudine asks Dr. Richards.

His eyes flick to me, then back to Claudine. I don't miss the flash of nervousness before nodding. "Yes, I am forcibly retired."

"Have the police found anything?" Dr. Sakura asks.

"Not yet," Dr. Richards says dejectedly and then steps away with his wife.

"What happened to him?" Scar asks Claudine.

"He was assaulted near his home by some thieves," she murmurs. "And they stabbed his hands before taking off with his money. Police think it might have been a family member of one of his patients who perished."

"Brutal," Scar comments before Claudine turns her attention to the next guest.

Scar and I stand there for a few more minutes before my legs start to burn and I convince her to escape to the kitchen with me. The place is bustling with chefs shouting orders and wait staff carrying trays of hors d'oeuvres. We manage not to get in the way as we squeeze over to the small table the kitchen staff set up by the windows facing the backyard.

Scar and I eat a quick dinner with a glass of wine, knowing it'll be our last chance for proper food before having to face the droves of people and socialise. We don't typically attend these events; usually Scar and I hide upstairs or go out for the night, but this big surprise is important to Claudine.

"I don't want to go out there," I confess, taking a mouthful of wine.

"Same, but we have to," Scar says, grabbing my hand across the table.

Claudine appears in the kitchen and spots us through the throng of staff. "There you are. Let's go ladies, enough hiding."

Scar and I gulp down the wine before shooting up and following Claudine through the house to the ballroom.

The entire space is dimly lit, but warm. Round tables are spread out through the whole space, and many people loiter around, filling the spaces between them. A woman croons jazz songs on the stage with a small band, her amazing voice piercing through the hum of many conversations.

Claudine, Scar, and I cross the room, occasionally being stopped by guests wanting to speak to Claudine, but eventually we make it to a table near the front of the stage where Dr. Sakura is in a deep conversation with someone I didn't expect to be here.

"Mr. Dragone," Claudine says. "I didn't think you'd make it."

Raph and his father both turn to Claudine with soft smiles. Raph's eyes land on me and his smile falters. He looks shocked. To see me? He knows I live with the Sakuras.

"Del," Mario breathes. "*Sei bellissima.*"

I smile. "Thanks, Chef."

Raph recovers from his shock, returning his attention to Claudine and kissing both cheeks. "We closed the restaurant for tonight. We both deserve a break."

Raph greets Scar the same way before stepping up to me and planting a kiss on my cheek, his hand resting on my waist.

"You look incredible," he whispers into my ear before pulling back.

I clear my throat, stepping away from his touch. "Impeccable suit, as always."

His crisp black suit is expertly tailored, and his matching tie is perfectly straight. He nods in thanks, returning to his father's side, engaging Scar and Claudine in conversation.

I take a glass of champagne from a waiter passing by, the fizz distracting me as I look at my phone screen, checking the time.

A message from Enzo appears.

ENZO

Raphael should keep his hands to himself.

SEVENTEEN

— Q —
♠

DEL

I ALMOST CHOKE ON my drink. Is he—

"Claudine," Vivienne's voice burns my ears as I look up and see her approach with Matteo and Enzo. Well, shit.

"Mrs. Herrington," Claudine says in a clipped but polite tone as they exchange one of those weird fake hugs.

"What a stunning house you have," Vivienne croons, stepping back and wrapping her arm around Enzo's. A tendril of possession curls in my stomach as I force myself to look away from the touch and take a sip of my drink.

"These are my daughters, Scarlett and Del," Claudine says, her smile not reaching her eyes. She doesn't seem to like Vivienne very much. Same.

Matteo's smile beams as he bows slightly, holding out his hand to Scar. "I'm Matteo."

She places her hand in his. "I know who you are, Mr. Herrington."

"Please," he purrs, kissing her knuckles, "call me Matteo."

I roll my eyes, drinking more champagne as Matteo straightens, turning those beautiful blue eyes on me. "Del, we meet again."

"*Matty*," I mumble as he does the same as Raph, stepping forward and touching my waist, kissing my cheek. I step away, my skin crawling. Too many people have touched me today.

"Delphine is *your* daughter?" Vivienne asks Claudine, trying to coax out gossip.

"Yes," I say, my tone daring her to question me.

A waiter approaches our group with a tray of champagne. I empty my glass, replacing it with a new one as everyone else clears the tray.

"Mr. Dragone," Enzo's low timbre pierces through the space, demanding my attention.

I finally take a good look at him. He's in black everything—suit, shirt and tie. Even his watch is black. His hair is styled away from his face, the sides freshly cut short, and the top left longer. He hasn't shaved yet, the few day's growth adding to his ruthless perfection.

"Lorenzo," Mario says, raising his glass. "Condolences."

"Thank you, Mario," Vivienne answers, leaning further into Enzo, her perky, fake-looking breasts caressing his arm.

"If you'll excuse me," I say, turning and heading for the bathrooms before I tackle Vivienne to the ground.

I drain the entire glass of champagne on the way, giving it to one of the wait staff as I walk past the bathrooms and slip through the 'staff only' door. I startle some of the staff on their break as I rush past and lock myself in their bathroom.

My hands tremble as I kick off the stupid heels and pace, trying to calm my breathing. I don't know why I even care if he's fucking his father's widow. That just means I can get out of whatever vague arrangement we made last night.

I'm not going to be a side piece. I don't need that drama in my life.

Soft taps sound at the door. "It's Scar, let me in."

I unlock the door, letting her in before locking it again. She takes a seat on the closed toilet lid.

"I thought you might have been in here hyperventilating, but you look like you're about to punch a bitch."

"Mmm," I hum, starting up my pacing again.

Scar gasps, standing ramrod straight. "Which one is it?"

I pause mid-stride. "What?"

"Church guy," she explains, as mischief sparkles in those brown depths. I don't say anything, just resume pacing, and she crosses her arms. "From this murderous energy wafting off you, I'm going to say it's Enzo."

I stop again, looking at Scar. Her mouth pops open.

"*Delphine*," she gasps. "You fucked *Lorenzo Herrington?*"

"And now I have to get checked for a disease since apparently he's fucking his step-mum."

"First of all," Scar says, grabbing both my forearms, "you're making me dizzy. And if you waited twenty more seconds, you would have watched the harlot slide up to Raphael."

"Whatever," I grumble, pulling away and checking my make-up in the mirror. My phone vibrates on the counter with a call and Enzo's name flashes on the screen. Before I can decline the call, Scar snatches up the phone and answers.

"Enzo," Scar answers, drawing out his name. She listens to the phone for a second and then scoffs. "No... You don't hear 'no' often, do you?" Scar rolls her eyes. "Bye Enzo," she sings and then ends the call.

"You're a crazy bitch, but I fucking love you."

"I got your back, baby."

I hold out my hand for the phone. "What did he want?"

"He wanted to talk to you," she says, handing the phone over. It vibrates in my hand.

ENZO

> Where the fuck are you?

It's my turn to roll my eyes.

> I'm around.

ENZO

> Outside. Five minutes.

"This prick," I whisper, furiously typing out a response.

> I don't want to play this game anymore.

ENZO

> Four minutes.

I let out a frustrated sigh.

"I can get him escorted out," Scar offers, smoothing down her hair.

"It's fine, I'll deal with him."

Scarlett helps me back into my heels and we exit the bathroom, making our way back into the ballroom. Scar heads towards her mum, where Vivienne is indeed hanging off Raph, and I make my way towards the glass doors leading to the huge deck.

The breeze is soft but freezing as I curl my arms around my waist, scanning the guests dotted around smoking and drinking. My phone buzzes again in my hand.

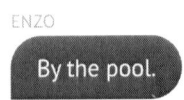

I cross the deck, descend the stairs, and walk the path to the other side of the house. The pool area is surrounded by high hedges, except for an archway cut into them for the glass gate. Lucas stands guard at the entrance, stoic as ever.

"I didn't know you were here," I comment when I'm in earshot.

"I'm always around, even when you don't see me," he says as he opens the gate for me.

"Stalker," I say with a smirk as I cross under the arch. The pool is my favourite place on the property, especially at night. The pool lights cast a blue glow throughout the entire area, illuminating the raised deck at the other end of the large pool.

Enzo paces slowly with his hands in his pants pockets in front of the sunbeds on the deck, looking calm and composed.

"This area is not for guests," I call, slowing my approach toward him.

"I don't give a shit," Enzo says, continuing his leisurely pace.

"You really don't know what the word 'no' means," I point out as I climb the two steps onto the deck, stopping at the edge.

Enzo turns slowly at the other side. "Why do you keep running?"

"I don't want to be some piece of ass you use up and throw away."

Enzo stalks closer, his face stony. My heart rate picks up, the warning bells in my head telling me I should probably run out of here.

I swallow the panic, forcing myself to stay where I am. "I don't want to get between whatever is happening between you and Vivienne."

Enzo pauses mid-step. "You think I'm fucking my father's widow?"

"You're pretty cosy with her every time I see you."

A wicked grin lights his face as he continues towards me again. "Are you jealous, sweetheart?"

"No," I breathe, as he stands toe-to-toe with me, my chest just brushing his suit jacket. Spiced grapefruit, sandalwood, and that mysterious sweet scent swirl around me, tempting me to taste, but I keep my tongue to myself.

The reflection of the pool lights dance in his cerulean eyes, making them look inhuman as his head tilts closer to mine.

"I'm jealous," he confesses. "It drives me fucking crazy when anyone else touches you."

"Even your brother?" I ask.

"*Anyone*," he growls.

"So, if I go back in there and wrap myself around Matteo—"

"Then I will gut him where he stands." Enzo crushes his mouth to mine as a strong arm curls around my waist.

My body relaxes into his touch, like the unwanted touches and the ghosts of my past have washed away. The noise in my brain quietens as I open my mouth to Enzo's demanding tongue, revelling in his smoky taste. My teeth graze his bottom lip as our tongues play and my hands sink into Enzo's hair.

I pull away from his lips, panting. "I lied."

"About?" he asks, his eyes narrowing.

"I am jealous." My hands clench in his hair. "I don't want anyone touching you."

"Then they won't." Enzo's hands slide down to my ass, and he pulls me closer, his erection pressing into me. "This is what you do to me," he growls. "*Only* you, sweetheart."

"Good," I murmur, swiping my tongue across Enzo's bottom lip.

"Dress off," Enzo demands, stepping back.

I smirk, taking a step back down the steps, continuing backwards. "Definitely not."

"Sweetheart," he warns, following me.

"Once I get this dress off, it's not going back on."

"That's fine with me."

I laugh. "We both have to suffer through this stupid gala."

"Or we could leave," Enzo offers, continuing to follow me as I approach the gate.

"I can't, not yet anyway," I say, stopping at the archway. "And we should probably keep *this* quiet for now."

Enzo traces my jaw from my ear to my chin, then drops his hand. "Why?"

"I don't think it will please Claudine that I'm involved with a man who's twice my age."

"You're an adult."

"Obviously, but the Sakuras have been good to me. Claudine has to be eased into the idea."

Enzo frowns but nods once, and then surprises me by taking my hand and pulling me through the open gate into the gardens.

"Dragone needs to know that he can't touch you anymore."

I smirk. "Well, we can use your brother for that. Just promise you won't kill him."

"I can't guarantee that," Enzo huffs. "Matteo lives to push my limits."

We walk in silence, hands still clasped together, with Lucas trailing behind us. Apart from the fact that Enzo is a criminal and one of his henchmen is trailing us, this feels so... normal.

Dread seizes my heart and I slip my hand from Enzo's, quickening my pace. My hand drifts up to my neck, looking for those damn beads. I force my hand down.

"There you go again," Enzo mutters behind me. "Running."

I stop in my tracks. "I'm not running from you."

My body tingles as Enzo steps closer but doesn't touch me. "Then where are you going?"

"I... I just... I need a minute." I take a few steps and then turn back. "It's not you."

I don't give him a chance to answer as I rush onto the deck, slipping into the ballroom unnoticed and slow my pace towards the Sakuras, where another familiar face is standing with Claudine.

"Del," Claudine calls, holding out her hand to me. "This is Austin Michaelson, a colleague of mine."

The Barrister is also here—why am I not surprised? I hold out my hand. "Mr. Michaelson."

He accepts my handshake. "Please, call me Austin." Austin's grey eyes flick up behind me. "Enzo."

"Michaelson," Enzo rumbles behind me, sticking his hand out for a handshake, brushing my arm as he goes.

"Keeping out of trouble, I hope," Austin comments, his gaze flicking between me and Enzo.

"I pay you a ridiculous amount of money to keep me out of trouble." I can almost feel the words vibrating from Enzo's chest on my back. He ignores the word 'no' *and* doesn't understand personal space.

Austin shakes his head, turning back to Claudine, and they walk over to Dr. Sakura by the stage.

"Is this an underworld convention?" I mutter more to myself than Enzo.

"Wolves hide among the sheep," Enzo muses, stepping to my side and dropping his bright eyes to me. "Disguising themselves as one of the flock. That's how they get away with devouring unsuspecting lambs; they never suspect their own."

"God, I hate sheep."

Enzo leans closer. "That's because you're a wolf."

I frown. "Am I?"

A knowing smile plays across Enzo's tempting lips as he straightens, saying nothing else.

"A broken wolf," I mutter, stepping away and circling the table until I find my name scrawled on a card and take a seat. My phone buzzes in my hand.

ENZO

Not broken, just lost.

I look up at Enzo sitting a few tables over, with Matteo and Vivienne.

I reply to his message.

I feel like I'm suffocating in all this wool.

I watch Enzo look at his phone and then taps away. I look down when my phone screen lights up.

ENZO

Don't forget you're the one with teeth.

EIGHTEEN

— Q ♠ —

DEL

THE MUSIC FADES OUT as Claudine and Dr. Sakura climb the stairs to the stage, and a hush crawls through the whole ballroom. Claudine steps up to the microphone with a beaming smile.

"First of all, my husband and I would like to thank everyone in this room for their contribution over the years to the children's hospital and supporting the Sakura Foundation." Applause rolls through the room before the attention is back on Claudine. "As most of you know, Benjiro and I believe we were brought together to change the lives of those children who need a safe haven to heal and to thrive, and we are thankful every day to the universe for leading us to such special and wonderful children."

Claudine's eyes shine as she looks over to me and I force myself to keep the smile on my face. As much as I want to feel joy, to feel her love, my stomach rolls at the thought.

She launches into a speech about all the amazing things the foundation's money is going toward, and I slump back into my seat.

Awareness prickles my skin, like eyes are on me, and I look up to Enzo. He's watching me, his face neutral, but the slight narrowing of his eyes looks pensive. He's probably reconsidering attaching himself to damaged goods.

"... Finally, we have a new project we are ecstatic to announce tonight." Claudine's voice snags my attention and I look toward her. "In honour of our two youngest daughters, we have started the Voices of Angels Project."

Claudine turns to the large screen behind her and Dr. Sakura presses a button on a remote he has in his hand. The screen shows the schematics for a beautifully designed three-story building and a list of services.

"Voices of Angels will provide medical, financial and legal aid, as well as emergency accommodation for anyone, but more particularly children, suffering through domestic violence or other harmful situations..." Claudine's voice fades out, my heartbeat pounding in my head. I can't feel my limbs, and pain tightens in my chest.

A small hand snakes between mine, which are clasped together tightly in my lap. The touch pulls me back to reality, and I turn to Scar.

"We'll get out of here soon," she whispers, a smile still on her face, but pain shadows her eyes.

"Thank you," I murmur back, squeezing her hand between mine and breathing a little easier. I thought Scar had a similar background to my own, but I really hope it wasn't as bad as mine.

"They should have told us about this before tonight," Scar whispers.

"Damn straight," I whisper back.

Claudine finishes up her speech about the new project, and a thundering applause follows them off the stage.

Scar squeezes my hand once more and then stands. "I'm going to go politely berate those two. Care to join me?"

"She will in a moment," Enzo's deep timbre announces behind me.

"Del?" Scar asks, crossing her arms over her chest, sending a death glare in his direction.

"I'm good, Angel Face," I say standing. "I'll see you later."

Her eyes drift to me, and I give her a reassuring smile. She sighs softly, nods, and heads over to her parents. I turn to Enzo, who's with Matteo as well, both of them watching Scar leave.

"I like her," Matteo announces.

"Off limits," I warn.

Matteo chuckles, wrapping an arm around my shoulders. "We'll see."

"Matteo," Enzo warns, his jaw clenching.

"This is *your* idea," he laughs, pressing me closer to his side. "I'm just selling it."

Enzo inhales, his eyes roiling with anger, before he rolls back his shoulders, indifference masking his face. "Let's go."

"Where are we going?" I ask as Matteo pulls me along, both of us following Enzo towards the back doors.

"We have a business meeting," Matteo croons, his hand slipping from my shoulder to my waist. "Enzo wants you close by."

"You might want to watch where you put your hands," I murmur.

"Oh, I know, baby," he whispers into my ear. "Enzo never liked sharing his toys."

I stop in my tracks and grab Matteo's tie, forcing his face closer to mine. "I'm not a toy, *Matty*," I whisper against his lips. "I'm a nightmare."

Matteo's tongue darts out, swiping across my bottom lip. "It's okay, both of the Herrington men like their women volatile."

"Are you wanting to be cremated or buried?" I whisper, my lips brushing his as I speak. "I'll make sure the funeral director knows of your final wishes." I push away from him, releasing his tie and stalk towards the back door.

Matteo's laugh trails behind me as he catches up and resumes his hold on my waist. "If you want to fuck, you can just ask. You don't need to turn me on with the promise of murder."

"Enzo might be your brother, but he won't hesitate in cutting off your hands and leaving you to bleed to death."

"We call that a typical Saturday in our household."

I try to tug out of his arms. "Matteo, seriously—"

He laughs, stopping us short of exiting to the deck. "You're ruining my fun, Del. This is the first time my stoic brother seems to have an *actual* interest in a woman, and is not just keeping them around for convenience. I'm going to milk this opportunity to piss him off as much as I can."

The *first* time? I doubt it. I narrow my eyes. "Do you also have to piss me off while you do it?"

He smirks, pulling us out of the house. "Absolutely. You're also so fun when you're annoyed."

We approach the dark end of the deck, where Raph, Enzo, and Austin lean against the railing, smoking cigars. Raphael straightens as he catches Matteo and me, turning to Enzo. "She doesn't need to be here."

"You're the one who pulled her into this," Matteo points out.

"Anyone aware of what we do needs to be warned about the risks associated," Enzo states, drawing on his cigar and releasing the smoke.

"Are there any leads about who hit the warehouse?" Austin asks, bringing everyone's attention back to the issue at hand. They must be discussing last night.

"The cameras were taken out," Raph murmurs, taking a sip from his tumbler. "We only got a glimpse of them."

"Anything we can identify?" asks Matteo.

Raph shakes his head. "They were in ski masks, but they were organised."

"Couldn't be the bikies then," Enzo muses, looking off into the gardens. "They're too brash to do something this stealthy."

"Another player in the game?" Austin asks.

"Has to be," Raph sighs. "They cleaned us out." Another crime boss in Melbourne? Do we not have enough?

"When can you get another shipment?" Matteo asks, his fingers flexing on my waist slightly.

"There's more coming next weekend," Raph says, his eyes drifting to Matteo's hand before flicking back up to his face. "But where are we going to store it?"

"Do you think they'll hit again?" Matteo asks.

"If it's a new player trying to set up shop, then yes," Austin says as he swirls his drink in the glass.

"How did they know where it would be?" Raph asks, taking a drag of his cigar.

"There's a leak somewhere," Enzo surmises, rolling the cigar between his finger and thumb, watching the lit end glow.

"Split the product between the two of you and see which site gets hit," Austin suggests. "But use different shell companies: I've dissolved the last ones." He extinguishes his cigar and excuses himself.

"I'll organise transport," Raph says. "Just tell me where to take it."

Matteo chuckles low. "It's probably best neither of us know where the new locations are, not until we clean out the rats."

"And I still want to meet your new import connection," Enzo adds.

"They've agreed to meet next week when the shipment comes in," Raph says.

"Good," Enzo surmises.

Raph's eyes narrow as he squares his shoulders. "I'll send you the details." Raph looks at me, and something like regret or maybe disappointment flashes in his gaze before he stalks off towards the house.

"How many people did they kill?" I ask no one in particular.

"A dozen," Enzo answers, as he extinguishes his cigar and puts it into a tube from his pocket. "Equal amount from either side."

"Our people are loyal," Matteo says, finally moving away from me. "It has to be from Raph's side."

"Looks can be deceiving," Enzo says as he steps closer to me. "I want everyone to be looked into. The whole organisation."

"On it," Matteo mutters, pulling out his phone and stepping away.

Enzo brushes his knuckles over my arm softly. "Come home with me."

"I can't tonight," I whisper, keeping my eyes on his chest. "There are things I have to sort out here."

"Do it tomorrow," he murmurs. "Let me distract you tonight."

"I can't avoid this one," I say, caressing the lapel of his jacket. "Raincheck?"

"*Tomorrow*," Enzo declares, "you're mine."

"Okay," I whisper, rising up on my toes and planting a soft kiss on Enzo's lips. He stills, the move shocking both me and him. I step back, smiling. "See you tomorrow."

Scarlett and I stay for another hour before we both decide to call it a night. We sneak out two bottles of champagne and a tray piled with food from the kitchen before disappearing upstairs.

I put the bottle down on my desk, immediately kicking off these damn heels, and try to reach the zip of my dress. "Please get this thing off me before I scream."

Scar giggles, putting down the tray of food and unzipping my dress. My shoulders drop as I'm released from the cage of glamour that I am never at ease in.

I grew up in a comfortable household, nothing flashy or extravagant, but even as my family got wealthier, I never liked this world of shiny.

I know I'm lucky to have met the Sakuras; I could be in a much worse position right now.

I help Scar out of her own glamour trap and we both wash our faces and get into comfortable clothes, Scar borrowing one of my t-shirts that's long enough to be a dress on her.

We pop a champagne bottle and sit in the centre of my bed with the food between us, passing the bottle back and forth as we eat.

"I'm dying to know," Scar blurts out.

"Which part?"

"All of it," she says, taking a bite of a sandwich, her big, brown eyes expectant.

"You know most of it already," I sigh. "I didn't know who he was when we first met, and then he was at the baptism."

"You're holding back, I can tell."

"Okay, fine, he came into Raph's restaurant before the baptism." I lean forward to take the bottle out of her hands, but she pulls back.

"You don't get any of this until you tell me *all* of it," she demands.

I roll my eyes and tell her everything up to last night, leaving out anything mob-related. When I finish, Scar is frowning. "So Enzo isn't part of Raphael's drug ring?"

My mouth falls open, and I'm speechless.

Scar bursts into laughter, thrusting the bottle into my awed face. "You didn't think I knew that?"

"How?" I breathe, taking the bottle and taking a long drink.

"My mum is his lawyer, and I'm a snoop," she says, her eyes dropping to the tray between us. "I would have told you ages ago, but..."

"I was traumatised?" I surmise.

Scar nods, her eyes returning to mine. "I remember what it was like those first few years after you've escaped Hell."

"What... What happened to you? You know, before."

"The Sakuras took me in when I was seven," she says as she gets off the bed and takes the tray, moving it to my desk. "And let me tell you, I was a wreck."

I crawl up the bed and slip under the blankets, Scar slipping in next to me and taking the bottle. "Both of my parents were heavily into drugs, any they could get into their bodies. And they did *anything* to get them." She finishes off the bottle and grabs the other one.

"Were you... used to get drugs?"

Scar pops the fresh champagne bottle, passing it to me. "I was never used as currency, luckily, but there were many times I was either left at home starving and dirty for days at a time when my parents forgot they actually had a child. Or I was shoved into a wardrobe while my mum used herself as payment."

"Is that where the claustrophobia comes from?"

She nods. "Yeah, they would lock the wardrobe from the outside, and it was pitch-black in there. I was forgotten more times than I want to think about." Scar finds it hard to be in tight spaces and the dark; we always have some sort of light on at night.

"How did you get free?"

"My mum overdosed at a party and an ambulance was called. She died that day and my dad split, but luckily the hospital went through her medical history, which said she had a kid, and they sent the cops to the house." Scar pulls the bottle back to herself and takes a healthy swig. "I was a rabid animal when they picked me up. I tried to stab a cop with a fork as they wrestled me out of the house."

"Violent tendencies," I murmur, and we both laugh.

"Yeah, I was a little shit. When they got me to the hospital, a nurse actually wept at the state of me. I was so tiny for my age and I struggled to eat proper meals because I would throw up. I was in the hospital until I was physically healed, but my brain was broken. I ran from four foster homes; I couldn't stand being in a home. I much preferred the hospital."

"Is that where you met Dr. Sakura?"

"Yeah," Scar says smiling. "The last time I came in, screaming my head off about not going back to my foster place, he was the first person to take the time to work out why, and from then on I was attached to him. He got me admitted to the psychiatric ward, not only because I needed the help but also so I had a bed at the hospital."

"You liked the hospital because you were never alone," I surmise.

Scar nods. "And there was always a light on. I didn't feel trapped."

Scar gives me back the half-empty bottle and scoots down the bed, pulling the blankets up to her shoulders. "Mum came in to see me often after Dad told her about me. She worked with Child Services to get the adoption processed quicker. They would bring me here for day trips for almost a year, letting me warm up to the house; I really loved all the windows and the high ceilings. They also let me pick out a room and furniture, so I never felt trapped."

"I swear both of them were gifted from God to heal the world," I murmur, then drink the remaining champagne in one go. The alcohol burns in the pit of my stomach, but the buzz I have eases some of the tension in my body. I slide further down the bed, facing Scar. "How are you so positive about life?"

"It's taken me a long time," Scar murmurs, turning toward me, "and being here almost reset the clock. I still got to have a good childhood, even though the first half was trash."

"I wish I got out earlier," I mumble, closing my eyes. "There are things I shouldn't have known about so young."

"What happened, Del?" Scar whispers, her small hand threading through mine.

I squeeze my eyes shut, my heart pounding as memories rush through my mind. "My mum once told me that the day I was born was the worst day of her life."

"*What?*" Scar whispers.

I take a shaky breath. "My biological dad died in a car accident two months before I was born. My mum and Isaac were with him, but they survived. He was Eleanor's second husband, and according to her, her *person.* The absolute love of her life." I roll back onto my back. "She blames me for the accident—they were on the way to a doctor's appointment when the drunk driver hit them."

"This woman makes my murderous," Scar growls.

I snort. "You'd think being his kid, she'd be grateful for having a piece of him for life, but it's like she didn't want the constant reminder of what she lost, so she palmed me off to my grandmother like I never existed."

I turn back over, facing Scar. "She loved me, but she was a God-fearing woman, and raised me to be a good Catholic girl until she died when I was five."

"So you went back?" Scar asks softly.

I nod. "When I got back, she was married to her third husband, my stepdad." Panic seizes me, and my neck stings from phantom beads digging into my flesh. I grab Scar's hand. "He was fine at first—great even. I was still an inconvenience to my mum. Isaac was her only priority, but he doted on me. He changed my last name to his, gave me anything I wanted, took me to dance classes. He took me to church every Sunday, as he was also religious. He even gave me his mother's rosary beads, which I rarely took off."

My free hand slides to my bare neck. "It didn't last long, the good times. He had two sides of him: the doting family man and the aggressive monster."

"What... what did he do?" Scar asks hesitantly.

"He liked to use the words of his Lord as justifications for..." My stomach rolls, threatening to bring up the champagne. "You know, my mum *never* considered leaving him the entire time they were married. We weren't rich, but we were comfortable, and he worked hard to provide the life she wanted. Even when..."

Tears slide down my face as I stare at the ceiling, drowning in every nightmare inflicted by that man racing through my body.

Scar shifts closer to me, stroking my arm soothingly. "You don't have to tell me the rest."

"I want to," I croak. "I *need* to."

I turn to those big brown doe eyes shining with empathy. I love her so much.

"I was seven when it started. He would beat the shit out of me like he did to my mum and Isaac, but he... he touched me, in other ways. He made it seem so normal, like it was something I was supposed to do, like something I was supposed to *enjoy*. He used to use it as an apology for hitting me, but also convinced me it was some perverted teachings from the Bible."

"Del..." Scar whispers.

"He made me promise to hide it from my mum and Isaac, but I think... I think they knew. At least my mum did later, after Isaac left, and she did *nothing* about it," I choke out around the knot in my throat. "She let it go on for years, and when I finally ran off to the hospital at fifteen, she changed her tune, played it up to the police that she never knew."

"Did you tell the police that she was a dirty liar?"

"I exchanged my silence for my freedom," I murmur, turning back around toward her. "I told your mum everything, and I've never seen her so fucking livid. She managed to get my stepdad put in prison and me emancipated from my mum. She wiped my entire existence away and gave me a new life, then took me in. Just like with you, she knew that I needed a family, someone who actually gave a shit about me, but I needed to know that the option to leave on my own was there."

"That's why they never officially adopted you," Scar breathes. "I always wondered why."

"I'm so grateful every day they allow me to stay here."

Scar clutches one of my hands in both of hers. "My parents are *your* parents, too. You were one of theirs from the day they met you."

More tears leak from my eyes. "I wish I could let them in like that, but I can't... I don't know if I will ever be able to."

"It's okay," Scar whispers, wiping my cheeks with her free hand. "We're still your family. We all love you regardless. But know that I'm attached, and you can't get rid of me."

"I'm not worthy of your commitment," I sob. "I don't know if I can ever give you all that you deserve."

"You don't have a choice," she says sternly, wrapping herself around me tightly, resting her head on my shoulder. "You're my best friend and my family, and I'm not letting go."

My heart fills with so much light, it feels like it might burst out of my chest. To know that someone won't leave despite seeing the darkest parts of your soul is *everything*.

"Del," Scar whispers as she settles into my side. "What ever happened to the rosary beads?"

"I burnt those fucking things to ash the moment I was free."

NINETEEN

DEL

I NCESSANT BEEPING ECHOES IN the back of my mind.

"Del, turn off the fucking alarm!" Scarlett bellows from the other side of the bed, jolting me awake.

I reach over from the cocoon of blankets and bash the screen of my phone.

"Jesus Christ, Scar, you don't have to be such a harpy in the morning," I groan, tucking myself back into the warm blankets.

"Why do you have the alarm on?" she whines.

"My drunk ass forgot to turn it off," I grumble. As I'm starting to drift off again, my phone chimes with a message, resulting in a pillow being thrown at me.

"Who has their sound *on?*" Scar says, appalled.

I ignore her and pull my phone into the blankets, squinting at the screen.

ENZO

What time am I picking you up?

I laugh softly.

> Someone is keen at 8am on a Sunday. I'll drive to you, just let me know where.

I'm expecting him to argue the point, insist on picking me up, but he doesn't.

ENZO

> I'll be at Luxuria. Lunch will be served at two.

> See you then.

I reply, then put my phone on silent and go back to sleep.

After a long shower and way too long in front of my wardrobe trying to decide what to wear, I'm finally pulling out of the Sakura property. I turn up the rap music and put the windows down, enjoying the rare sunny late-May day.

For some reason, I'm overly nervous. Maybe because it's the first meeting between Enzo and me where it hasn't been provoked or circumstantial.

The man has literally been *in* me; I honestly don't know what I'm so worried about.

It doesn't take me very long to get to *Luxuria*, with the traffic being light, and I pull up to the valet driveway. An energetic valet attendant opens my door and greets me by name, taking my car key and giving me a valet ticket.

I stuff the ticket into my handbag as I enter the hotel. Before I have a chance to line up with the other guests, a manager comes over with a beaming smile and a black keycard, also addressing me by name. Rose seems to have done her job well.

I get into the elevator and hit the top floor button, my stomach churning with nerves as the elevator shoots up. I pull out a compact mirror from my bag and check my face. Should I have worn more make-up? All I did was cover my dark circles and put a sweep of mascara over my lashes.

I close the mirror, shaking my head. I just need to be me, and if he doesn't like it, then I can go.

The doors slide open, and I approach the double doors. Should I knock this time? I swipe the keycard, letting myself in. The penthouse is stunning in the daylight. The sun glitters along the polished floors, lighting up the dark furniture and finishings. It feels warm, despite the imposing selections and hard angles.

"Just so you know," I hear a familiar voice echo through the open space as I walk toward the living area where Matteo sprawls across the black lounge. "Enzo doesn't like surprises."

"Don't give me a key if you don't want me to use it," I counter. Matteo is dressed in a t-shirt and jeans, his hair ruffled, and holy hell, the man is stunning.

"You look good," Matteo comments, his eyes taking me in from head to toe. I pulled out a flowing, knee-length dress and paired it with my favourite leather jacket and combat boots.

"Thank you," I say, shifting on the spot.

Matteo flashes his perfect teeth, mischief swirling in his dark blue eyes. "He's in his office."

I return his smile and continue toward the office down the hall.

I walk in like I own the place. Enzo's sitting behind his desk, staring hard at his laptop screen with his phone to his ear. The sun shines in from the windows behind him, lighting up the whole room, but it's almost like the light avoids Enzo.

He's darkness in a sea of light, and I'm drawn to it.

"Justify these expenses to me," he demands to the person on the phone, not looking away from his computer.

I close the door softly, and approach one of the chairs on this side of the desk, dropping my bag and wandering over to the bookshelves. Each wall is lined with shelves, the books in each row neatly stacked and dust free. I don't think any of these books have ever been read. I run my fingers over the spine, enjoying the rumbling sounds of Enzo's voice as he talks about finances.

I cross the room to the other bookshelf, pick a random book out and flip to a page in the middle. I'm immersed in the anatomy book, learning about the structure of a hand when a strong arm wraps around my waist and pulls me into a warm body.

Enzo buries his nose into my hair and inhales, his body relaxing behind me, pressing further into mine.

"Get your ass on my desk," he murmurs.

"Oh hi, Enzo," I mock, "how are—"

"*Now*, sweetheart," he says, wicked heat blazing through my body at the warning in his tone. "Don't make me ask again."

I close the book and put it back in its place. Enzo lets me go and I circle around him, toward his chair. "Do you ever take a break from work?"

"No," Enzo says, his voice close behind me.

I turn to him and see the flash of heat in his cerulean eyes before his mouth consumes mine, hard and demanding. His spiced grapefruit and sandalwood scent sinks into my being. All my nerves and stress melt away, my mind falling into a quiet lull as our tongues and teeth dance. I don't know how he does it, or why only Enzo has the ability to turn my brain off and give me the space to breathe.

I wrap my arms around his neck, and he walks me back until my thighs hit the desk. Enzo reaches under my leather jacket, pushing it off my shoulders, letting it drop onto the glass top.

He rips his mouth from mine, his eyes blazing with so many things; I can't decipher any of them.

"Church," he pants.

"What?"

"If you want any of this to stop, say it, and it all stops immediately."

I pause, taking in what he's saying, what he's giving me. I...

I swallow and nod, too floored to form words. I have an out, something I've never been gifted before. Before I can mill over the odd feelings that brings up, Enzo spins me, and pushes my torso flat onto his desk. He pushes up my dress to my waist and *tsks*.

"Trying to make it harder for me, are you?" he asks. Pain blooms as he smacks my covered ass cheek.

"Thighs like mine, chafing is a bitch," I mumble.

"You should always be ready to fuck me," Enzo breathes, his hands grabbing the waistband of my shorts and panties, pulling them off, "no matter where you are."

"Wear skinny jeans next time, got it." My comment earns me another hard slap across the other ass cheek, the sting pulsing through my body, arousal flooding my system. Enzo pulls me up and turns me, my tender ass perching on the edge of the desk as he sinks to his knees in front of me.

He grips my hips and looks up with a burning gaze. "Lay down."

I do as I'm told for once and recline onto his desk. Enzo pulls my ass to the edge of the desk, hooking his hands over my thighs and spreading them wide.

My body trembles in anticipation, fear, and arousal as Enzo's cool breath plays across my wet core. He hasn't even touched me and I'm already too hot, finding it hard to stay still. One thick finger circles my clit, then slides down and pushes into me, enticing a groan out of me.

"How many people have had the pleasure of tasting you?" he asks.

"What?"

"Tell me," he demands, pushing another finger in, curling them up, finding that sweet spot that has my eyes rolling closed.

"Does it matter?" I breathe. My mind is spiralling into another dimension.

"Tell me, Delphine," he demands again, pumping his fingers into me lazily.

"It's just Del," I bite back, trying to buck him out of me. This was a fucking mistake.

Enzo's other hand clamps down on my thigh, holding me in place, his fingers still in me as I feel the air shift and his body pressing into me. I open my eyes to fury hardening his beautiful face.

"Answer the question."

"No."

"Are you embarrassed, sweetheart?" he says in a low tone, pulling his fingers almost all the way out of me and then slamming them in again with another one added. I bite back the whimper, holding his angry gaze. "Were you a dirty little whore before you met me?"

"Jealous you're not the only one to touch me?" I huff.

A cruel grin twists his face. "It's probably best not to tell me," he muses, his fingers moving in me again. "Because I will kill them all."

"You know you have issues. Right?" I pant, my thighs burning from holding them still.

"And you have a smart mouth," Enzo retorts as his thumb finds my clit, circling as his fingers pump faster. His mouth captures mine as he continues their torturous rhythm, his hands formidable, pushing my arousal higher and higher until the pressure plunders through my body so hard and fast that I'm coming in the next stroke.

I choke on a moan as my legs lock around Enzo's waist, trapping him as my body trembles.

"Good girl," he breathes against my lips as I loosen my legs, coming down from the orgasm. He sinks back onto his knees. "And now you'll do it again."

That's the only warning I get before his tongue is on my clit, demanding and possessive, swirling hard over the sensitive flesh as his fingers start that fast, relentless rhythm again.

Pressure surges forward, my body on the edge of another blinding orgasm, but I force it under submission, keeping it at bay. It's almost impossible; he's almost *too* skilled not to wring it out of me, but I hold on for dear life. He can work harder for it.

But I don't expect his teeth as he sucks my clit into his mouth and bites down. The pain shoots straight through my hold as I explode, choking on a scream before clamping my hand over my mouth, muffling the strangled noise.

Waves of intense pleasure sear my nerve endings, but Enzo doesn't give me long to recover as he starts another punishing assault on me, rolling me into another orgasm.

Tears stream from my eyes as I shout into my palm again. What fucking voodoo shit is this? I've never come so many times in a row. He warned me he'd do this, and he's expecting me to beg him to stop. I won't give him the satisfaction.

As I'm trying to return to my body from this last orgasm, he chuckles, his tongue darting out to circle my clit once more, my hips bucking up at the almost painful jolts of sensation.

Enzo's fingers slip out of me and he stands, unbuckling his belt. "Are you on contraception?"

The question forces a laugh out of me. "You've already come in me once, and *now* you're asking me?"

"Delphine—"

"Use that name again, and I'm out of here," I warn. His hands are still on the waistband of his pants, waiting for my answer. I point to the tiny scar on my upper arm where my contraceptive implant sits under the skin. "We're good."

"Grip the edge of the desk above you."

I do as I'm told, watching as his cock springs out of his pants—God, I want to taste it again. He bends over me, one hand bracing on the desk beside me as the length of that glorious cock slides through my arousal, coating himself, making me writhe under him, wanting to be filled.

"Tell me you're mine," he growls, his eyes feral.

"No," I grind out.

One of his hands grips the back of my neck, pulling my face closer to his. "Say the words."

"No," I breathe against those wicked lips. "You don't deserve them."

He lets go of my neck, grabs my hips with both hands and slams his whole length into me. It's painful, so painful, and so full, and so fucking *good*.

"You think a little whore like you can tell me what I *deserve*?" he booms, thrusting in and out of me, our skin slapping together, my body responding to his words, already on the edge of coming again.

"Temper tantrums won't get you anywhere," I gasp.

"Watch your mouth," Enzo growls, never relenting on his fast and hard pace. His thumb presses into my clit, and I struggle to hold back my orgasm. Enzo chuckles, his thumb rolling in small, tight circles. "Give it to me, sweetheart."

I'm concentrating on locking down my impending release to think of some smartass comeback, but Enzo's figured out this game already. His free hand snakes up my body and pinches a nipple through the dress hard, the pain merging with the overwhelming pleasure, and I break, coming hard.

Enzo finds his release in another two hard strokes, half collapsing onto me. We take a moment to slow our breathing. My body is wrecked, sweaty, and completely sated. Am I even going to be able to walk out of here?

I shift under Enzo's weight, pleasure shooting through my oversensitive skin.

Enzo lifts his head, his eyes meeting mine, a satisfied smile on his lips. "Ready to go again?"

I scoff. "No, you're heavy."

He chuckles as he stands upright, tucking himself back into his pants, smoothing out his shirt and putting his jacket back on. I sit up, covering my legs, and look around for my underwear.

"Don't bother," Enzo says, holding out his hand.

"You want me without panties near Matteo?" I ask, placing my hand in his, allowing him to pull me off the desk.

"Yes," he breathes, pulling my body flush to his. "So try not to bend over."

I open my mouth to say that's exactly what I'm going to do, but the words die in my throat as wetness rolls down my leg.

"I need to freshen up," I mutter, pulling away from Enzo, but his arm locks around me.

Feral heat sparks in his eyes as he shifts lower, his hand gliding up my leg, capturing the spill on my thigh with his fingers. I find it hard to breathe as he straightens, pushing his fingers into my mouth. I hold his hungry gaze as I swirl my tongue around his fingers, tasting his come and mine.

"All clean," Enzo rumbles, pulling his fingers out of my mouth, and threading them with mine as he pulls me out of the office.

TWENTY

— Q ♠ —

DEL

MATTEO IS DRAPED OVER a dining chair in front of a huge spread of food.

As we approach, his smile is wild; he knows exactly what just went down. I should be embarrassed, but weirdly I'm not. Enzo leads me to the chair next to Matteo, pulling it out and motioning for me to sit. My bare ass smarts as it hits the wooden seat, and I fight the wince as Enzo claims the chair at the head of the table on my other side.

"Sore?" Matteo asks, leaning forward.

"Jealous?" I counter.

Matteo picks up a bottle of red wine. "Why would I be jealous? You'll be over my desk soon enough."

I scoff. "In your dreams."

"Every night, babe."

"If you want to keep your tongue, Matteo," Enzo says calmly, picking up the pitcher of water. "I suggest you stop."

Matteo chuckles, pouring himself some wine. "Save your threats, bro, because I definitely will not stop."

"Reckless," I mutter as I stand and lean across the table to grab a bottle of white wine. Matteo asks Enzo about legitimate business things as I pour myself a glass and take the time to watch them.

They're so similar, yet so different.

Matteo has a confidence that's warm, inviting, and easy. I wouldn't be surprised if he's always got a woman in his bed and a trail of broken hearts in his wake. His dark features, blue eyes and solid but lean build give him a charismatic Prince Charming edge.

But Enzo?

Those same dark features and large frame scream villain. I don't think he leaves behind broken hearts, but broken people, forever destroyed by the darkness he revels in. Good thing that I've already been tainted.

We pick through the food, and I'm refreshed to know that neither of these men seem to believe in polite serving sizes. If anything, both Enzo and Matteo encourage me to eat more.

"I didn't think some cock and good food would render you speechless," Matteo comments, sipping on his third glass of wine.

"I'm not a blabbermouth like you, *Matty*."

"Oh," Matteo purrs, leaning forward slightly, "so you want to play?"

"I don't play those games with you, *Matty boy*."

"Call me that again and I'll take you across my knee."

"Oh, really?"

Matteo rolls his neck, putting down his wineglass. "Care to find out?"

I turn in my seat as he pushes his chair away from the table, angling toward me, that cocky grin lighting up his face, his hands lying flat on his thighs.

My eyes drift down his body, then back up to his face. "You probably hit like a bitch."

The same darkness that often pours out of his brother burns in Matteo's eyes, and a small part of me thinks I might have fucked up. Matteo barely jerks forward before my whole seat is shifted back.

"You shouldn't tease Matteo," Enzo chastises. "It would be a waste when I have to take his life."

The darkness still simmers in his eyes as Matteo clears his throat and excuses himself from the table, disappearing further into the penthouse.

I turn to Enzo. "Did I piss him off?"

"You provoked a part of him he finds hard to control," he says, taking my hand and pulling me out of my seat. He spins me and pulls my hips back, my ass landing in his lap. "He'll be fine when he cools off."

"Has he ever had female friends before?"

Enzo smirks. "They all end up with a broken heart."

"This will be a new experience for him, then." I get off Enzo's lap, but he grips my hips, turns me, and plants me back on his lap, forcing me to straddle his thighs.

"And where are you going?" he asks with a raised brow.

"To go apologise to my new best friend."

"We aren't done here."

I frown. He looks... "Are you mad at me?"

"Yes," he says. "You bent over."

"When I reached for the wine?" I ask, and he nods. I hold back the laughter bubbling in my chest; probably best not to laugh in Enzo's face. I clear my throat. "Sorry?"

A cruel smile spreads over his face. "Apologies won't help you now."

His cerulean eyes hold me captive as his hand slides up my thigh. His thumb skims my inner thigh and dips into the slick heat, finding my clit. A satisfied grin heats his face as he circles over the sensitive area, making me jerk back.

"Oh no, sweetheart," he rumbles, "you'll take your punishment like a good girl."

"Punishment?" I croak, leaning back and resting my elbows on the table behind me. "This seems like a reward to me."

"Mm," he hums as his thumb picks up in speed. Pressure builds low in my stomach and goosebumps coat my body as adrenaline and lust courses through my veins. My brain is going hazy, and I drop my head back. I'm too hot. My body clenches at the overwhelming sensations pulsing through my clit, and my thighs tremble.

I try to pull away from Enzo's torture, but in this position, I'm trapped, so I try to breathe through it, but I'm tumbling toward another devastating orgasm.

I moan, so close, and just as I'm about to fall off the edge, Enzo pulls his hand away. I pull my gaze back to him, panting, and his wicked grin aggravates me. Before I can move or speak, his hands are on me again, teasing me to the edge and retreating at the precipice of orgasm.

My mind can't string together any thoughts apart from those hands on my body, and my whimpers become more and more desperate.

"Beg me," Enzo pants, drawing my head up.

Enzo's always so refined, and in control, but this is something entirely different. His eyes are wild, watching my body react to his torture—I tremble at the sight as heat pulses through my veins.

He looks up, staring directly into my *soul*. "I want to hear that smart mouth beg me."

I shake my head, not wanting to give in. He won't get those words out of me.

But his hands are on me again, this time in me as he thrusts two fingers in and I choke on a sob, my core clenching hard around him. I'm so incredibly wet, and hot, and *desperate* for release.

"Please," I plead, tears filling my eyes. "Please, Enzo, I'm sorry. Please let me come."

Cruel satisfaction heats Enzo's face as he leans forward, forcing his fingers deeper into me, my mind fracturing even further. "Will you do as you're told?"

"I..." Honestly, probably not. "I will. Please, Enzo, I need to come."

"Very well," he purrs as he sits back, his thumb finding my clit as he works my body hard and fast. I come so hard that my whole body spasms, and I throw my head back and scream so loudly that I'm sure Matteo can hear it.

But I don't care. I'm undone. My mind is so incredibly quiet that I think for a second, I might be dead.

At some point, Enzo's hands disappear and the trembling in my body stops. I look up, still panting, and I'm met with cold eyes. What...

"Get yourself cleaned up," Enzo says, pushing me off his lap. I stumble onto my feet and Enzo stands, walking towards his kitchen. What the fuck just happened?

I want to say something, but his back is to me, like I don't exist. I clench my jaw and stomp toward his office.

Matteo's words from last night come back to me. *This is the first time my stoic brother seems to have an actual interest in a woman, and is not just keeping them around for convenience.*

Why the fuck did I for one millisecond think that Enzo sees more than a convenience?

I push into his office and Matteo lifts his gaze from the laptop with a cocky grin. It disappears as soon as I slam the door behind me. My shorts, panties and jacket are sitting in a neat pile next to my bag.

"What happened?" Matteo asks.

"I have to go," I force out, as I cross to my things and pick them all up, not bothering to put any of my clothes back on. I just need to get out of here.

"Del—"

"Whatever you're about to say," I warn, "I don't care." I turn, fighting the unexpected tears.

"Wait," Matteo pleads, as my hand lands on the doorknob, making me pause.

"There's nothing here," I croak, wrenching the door open and walking away.

When I get to the living area, Enzo is, of all things, clearing the dishes from lunch. I'm so fucking angry at myself for even coming here. So fucking angry at people taking advantage of me every chance they get.

He doesn't stop me as I storm out. As I close the door behind me and head to the elevator, I hear plates smashing.

TWENTY ONE

K
♠

ENZO

PLATES AND FOOD EXPLODE across the floor as rage burns through my veins. I pace in front of the destruction, my mind reeling. She's infuriating and intoxicating and fucking with my head. Strawberries and goddamn frankincense are imbedded into my skin—I can smell her everywhere.

She left *again.*

Matteo storms out from the direction of my office and stops by the fireplace as he sees the mess on the floor.

"What did you do?" he demands.

"Fuck off, Teo."

"Enzo—"

"She's none of your fucking concern," I growl, charging toward him.

Matteo doesn't back down and barely moves as I shoulder check him, heading for my office.

My phone buzzes on the desk as I sit down. "Are you following her?"

"Yes," Lucas answers.

"Good."

Rage still courses through my veins as I toss the phone onto the desk and close my eyes. I saw it, just for a moment, when those emerald green, lust-drunk eyes sparkled with light.

If I let Delphine anywhere near the poisoned part of me that was once occupied by a soul, she'll try to neutralise it with those sparkling eyes, and sweet noises, and the last threads of *purity* that hold on to her for dear life.

Fury explodes through my body as I take it out on my desk, flipping it onto its side, the contents that were on top exploding across the floor.

I can't be fucking saved—I don't *want* to be saved. But she won't fucking leave me. The dark, consuming, *obsessive* part of me she's coaxed out whispers in my ear.

What if she likes the poison?

She's in my head. In my waking hours and in my dreams, she's all I can think about.

It's been torture to refrain from showing up at her house or school and locking her up in my penthouse. I know Delphine's exact routine—school, home, work on repeat. It could be easy to pick her up on her way home and—

Fuck, *no*, I can't kidnap the woman.

My phone buzzes with a message from Lucas. He's going to demand a raise after I've forced him to keep tabs on Delphine all week.

She's home. Do you want me or Peter at the meet?

I'd prefer Lucas at this meeting, but something about Peter knowing where Delphine lives makes my jaw tense. I send back a message.

Stay with Delphine.

I toss my phone on the desk and cross to the small bar in my office, pouring myself a bourbon. I need to see her, but I don't know how to convince her *without* forcing her hand—I know my stubborn little siren is upset with me.

Should I organise a dinner at *Seduzione*? No, I avoid Raphael as much as I can, so he'd be suspicious if I'm there for anything other than business.

Maybe I *should* pick her up from school one afternoon?

I sigh, draining my drink—once again, I cannot kidnap the woman, no matter how easy it would be, and how much I itch to do so.

I head to my room, needing to change. Despite my grievances, Raphael's new import connection wouldn't meet anywhere but at the docks, so I select a black suit and a heavy wool coat before getting into the shower.

I dress in a black shirt, suit pants and dress shoes, before pulling on a custom-made brown leather shoulder holster, and pick up my jacket and coat before heading for the office.

I open the safe stored behind one of the bookshelves and pick out a handgun, checking the ammunition before fitting it into the holster, then pulling out a couple of knives and putting them in their slots on the other side.

I'm not the biggest fan of guns; my preference is knives or fists, but in this business, you prepare for everything.

Peter is at the elevator when I exit the apartment and we ride it to the basement car park in silence. He's relatively new to my payroll, and he's a good asset with his connections to the bikers, but there's something about him that makes me wary.

I have this feeling he isn't as loyal to me as he claims to be—I guess tonight will be a good indication.

I climb into the back of the black sedan, Peter getting into the driver's seat, and we pull out of the car park. As the city buzzes by, my mind drifts back to Delphine.

Possession slithers in my chest. I've told myself so many times this week that I should leave her be, let her escape a life tainted by the darkness of mine. Avoid the possibility of her trying to *fix* parts of me that are too far gone. But the thought of her moving on, of her allowing someone *else* to touch her, makes me want to slit throats—a lot of them.

I can't let her go.

She's mine, even if she runs from me. Even if she *ruins* me.

I pull my phone out of my jacket, about to demand an update from Lucas, but it buzzes in my hand with a message.

LUCAS

> She's gone to another student's home with Miss Sakura. Looks like a house party.

I frown. That's not part of her routine. She should be working today.

> Watch her.

I respond as we pull into the docks.

Peter turns right and brings the car to a stop near a stack of containers where two of Raphael's men stand guard. They recognise Peter and nod, motioning for him to continue straight through the rows of containers.

"Is it just us, boss?" Peter asks as we approach an open space.

Three cars are parked to one side, and a few guys are milling around. Raphael, his second-in-command Jace, and another man converse in front of an open container on the opposite side. Peter reverses the car next to another—smart move in case we have to get out of here quick.

I ignore his question and slip out of the car, not bothering to wait for him.

Raphael isn't stupid enough to take me out, just like I know not to do the same to him. Both of us hide enough of our side of business that one could not function without the other.

Also, both being prominent members of the community, it would be rather suspicious if either of us disappeared or wound up dead.

I stop a short distance away, drawing their attention as Peter catches up, flanking my left.

"Dragone," I say in greeting.

"Herrington," he acknowledges and then gestures to his associate. "This is Adrian."

"Just Adrian?"

Adrian flashes me a white smile that's a stark contrast to his brown skin as he crosses the distance to me, his hand out. "I'm here on behalf of the Navarro family." The Navarro cartel is one of the largest growers and producers of cocaine in Colombia. "It's a pleasure, Lorenzo."

I try not to grind my teeth at his casual use of my first name as I shake his hand. "We've never met."

Adrian chuckles, releasing my hand. "No, we haven't, but you can't live in this beautiful place and not know of Lorenzo Herrington—you own most of the city."

The man is tall, but I'm still easily a head taller. He's of slim build, but fit, and dressed well in a navy suit, with his dark brown hair styled back neatly. He seems almost overly relaxed as he meanders back to Raphael and Jace, his back turned to me. You should never have your back turned in a situation like this.

"Raphael tells me you were very eager to meet with me," Adrian drawls. He gestures at one of the men by the open container and barks orders in what sounds like Spanish, and then turns back to me.

"I want to know who I'm doing business with."

Adrian dips his chin. "I respect that."

"Where's Matteo?" Jace asks, drawing my attention.

Where Adrian looks relaxed, both Raphael and Jace are a little too stiff. Raphael's eyes have a cold gleam, and they keep taking in everything around him, like he's waiting for an ambush. My instincts bristle—what is he anticipating?

"He'll be here soon," I say, adjusting my jacket sleeve.

As if summoned, the rumble of Harleys ricochets off the containers as three bikes, Matteo's gunmetal grey sports car and a truck appear in the space. The truck backs up close to the container as Matteo and the Harleys park near my car.

"Dragone," Creed drawls as he prowls toward the truck, pulling out a smoke from his pocket. "I see that there's actual product this time."

"If your boys weren't so incompetent, you'd have more," Jace spits, making Creed chuckle.

Raphael rolls his eyes as he starts instructing men to load the truck. Forklifts come out from the fringes and start pulling out pallets of cigarettes in which bricks of cocaine are hidden between—it's an efficient way to get through customs, apart from the considerable bribes to government officials and threats of violence to their families.

Adrian introduces himself to Matteo and Creed.

"You one of the Navarro sons?" Creed asks. Apparently, there's a couple of them.

"A very close cousin," Adrian corrects. I would normally get Lucas to look into this guy, but if he's related to the Navarros, I don't want to start a war with the cartel by getting in their business—best to keep it cordial.

"How long have you been in Melbourne?" Matteo asks.

"Born and raised, *hermano*," Adrian says.

"And we're only just working with you now?" I ask. If he was a player in this game, we would have been working with him already, or he would have been eliminated.

"I've been over with the Navarros for a few years. I only got back in the last three months."

"Seems like all things are going well over there," Matteo comments. "The product is clean and potent."

A haughty smile spreads across Adrian's face. "I expect only the best."

The feeling of being watched brushes against my senses, and I go on high alert. I force myself not to have a visceral reaction, but I can see Peter step closer in my peripheral—at least he's picked on something being wrong.

Creed and Matteo are talking to Adrian about the product, and Raphael is looking at his phone, completely oblivious to everything around him.

Jace seems to bristle and starts looking around, his hand slipping behind his back, probably going for his piece.

My gun is out and aimed at the container opposite the truck as two men peek out from the roof of a container, cameras raised toward Matteo and Creed. I fire, dropping both of them before anyone else has the chance to draw their weapons.

Suddenly, almost everyone has a gun out. Peter has stepped slightly in front of me with two guns, one pointed at Raphael and the other at Adrian.

"Who the *fuck* are they?" Raphael growls from behind Jace, who has his two guns pointed at me and Matteo.

"Someone not meant to be here," I say, holstering my weapon.

Jace barks out an order to one of his men, who disappears behind the container and then reappears on the roof. He feels around in their pockets, pulling out phones and wallets, and looks at the items before dropping them like they bit him.

"They're fucking cops," he says, scrambling away from the bodies.

Jace's narrowed gaze swings between me and Matteo. "How the *fuck* did the cops found out about this meeting?"

Matteo scoffs, his gun steady on Jace. "You're the mob boss, Dragone; they sure as fuck weren't following us."

This is why I didn't want this meet here—it's too open.

"Creed is the president of the Savage Wings," Raphael points out. "They could have been following him."

Creed chuckles, putting his gun away. "I know every fed and local cop watching us, and those two are not any of them."

"If either of you are compromised, perhaps I should reevaluate our working arrangement?" Adrian asks. He never drew a weapon, but his men surround him, guns drawn.

"We've cleaned house," Matteo says towards Adrian, "so if you want to drop Dragone, we're happy to discuss direct business."

Jace swings both guns to Matteo, making him smile.

"You *dare* steal business from us?" Jace warns.

"Might want to shut your lapdog up, Dragone," Creed says, "before he gets put down."

My phone buzzes in my pocket—probably a message from Lucas about Delphine. My hands itch to pull out my phone, curious to know what my devilish woman is up to.

"Let's go, Peter, I've got other business to attend to."

"You're really going to leave when there's two dead cops here that *you* shot?" Raphael asks.

I smirk as I begin to step backwards to my car. "You should be thanking me."

"For what?"

"For allowing you to continue to breathe, since you've become a fucking problem."

TWENTY TWO

— $\underset{\spadesuit}{Q}$ —

DEL

I FEEL LIKE I'M on a boat in the ocean, bobbing up and down and unable to stop.

My stomach burns as I slam the shot glass down and shove a lime wedge into my mouth. Scar giggles at my discomfort as she wipes her mouth with the back of her hand.

"I love your face," she slurs as she twirls away and dances to the music pulsing through the living room.

Scar dragged my moping ass to some random house party and proceeded to force-feed me tequila shots all night. I'm glad to be drunk right now, because there are people *everywhere.*

I start to sway to the music, drifting toward Scar, letting the music take over any thoughts or feelings that have plagued me for the last week.

As far as I'm concerned, Enzo is done, gone, never to be in my life again. All that man has done is make the nightmares of my past come back and make my body desperately crave his touch in the dark.

I shake out the thoughts of his beautifully wicked body, and close my eyes, moving to the music and giving no fucks about anyone around me. I hope someday my life will settle in a soft, boring lull where my nightmares don't taint every moment, and crime lords aren't fucking with my head.

Normal. Boring. That's what I want.

What a fucking lie.

Frustration bubbles in my chest. I know in my bones that my life will never be normal, not after everything that has happened to me.

I open my eyes and the sting of bright, colourful lights makes my stomach roll uncomfortably. I leave Scar dancing and push through the crowd until I get to a short hallway and find the bathroom.

My reflection in the mirror swirls as I try to settle my churning stomach. Saliva fills my mouth and I jolt for the toilet, emptying my stomach contents into the bowl, most of it being tequila.

After the heaving stops, I flush and rinse my mouth out at the tap, my reflection no longer spinning. I toy with a tendril of my hair that's escaped the high bun, twirling the faded red end around my finger.

Enzo seemed to like this colour.

I shake my head and frown, dropping my hand. No, I'm not supposed to be thinking about him.

I pull my phone out of the pocket of my leather jacket, and find Enzo's name in my messages, and start typing out a message.

> You're a bastard.

I smirk at myself and set my phone on the counter as I undo my hair to re-tie again. It buzzes with a notification as I finish, and I scoop up the phone.

ENZO

> My parents were married when I was born, so technically, I'm not.

I huff, thumbs flying across the keyboard.

> I'm over you.

ENZO

> Then why are you messaging me?

> To tell you.

ENZO

> Has anyone else touched you?

> Not yet. But they will.

ENZO

> Do you really want someone's demise to be on your hands?

I roll my eyes at his threat.

> Why did you have to choose me?

ENZO
Because I wanted you.

If I had said no, would you have let me go?

ENZO
Most likely not.

I didn't ask for any of this. You came into my life and fucking ruined it. You're a Herrington, you can have anyone you want, so why did it have to be me?

My phone starts ringing, Enzo's name lighting up the screen. Fuck.

I answer, putting the phone to my ear but saying nothing.

"I ruined *your* life?" Enzo asks in a quiet but deadly tone. "I own this city, and all I think about is that I don't own you."

I swallow, not knowing what to say.

Enzo chuckles on the other end of the line. "If you think I've ruined your life now, just wait. Remember, *you're* the one who started this, sweetheart. Be prepared for the consequences when I catch you."

My heart is pounding as I hang up, blinking at the screen. Surely, he's joking?

But Enzo doesn't *do* jokes. He means every wicked syllable that comes out of his mouth.

Banging on the door stops me from calling Enzo back to either give him a piece of my mind or beg for a reprieve—I don't exactly know which one.

"Hurry *up*," I hear Flynn whine on the other side of the door.

I shove my phone back in my pocket and wrench the door open.

Flynn tilts forward as he was leaning on the door and barely catches himself before crashing into me. "What the fuck?"

"There are other bathrooms in this house, puppy."

Flynn's eyes are glazed over as he smirks and steps into the bathroom, forcing me to step back, and closes the door, trapping me. He stalks me further into the bathroom until my back hits the glass of the shower.

He places his hands on either side of my head and leans in, our noses almost brushing.

"You know, you're kind of pretty for someone your size," he slurs, the stench of bourbon wafting over my face.

Memories flash through my head, and I try with everything in me not to dissolve into a panic attack at this very moment. I need to get out of here first.

"I need to leave, Flynn," I bite out, keeping myself very still.

Flynn chuckles, pressing his body into mine. "You can't tell me you don't want to fuck me. I've seen how you look at me."

I scoff. "With disgust?"

"Come on, Del, I'm letting you fuck someone *way* out of your league."

I laugh in his face. If only he knew.

Flynn's face turns cold, and he crushes me further into the glass, his hand going to my throat. "You stupid bitch. You're nothing but some disgusting stray the Sakuras scraped out of the gutter, just like Scarlett."

Rage pours through my veins as I shove Flynn off me. I take advantage of his surprise and swing, connecting my fist with Flynn's eye. He crashes to the floor, and I connect my boot with his ribs as hard as I can.

"Touch me or Scarlett again, and I will fucking *kill* you."

I step over the cowering mess on the floor and escape the bathroom. My whole body shakes as I find Scar's jacket thrown over a couch, and the tiny drunk mess making out with a girl in front of a bunch of guys. I yank her back and they boo as I pull her through the crowd and out the front door.

She tugs me to a halt. "Del, what the hell?"

"I need you to stop taking me to these fucking parties," I practically growl, shoving her jacket into her hands.

Her big, brown eyes soften slightly. "I know you're not upset at me. What happened?"

"Flynn. The little fucker," I mutter, shaking out my hand as it starts to throb.

"What did he do?"

I blow out a breath, tilting my head back to the night sky. "He trapped me in the bathroom and tried to make me fuck him."

"He did *what?*" a deep voice asks.

My head whips over to Lucas, storming up the driveway.

"Lucas, what—"

"Get in the car," he orders, his eyes focused on the house behind me. "I'll take you both home."

"We're fine. We can—"

His dark eyes promise murder as he glares at me. "Get in the car."

A small hand wraps around my wrist. "Let's go," Scar whispers as she tugs me down the driveway.

Instead of following us, Lucas disappears into the house. I get shoved into the back of a warm SUV before I can follow him. Scar holds my hand as I stare out the window, waiting for Lucas to reappear. I really hope he doesn't kill Flynn. He might be a dick, but he's the son of a judge, and his father wouldn't rest until someone was in prison.

After what feels like an eternity, Lucas walks out of the house, suspiciously calm. He has his hands in his fucking pockets—I doubt the man just *spoke* to Flynn.

"Did you kill him?" I ask as soon as he slides into the driver's seat.

"Unfortunately, no," is all he says as he pulls onto the street.

"Did Enzo call you?" His possessive boss must have told him to collect my drunken ass before I made good on my threat to let someone else touch me.

"Yes."

I blow out a breath. I know I'm not going to get anything else out of him with that finality in his tone, so I resume looking out the window. It's a short drive back to the house, but the adrenaline drains from my body and my eyelids grow heavy.

Red and blue flashing lights zip past as I fall asleep.

Bourbon breath wafts over my face, the saccharine stench sticking in the back of my throat. It's pitch black. I can't see him, but I can *feel* him, his huge body looming around me. I'm too warm. Why won't he leave me alone?

"Kitty," he breathes into my ear. God, I hate the sound of his scratchy voice. I swallow, not making a single noise. He hates it when I complain.

Big, clammy, rough hands grasp my knee. Please stomach, please don't empty all over him again. Remember what happened last time. I swallow back the bile burning my throat as his hand slides higher, and higher, and higher.

When will this torture end?

The last two weeks have been exhausting.

Rumours of me being an alcoholic have taken over the school, and I'm over the snickering of students and the worried expressions of teachers that hound me every day.

My nightmares have come back with such force that if I do manage to fall asleep, I'm soon being shaken awake by Scar or Claudine, because I'm screaming.

The only good thing right now is that I haven't seen Flynn since that stupid party. Three broken ribs, a black eye, a broken nose and three fractures in his arm have kept him home—Lucas didn't kill him, but he definitely beat the shit out of him. I'm pretty sure at least one of those broken ribs was me, so I helped.

I'm sitting in my history lesson half-asleep when the vice principal interrupts the class, speaking quietly to the teacher.

They both turn to me. "Miss Blaire, they need you in the office."

Fucking great. I pile up my things and follow the vice principal; the whispering chasing me out. We cross the school to the main building where the reception and offices are. We climb to the second story, and I'm led to a meeting room. The moment I open the door, I fight the urge to leave.

The principal, my mother, and Isaac sit around the conference table.

"Please, Miss Blaire, take a seat," the principal, Mr. Fernandez, says.

"You know she's not my guardian, right?" I point out. Fernandez's frown deepens; he's not going to kick her out. My day is about to get worse. Lovely. I drop my books hard on the table at the far end and drop into the seat.

"Darling," my mum purrs, "you look so tired."

"Thank you," I say, crossing my arms over my chest and turning my attention to Fernandez. "What do you want?"

"It's been brought to my attention by some teachers that there may be some concerning behaviours that need to be addressed."

"And what would they be?" I ask. I know exactly what this is about.

He sits a little straighter. "They have heard from some students that you may be suffering from substance abuse issues."

"We're worried about you, darling," my mum coos, her face soft with concern.

I ignore her and glare at Fernandez. "What's your evidence?"

"Reports of being withdrawn with your peers, excessive tiredness, and—"

"How are my grades?" I ask, cutting him off.

He blinks a few times. "No change there, but—"

"But nothing," I argue, "nothing has changed in my behaviour. I come to school every day on time, I do my homework, I haven't missed any hours at my paying job, and I don't start trouble. The only thing that has changed is the bullying that I'm receiving, but you don't see me reporting it. So, are we done now?"

"We have a strict policy on drugs and alcohol in this school," Fernandez chides, "and if you would like to graduate, you will need to prove to us you are free from the influence of all substances."

Isaac clears his throat and sits forward. "Del—"

"Is that why you're here?" I say, laughing. "You bought in a fed to do a rudimentary drug and alcohol test?"

"I was worried about you too," Isaac counters.

"Did your dear *sister* tell you of her concerns?" I spit.

"We're just trying to help you, Delphine," my mum says.

"You're trying to meddle with my life, Eleanor," I say, standing up. "One that you *legally* have no right to have any say in."

"Miss Blaire," Fernandez warns.

"Let's get this shit over with," I huff, rounding toward Isaac.

He stands, placing a small bag on the table and pulling out an alcohol breathalyser. He makes me blow into the tube until the machine beeps and shows Fernandez the '0' reading. Next, he pulls out a roadside drug testing kit. I do as instructed, scraping the small pads along my tongue and hand back the small tab.

"We need a saliva sample as well," Isaac murmurs, pulling out a test tube with a long, clean swab in it. I don't say anything as I open my mouth and let him swipe both sides of my cheeks with the swab before putting it into the tube.

Isaac picks up the other drug test. "This one is clean. The other analysis will get back to you by Monday."

I walk back to my books and scoop them up. "Now that you've ruined my Friday, I'm going to go home now."

"We haven't finished, Miss Blaire," Fernandez says as he stands.

"Unless you want me to get lawyers in here, we are," I say as I walk out of the office. The bells shrill as I walk out of the building, heading to my locker.

Scar is already there with my bag and hers on the floor as she paces back and forth, wringing her hands. When she spots me, she runs over and slams into me, almost knocking me over as she hugs me fiercely.

"Please tell me you didn't get expelled," she pleads.

"Not yet," I breathe, pulling out of her hug. "Let's get out of here."

Scar nods, handing me my bag and picking up her own. I shove my things into the overstuffed bag and get to the parking lot before the major rush of students. As I'm pulling out of the park, we drive past Isaac and my mum, walking out of the main building.

"Is that your *mum*?" Scar asks as I peel out of the parking lot and race a little too fast down the street. "She can't be here."

"They made me take a fucking drug and alcohol test," I explain to Scar.

"My mum is going to sue the *shit* out of Silvia," Scar announces. "This is defamation."

I suddenly feel exhausted, the adrenaline evaporating. "If they want to drug test me once a week, they can go right ahead."

"Say the words, Del, and I will fuck up Silvia's whole life," Scar promises.

"I just want to get through this school year and then disappear from everyone's lives."

"First of all," she says, grabbing my hand that's clutching the gear stick, "you can't disappear. And secondly, fuck them all."

"I'm just so tired of all this shit," I sigh, pulling my hand out of her grasp to use the indicator.

"You know what? I know what I want for my birthday," Scar announces. Her eighteenth birthday was yesterday, and she hasn't decided on what she wants to do to celebrate. "We're going out tonight, just the two of us. And we are going to get completely trashed."

"Scar, we are not—"

"No rules, except that we stay together," she says, before turning the volume up on the music to an earsplitting level.

Well, I guess that's that.

TWENTY THREE

—Q—
♠

DEL

SCAR AND I HAVE dinner with the Sakuras, filling them in on my eventful afternoon, which makes Claudine livid.

I stop her from calling the school or Silvia's parents to start a war, but I promise to call her if the school tries to make me do any more tests.

We let the Sakuras know we are going out tonight, before Scar drags me upstairs to get ready.

"We're getting this party started early," Scar announces, pulling out a bottle of tequila from her wardrobe. "And this is a big fuck you to Fernandez."

I laugh, pulling the bottle from her hand and opening it. "Happy birthday! I love your crazy ass."

"I love you too," she croons as I take a swig from the bottle. It burns from the moment it hits my tongue, and I try not to gag as I thrust the bottle back into Scar's hands.

"You are so bad with tequila," she teases as she takes a swig without flinching.

"It tastes like poison."

"But it gets the job done," she counters, taking another swig.

I pull the bottle from her, brave another mouthful, and then set the bottle down. We take turns having quick showers, do our make-up and hair, and then contemplate what to wear.

I'm thoroughly buzzed by the time I'm dressed in tight, black skinny jeans, a loose black camisole with a deep V-cut neckline, and a gold sequined jacket. I sit on the floor and zip up a pair of my nicer biker boots as Scar pulls her leather mini skirt over a red bodysuit, then stumbles toward me.

"Zip this for me," she slurs slightly.

"Enough tequila for the both of us until the club," I say as I zip her up.

"Agreed," she mumbles, as she sits on the edge of her bed and pulls on the thigh-high boots. I don't know why this woman wears heels when they always end up off her feet, but at least these boots have a thick heel, so she might last a little longer than normal.

I scramble off the floor, a little dizzy when I'm upright, and put on the hoop earrings picked out for me, then fasten the necklace Scar chose around her neck.

"Are we ready?" I ask, taking both of our phones off charge and passing Scar her bag and leather jacket.

"I'll order the ride," she says as we leave her room.

"I feel like trouble is brewing," I mumble as I hook my arm through hers.

"We are the trouble, baby," she says as we descend the stairs in a fit of giggles.

I'm pretty sure we are the most entertaining ride this driver will have all night. We delight him by asking him to turn up his eighties music and sing along to every song.

I don't even know where we're going, but I'm already having a great time. We travel deep into the centre of the city and the car stops in front of *Decadence*, one of the most popular clubs in the city.

A thick line of people hugs the entire length of the building.

"Scar," I complain as we get out of the car, "we're going to be in this line forever."

"Girl, we don't stand in lines." Scar walks straight up to the bouncer.

He looks down into her face, eyes hard. "Back of the line is over there."

"Call your boss. He knows who I am," she demands sweetly.

He scoffs. "You're not the first one to claim that tonight, love."

"I'm not everyone, babe," she says, crossing her arms over her chest. "Tell your boss over your little earpiece that Scarlett Sakura is here."

I tug on her elbow. "Let it go, Scar."

She stands her ground as the bouncer rolls his eyes and talks into the little radio at his shoulder. After a few seconds of fighting the biting June air, his eyes widen and he stands a little straighter, looking down at Scar.

"I need your IDs," he says, holding his hand out. We both pull out our cards and he lifts the rope, letting us through to the small security podium, giving our IDs to the other bouncer who scans them and hands them back.

We walk through the dark hallway; the only lights are the red lighting that glows on the floor.

"How on earth did you just pull that off?" I ask as we shuffle arm in arm to the admission desk where they wave us through, not wanting the cover charge.

"We're friends with the owners," Scar explains.

"Are we?"

Her smile is downright cheeky as we push through a heavy door and drown in lights and music.

The place is packed, people teeming everywhere, dancing or drinking or both.

Scar pulls me through the crowd to the bar and she orders two shots of tequila and two cocktails, the drinks also at no charge. We shoot back the tequila and chase it with the cocktail, then Scar pulls me through the crowd again, towards the dancefloor.

Scar picks a spot in the middle of the gyrating crowd, and we start to move with the music. I dance, laugh and drink, letting the music course through my veins and the alcohol drown all the shit that has happened to me since... well, since the day I was born.

I become just another body swaying to the music, just another person forgetting the consequences and doing whatever the fuck I want.

"More drinks?" Scar shouts into my ear, bringing me back to reality. I nod, letting her drag me back to the bar.

"Okay, you have to tell me," I say to Scar as we wait for our drinks, "who are you screwing to get us free drinks?"

Scar wiggles her eyes at me. "I'm not fucking anyone, *you* however..."

Realisation hits me like a bucket of ice water. "You mean—"

"Being in bed with a Herrington gets us perks," Scar says, accepting the drinks from the bartender.

As if summoned, a tall figure approaches Scar's side and Matteo's beautiful face comes into my hazy view.

"Ladies," he says with a wide grin, "you both look *hot*."

"We know," Scar says, saluting him with her cocktail.

"What's the occasion?" Matteo asks.

"I'm finally legal," Scar says, sipping on her drink.

Matteo's face beams as he steps forward and goes to wrap his arm around Scar, but she bats at his chest, giggling. "No chance, buddy."

I drown out their bantering as my head spins.

Is he here?

I scan the crowd, looking for his huge frame; he'd stand out.

My eyes lift to the balcony that overlooks the dancefloor. There's another bouncer by the stairs to get up there, so I assume that it's the VIP area, and being his club, he'd probably be...

Leaning on the railing with a drink dangling from his hand, the Devil is staring straight at me. My heart pounds. I haven't spoken to him since I drunk-texted him two weeks ago, and I haven't seen him since the penthouse the week before that. But he continues to haunt my dreams and my nightmares.

"Are we doing more shots?" Matteo asks from next to me. But I can't look at him, transfixed by Enzo's stare.

I can't tell if he's pissed off or smirking at me, but there's something about him that feels... volatile.

He looks pristine in a dark suit and white shirt, not a hair out of place on his head. I hate that my body reacts to just the sight of him, my traitorous hand tingling at the thought of touching him.

No. He threw me out the last time I was with him—there's nothing between us. He's just a demon in a cold shell of a human—cruel and incapable of anything that resembles decent emotions. I've already been ruined by one demon, and I'm not about to do it again.

I force myself to turn back to Matteo and Scar with a feigned smile, watching the bartender pouring out a row of six pink shots. Matteo divides them, putting two in front of each of us and then raises one, waiting for us to do the same.

"Happy birthday!" he shouts over the music and takes the shot.

I drink mine back-to-back, letting the fruity concoction slide down my throat before asking the bartender for another round.

"Damn, Del, you're here to play," Matteo muses.

"I hope you can keep up, Teo," I shout, pushing another shot toward him.

He chuckles, shaking his head slightly before knocking back the drink. Scar does the same, and then I take both of their hands, pulling them to the dance floor.

I peek up to the railing, and Enzo tracks us through the crowd, sipping on his drink. I make sure we're in the middle of the sea of people, but directly in Enzo's line of sight.

The three of us laugh and dance, the rest of the crowd around us thick enough that we're all dancing intimately close. I put Scar in between me and Matteo, and he pulls both of us closer, pressing both of us into Scar.

"Are you trying to make all my dreams come true?" I hear Scar ask Matteo over the music as she wraps her arms around his neck.

He smirks, his grip on my hip tightening. "I can give you anything you want, sweet thing."

I rest my chin on Scar's shoulder, grabbing Matteo's shirt and tugging him forward so he's plastered to Scar's front. Wildfire dances in those familiar blue eyes as he leans closer to me, our noses brushing.

"I think he's trying to make his own fantasies come true more than yours." I muse, Scar shaking with laughter. "If it was Scar's fantasy, I would have a cock."

Matteo's smile is feral as he presses his mouth to mine, surprising me.

He pulls back and looks at Scar. "Good thing they sell those."

I laugh and pull away from the Scar sandwich and turn with my eyes closed and my head tipped back.

Arms slither around my body and a warm body presses against me. I open my eyes and death incarnate stares down at me. Enzo doesn't have a drink anymore, and he's gripping the railing like he's about to sail over it.

I tilt my head forward and look into a strange set of brown eyes. The guy is tall and handsome as he directs our bodies to the tempo of the beat, a cocksure grin across his face.

"You are stunning," he says, his voice vibrating through me.

"So are you."

"Should we take this party elsewhere?"

I look up, locking eyes with Enzo. He exudes murder.

I smirk up at Enzo but answer the man. "Yeah, let's go."

He grabs the back of my neck, making me bring my face back to his as he crushes his lips to mine.

He tastes like bourbon, and I try not to have a reaction as I open my mouth to him, letting his tongue sweep in. He's a lousy kisser, probably even lousier in bed, but it's not like I'm going to let him get that far.

I pull back and force a smile on my face, looking into this guy's lust-drunk eyes. I can't help but look up. The balcony is empty. Shit.

This guy twines his fingers in mine and turns toward the exit. We take two steps before he's halted by a huge hand wrapping around his throat. Enzo looms over him, wrath blazing in those cerulean eyes.

Run. My survival instincts scream at me to get the *fuck* out of here before Enzo can get his hands on me next.

I let go of the stranger's hand and take a step back. The movement catches Enzo's attention, and he turns his death glare to me.

I don't dare back down or cower. *He's* the one who fucked this all up.

Stupidly, my body is exhilarated by challenging the Devil. Adrenaline floods my system. I don't know if I want to fuck or fight this man—who am I kidding? I want to do both. Preferably, at the same time.

A small hand slips into mine, breaking the trance. I now notice that the crowd has cleared a space around us, and the music is quieter.

I grip onto Scar's hand tight and pull her to the side, away from both Herrington men.

Enzo tracks my movements, still gripping the stranger by the throat. The poor guy is struggling, desperate to escape Enzo's death grip. I'm pretty sure he won't live past tonight.

"Who is he?" Enzo asks, his voice cold and empty.

"No one," I say in the same haughty tone.

He tilts his head slightly, his eyes narrowing. "So, you let anyone touch what's mine?"

I smirk. "You don't own me."

Enzo must squeeze the guy's throat tighter because he makes a choking sound. "Watch your tone."

"Oh, I'm sorry." I clear my throat. "You don't *fucking* own me, Lorenzo."

Enzo laughs, the sound devoid of emotion. "I've warned you, sweetheart, that your actions and your words have consequences."

I move in the direction of the exit, staying on the edge of the space around us. Enzo watches every step I take.

"You let me go, so you can suffer the consequences of your *own* actions." The crowd parts as I stick Scar behind me and step backward, facing Enzo the whole time. We're getting the fuck out of here.

"If you run, I *will* find you," Enzo warns.

Self-preservation flies out the door as I stop to blow Enzo a kiss. "Good luck."

TWENTY FOUR

K
♠

ENZO

MY WOMAN HAS A death wish.

I watch her retreating form until she disappears from sight.

I want to hunt her down, lock her in the penthouse, and punish her for the shit she's pulled tonight. Punish her for consuming my whole fucking life.

I turn my attention to the man struggling in my grip. My body vibrates with fury as I shove him back, heading toward the back of the club.

"Follow her," I growl to Lucas as I walk past and disappear through a staff door.

I drag the vermin down a dark corridor and into an empty office, tossing him on to the floor. Matteo enters behind me and shuts the door, trapping the guy in with two lethal predators.

He coughs and splutters as he scrambles back. "Please," he croaks, covering his head with his arms, "I didn't know she was yours."

"Actions have consequences," I say, echoing what I told Delphine before she ran off. Locking her in the penthouse sounds more and more appealing.

"Please, let me go man, *please*."

Matteo meanders towards the guy with his hands in his pockets. "This is not the sort of begging that I'm into."

Matteo's boot lands on his ribs, the man's shout singing to the dark part of my soul. My brother gets in a few more stomps to his chest before he grabs a fistful of his hair and his knee connects with his nose. Blood pours out of his nose as the guy sobs and slurs pleas for mercy, fuelling the demon within—but he wants *more*.

"What made you think you could come into my establishment and have your filthy hands all over my woman?"

"I didn't know!" he gurgles through his sobs.

"Not good enough," I say, pulling out my switchblade.

His tear-filled eyes widen at the blade, shaking his head violently as he tries to shrink back. "No. No! I have a wife at home, please, no!"

Matteo chuckles, sinking to his haunches, wanting to be closer to the violence. "Not only are you a perve, but you're a dog, too?"

"I should've known she was yours," he sobs, curling further into his body. "Don't kill me, man."

"You were dead the moment you laid eyes on her." My blade strikes out hard and fast, sinking into the soft flesh of the jugular.

Watching the shock, the *terror*, draining into the sweet nothingness of death, settles some of the burning fury in my blood. It clears the noise buzzing in my head and lifts a weight off my chest, letting me breathe.

The demon in my soul is satiated.

For now.

"What a waste of fucking space," Matteo mutters, watching in wonder as the blood pours down the dead guy's body.

I rip the blade out and move to the side to avoid most of the carnage, but it spurts out onto the sleeve of my shirt, staining it crimson, and sprinkling onto my shoes. I wipe my hand and blade on a clean part of the vermin's shirt as best as I can, then pocket the knife. I stand, rolling my neck and shoulders, feeling the muscles loosen slightly.

"What should we do with the body?" Matteo asks, standing and stretching lazily.

Flashes of him dancing with Delphine, of *kissing* her, flood my mind, and the edges of my vision go grey.

I slam my fist into his face before I know it, and go to swing again, but Matteo catches my fist, grabbing the front of my shirt. I hear the already-ruined shirt tear as he headbutts me, slamming into my lip, busting it open, and then he shoves me off.

"What the fuck, Enzo?" Matteo barks, wiping the blood sliding into his eye from the split in his brow.

I spit the blood pooling in my mouth at his feet. "She's *mine*."

Matteo arches his injured brow. "Is she?"

I launch at my brother, tackling him to the ground. Being leaner than me, he's faster, so he rolls to the side, and throws a punch, connecting to my jaw, the pain barely registering. Matteo slams his arm into my throat, cutting off my oxygen and pinning my chest to the floor. I manage to get to my blade and press it to the hollow part just under his chin.

"Lorenzo," he says, his burning blue eyes on mine.

"Touch her again and I will slit your throat," I spit through the restricted airway, the threat ringing through the room.

Matteo, the crazy bastard, smirks despite the blade cutting into his flesh. "Well, at least we know you're serious about her."

He pulls away from me and rises to his feet, holding out a hand to help me. I accept the gesture and stand, wiping the blood dribbling down my chin.

"Dump his body in an alley somewhere away from the club." Matteo nods and turns to the dead man. I pull my phone out and ring Lucas. "Have you found her?"

"The guys at the door said she turned down the next street, but she disappeared."

I clench my fist, reining in the rage threatening to bubble over. "Go to her house. Hopefully, she's smart enough to head home."

I hang up on Lucas and dial Delphine, but her phone goes straight to voicemail. I take a steading breath and forcibly stop myself from throwing the phone across the room.

Don't run. Answer when I call. No one touches what's mine.

My little siren likes to defy me at every turn.

I hope she's ready for the consequences.

TWENTY FIVE

— Q♠ —

DEL

"**W**HERE ARE WE GOING?" Scar asks as we step out into the frigid night, my lungs stinging as I gulp in clean air. "Del, talk to me."

"Enzo and I aren't...We're nothing."

"What? Why didn't you tell me?"

"It doesn't matter. Let's find somewhere else to go," I say, steering her down the street, needing to put distance between us and *Decadence*.

We walk a couple blocks in silence, Scar clutching my arm as we aimlessly wander the city. We turn down one of the city's many alleyways and navigate the cobblestones—there's a bar somewhere here that I've heard some guys at school talk about.

"Let's just go home," Scar suggests as the alley gets darker, her breathing starting to come out a little harder.

I'm about to agree, but a warm glow comes from another alley connecting to this one. I look around the corner and see a single security guard at a door with a yellow light above it.

"Shall we?" I say, tugging on Scar's arm, but she stops me.

"This place looks like I'll catch a disease."

I laugh. "Weren't you the one who said we were going to get wild tonight?"

"Yeah, but not at a seedy bar in an alleyway."

The door opens up the alley, and a man shoots out, falling to the ground in a heap as another guy steps out with a bottle of beer in his hand, looking down at him. I recognise the rings glinting in the light on those tattooed hands.

"Come on."

The Mechanic crouches down to the man crumbled up on the floor.

"Don't come back here, or you won't leave alive," his harsh, deep voice bounces off the walls as I drag Scar up the alleyway.

The security guard sees us approaching and steps forward. "Private club."

The Mechanic looks up and recognition lights his honey-brown eyes. "Siren."

"Mechanic," I say in greeting as he stands, taking a swig of his beer, his other hand pushing the longer top parts of his hair away from his face.

"Siren?" Scar whispers, drawing the Mechanic's attention. His eyes roam her body, and something like surprise flashing in his eyes, like he's never seen anyone like Scar before. Which would be true.

"This is Songbird," I say, gesturing to her. She turns to me, confused, and I just shrug. "This is the Mechanic."

"Is that the name your mother gave you?" she asks.

The Mechanic chuckles. "No."

Scar smiles sweetly. "Where can a girl get a drink around here?"

The Mechanic chuckles as he shakes his head and motions for us to follow him. The security guard returns to his post as we enter a dark hallway, Scar clutching my arm a little harder. This hall even makes me a little claustrophobic. Thankfully, it's short and the Mechanic pushes through a door into a packed bar.

If you didn't know the Mechanic was a biker, you would now by the number of men sporting the Savage Wings leather cuts.

All heads turn to us as the Mechanic leads up directly to the bar. He meets the eyes of everyone in the bar, holding their attention.

"This is Siren and Songbird. They're not on offer, boys."

Many groans and expletives rumble through the space as they return to their drinking.

"Everything is on the house," the Mechanic says, taking one more long look at Scar before dissolving into the crowd, heading to a pool table.

"You really know every bad guy in the city," Scar comments as she flags over the bartender.

Scar coaxed a group of bikers into a darts tournament, and I honestly don't know how she's winning with this much alcohol coursing through her veins.

I can drink almost double what she can handle, but I'm struggling to string two sentences together.

I've switched to water, trying to sober up a little if I'm going to last until the early hours and get us home safely.

"You need a pick-me-up," the Mechanic says as he sidles up next to me at the bar.

"I need to sober up," I say, jiggling the half-drunk water. "I have to watch Songbird before she ends up with four biker boyfriends."

"That won't happen," Mechanic announces almost forcefully. He takes my water and puts it down on the bar, then digs into his pocket. "This will help you out a lot more than water."

He shakes out the tiny bag in front of me.

"Oh, no, I don't—"

"It's your boyfriend's product, the best on the market."

Scar's giggles come closer, and she wraps her arms around me from behind, resting her chin on my shoulder. "What's happening over here?"

"Want to make this night more interesting?" Mechanic asks, showing Scar the cocaine.

"I'm down if Del's in," Scar says.

I'm not surprised by Scar's willingness—she's always chasing the adrenaline and danger—but the Mechanic is. Delight heats his face as his attention returns to me, the question in his eyes. The irony is not lost on me that I took a drug and alcohol test earlier today. But honestly, what's stopping me?

"Come on," Scar purrs into my ear, "let go. Let's get crazy."

"We stick together," I say, "no running off with a biker."

"*Fine*," she whines, squeezing her arms around me.

I nod at the Mechanic, and he smiles, motioning for us to follow him. He takes us to a small office off the bar and takes a seat behind it, pulling out a mirrored tray with a small razor blade.

"Have either of you done blow before?" he asks, pouring out the white substance and slices through the stuff with the blade.

"No," Scar answers.

He nods, pushing the pile into three thin uniform lines. He picks up the small clear straw. "I'm going to do the first line, so you know I'm not trying to poison you."

Both Scar and I watch as the Mechanic leans down and snorts the first line and then offers the straw over. Scar doesn't hesitate, mimicking the Mechanic, cleaning the next line off the plate. She sniffs a few times when she comes back up, and then holds out the straw for me.

"Fucking hell," I breathe, taking the straw and following suit. The first thing I notice is the bitter taste hitting the back of my tongue, and my nose tingles, burning a little.

The Mechanic has a satisfied smile across his face as he pours out some more and starts cutting it up with the blade again.

"Is my tongue supposed to feel numb?" Scar asks, her face flushed.

"I kind of like the feeling," I comment, noticing the numbness now.

"You should lick the blade," the Mechanic says, dividing the product into three thicker lines this time, holding out the straw to Scar and the blade to me.

I hold his gaze as I lick both flat sides of the blade, the bitter taste intense and my tongue loses more feeling instantly. Scar clears her line and gives me the straw, and I follow her lead then pass it to the Mechanic.

"I didn't think you were such a rebel, Siren," he muses before taking the last line.

"She's never like this," Scar comments, her eyes a little wide as she sways, like she's dancing to music that isn't there.

"And you, Songbird?" Mechanic asks, sniffing as he sits back.

"I was born into this life," she says, bursting into laughter.

"Is it hot in here?" I ask, suddenly feeling too hot, wanting to peel off my clothes.

"Let's go drink," Scar says, practically bouncing off the walls as she rounds the desk, tugging on the Mechanic's hand. He chuckles softly, pulling her into his lap, Scar giggling as she falls.

"Let's just party in here," he offers.

Scar shocks me by crushing her mouth to the Mechanic's and then slips out of his lap. "Another time, lover; tonight is girls' night."

Mechanic's eyes follow Scar like a hawk hunting its prey as she pulls me out of the room. I'm going to have to keep an eye out on that one.

The world is buzzing. I feel nothing other than a sense of euphoria. My brain is running a marathon, but it's also empty for the first time in the last three weeks and I'm relieved; this break is heaven sent.

We've been snorting lines all night, the drugs enhancing the effects of the alcohol, so Scar and I are practically hanging off the bar by the time the bartender cuts us off.

"But you make the best White Russians," Scar slurs, pleading with the poor man.

"I agree with him," I hiccup. "We're done for the night."

Scar's heavy eyes look at me, pouting, but she nods. "Fine. Let's go."

The Mechanic, who's been watching Scar a little too closely all night, sidles up to her and wraps an arm around her waist. "How are you two so wrecked, but still look this hot?"

"Black magic and ritual sacrifice," I declare, pulling Scar to my side, out of his arms. "We have to go now."

"You can't possibly get home in this condition," he argues, crossing his brawny arms over his chest. "You can crash at my place. It's not far."

"We have other arrangements," I say, pulling the giggling Scar toward the exit, "and we don't want to piss off the Executive."

The Mechanic follows behind us. "I think he'll be more pissed off if I let you ladies wander the city by yourselves."

I might not be speaking to Enzo right now, but the association is keeping us safe in a bar full of criminals. I sigh. "Do you have a car?"

He smiles and nods, leading us to the other side of the bar, away from our original entrance we came through. We pass through another hallway, this one well-lit and with a few other doors, before pushing through into a motorbike retail shop. We pass lines of shiny bikes and leave the front door where a huge utility vehicle is parked out the front with a motorbike on the tray.

The Mechanic opens the passenger door and scoops up Scar in his arms. "Please don't puke in my car."

She giggles, tapping softly on his cheek. "No guarantees."

He puts her into the seat and buckles her in as I slide into the back passenger side, belting myself in, then he gets behind the wheel.

"Where to?" he asks.

"*Luxuria*," I say, laying my head back on the headrest. I don't want to go there, but I don't want the Mechanic to know where we live. We're also way more wasted than I thought we'd be, and if we go home, there will be *a lot* of questions. We'll get a room under a fake name and slip out of there in the morning.

The lights of the city burn a little too bright and the colours are vivid as we cross the city. The drive is not very long as the

Mechanic rolls right up to the door and hops out, heading for Scar's door. I slip out of the car as he's lifting her half-conscious body out.

"Are you sure you're going to be okay?" he asks, putting Scar on her feet and slinging her arm over my shoulder.

"We're good, thank you," I say, pulling Scar into the hotel. I approach the front desk and see none other than Rose.

"Miss Blaire," she says as a greeting, her eyes a little alarmed at the state of Scar. "Keys for the penthouse?"

"No," I say immediately, "another room. Don't tell anyone we're here."

She nods, tapping away at her computer, and then frowns. "We are booked out tonight," she muses, "but I'm sure I can find something. It'll take me a couple of minutes."

I nod, leading Scar to an armchair and sit her down. She sinks into the seat, bringing her knees to her chest and hugging her legs.

"I'll just sleep here," she sighs.

"Don't pass out on me now," I grumble, as I perch on the arm.

The soft music playing in the space gets muffled like I'm underwater as I focus on dozens of artistically hung bulbs above the front desk. The lights dance and swirl together so beautifully. A high-pitched *ding* pierces through my reverie, and I hear footsteps behind me. I look over toward the elevators and shoot up from my seat as Enzo and Matteo storm through the foyer.

I've never seen Enzo so unkempt. He's still in dark suit pants, but his shirt is in complete disarray. It's unbuttoned, no, *ripped*, halfway down his chest and the sleeves are rolled up. One sleeve isn't white anymore, but a reddish-brown. My stomach twists—that's *definitely* blood.

As he gets closer, I see the busted lip, the wild hair, and I gape at the feral inferno burning in his eyes.

"Where the *fuck* have you been?" he booms as he clutches both my upper arms, shaking me slightly.

"Why do you care?" I ask.

Matteo steps around me, and I notice he's a little banged up as well, sinking to his haunches next to Scar. I try to pull away from Enzo, but he grips me tighter, forcing me to stare into his terrifyingly beautiful face.

He leans down, his face close to mine as his eyes bore into me. "Are you fucking high?"

"And I ask again," I say with a little more conviction, "why do you *care*?"

"What did you take?" Matteo murmurs behind me. Why do either of them fucking care? We aren't—

"Delphine," Enzo barks.

I lift my hands and shove hard against Enzo's chest. The move surprises him and he actually releases me, staggering a few steps back. I turn and shove Matteo away from Scar, who falls on his ass.

"We're going," I say, hauling Scar up, making her groan in protest.

Matteo shoots up from the floor and picks up Scar before I can take two steps, then heads for the elevators.

"I will call the fucking cops," I shout, trying to go after Mattco, but a grip on my elbow wrenches me back, and I fall against a hot, hard body.

"They aren't going to do shit," Enzo growls into my ear. "They look the other way, or I pull the Herrington funding."

"You're a piece of shit," I spit, trying to shake his hold. "Let me go."

"No," he states.

"Let me go," I bite out as I glare up into his face. I need him to let me go, release all ties, and just pretend I never existed.

"I can't," he whispers, his eyes blazing with so many things. "I won't."

TWENTY SIX

DEL

ENZO WRESTLES ME INTO an elevator, never letting go of my arm as we journey up to the penthouse in silence. My heart is pumping in my ears and my stomach dips. I need to lie down.

The elevator doors slide open and Enzo pulls me to the door, opening it and shoving me inside. I immediately set off in search of Scar, checking the kitchen, lounge room and then head for the hallway towards the office.

Arms circle around my waist, halting me by the fireplace. I drive my elbows back, trying to dislodge Enzo, but he has me pressed into his body so firmly that I can't get leverage.

"Where's Scar?" I demand, fighting his hold.

"I'll take you to her if you tell me what you took."

I stop fighting him. "Coke. Your stuff."

"Who were you with?" he asks, his chest rumbling through mine. I close my eyes. I don't need to think about how fucking amazing that feels, or how wet I'm about to be if he doesn't let me go.

"Friends," I mumble.

"Did they touch either of you?" Enzo asks, his lips grazing my ear.

"No," I whisper, finding it very hard not to press further into him, to let him touch me. Why is my body a traitorous harlot for this man?

"Why did you leave?" he asks, and I'm not sure if he's asking about leaving the club or leaving the penthouse three weeks ago.

"Why stay where I'm not wanted?"

Enzo turns me in his arms and grips each side of my face. "Delphine—"

"Take me to Scarlett," I ask, trying to catch my breath.

I'm drawn straight back into his vortex. I want to taste his darkness every waking moment until all I can taste, see, and feel is Enzo. He's more potent that any drug I could ever put in my body.

Enzo opens his mouth to say something but then locks his jaw and nods, loosening his hold and walking toward the kitchen. "Bedrooms are this way."

I follow him to another hallway past the kitchen and he knocks on the first door on the right. Matteo opens the door shirtless in tracksuit pants, his right eye swollen and half-closed.

"Where's Scar?" I ask softly. Matteo opens the door a little wider. Scar is passed out in the middle of a huge bed, hugging a pillow, in a t-shirt that clearly isn't hers.

"Before you berate me," Matteo murmurs, "she said she didn't want to sleep alone, *and* she changed on her own. Without an audience."

"Touch her and I will beat the shit out of you," I whisper.

"Yes, boss," Matteo whispers, softly chuckling.

"Keep the bathroom light on and the door ajar."

Matteo doesn't say anything, but nods and then closes the door.

I step away from the door until my back hits the wall opposite, keeping my eyes on the floor. "I'll come back for Scar in the morning."

"You're not going anywhere," Enzo states.

I refuse to look at him. "Get Lucas to take me home or I'll call a ride."

Enzo's shoes come into view in front of me. His fingers tilt my chin up, forcing me to look at him. "No."

"You can't—" His lips swallow my complaints, and steal all the oxygen in my lungs.

He does it again, ridding my body of any tension and filling my head with the quiet I crave. Before I have a chance to get my bearings, Enzo pulls back and takes my elbow, pulling me into the door at the end of the hall.

I don't see much of the dark room, as Enzo's mouth is on mine again. His hands pull off my jacket and I rip open the rest of his ruined shirt as our tongues fight for dominance. The metallic tang of his blood floods my tastebuds. Enzo pulls back, a wild energy pulsing off him as he pulls my top off, leaving me in just a lace bra.

I side step, escaping his hold, and covering myself as I stalk toward the large windows showcasing the sparkling city. "I'm not doing this again."

A large hand clutches my jaw, turning my face to the side as Enzo's towering body crushes me into the cold glass.

"Let go of me," I huff.

"Never going to fucking happen. Ever."

"Fuck you, Enzo."

He laughs, the sound brutal. "I plan on fucking you until all you can think about when you move is me."

"No," I say, struggling under his hold.

He turns me around, pushing my back into the glass, his hand clutching my throat firmly without cutting off my airway.

"Say it, then," he challenges, his eyes boring into mine.

"Say..." Church. *Say it, and it all stops immediately.* Our safe word. On one hand, I want to scream it at the top of my lungs. I *should* say it. But... "I hate you."

"The feeling is mutual," he says, crushing his mouth to mine, forcing his tongue into my mouth. My skin breaks out in goosebumps, my insides melting under his harsh touch. I hate that he's the *only* person that can do this to me.

He pulls away from my mouth, his hand still gripping my neck as he pulls me to the huge bed and pushes me down.

He unclasps my bra, pulls off my boots, jeans and panties in quick succession, then tears at his own clothes.

If he looks imposing fully clothed, he looks down right predatory naked.

Every part of him is carved with precision, his skin marked with scars in quite a few places, and he has a massive tattoo that twists along the right side of his torso, disappearing onto his back.

I don't get a chance to get a closer look at the tattoo before Enzo grips my ankle and pulls me to the edge of the bed, my ass almost slipping off the edge. Enzo drops to his knees and that wicked tongue is on me before I can protest.

His hot tongue drags up to my clit in a hard, deep stroke, making my hips buck. Enzo wraps his arm across my hips, holding them down as he sinks two fingers into me, his tongue swirling over my clit.

I bite down the whimper as my eyes roll back, and fight Enzo's hold as the impending orgasm builds in ferocity, almost painfully. My breathing is hard, my brain melting into a sea of pleasure and fury.

Why am I allowing him to have his tongue or his hands on me?

Why do I never want it to end?

My body tightens at the edge of ecstasy. A few of the right strokes and I'll be screaming. But no. *No.* Enzo doesn't want me, despite his mouth completely destroying me right now like his life depended on it. And I don't want him—he threw me away the last time I saw him.

I force my body to hold off on the impending orgasm, using the same techniques I used when—

Enzo growls against my clit, almost tipping me over the edge. He pulls away from me and rises from the floor, his body covering mine as he thrusts into me. I let out a strangled breath as the

263

searing heat from his cock stretching me makes me both wince and tremble; the pain increasing the pleasure.

"Stop hiding from me," Enzo growls into my face, his hand sinking into my hair, his eyes demanding my full attention.

"I can do whatever the fuck I want," I pant.

"Why are you doing this?" Enzo asks, his eyes scorch me with so many things I don't want to see.

I close my eyes and shake my head. I try to move my pinned body, wanting, no *needing*, him to move, to fuck me until I feel nothing.

Until I am nothing.

Enzo's hand slips around my throat. "Look at me."

"Fuck me," I breathe, keeping my eyes closed.

"*Look* at me," Enzo demands.

I open my eyes, the intensity still burning brightly in his cerulean irises. I hate that I'm obsessed with these fucking eyes. I hate that he's the only person I allow this much control over my body. I hold Enzo's gaze as he pulls almost all the way out of me and then thrusts back in deeper, harder.

"Stop fucking leaving," he grits out, thrusting in and out again.

"You threw me away like garbage," I say, the last word breaking as he thrusts into me again.

"Delphine—"

I cup the back of Enzo's neck. "I don't give a fuck about your excuses. Just fuck me and then get off me."

Fury darkens Enzo's face as he wrenches my hand off him, pinning it to the bed, his hold on my hair going to my throat as he starts pounding into me.

"Why are you so fucking defiant?" Enzo growls.

I make a choking sound as panic courses through my veins. Instead of Enzo's hand, it's phantom beads digging into my throat. It's broken wrists and bruised ribs. It's Bible verses and false sweet nothings. I grip Enzo's wrist with my free hand as tears stream down my face, trying to anchor myself to the present and not drown in the past.

Enzo's hand twists, releasing my throat and grabs my hand, holding it, then pins it above my head. I blink tears out of my eyes and his cold, beautiful face comes back into view.

"You drive me to fucking violence," he grits out as he thrusts into me to the hilt and stills. Leaning down, he stares into my very existence. "Get it through that pretty head of yours that there's nothing else for you but *me*."

"To what end?" I whisper.

"Until I'm done with you," Enzo growls.

His mouth claims mine as he starts moving again. This time his movements are erratic, harsher, punishing. His hand slips from one of my wrists and lands on my clit, working my body like he owns it. Because he fucking *does*, and it pisses me off.

The orgasm I was holding off rips through me so hard that fresh tears fall freely and my legs lock around Enzo's hips in a vice grip.

My mind is fracturing; the past, present and future all burning away in the inferno engulfing my body. I can't breathe and can finally breathe all at once. My heart is pounding in my ears. I want to throw up and laugh. I'm falling into an ocean of tainted euphoria, and I can't decide whether I want to revel in the depths or drag myself out and never test these waters again.

My name being groaned into my ear draws my attention; Enzo is buried deep and collapsed on top of me, panting, his face nestled into my neck. As we lay here, bodies pressed together, listening to each other breathe, I'm... calm.

Enzo lifts his head, his gaze heavy, but still pissed. I don't know why I expected anything less, but unshed tears still sting my eyes. Why does the person who makes me feel like an *actual* person have to be so impossible to understand?

Enzo pulls out of me, the throbbing ache settling into my body as he gets off the bed and pulls on his pants. He disappears into what looks like a dressing room and then comes back with a t-shirt in hand. He holds out the black top and I accept it without a word, pulling it over my chilled body as he heads for the door.

"Del," he says softly, stopping with a hand on the door handle, turning back to me. It's the first time he hasn't used my full name. "I don't think I'll ever be done with you."

TWENTY SEVEN

DEL

I **WALK DOWN THE** stairs of my childhood home, clutching my rosary beads.

My hand gripping the rail is clammy. I force my feet down the stairs to *his* office. I hate his sterile office.

Nothing good ever comes out of a visit there.

My knees tremble as I approach the door and knock softly. *He* tells me to come in, his voice scratchy, chilling me to the bone. I don't want to—

A warm arm tightens around my waist, waking me up as it pulls me closer to a hard body. I open my eyes to a dim room. Not my room, there are too many windows.

Last night flashes through my mind. The club, the Mechanic, and Enzo.

"Are you okay?" Enzo's deep voice is thick with sleep, his breath heating the back of my neck.

"I'm fine," I murmur, closing my eyes.

The arm I'm apparently using as a pillow flexes under me. "You were begging someone to make him stop."

"Was I?" I knew I sometimes screamed in my sleep, but I didn't know I talked.

Enzo kisses the side of my neck. "Who is he?"

I turn in his arms, burying my head under Enzo's chin and fitting one leg between his, inhaling his spiced citrus and sandalwood scent. He always smells so good. "It doesn't matter."

"Did he hurt you?" Enzo asks, his hand tracing soothing circles along my spine.

"So many times," I admit.

"Del," Enzo says, his other hand tilting my chin up to face him. Hair is rumpled, and his eyes are heavy with exhaustion, but determination glows in his hard expression. "Tell me."

"He's gone. That's all that matters." I trace his mouth with a light touch, avoiding the injury, and across his jaw, enjoying the feeling of the facial hair beneath my fingers. "Are you growing a beard?"

Enzo smiles, tilting his chin down and nipping my fingers. "I've been too busy to shave."

"I like it," I muse, lowering my lips to his jaw, kissing and nibbling toward his ear. This side of Enzo is one I haven't seen. It's warm and comfortable. I don't feel the need to run.

"I like your brand of distraction," Enzo rumbles, rolling us over so his heavy body is covering mine. He lifts his head slightly so he can look at me. "But I want to know."

"Why did you throw me off you the last time I was here?" I ask.

The question distracts him. He rolls to my side, and pulls me over his chest, tracing circles on my back again as I wrap myself around him, taking the opportunity to enjoy this rare moment of tranquility.

I don't think he's going to answer me, but then he sighs heavily. "My father kicked my mother out when I was ten. He told me that day that women are only good for two things: giving you sons and wearing your bruises. If they couldn't do either of those things, they needed to be replaced. He lived by that philosophy until the day he died."

I bite my tongue, swallowing my response.

"He was a bastard," Enzo continues, echoing my unshared thoughts, "and so am I. His carbon copy. Cold, stubborn, heartless."

I lift my head, frowning at him. "Do you really believe that?"

He stares at the roof as he chuckles softly. "Teo says I show more emotion when I'm slitting someone's throat than I do with a woman. I don't keep them around for long. There's always a point where they try to fix what's broken in me, and that's when I leave. They don't understand that I don't want to be fixed."

"So what? You think I'm going to try to fix you?"

His cerulean eyes meet mine with a sigh. "You will. They always do."

I slide my leg over Enzo's hip, lifting myself to straddle him, my hands stretched over his chest. "Mr. Herrington—you're a business tycoon worth billions. How are you *this* stupid?"

His eyes harden. "Excuse me?"

I roll my eyes. "You think I'm some soft little socialite that wants to tame the big, bad wolf? When did I *ever* give off that impression?"

He starts to lift off the bed, but I press his chest back down. "I grew up with a family who didn't give a shit about me, and broke me until I was nothing. Why would I want to fix someone else when I can't even fix myself?"

"Surely, your mother—"

It's my turn to laugh. "My mother doesn't care about anyone but herself. She left Isaac's dad because he was too soft, even though that man is still obsessed with her. She blames me for my biological father dying in a car accident two months *before* I was born. And don't get me started on my fucking asshole stepdad." I fight the tremors wanting to shake my bones. "William is just the convenient, *wealthy* choice. She cares about nothing but status and keeping her greedy hands stuffed with cash."

Enzo doesn't move or say anything as he stares angrily at the ceiling. I can practically see his mind working behind those beautiful eyes. I run my hands up his chest slowly until my chest is just brushing his. "I don't want you to try to fix me, either."

"You don't need fixing," he rumbles, curling an arm around me.

"Neither do you," I say honestly.

His eyes flick to mine, searching my face, confused.

"Which one are you?" I ask. "The one too attached, the one that got away, the asshole, or the convenient choice?"

He frowns, eyes cold. "I'm a bad man."

I laugh, the sound flat. "I know that."

"Logically, I'm the asshole."

"Let's hope not." This will be the end of the line if Enzo is anything like *him*.

Something in my tone or my face melts the coldness in his eyes slightly. "What happened to you?"

"Nothing."

Enzo gives me a hard stare, expecting answers.

I smile, the motion feels tight. "Maybe you're the one who'll get too attached, but perhaps you're just the convenient choice."

Enzo's arm tightens around my waist as he sits up, our bodies plastered together. "Do you want to know what choice I am to you?"

He brushes my hair behind my ear, his fingers trailing along the sensitive skin towards the nape of my neck, then grips a handful of hair, pressing our foreheads together. "I'm the worst choice."

"Why?"

"Because you're my *only* choice, and I'm not letting you go," Enzo says fiercely, his eyes blazing intensely.

My heart pounds in my ears, his words wrapping a vice-like grip around my mind. My chest burns, begging for oxygen, but I can't breathe.

His only choice.

"You," I sputter, finally taking in a shallow breath. "You don't want that."

"I do," he reassures me, his hold on my hair loosening. "I want to own you mind, body, and soul."

I shake my head. "There's no value in any of that."

"Del," he grumbles.

"I will ruin you."

He barks a harsh laugh. "Last night, I killed that man who kissed you," he says as his hands slip down my back, gripping my ass. "Slit his throat without mercy."

He grinds my naked core over his hardening cock, sending jolting pleasure through my body. "As that vermin bled on the floor, I threatened to do the same to Matteo for touching you, then clocked him in the face."

"Seems like he got in a hit or two," I say in a shaky tone, my hips rolling over Enzo's hard length, coating him in my arousal.

"The day you left this penthouse, I trashed the place. I lose my fucking mind when you're not around me. You've already ruined me, sweetheart. You have ingrained yourself so far into my subconscious from the day you slammed into me in that church. So far that I will never get you out. And I don't want to."

I slam my mouth onto his in a clash of lips and teeth.

I don't want to think about the words he's saying to me, the feelings he's alluding to. I can't let someone in like that; the walls around me are thick steel for a reason.

Enzo kisses me back with the same fervour, gripping me tight as he turns over and lays me on the bed.

He pulls back, panting, his hips pinning me to the bed. "Say yes."

"To what?" I whisper.

"To being mine," he breathes, those hooded eyes searching mine.

"I..." I can feel the words stuck in my throat.

I watch the cool indifference wash over Enzo, and his jaw clench at my silence. "Very well."

I reach out and cup the back of his neck as he shifts to move off me. "My answer isn't no."

"Then say yes," he murmurs.

"Just give me some time," I whisper, loosening my grip on his neck, "I just need time."

He leans down, kissing me softly. "*Today,*" he says against my lips, "I want to know today. I don't do half answers."

"Okay," I mumble, pressing another kiss on his lips. "Today."

I leave Enzo in bed dozing as I make my way to his kitchen. It's still early in the morning, the sun barely lighting the sky, but everyone will need breakfast, and I need space to think. I find the pantry and fridge stocked full of food, so I get to work on making pancakes.

I'm in search of a pan when Scar's humming echoes through the room as she enters the kitchen in the same t-shirt she was in last night.

Her soft smile drops as she sees me. "You're making pancakes."

"Yes," I say as I open another drawer and find a pan.

"You're cooking, which means trouble," Scar points out as she steps to my side, pulling me to face her. "What's wrong?"

I sigh, closing my eyes. "I don't know what I'm doing, Scar."

She rubs the back of my hands with her thumbs. "Do you want to talk about it?"

I open my eyes and give her a small smile. "Grab the butter."

Scar and I work together to make a mountain of pancakes, grill up some bacon and put them on a tray, sliding it into the oven to stay warm as I talk her through everything Enzo-related.

"So he's kind of obsessed with you," Scar says as she washes the pans at the sink. "And there's a problem with that?"

"It's too soon, is it not?" I ask as I slice up strawberries next to her, putting them in a small bowl. "I'm a shiny new toy. Surely the novelty will wear off soon enough."

"Will it though?" Scar asks, pulling the bacon out of the oven and putting in on a plate.

"He told me he's never kept anyone before," I point out, following Scar to the table with the heaving plate of pancakes and the bowl of strawberries. "What's to say he won't go back to his old ways?"

"Okay," Scar sighs, "without thinking about it—if you say no, are you going to regret it?"

"Yes," I respond immediately.

"Then there's your answer."

"But, what if—"

"If he's stupid enough to let you go, then you pick yourself up and keep going."

"This feels different," I counter, walking over to the fridge and pulling out the juice I spied earlier.

"Does it feel different because he isn't forcing you into it?" Scar asks softly behind me.

"It..." I turn to her at the stove. "Shit. Yeah."

At every point, even last night, he gave me a choice, an out. Even now, he's giving me the choice.

"Most people aren't trying to take something from you," Scar says, taking the whistling kettle off the stove and pouring the hot water into a massive teapot. "Enzo is broody, and demanding, and fucking terrifying. But maybe he's not always the monster he's portrayed as."

"I think he's *exactly* the monster he's seen as," I counter, turning on the drip coffee machine. "But I think I like it."

We both walk over to the table with beverages and glassware, setting them down. Scar takes both of my hands in hers, her big brown eyes staring hard at me. "Just don't lose yourself."

"I won't," I promise. I can't afford to lose any more pieces of myself to a man.

Scar stares at me for a few more seconds before nodding once and spinning towards the bedrooms, skipping away as I go back and check on the coffee.

I pull the pot out and open an overhead cupboard to take out mugs, but a long, muscled arm reaches out from behind me and plucks out the mug I was reaching for. Enzo presses his warm body into mine, his nose burying into my hair.

"Hi," I whisper, pulling out three other mugs.

"I like seeing you in my clothes," Enzo murmurs, his free hand roaming down my hip, slipping under the t-shirt and sliding up to palm my breast. "But I would much rather you were naked."

"There are other people here," I mumble as I tilt my head back into Enzo's clothed chest, my eyes fluttering closed as he rolls my nipple with his thumb and finger.

"Let's go back to bed then," he murmurs into my ear. "They can listen to you scream my name."

I push my body further into Enzo, feeling his erection at the base of my back. "I'm sure they'll appreciate that."

"Like I fucking care," Enzo growls, pinching my nipple hard, sparks of delicious pain making me shudder.

I let out a breathy laugh, forcing my eyes open and turn toward Enzo. He's in a t-shirt himself, something I thought I'd never see. "I made pancakes."

"I saw that," he muses, his hand now slipping into the briefs I borrowed from his drawers last night and cupping my ass, making it very hard to concentrate.

"Let's not waste my efforts," I rasp before clearing my throat and reaching for the mugs behind me.

Enzo chuckles, the sound doing things to my body, as he takes his original mug and coffee pot, following me to the table. Scar and a shirtless Matteo appear from the direction of the bedrooms. Matteo's eye isn't as swollen as it was last night, but the bruising is starting to darken his cheek and brow.

They take a seat next to each other as Enzo and I claim the other two seats opposite them.

"Damn, Del, this looks good," Matteo groans as he stabs his fork into the piles of pancakes, stacking them on his plate.

"Hey, I helped," Scar complains, batting Matteo away from the food.

He laughs, planting a chaste kiss on Scar's cheek. "Don't worry, I'll just marry both of you."

"Should you really provoke your brother?" I ask, gesturing to his face. "Looks like it didn't work out too well for you last time."

Matteo barks a laugh. "I can take him if I want to."

"Oh, really?" Enzo asks, his hand sliding onto my thigh as I start serving both of us food.

"I was feeling bad for you last night," Matteo explains, pouring Scar some tea. "You were having a bit of a tantrum."

Enzo's hand squeezes my thigh.

"Well," Scar interjects around a mouthful of pancake, "we had a super fun time last night. We made so *many* friends."

I give Scar a pointed look. Her innocent smile makes me roll my eyes. She loves provoking demons. Incorrigible adrenaline junkies.

"Where exactly did you end up last night?" Matteo asks, shoving a forkful of pancake into his mouth.

"Honestly, I don't know," Scar answers, sipping on her tea.

"They ended up at Creed's," Enzo says, picking up the coffee pot, his hand leaving my thigh. I'm assuming Creed is the Mechanic.

"He's still alive, right?" Scar asks, alarmed.

"Yes," is all Enzo says, but I can feel the tension radiating off him.

"He must have gotten *some* lecture," I muse, sliding my mug over to Enzo.

Enzo hums his agreement as he pours me some coffee. I'm sure Enzo ripped into Creed for supplying us with drugs and booze all night without calling earlier, but since he's still alive, I guess getting us to the hotel safely allowed him to keep his body parts.

As Scar and Matteo exchange stories about wild nights out, I take a moment to just be. The fact that I can just sit here and observe, and not feel like I have to put on a fake smile, is refreshing. I rarely feel comfortable anywhere, but here, sitting next to one of the most dangerous people in the country, is like a home I never had.

I should probably fill the missing pieces of myself with light, but I'd honestly rather fill them with decadent darkness and thrive, rather than be a disappointment when I'm not shiny enough for the light.

The realisation settles some of the questions rattling around in my brain and clears away the weight of anxiousness that held me down earlier. I slip my hand onto Enzo's huge thigh, the answer to his question warming my chest. I turn to him, his cerulean irises glowing in question.

"Yes," I barely whisper, squeezing his thigh for effect.

So many emotions flutter through Enzo's eyes: realisation mixed with something like relief, and then blazing hot wickedness.

I feel heat warm my cheeks as I turn back to the table, Scar and Matteo still chatting away, as I pick up my coffee. Enzo places his hand over mine on his thigh, guiding it across to rest on his very obvious erection. I smirk into my cup, pulling my hand away and standing from the table.

"You two can clean this up, right?" I say abruptly, stepping around Enzo's chair and grabbing his hand, pulling him away from the table.

TWENTY EIGHT

— Q ♠ —

DEL

I SCREAMED ENZO'S NAME for most of the day—in his bed, against the window and in the shower. Dressed in another one of his t-shirts, a pair of his tracksuit pants and socks, we finally emerge from his room.

Enzo leaves me in the living room, needing to do some work in his office. I curl up on the huge couch, turn on a movie, and nestle under a thick blanket. Scar finds me eventually, and we both make ourselves at home.

"Does your mum know we're still alive?" I ask, half dozing off.

"Yeah, I told her we probably won't be back until tomorrow," Scar murmurs.

I chuckle. "Having too much fun with Matteo?"

Scar kicks me in the shin. "Bitch, I'm not the one that screamed the penthouse down all day. I did it for you."

"Sure," I drawl, sitting up, "it's not because Matteo is just panting—"

A pillow whacking me in the face cuts off my teasing as I laugh at Scar's huffing at the thought. I know she's *soaking* up his attention.

As if summoned, both Herrington men walk into the living room.

"Please tell me you're about to have a pillow fight?" Matteo pleads, with excitement burning in his eyes.

Scar scoffs, pulling herself off the couch, stretching her arms above her head. "Del and I don't pillow fight, we wrestle to the death. And *no*, you will never see it."

Enzo rolls his eyes at his brother's groans of protest as he crosses to stand in front of me, his hand out. "Did you two have dinner plans?"

I slide my hand into Enzo's offered hand, letting him pull up and wrap his arm around my waist. "No, but I am starving."

"Me too," Scar agrees. "We should check out that new Japanese place along the river."

"Doesn't that place have a four-month waitlist?" I ask.

Scar turns her big brown eyes on Matteo, batting her eyelashes. "A little birdy told me that a certain family owns that restaurant."

Matteo chuckles, slinging his arm across Scar's shoulder. "Come on, Little Songbird, let's go get ready."

Scar's intel was right, and we have no problems getting into the restaurant as the Herringtons do, in fact, own it.

I traded Enzo's tracksuit pants for my jeans, keeping his t-shirt and pairing it with one of Matteo's bomber jackets that he insisted I wear, since Enzo only owns suits or comfy clothes. He also finds Enzo's annoyance very entertaining.

Scar tucked one of Matteo's smallest t-shirts into her skirt and wore her leather jacket with her boots, and both men are dressed in suits.

The four of us are taken to a large, private table at the back of the restaurant by the doting manager, who takes our drink order as Enzo and Matteo pull chairs out, and promises to bring out a feast.

Just like breakfast today, I'm just able to *be.* No one expects me to put on a facade and pretend that I'm someone that I'm not. Conversation flows between us all, Scar's bright and chatty aura matching Matteo's sweet and suave charm, with Enzo and I only occasionally chiming in.

He might not be much of a talker, but Enzo's hands are not far from me during the whole meal. He grips my thigh, or brushes his fingers across my forearm, or rests his arm along my chair, playing with a tendril of my hair.

I didn't expect Enzo to be this tactile, and I thought I'd hate it with my aversion to touch from most people, but every connection between us fills me with reassuring warmth. I know he's here, and he's aware of me.

After an endless amount of food and drinks, and Matteo insisting on paying despite the manager's protests, Scar convinces Matteo to take her to a bar.

"Have fun!" Scar shouts over her shoulder as she drags Matteo into the night.

"She's a little shit," I chuckle.

"She's very good at reading a situation, though," Enzo muses.

I turn to ask him what he means, but my question is swallowed a bruising kiss. I trap Enzo's bottom lip between my teeth, tugging slightly. Enzo's replying hard smack on my ass makes me yelp and release him.

Enzo *tsks*. "You think a few niceties between us and I was going to be soft on you?"

"You keep forgetting that your hands on my ass don't mean I'm going to wilt for you."

Enzo's smile turns dark. "It's going to be so satisfying when I break you."

I step back in the direction of the car. "Don't be too disappointed when you fail."

I turn and walk through the alley that goes to the street behind the restaurant where Lucas will be with the car. I get about halfway down when I'm shoved sideways; the back of my head connects with Enzo's hand but the rest of me hits a cool brick wall roughly.

Enzo's facial hair rubs against my cheek as his hot breath caresses my ear. "You think you can just walk away from me?"

I huff out a laugh. "You forget intimidation doesn't work."

"If I decided to fuck you right here, I know I'd find your cunt dripping." Enzo presses his body harder into me, his hard cock pressing into my lower abdomen.

"What are you waiting for?" I pant, my body vibrating with adrenaline.

Enzo pulls his head back, his nose brushing mine. "I'm waiting for you to beg."

"Please," I whimper, looking up through my lashes. "Don't hold your breath waiting."

I buck my hips forward and spin us around so he's pinned to the wall. My tongue flicks out and sweeps across his lower lip.

Enzo's eyes burn in violent annoyance as he fists my hair, angling my head up almost painfully, exposing my neck. "You forget who's in charge here."

I hiss at the tug on the strands as my hands fall to his belt. "Should I get on my knees and ask for forgiveness?"

Enzo's smile soaks in cruel satisfaction as he releases me. "Like a good, *pious* woman." His head falls back on the brick. "At least you're learning your place."

I press my chest to his as I unbuckle the belt and unzip his pants, slipping my hand into his boxer briefs. His eyes fall closed, and he hisses as I wrap my hand around his cock; his reaction sends a thrill through me. I pump him slow and firm, watching his throat bob up and down.

"Do you like that, Enzo?" I whisper, continuing the lazy rhythm.

He tips his head forward, his lust-drunk, hooded gaze meeting mine. "On your knees, sweetheart."

I give his cock one last stroke before pulling my hand out and stepping away from Enzo, continuing backwards toward the end of the alley. "You coming?"

Enzo chuckles, the sound terrifying as he rights his clothes. "You have no idea how much you've fucked up."

My heart pounds wildly in my chest as I turn and pick up speed, the car coming into view. I get into the front passenger seat, surprising Lucas, as Enzo exits the alley, completely unfazed, and slides into the backseat.

I relax slightly into my seat, and hum along to the radio as we drive back to *Luxuria,* but I can feel the tension emanating from Enzo behind me. The drive is short, and soon as soon as we pull into the driveway, I'm out of the car and cutting through the foyer toward the elevator.

I hit the button to call the elevator and turn to peek at Enzo. He's leisurely crossing the foyer with his hands in his pockets, like he has all the time in the world.

The instinct for recognising danger is blaring in the back of my head, but my god, are my panties getting wetter with every step he takes closer to me.

I try to calm my heart rate as the elevator door opens and I step in, Enzo close behind me. We stand on opposite sides; the tension suffocating in the small space. The doors slide open, and Enzo sweeps his hand out, allowing me to exit the elevator first. I practically dash out, pulling the keycard from my bra and opening the door.

I take two steps into the penthouse when Enzo grips my elbow tight and marches me to his room, thrusting me in and closing the door behind him. He pulls me toward him, our bodies clashing together as his mouth claims mine. Both his hands sink into my hair, holding me captive as his tongue tastes mine and his teeth nip at my lips.

Enzo pulls away, his eyes burning with a cruel heat. "Clothes off, now."

"No," I breathe.

Enzo pulls hard on my hair, the searing pain making me hiss. "When I give you a command, I expect you to obey immediately."

"Sorry, I don't think I heard you right," I muse, the smile playing across my lips making Enzo narrow his gaze. "What was it that you asked me to do?"

"Clothes. Off." He bites out both words with such authority that my knees almost give out as desire tries to drown me. He keeps a firm grip in my hair as I make quick work of my pants, jacket, and boots. He releases me to watch my t-shirt disappear over my head and my bra fall away, his eyes consuming every inch of naked flesh.

"So fucking beautiful," he muses, his hand trailing down my sternum. "Are you wet, sweetheart?"

"Very," I almost moan.

An approving sound rumbles from Enzo's throat as his hand slides further down my body, but tapers off and he steps back. His eyes never leave me as he starts to loosen his tie and remove his jacket. "Do you remember our word?"

"Church," I croak, arousal frying all my nerve endings.

"Good," he approves, "because you're about to be punished for all the shit you've pulled in the last couple of days."

My instinct to run overrides everything as I try to dart around Enzo to the door, but I slam into his hard chest and caged by powerful arms.

That cold, dark chuckle rumbles through his chest. "There's no point in running, sweetheart."

I struggle in his arms. "Let me go."

He sighs. "Begging now won't help either."

I shiver as he walks me over to his bed and deposits me on the end, his hand now around my right forearm as he reaches down under the bed, pulling out a black cuff attached to a solid-looking chain.

He tugs me up and turns me so that I'm facing the bed, pulling my naked body into his still-clothed one. "Be a good girl and lay your chest on the bed, hands out."

I scoff. "Make me."

His hand moves from my arm to the nape of my neck and he shoves me face first into the bed. He releases my nape and grabs my right wrist, his elbow digging into my back as I try to roll away. He manages to cuff my wrist quickly and then does the left one. My legs burn from the bent position as I pull on the leather cuffs, the chains clanging but not budging. Damn it.

I watch Enzo walk to his side of the bed and grab two pillows, then disappear behind me. The pillows slide between my pelvis and the bed, elevating my ass into the air and taking some pressure off my legs.

"I'm going to test your limits, sweetheart," Enzo murmurs behind me as a loud, hard slap lands on my ass cheek. It hurts, but I don't react at all. Another slap lands on the other cheek, and it's loud and hard, but again, I don't react to it.

I lean on a shoulder and crane my neck back, catching Enzo's hard stare. "Spanking is beginner's play. What else you got?"

Thunderous clouds darken Enzo's eyes as he crouches down behind me and disappears out of view. Enzo's warm hand slides down my right thigh all the way to my ankle and pushes it out toward the corner of the bed. Then I hear the clinking of a buckle, and feel another cuff wrap around my ankle. He gives the other leg the same treatment and cuffs my other ankle. My legs are spread wide and I'm completely at his mercy.

I shiver in anticipation, my ears keenly listening for movement or another command. But there's nothing, no rustling of clothing, or breathing or shuffling of feet. Nothing at all. I try to turn again, to see what he's doing, when suddenly his tongue is on my clit.

I gasp at the contact, trying and failing to buck forward, away from the intense sensation. Enzo's tongue licks a hot, hard path up, all the way to my ass before disappearing, and teeth sink into my left ass cheek, making me yelp.

He does it again, starting at my clit, moving up and then biting my other ass cheek. My legs are quivering again, my body too sensitive from being this exposed to Enzo's relentless tongue. Enzo decides to give his full attention to my clit, making me fight the whimpers trying to escape my mouth as I barely register the sound of something sliding across the floor.

Two distinct clicks that sound like the opening of a briefcase echo in the room. I want to ask what the fuck is going on, but

Enzo's tongue is doing this swirling thing that has me pushing my pussy into his mouth and panting loudly. If he keeps doing what he's doing, I'm going to come so hard.

My heart and breathing pick up in speed, and just as I'm about to come, his tongue disappears. I growl in frustration, trying my luck against the restraints again.

Enzo chuckles softly behind me, and then items start landing on the bed. "Any of these interest you?"

A suede paddle and flogger, a leather riding crop, and a bamboo cane all line up beside me and I think my brain stutters. "I... all of them?"

"Are you sure, sweetheart?" Enzo warns, his hand stroking the cane. "This has more bite than you think."

I scoff. "You won't break me, Enzo."

His hand pauses for a moment, and then he reaches for the paddle. "Remember your safe word."

The contact of the paddle to my thigh makes me jerk forward in surprise, but I bite down the yelp. Now, that *stings*. He matches the strike on the other thigh, and I jerk again, chewing on my bottom lip. The heat radiating up my legs is exhilarating, and my thighs try to clench together.

Enzo chuckles. "Are you enjoying yourself, Delphine?"

"Motherfucker," I huff as he lands another strike, this time over one of his hand prints, pulling out a hiss.

"Mind your language," Enzo chastises, landing another strike on the other handprint.

He strikes the untouched skin of both ass cheeks and down my thighs. I can't hold in the groans, the sting and pain of the strikes turning me into a throbbing mess. I need Enzo to make me come before I actually lose my mind.

No, I'm not going to let him win.

I take a deep breath, trying to rein in my body and get a hold of the heady lust pumping through my veins.

As I get a grip on my body, a sharp burning pain lances across my entire ass and I choke on a yelp. My eyes flick to the bed and the cane is gone. Another burning lash sears across my already sensitive flesh and goosebumps explode across my body.

"Just as I thought," Enzo breathes, "your skin marks up so pretty."

He strikes me again, and I choke out a sob. The pain is searing, and I'm pretty sure he's broken skin. "Please, no more."

"You get six more. Count them out."

"No, please, Enzo, stop," I sob, but the cane bites across my worked-up skin.

Tears track down my face as he strikes again, on my thighs this time, and I whimper.

"*Count*, Del," Enzo demands.

"Two," I whisper. I want this to end. Strike. "Th-three." But do I? The pain is intense. Strike. "Four." I can't help but notice my body clenching, getting wetter with every strike. I sob as the next strike lands across the very top of my thighs, the bite of the cane lancing across my core. "Five." My voice is barely a whisper as the tears dampen the sheets.

"Last one, sweetheart," Enzo pants.

I sob and then scream 'six' as the hard strike settles into my skin. The cane lands softly on the bed next to me and I listen to Enzo's heavy breathing.

"So fucking beautiful," he huffs. "I want to see my marks on you at all times."

His hand caresses my sore ass so reverently that I hiss and tremble at his touch. His fingers slide through to my clit and he groans. "Christ, you're dripping."

"Enzo," I groan, "please." I don't know if I'm begging for him to let me go, or keep going. I just... *need*.

Enzo releases my wrists, but leaves my ankles cuffed. He drapes himself over my body, the fabric of pants rubbing against my tender flesh as he peppers kisses across my shoulder until he reaches my ear.

"I'm going to fuck you now," he whispers, "and you're not going to come until I say you can."

I nod stiffly. He stands back up and I don't dare move, as I hear his clothes fall to the floor. One hand returns to grip my hip, and the other one strokes up my spine until it curls into my hair. Enzo sinks into me in one stroke. I almost come on the spot, but I hold that bitch in, not wanting any more punishment, just wanting all the pleasure.

Enzo's hand on my hip snakes around my waist as the hand in my hair pulls me up, and I'm about to pass out. This angle, with my ankles still bound apart, and with Enzo buried in me to the hilt, that curved cock hitting certain places—I don't think I can breathe.

And then Enzo starts moving.

"Oh my fuck," I choke. Enzo's hips slam into my tender ass, sending shocks of pain through my whole body, intensifying the pleasure flooding my system, and I'm about to combust.

"Enzo," I pant, "I can't hold it... I'm going to come."

"Not yet," he growls into my ear, his thrusts getting harder, my mind losing all function.

I might actually die here.

My knees are buckling, my hands are clawing at his arm around my waist. "Fuck, Enzo, please, I *can't.*"

His arm slides from my waist, and two fingers press into my clit. "Now, sweetheart."

It takes two strokes and I explode. The world goes white. I burn so hot that I'm sure this is what it feels like to be a dying star. I don't know if my heart is beating or if I'm breathing.

If it's even fucking possible, I come down ever so slightly from the mind-bending orgasm, but Enzo's still fucking me so hard and working my clit that I roll into another one. I slam my hips back into Enzo's and he groans, both of us collapsing onto the bed.

My whole body convulses as overwhelming pleasure burns every part, right down to my very soul.

If I never move again, I would be fine with that.

TWENTY NINE

DEL

SCAR AND **I** WALK into our history lesson, both in good moods for a Monday.

I slide onto my usual chair and wince. Enzo's marks from Saturday are still bruised and tender. A flush creeps up my face as I remember the hard blows and the unbelievable orgasms that followed.

Enzo's soft touches of yesterday were amazing, but I definitely like his firm touch more than I probably should.

Silvia and her gaggle of fake friends stop by our table. "You two are cheery today. Did we get into Dr. Sakura's liquor cabinet for breakfast?"

Her friends snicker at her remark. I sigh and sit back in my chair. "You need to come up with new material for your insults, babe."

"Ah, kids these days, they have no respect for their elders," Scarlett murmurs, opening up her textbook, dismissing Silvia. I chuckle as Silvia stomps toward her spot at the back of the class with her little followers.

"She'd be screeching with jealousy if she knew what we did this weekend," Scarlett says.

I swat her on the arm. "Let's not talk about that *too* loudly."

"I wish we could throw it in her face that you're getting railed by a Herrington," Scarlett whispers as our teacher rushes into the class.

"Such a filthy mouth, Angel Face," I mutter.

"It's Songbird now, thank you very much."

I roll my eyes, opening up my notebook. The day breezes by with no other comments from anyone, and it's nice for a change. Scar and I are in separate classes until lunch. We meet and grab a few things to eat before making our way to the side of the science building: our usual spot we sit at lunch.

A few random people join us to speak to Scar and ignore me, which is wonderfully fine. I'm trying not to doze off while I watch the dark clouds in the distance, when my phone buzzes in my pocket. I pull it out and smile at the message

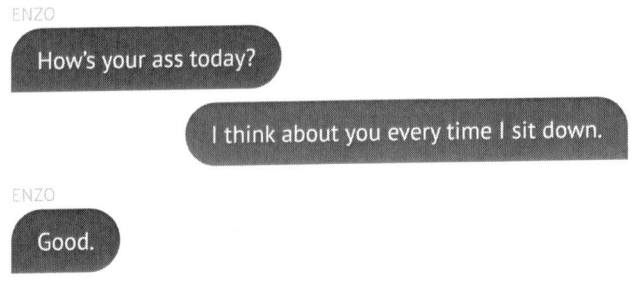

ENZO
How's your ass today?

I think about you every time I sit down.

ENZO
Good.

> Shouldn't you be working right now?

ENZO

> I own this place. I can do whatever I want.

I roll my eyes as the bell shrills.

> I have to go back to class. Stop bothering me and go run an empire, Mr. Executive.

ENZO

> That smart mouth of yours has just guaranteed you a punishment, Siren. See you later.

Wicked, heady anticipation heats my blood at the thought of Enzo's hands on me again.

Enzo hasn't given me a night to myself in the last couple of days. He lets me go home for a couple hours to do homework, change and pack a bag, before expecting me at the hotel for dinner, and after we fuck until both of us pass out.

The man is insatiable.

Today I'm rolling up to *Luxuria* after dropping Scar off at home, still in my uniform. I give my key to the valet, telling him to keep the car in the driveway as I rush in with nothing but my phone and approach the front desk.

"You're on day shift today, Rose," I muse as she looks up from her computer, surprise in her eyes.

"You're in—"

"Final year, I'm almost nineteen," I say, easing the tension in her face.

"He's on level six today," Rose says, handing me a key card. I thank her and head to the elevator. I walk into the reception area from the poker night. The same beautiful receptionist is standing at the desk, chatting with Peter. He still gives me the creeps.

They both turn at the sound of me approaching and frown at my uniform.

"Is this some weird roleplay thing?" Peter says, his eyes stuck on my skirt.

"I need to see Enzo," I say to the receptionist, ignoring Peter's leer and the crawling sensation across my skin.

"*Mr. Herrington* is in a meeting right now," she says in a clipped tone, obviously disapproving, or jealous, at my casual use of his first name.

"Can you call him?" I ask.

"He doesn't want to be disturbed."

I roll my eyes, pulling off my school jumper—probably not the best idea to go into a crime meeting displaying my school emblem—and toss it onto the reception desk. The receptionist looks pissed as I step around the ogling Peter and through the black curtains before he has a chance to stop me.

The first thing I notice is the smell of iron and sweat. The room is dark, except for the circle of low light from the one large overhead light where the poker table should be. Today, a lone man tied to a chair is directly under the light.

I should really find this whole situation terrifying and run out of here screaming, but it whispers to the dark stain across my heart, beckoning me towards the chaos. My head would be a psychiatrist's wet dream.

I can see his light hair is plastered to his head, the ends tinged pink, as I edge closer. His white shirt is slashed up, and covered in blood, and his face is swollen and bleeding from the decent beating.

At the edge of the circle of light, two figures loom in the darkness, staring at the man in the chair. Enzo doesn't have his suit jacket on, but he looks pristine in a black shirt and suit pants with his arms crossed over his chest and a deep frown on his face. Lucas, next to Enzo, has his usual stern look across his face; he almost looks bored.

A glint of light catches my attention and I notice Matteo crouched down next to Lucas with his elbows resting on his knees, rolling a large, bloodied blade between his hands. He looks fucking *feral*; his grey shirt, forearms, and hands are covered in blood and his eyes are dancing with predatory energy as he glares at his prey.

Lucas is the first person to look over at me approaching. He leans closer to Enzo a fraction, murmuring something. Enzo's head turns to me, surprise flashing across his eyes before they settle back into hard concentration.

I stop at Matteo's side, looking at the panting man in the chair. "What did he do?"

I feel Matteo stand up slowly, the air around him charged as he turns his body to me. My heart is racing as I turn to face him.

When you're facing an aggressive dog, they tell you not to look at them in the eye and remain still, so I guess I have a death wish when I look at Matteo directly.

His eyes burn hotter and his nostrils flare slightly as he heaves in a breath.

"He's a rat," Enzo murmurs behind Matteo. The guy in the chair starts gurgling something, but I'm suspended in Matteo's wild stare.

He looks like he's about to eat, fight, or fuck me, or possibly all three.

I don't know why I do it, but I reach up and push the escaped tendrils of damp hair off his forehead, scraping my fingernails softly across his scalp as I push it back into place. His eyes shut and his head drops back at my touch as he shivers, his breathing stuttering out.

I step around him as I pass behind Lucas, squeezing his elbow softly in greeting, and then pressing myself into Enzo's back, wrapping my arms around his waist and pressing the side of my face on his back.

Who thought the sight of torture would make me so... touchy?

"We saw your texts to an unknown number," Enzo says, the words vibrating my cheek. "You gave the exact location of the warehouse and run sheet."

"It was one of Raph's m-men," the guy stutters. "Please, I swear on my children's lives, he was p-part of the crew."

"Raph's people wouldn't be asking *us* about that information," Lucas points out. "They would ask their boss, would they not?"

"You have the messages," the guy wails. "H-he said that he was told to ask us."

"And you didn't find that suspicious?" Enzo asks, one of his hands now stroking my arm slowly. "I didn't think you were that fucking stupid."

"Boss, *please*," he begs, "I thought it was new protocol!"

Enzo sighs, his hand sliding across my arm and then down my side, resting on my hip. "Your stupidity got six men killed and almost a million dollars' worth of product stolen from me. You signed your own death warrant."

I can hear the guy start sobbing and thrashing around in the chair as Enzo turns in my arms. I rub my cheek over his chest, inhaling his addictive scent as both of his hands settle on my ass.

"You're here early," he murmurs.

I sigh, lifting my head to look at him. His face has softened a fraction, and he's sporting a smirk. "I wanted to see you before work."

His face drops. "No."

I snort. "You can't say 'no'."

"I just did."

I roll my eyes. "I finish at ten. I'll be back after."

I try to step back, but his hands grip my ass tighter, cementing me to the spot. A scream bursts out of the guy behind us. My eyes dart to where Matteo was standing a moment ago, but he's not there.

"We have dinner plans," Enzo says, drawing my attention.

"I have work plans," I counter, narrowing my eyes at him. "You can't keep me locked in your luxury tower. I do have responsibilities."

"I don't want you near Dragone or his people."

I laugh softly. "God, are you *still* stuck on that issue? I told you—"

"It's not about whether Raphael wants to fuck you or not, because we both know he does. It's the fact that he has a rat in his camp, and I don't trust you to be in his territory." The guy's screams have fizzled out behind Enzo. He's either dead or passed out.

I place both of my hands on his chest. "Well, as you like to point out, Raph has a soft spot for me. He won't let anything happen to me."

"Is it a money thing? How much do you need?" Enzo asks.

"I'm not taking your money. I'm going to work." I push on Enzo's chest; he tenses a fraction before loosening his grip and letting me step back.

"Message me every hour," Enzo says, wrapping a hand around one of my wrists.

I raise a brow. "You're being a little paranoid."

Enzo grips my chin and leans down, capturing my lips in a harsh kiss. My legs quiver as his teeth nip at my lower lip. "I want to cuff you to my bed in this uniform."

"Maybe later," I murmur, stepping back from Enzo, missing his heat and his scent already. I walk toward the exit, only seeing the carnage of the guy in my peripheral.

"Every hour, Delphine," Enzo warns as I approach the heavy drapes.

"I'll try, Lorenzo," I call back before slipping out.

I manage to sneak a message to Enzo in the first two hours of my shift, but the place is fully booked tonight and Queenie is sick, so I'm stuck hosting and serving. Raph is helping with the hosting duties, but he's distracted, and constantly disappearing with Jace into the kitchen.

I get into a good routine, with the help of Stella and Florentina, and the floor settles at around eight, giving me a few minutes of peace at the host desk. I pull my phone out of my apron to find six missed calls from Enzo and a string of messages demanding me to answer his call.

I scramble out a text, telling him I'm okay, and then slip my phone back into my apron as another guest arrives. They're regulars, so I take them to their usual table and confirm their drink order. I put the order in on my tablet on the way back to the host station, where a group of people is waiting.

"I'm sorry for the delay—" I say, looking up into hard cerulean eyes. "En—Mr. Herrington, good evening."

"I wasn't expecting you today, Herrington," I hear Raph say behind me. I can feel his suit jacket brushing my elbow.

Enzo's eyes darken slightly as they flick over my head. "We have a few things to discuss."

Raph steps to my side and sweeps his hand to the stairs. Enzo, Lucas and Peter climb the stairs, followed by Raph and Jace. I turn to see Matteo staring at me. He's not covered in blood anymore, dressed in a crisp grey suit, but that wild fire still simmers in his eyes. He steps up to the host station and leans forward.

"Why did you leave?" he asks, his voice low but strained.

"I had to work," I respond, a little confused.

"You touched me," he states.

"Yes."

"Why?" he asks, leaning closer. I shrug, not sure what to say. I don't know why I touched him, it just felt *right* at the time.

"Raph wants you and Matteo upstairs," Jace says from the stairs, breaking off the intense stare off between us. I blink a few times and turn my attention to Jace, who's frowning at Matteo.

"We're down a person tonight, I—"

"I've got it covered, *bella*," Mario says as he sidles up next to me, straightening the suit jacket he's changed into. I give him the tablet I'm clutching and step around to pass Matteo, but he catches my hand.

He puts it in the crease of his elbow, keeping me close to his side as we pass Jace, his face pinched in suspicion, and climb the stairs. Peter stands to the side, keeping his eyes off me surprisingly, as we reach the top and cross over to the bar. Raph is pouring drinks behind it, with Lucas and Enzo standing in front of him.

Raph's gaze narrows on me as Matteo stops next to Enzo, not releasing me from his side. I tug softly, drawing his attention.

I give him a small smile. "Do you want a drink, Mr. Herrington?"

Matteo takes a second to get the hint and releases me, nodding. "Gin on the rocks."

I slip behind the bar and reach up to the top shelf gin, turning to face the Herrington men as I prepare Matteo's drink. Raph doesn't exit the bar as I thought he would, but instead shuffles closer to me, his arm brushing mine. I ignore the touch, knowing if I react to it, Matteo or Enzo will lash out.

I put all my focus into this drink, reaching for a whole lemon, the small cutting board and a paring knife.

"Why are you here, Enzo?" Raph asks as I carve a perfect slice of lemon rind.

"Have you found the leak in your ship?" Enzo's tone is low, the warning to not bullshit him laced through his words.

"Everyone has checked out," Raph brushes off.

"One of our men told us that someone from your crew tried to get information out of him about the stolen shipment." Matteo comments, as I pour the double shot of gin over the two large ice cubes.

"None of my soldiers have contacted your men," Raph reassures as I twist the rind above the drink and then drop it into the glass.

I finally look up to see Matteo watching me. I hand the drink over and his hand brushes over mine as he takes the drink with a curt nod.

I peek at Enzo, who's giving Raph that hard businessman stare. "You're either blind to the holes in your operation, or you're trying to screw me, Dragone."

Raph presses his hands into the bench as he leans a fraction closer to Enzo. "You're stupid to threaten me in my own establishment."

I can feel the electricity crackle between the three men, all of them seconds away from striking. I step closer to Raph and grip his elbow, tugging it back. "Bickering like children won't get either of you anywhere."

The tension simmers down as Raph steps away from the bench. His arm slips behind me, curling around my waist. I freeze, my eyes bouncing between Enzo and Matteo. Enzo's eyes darken slightly, but he schools his face into neutrality almost immediately. But Matteo... his blue eyes simmer in that Herrington darkness. He looks like he's about to jump the bar and rip Raph in half.

Raph, the fucker, knows exactly what he's doing as he flexes his hand on my waist. "Is there anything else? We have to get back to our evening."

"We'll continue this discussion at the tournament," Enzo says.

Raph sighs softly, his breath tickling my bare neck. I try not to flinch away. "We'll be there."

Enzo nods, stepping away from the bar, abandoning his untouched drink. Lucas appears at Enzo's side, waiting for Matteo, but he's still glaring at Raph's arm.

"Matteo," Enzo calls, turning to the stairs, pulling out his phone. Matteo drags his eyes to me and then Raph before backing away slowly, only breaking eye contact with Raph when he gets to the stairs.

I try not to sag in relief that neither Herrington man drew weapons, because I was waiting for it. I move to step away from Raph and collect the untouched drinks, but I'm spun around and Raph pulls me to his chest.

"What did I say about the Herringtons, Del?" he growls.

I frown. "Let me go."

His hands on my biceps squeeze a little tighter. "I told you to stay away from them."

"You have no fucking right to tell me what to do, Raphael." The fucking gall of this man.

"I'm just trying to protect you." His eyes beg me to understand.

"If you wanted to do that, you wouldn't have dragged me into this bullshit." I tug at his grip.

He sighs, finally letting me go. "I just... I wanted to..." He runs a hand through his hair. "Why not me?"

I blink, taking a step back, my ass hitting the bench. "What?"

"Why Herrington and not me?"

I blow out a breath. "First of all, there's nothing there." With Matteo. "And there are so many reasons, Raph."

"Tell me," he demands softly, stepping up against me, his hand tracing my jaw.

I look up to his sculpted lips and slanted nose, then into those grey-hazel eyes. I could drown in the want in them.

"You're my boss. I need this job. You fall for every attractive female you see. You are part of the *family business*. You never had any interest until it looked like someone else did. Pick any of those."

He frowns. "Matteo is also in a dangerous industry."

I slip to Raph's side, away from his body. The dejection in his eyes would be heartbreaking if I cared. "Nothing is happening with Matteo."

I abandon the bar and mezzanine, racing downstairs and darting into the break room. My skin is crawling from the touching. I feel a little breathless, needing to get out of here. I pull out my phone from my apron and read the unread messages from Enzo.

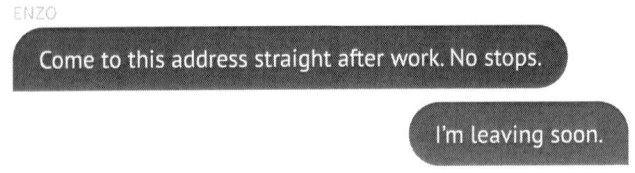

I need to see him, have him erase this crawling feeling from me. Another message pops up.

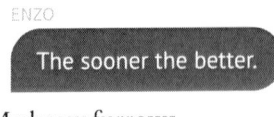

My brow furrows.

What's wrong?

ENZO

Just get here as soon as you can.

Something's off. I hastily change out of my uniform into gym shorts and a hooded jumper, shoving all my things into my bag and grabbing my car keys.

Fuck Raph.

THIRTY

DEL

I PARK ACROSS THE road from a stunning two-story Victorian mansion in the silent streets near the Fitzroy Gardens.

Solid, Roman-style arches wrap around half the house, hiding heaps of narrow, floor-to-ceiling windows along the house; the other half of the front has bay windows on both levels.

The front garden is perfectly manicured, with a softly lit path to the front door, and black iron fencing wrapping around the entire corner property.

I think I'm in the wrong place, but Enzo walks out of the huge double doors, running a hand through his hair. I climb out of the car, pulling my bag out of the backseat and head for the gate.

Enzo's body seems stiff as I walk up the gravel path and onto the smooth concrete portico as he stares off with a hard expression and his hands in his pocket.

Before I can say anything, I hear the crashing of something somewhere in the house. A small noise of surprise falls out of me, drawing Enzo's attention.

"You came," he says.

"Where are we?" I ask.

"My home."

I frown. "I thought you lived at *Luxuria*."

"Matteo and I spend more time there since Vivienne moved in here."

I nod, and more crashing echoes through the house. "Is that Matteo?"

Enzo nods. "He's... lost to us at the moment."

"Lost?"

Enzo crosses over and pulls me to his chest. I rest my cheek on his chest, listening to his strong heartbeat, soaking up his heat. We stand there for a few seconds before he pulls back and those cerulean eyes simmer. "I won't let him hurt you."

"Why would he hurt me?" He's talking about Matteo like he's possessed.

Enzo doesn't answer as he takes my bag and leads me into the house.

The outside might be beautifully restored, but the inside has been completely modernised. A black staircase takes up almost all of the foyer area. The large opening on the right shows a formal looking living room in rich warm tones with an open fireplace.

Enzo leads me to the left through another smaller sitting room, also in warm tones, and a study which is basically a fucking *library*, and into a more informal living area. It's larger than the front seating area, but cosier, with the plush U-shaped lounge facing the huge television against a wall lined with more books.

The only light in the room is streaming in from an open door. Enzo drops my bag on the lounge, and then leads us across to the door and stops, putting himself in front of me, blocking the entrance.

I stretch onto my toes and peek over his shoulder. Vivienne is standing by a window on the other side of the room with her hands wrapped around her middle, her face twisted with worry. She looks much younger, dressed in a simple black dressing gown and her hair piled up in a bun.

Matteo crosses the room, which I'm assuming is a kitchen, turns, and stalks back out of view. He's pacing like a wild animal stuck in a cage, and it sounds like he's breathing fast, like he can't get enough oxygen into himself.

My eyes flick down to where a round glass table is in pieces across the floor, with fallen chairs, broken plates and spilt liquids among the mess.

"Teo," Vivienne pleads, "how can I make this better? How can I help you?"

"Fuck *off*, Viv," Matteo growls, his tone making her flinch.

"Matteo," Enzo rumbles calmly. "Look at me."

"You can fuck off too, Enzo," Matteo spits, continuing his pace. "You should have let me kill him."

"You know you can't do that."

"I *can* and I *will* if you let me out of this fucking house," he booms. Is he talking about Raph?

Enzo looks at me over his shoulder and tilts his head toward Matteo.

"Matteo?" I ask softly.

My voice draws Vivienne's attention and her eyes narrow, but she doesn't move. I can't see Matteo, but it sounds like he's stopped moving.

"Teo?" I ask again, a little louder. "It's Del."

Matteo steps into view. Wildfire and cold darkness clash in his eyes. His clothes are dishevelled and his hair sticks up in all directions, like he's been tugging at the strands.

I frown. "You're bleeding." He has a cut on his cheek, and blood tracks down to his jaw.

"You're here," he breathes. I can't tell he's relieved or annoyed.

"I'm here," I reassure him.

Matteo takes a few steps towards us, but Enzo pushes me firmly behind him.

"Move," Matteo growls.

"You can't have her," Enzo seethes. I hear the *snick* of a switchblade. Fuck.

Enzo jerks forward to stop Matteo, so I manage to squeeze around him and grab his wrist holding the blade, stepping in between the brothers, my back to Matteo. An arm wraps around me as Matteo presses me into his body, burying his nose in my hair. Enzo's eyes blaze hotter than the sun as he looks between me and Matteo.

"That's enough bloodshed today," I say firmly, holding Enzo's inferno glare.

Enzo pulls his wrist out of my grasp and pockets the knife, lifting that burning gaze to Matteo. "I will fucking kill him."

I don't think Matteo is even paying attention to the threats on his life as he inhales deeply and his body relaxes against mine. "She's ours, Enzo," he murmurs, "*ours.* And if Raphael ever puts his fucking hands on her again, he won't live another day."

Enzo presses closer to us, like he's about to snatch me away. I press my hand into his chest. "It's okay."

His eyes drop from Matteo to me, and the heat in his face turns to cold indifference almost instantly. He turns away and leaves. Did he just—

Soft footsteps approaching us make Matteo tense. Vivienne does the smart thing and walks past us, giving Matteo a wide berth, but I don't miss the disgusted look she throws my way as she follows Enzo's path and disappears.

"Let's get you cleaned up," I murmur, pulling away from Matteo and facing him.

He looks a little dejected as he nods once, his eyes falling to the floor. I was right about this room being the world's most beautiful kitchen, so I take Matteo's hand and walk him away from the broken furniture.

I stand him next to the industrial-size sink, and rummage through the drawers in the massive island bench until I find a tablecloth. Matteo wraps a hand around my arm gently as soon as I'm next to him again. He doesn't speak as I soak the cloth with lukewarm water and wring it out, then work on wiping the blood off his neck and face, careful around the wound.

His eyes have dimmed to a cold, dark blue, and he's not full of fury anymore. He almost looks empty, and my heart twists in worry.

I leave the cloth in the sink, noting to find the laundry in this place later, and take Matteo's hand again, leading him to the living room. I stop him in front of the lounge and push him down softly, indicating for him to sit. Maybe if I get him some food, it will put some light back in his eyes.

I don't even take a step away before Matteo pulls me down to sit at his side, and lowers his head into my lap, curling an arm over my knees.

"Don't leave again," he murmurs.

"I was going to get you some food," I say, absently running my hands through his hair.

He shivers at the touch, his arm squeezing my knees slightly. "Don't leave."

"Okay," I whisper.

I lean forward and grab the remote from the coffee table in front of me, and settle further into the plush lounge, continuing to stroke Matteo's hair. I eventually find something to watch, and try to follow along with the movie, but my mind and body are too hyper-aware of Matteo.

His breathing is even and deep, and he hasn't moved a muscle in a little while, so I think he might be asleep. I manage to pull my bag over from where Enzo dropped it, and get out my phone.

I message Scar, telling her about tonight and that I won't make it home until late, and she immediately offers to meet me here with fresh clothes for tomorrow.

I message Enzo.

> Can Scar and I stay the night here?

His message doesn't come through for several minutes.

ENZO
> Do whatever you need.

I frown.

> You're upset. Why?

I send Scar the address while I wait for a reply, but after another ten minutes, I give up. Frustration burns in my chest. He walked away from me earlier with that cool indifference, and now he won't tell me why he's upset with me. Broody bastard.

It takes Scar just over half an hour to text me saying she's out front. I try to slide out from under Matteo, but he stirs, tightening his grip across my knees.

"Scarlett's here," I whisper. "I need to let her in."

Matteo grumbles something unintelligible, but he lets me move. I tuck a pillow under his head and find my way through the maze to the front door.

I open the door to a wide eyed Scar. "This place is huge."

"It's just as amazing on the inside," I comment, ushering her in. I take her through the house, her eyes growing wider with each room, until we reach Matteo, still splayed out across the couch.

Scar's whole face melts into a soft look as she takes my spot on the couch next to Matteo's head. He lifts his head to see her, and abandons the pillow, pulling Scar over to lie across her lap.

I kiss the top of Scar's head, and squeeze Matteo's bicep. "I'm going to try to find Enzo and go to bed."

"Upstairs. Black double doors at the end of the left hall," Matteo mumbles, settling further into Scar's lap.

"I've got this," Scar reassures softly. "Goodnight, babe."

I take my work bag and the clothes bag Scar brought me as I climb the stairs, turning left at the top and walking down the dimly lit hallway to the double doors Matteo mentioned. One of the doors is ajar, and I can see the room is dark. I slip into the room and close the door behind me, blocking out all the light from the hall.

The only light coming into the room is from the streetlights glowing through the windows along the opposite wall on either side of the huge bed, similar to Enzo's at *Luxuria*. Enzo is laying on his preferred side completely still, probably already asleep.

I step over to the desk facing the bay window to my left and place my bags softly on the floor beside it, pulling out a t-shirt, strip down to just my underwear and slipping it on. I head for the sliding door next to the other ones, walking through a dressing room lined with what looks like suits, and step onto cool tile of a bathroom, closing the door behind me.

I wince at the light when I turn it on, and then I almost fall over. There's marble everywhere, a huge double-head shower along the back wall, a double vanity to my right and the deepest soaking tub I've ever seen in front of a large window to my left.

Before I give in to the temptation of filling the tub right now, I rummage through the vanity drawers and find an unopened toothbrush. I brush my teeth, wash my face and use the facilities before turning the light off and slipping out of the bathroom, feeling my way through to the bed.

I grab my phone from my bag, turn an alarm on, and sit it on the side table as I slide into the soft sheets, curling up on my side. The quiet drags out the exhaustion in my bones.

When did my life get so... intense?

I work on clearing my mind, giving into the exhaustion and not to the incessant questions rolling around in my head.

I'm hovering at the edge of unconsciousness when the bed dips behind me, and Enzo presses himself to my back, curling an arm around me and pushing a leg between mine.

Tension in my body evaporates as I settle back into Enzo's heat and succumb to sleep.

I wake up shivering. My phone alarm hasn't gone off yet, so I roll over, seeking warmth from—

The sheets are cool on Enzo's side. I open my eyes and sit up, my eyes sweeping the dim room, the only light coming from the window. I hear nothing but the faint chirp of birds outside. I check my phone—no messages. He's still upset with me then.

I turn my alarm off and drag myself to the bathroom. The water heats up almost instantly as I strip down and step under one of the two huge shower heads.

Everything in this place is indulgently big, like it was made for giants. Well, the Herringtons *are* ridiculously tall men, and one in particular is built like he lifts boulders for fun.

The hard pressure of the water is heavenly on my body. I close my eyes and prepare mentally myself for the day. Scar and I have a couple of tests today, and then we're bailing out of school early to go hunting for clothes to wear for the tournament. I'm already exhausted and my day hasn't even begun.

The bathroom door slides open, drawing my attention. Enzo steps in, tracksuit pants and no shirt, breathing heavily with sweat dripping down his chest. My traitorous body reacts to the sight, heat pooling low in my belly. He's upset with me for no justifiable reason; I'm not giving into the temptation who has just stripped down to nothing and is now heading toward the shower.

I turn to face the wall, picking up the shampoo that I brought in with me and start scrubbing my hair. Cool air whips around me before Enzo's hands are turning me toward him. I screw my eyes shut, fighting my need to touch him as he wraps an arm around me. He tips my head back into the warm spray, rinsing out my hair.

Enzo steps forward, backing me into the wall. I finally open my eyes to cold eyes glaring at me as the water rolls down his back.

I open my mouth to ask him why he's pissed off, but Enzo pushes his tongue into my mouth, crushing my body into the cold, tiled wall. His mouth claims mine as he nips at my lip and wages war with my tongue.

He pulls back, turns me and shoves my chest into the wall. He grips my hair at the nape of my neck, pressing my cheek into the tile painfully as he kicks my feet wider and buries himself to the hilt in one hard thrust.

"Do you enjoy lying to me, sweetheart?" he asks, his voice menacing, as he starts to fuck me hard.

"What?"

"I knew you'd be just like the rest," he grits out as his thrusts become rough, painful.

"I don't know what you mean," I pant as the slight grit of the tiles grazing my hard nipples sends electric pleasure straight to my core.

I can feel the pressure of an orgasm building, but as I slip my hand down the wall to help it along, Enzo makes a disapproving noise and presses me harder into the wall without breaking his punishing rhythm.

His thrusts are hard and short, and his hand twists in my hair painfully. "Just another pretty thing trying to fix everyone."

He continues to slam into me without mercy and then shudders as he comes, breathing heavily into my ear.

My legs tremble, my body worked up to the edge, desperate for release, but Enzo holds onto me like I'm his only lifeline. "Do you get a kick out of trying to fix dangerous men, Delphine?"

What the fuck?

I push backwards, Enzo slipping out of me as I turn in his arms, glaring up in his beautiful face. "You asked *me* to come here last night."

"And it was a fucking mistake."

"This whole thing between us is a fucking mistake."

Enzo's face changes into the King of Sin—cold, cruel, ruthless. He grips my throat, squeezing tight, trapping me under him.

I can't breathe. Can't move. Panic pours through my very soul. "*Church.*"

The Devil mask slips, and Enzo's breathing stills. He releases me and steps back, confusion replacing his earlier anger.

My trembling hands stroke over my neck, and a choked sob escapes me, still feeling his hands around my neck—like those fucking rosary beads.

His eyes flick to my neck, and they flash with so many things. Before I can decipher anything, he turns and steps out of the shower.

My heart stutters, my chest burning as I slide down the shower wall, my breathing erratic. Tears burst out of me as I break.

It's too much.

If this thing between us doesn't stop, then it will kill me.

I stay on the floor until my breathing is manageable and the tears stop, then stand and step back under the hot spray and hastily clean myself up.

I towel dry my body and hair, throw on my uniform and shove all my things in my bags, then leave Enzo's room.

THIRTY ONE

— Q ♠ —

DEL

SCARLETS ME STEW in my sour mood as we trudge through our week. It's Friday, so we've both decided to skip the rest of school at lunch and check out with reception.

"I'm thinking about wearing pants," Scar comments as she scrolls through her playlists whilst I back out of the car space.

"I'm not going," I grumble, shoving my sunglasses over my eyes. The audacity of the sun coming out today when I'm in this mood.

"You don't have to," Scarlet murmurs, "but I think En—"

"Lorenzo can go fuck himself," I bite back.

Scar sighs softly. "Are you going to tell me what happened?"

"*He's* the one who asked me to come to the house and help Matteo, but apparently because I stopped him from gutting his brother, *I'm* the dirty liar who's trying to save them from eternal damnation, or some bullshit."

"I don't think it's about that," Scar says, turning the music down to a whisper, "from what Teo told me—"

"*Teo?*" I ask, my eyes flicking to Scar before returning to the road. "He's *Teo* now? What exactly is happening between you two?"

I can almost hear her eye roll. "You're changing the subject. And it's not like that between us. We're friends."

"Mm, sure, Songbird."

"*Anyway*," Scar huffs, "Matteo told me that Enzo has never been this erratic about anyone, and he thinks Enzo might be having a hard time with, well, his feelings."

"His *feelings?*" I bark out a laugh. "He made his *feelings* pretty fucking clear to me last week. And none of those feelings were positive."

"That's where you're wrong," Scar counters as I pull into a car park in front of Scar's favourite boutique. "I watched him at dinner the other night. He couldn't keep his hands off you."

I turn to Scar. "That's because he's a possessive bastard who doesn't want other people playing with his toys."

"Del," she breathes, pulling my hands into her lap, "the man's eyes soften every time you speak. You wouldn't see it if you weren't looking for it, but it's there."

"We are talking about the same person, right? Because the mountain of a man I'm talking about has one facial expression, and it's anything but soft."

Scar rolls her eyes, releasing my hands. "You're rubbing on my violent tendencies, Delphine—don't make me hurt you."

"Don't use my full name, *Scarlett*, unless you want to brawl with me."

We get out of the car and head for Scar's favourite boutique, *Moda.* The owner, Bastille, immediately flutters over in his dramatic kimono jacket, like a rainbow butterfly. We spend the next hour being doted on by him as he persuades both of us to buy cocktail dresses and new shoes. We head home, listening to music way too loud, and then get sucked into homework for the afternoon.

Claudine calls us down for dinner, and we eat with her and Dr. Sakura. Claudine apologises again for springing the Voices of Angels Project on us unexpectedly, and launches into all the drama of the build.

After dinner, Scar and I head for our rooms. I put on some heavy metal music and flop down on the cold sheets, staring at the ceiling.

The thought of not sleeping next to that stupid bastard makes me a little sad. It's been only a week, and I know it's going to be next to impossible to actually rest. Scar is going to be a smug bitch when I ask her to curl up with me.

My phone buzzes next to my head, sending flutters through my gut. It's probably just Scar sending me something random. I try to ignore it, but that works for about a minute. I groan at my lack of self-control as I pull my phone up and squint at the bright screen.

ENZO

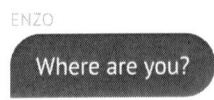

Don't answer him. Let him sweat. Don't do it... Fuck.

Home.

ENZO
Why?

I live here.

ENZO
You're supposed to be here at the house.

I scoff and stab out a reply.

Didn't want to be around and tempt myself into fixing someone.

His message lights up my notifications before I toss my phone away.

ENZO
Be at the house by four tomorrow.

When will he learn that I don't like being told what to do?

I planned on not going to Enzo's place at *all,* and abandoning this stupid tournament all together, but the other Herrington got into Scar's ear and she's dragging me out of the house at midday.

"Teo is going to teach me more about poker before tonight so I don't blow through my entire trust fund."

"I hate both of you right now," I grumble, slipping into the driver's seat. "I already need a nap."

"Nap at Enzo's," Scar comments before blasting pop tunes.

The thought of seeing him makes me nauseous. I don't know what mood he's in, but I know that I don't have the energy to deal with it today. Even with Scar curled up against me last night, I couldn't sleep, and when I did fall asleep, nightmares that had left me alone while I was with Enzo decided to come back with a vengeance.

It doesn't take us long to pull up at Enzo's home, and the nausea twists my gut as I stare at his beautiful home. My heart starts racing and my hands tremble on the steering wheel.

Matteo bounds out of the front door with a warm smile, like the other night didn't happen at all. Scar hops out of the car and into Matteo's embrace, before she starts pulling out garment bags from the back seat.

My chest is tight, the ability to breathe a little harder. I need to *go*. Where, I don't know, but I need some time on my own.

"I'm going to get some groceries," I say through the passenger window as Scar closes the back door, and I speed off down the street.

Tears track down my face as I struggle to breathe, my whole body trembling. The world starts to narrow around me, so I pull over and close my eyes.

My body saturates in full-blown panic and I wrench the car door open, vomiting onto the street. I haven't been able to eat, so all I throw up is water and bile, but it burns.

After the retching stops, I sit back in the seat and close the door, covering my sweaty face with my hands. I thought I was over these outbursts, but apparently not.

I ride through the whirlwind of emotions, trying to untangle them in my head and soothe them one by one.

I'm not trapped. The Herrington house is not my family home. I can leave whenever I want. I don't even have to go there.

One of my trembling hands drifts down to my neck. Despite everything that's happened, Enzo wouldn't hurt me like *he* did.

His words whisper back to me: *Just another pretty thing trying to fix everyone*. My soul aches at the fact that I'll probably never be able to convince him that I thrive in his darkness, but I was fine before him and I'll be fine now.

It was stupid to think that maybe whatever this thing we had was, might have been something else. I can dull the ache around my heart and put back the pieces I was willing to give him.

My breathing finally slows, and the tears stop as my brain quietens, settling into a sad lull.

I knew this wasn't going to end well, and that's *okay*. I have an entire life of potential joy and peace in front of me, and I'm not going to let one man drag me back into the despair I managed to escape.

I clear my throat, wipe my tears and navigate to the nearest supermarket. I get ingredients to make homemade pasta, needing to work the rest of the tension from my body into some dough, then head back to the house.

The front door is surprisingly unlocked, so I walk straight in and head for the kitchen. Scar and Matteo are set up on a new breakfast table in the kitchen area, laughing and bickering about poker. Matteo turns to say something, but Scar stops him with a shake of her head. She knows cooking is my brooding time.

I pull out all the ingredients, find some of the utensils I need, and get to work on the pasta. I go into that serene, methodical space in my head as I make the filling for the ravioli, and knead the dough on the marble top of the island bench.

The noise of Scar and Matteo's laughter and banter settles in the background as a soft, peaceful lullaby as I go in search of a pasta-rolling machine or a rolling pin.

The walk-in pantry is narrow but long, and packed to the ceiling with all sorts of kitchen appliances and food stores. I spot a pasta machine on one of the top shelves that I can't reach. Damn it, I'm going to have to actually form words and ask for assistance. I turn to leave, but bump into a wide chest.

I rock back and tilt my head, looking into beautiful cerulean eyes. My stomach flips, my heart squeezing in the knowledge that I won't be seeing these eyes for much longer. I take in a slow breath, fighting the eyeroll Enzo's scent tries to coax out of me, and point in the direction of the pasta machine.

My heart gallops as Enzo takes a step forward, pressing our bodies together, the heat of his body sinking into my bones. I tremble against him, but I don't move, trying to remember the angles of his face.

His face seems softer, less angry, maybe even concerned. Something about the way he's breathing heavily, or those eyes trying to see right down to my stained soul, makes me want to consider that maybe he regrets some of the things he's said.

His hand lifts as if he's about to touch my face, and I flinch.

My reaction makes that cold mask slip back onto his face as he reaches up and plucks the appliance off the shelf. He places it gently in my hands and backs away.

I shake off the pang in my chest and focus back on my pasta. I take extra care in rolling out perfect sheets, spooning the ricotta and spinach filling evenly and covering it with another perfectly smooth sheet, then cutting out the ravioli squares.

Matteo pulls out a huge pot for me and fills it with water as I pinch the sides of each ravioli, sealing the edges, and then returns to the poker training with Scar. I get to work on a simple Napoli sauce, letting it simmer on low, and clean up the kitchen.

Not ready to talk to anyone just yet, my eyes cast over to the arched glass doors that lead out to a small courtyard. I tell Scar to watch the sauce as I slip out into the chilled breeze.

A stone fountain bubbles quietly in the centre of the small space. An outdoor table with six chairs sits to the left and a fenced off pool to the right. I walk over to the pool fence and lean over it, watching splinters of dull light refract off the water from the cloudy day.

I register the door opening and closing behind me, probably Scar coming to coax me back to reality.

"What are *you* still doing here?"

The hairs on my neck stand up at Vivienne's whiny voice. I push any reactions down and turn to her with a cold stare. "Why do you care? Am I cramping your style?"

The small woman crosses her arm across her chest, her eyes narrowed at me. "Excuse me?"

"You're not trying to snag another Herrington for yourself?"

"That's disgusting to even insinuate," she spits. "They're family, I love—"

"Their money and their name's prestige. Everyone knows that." I take a step toward her, lowering my tone. "You were smart, you know, marrying the oldest Herrington. At least he dropped dead while you were still in your prime."

Tears shine in her eyes and I fight not to roll mine. "You don't know what you're talking about. Joseph and I were soulmates."

"And now you're desecrating that union by trying to fuck one of his sons, and *I'm* the disgusting one?"

"No wonder your mother abandoned you when she could," she volleys at me.

I laugh, the sound dripping with poison. "Oh Viv, it's really beneath you to believe all the whispers of upper society."

"You'll never be good enough for either of them," she sneers.

"And you think you are?" I take another step forward. "You're nothing but a gold-digging whore with a hole for a dumb rich man to fill and feel better about their sad lives."

"You disrespectful bitch," she seethes, storming toward me. "Enzo must have been high when he lowered his standards for trash like you."

"You really are stupid to attempt to intimidate me, Viv." I fill the space in front of her, pouring acid into my glare. "Trash like me knows how to ruin a whiny little thing like you."

I watch the flash of panic cross her face before she forces a pathetic attempt at nonchalance across her face to hide it. "Try it—you'll be slapped with assault charges."

I laugh in her face, making her flinch. "You aren't worth the jail time."

"You'll never be like her," Vivienne says, a shit-eating grin crossing her face as she leans closer. "Sienna will always have his heart."

I frown. "Whoever that is, I—"

"Oh, he didn't tell you about his wife?" she says lightly, tilting her head. "Must have slipped his mind."

I force any reaction behind an eye roll, even though I'm ready to combust with rage. All those words about not keeping anyone, and he has a *wife?*

Disappointment at the lack of reaction darkens Vivienne's face as I step around her towards the house. "I'll be out of your way soon, so you can continue your way through the Herrington men."

I walk back into the house and watch Scarlett and Matteo scramble to pretend they were playing poker and not watching the confrontation. I stop at the end of the island bench as Vivienne storms in and disappears further into the house without a word to anyone.

"Is what she said true?" I ask softly.

Matteo's shoulders stiffen, but he continues to shuffle the deck of cards. "Yes."

"Hmm," I hum, my chest hollowing out. Enzo has a wife. A fucking *wife*.

And I'm here in his house. *Her* house. Does he have kids? I push the spiralling thoughts aside, white noise filling my ears as I pick up my car keys, abandoning dinner, taking my garment bag draped over the couch and leave.

Sienna.

Her name keeps circling through my head as I carefully apply wine-red lipstick in the mirror in Raph's guest bathroom. Luisa could tell something was going on, so she insisted I ate something as soon as I walked through the door. After a pleasant dinner with Raph, Mario, and Luisa, I disappeared into the guest room Raphael showed me to get ready for the evening.

The dress Bastille picked out is all black, with long lace sleeves, a tight, plunging neckline, and a short flowing skirt that brushes my knees. He knows I don't like heels, but he sold me on a new pair of black leather boots with a slight heel.

I brush another layer of highlighter across my cleavage, the gold catching the light when I move, and I shake out the black and pink curls.

I put my ID, invitation, and phone into the pockets of the dress and pack away my things, slinging my clothes bag over my shoulder. As I open the door to leave, Raph is standing with a fist suspended in the air.

One of his blinding smiles lights his face. "You look stunning."

"Thank you," I respond with a small smile, stepping into the hall and heading for the front door.

"What's wrong, Del?" he asks as he catches up to me. "You've been distant since you got here."

Sienna is my problem. "I'm just stressed about school. Nothing I can't handle."

He doesn't ask me any more questions as he steps ahead of me and opens the front door, calling to his parents that we were leaving. I put my bag into the trunk of my car, and then slide into Raph's awaiting sports car, pocketing my key.

Raph fills the silence in the car with trivial conversation and I give half-hearted answers as I watch the city sweep past.

I just need to make an appearance, find an opportunity to slip out, get a car service back to Raph's place and then hide for the rest of the weekend and work out what I'm going to do.

We join the line of cars waiting for valet at *Luxuria*, and soon enough we're climbing out. The familiar valet attendants nod silent greetings as Raph offers me his elbow. I wrap my hand in the crook as he leads me across to the elevators and we ride them to level six.

Two huge security guards stop us, taking our invites and checking our IDs. As we approach the bitchy receptionist, her lips curl into a small, smug grin.

"Good evening, Dragon, Siren."

Raph's eyes flick down to me questioningly, but go back to the receptionist, who's holding out two black envelopes. "Take these to the cashier for your chips and your table allocation. Enjoy your evening."

We both accept the envelopes with our code names on them and then press through the heavy drapes. The room is teeming with people circling multiple poker tables. It's still pretty dark in here, the lights focused over the poker tables or the stage, where a solo jazz singer croons.

Security lines the walls, all dressed in dark colours, trying to blend into the shadows. As we weave our way to the cashier across the room, I spy politicians and celebrities amongst the crowd, blending in with businessmen and bikers. Everyone is dressed in their finest, even the bikers.

I wonder what they would say if they knew there was a man murdered in this room two days ago.

We approach a beautiful man behind the cashier's desk and pass over our envelopes. He pulls out the white cards in both and his perfect brows raise slightly.

"Dragon and Siren, you are both on the Platinum table which is over to the right of the stage. Your chips will be waiting for you there."

Raph thanks the cashier and steers me toward the stage. He leans down to murmur in my ear. "Siren?"

"Yeah," I say, giving him nothing more.

We see Lucas standing in front of the velvet ropes cornering off the poker table. If Lucas is here, that means...

"Siren," Creed, the Mechanic, draws out the code name from his seat at the table, drawing everyone else's attention, except Enzo.

There's an empty space between Austin, the Barrister, and Matteo. Scarlett sits to Matteo's right, with Creed on her other side. The dealer stands between Creed and the Politician, and there is an empty seat where the Surgeon would sit if he was here. Enzo sits with his back to us, next to the Surgeon's empty seat.

Lucas lifts the velvet rope. "Dragon, you're in your usual seat next to the Blade, Siren, you're next to the Politician."

The Blade must be Matteo, I surmise as I pull my hand from Raph and slip onto my assigned seat. I refuse to look at Enzo, but I can see his looming presence in my periphery as I start moving around the chips in front of me.

I frown at the chips as I mentally calculate the value. There's two hundred *thousand* dollars' worth of chips here. My eyes flick up to Matteo, my eyes narrowing. A smirk plays across his face and he shrugs, lifting his chin toward Enzo.

A waiter approaches my left, asking for a drink order, forcing me to turn toward Enzo. He's on his phone, lounging lazily in the chair, which is something I never thought I'd see. He's usually so... stiff.

"Double gin and soda, with a few lime wedges," I tell the pretty waiter. He nods and asks Enzo if he'd like a refill.

Enzo finally looks up from his phone and those cold cerulean irises catch mine.

Sienna, whispers through my head as I meet his cold stare with my own. He's baiting me with his glare, like he knows that *I* know. Matteo probably told him.

My eyes drop to his white shirt and black suit, before lifting again and catching his stare. I mirror the cold indifference he likes to give the world and then dismiss him by turning toward the table. I see his hand flex around his phone in the corner of my eye.

Matteo, Scar, and the Mechanic flick their attention between me and Enzo.

"Fuck," the Mechanic mumbles, sitting back in his seat, smiling with feral delight.

THIRTY TWO

DEL

ENZO PLAYS POKER LIKE an absolute savage.

He's quick with his decisions, bets risky, and is fucking intimidating. And I can't work out his tell, which is driving me insane.

I've been playing on the safer side, trying to read the table before making my moves, and only going for it if I have a really decent chance at winning. But I'm still down about forty thousand dollars, all won back by Enzo.

The waiter has been keeping my drink topped up for the last hour, and I'm buzzing from my third drink. Scar captures the attention of everyone on the table with her open smiles and flirty quips. She has all of these men by the balls, except for Enzo.

She's actually fairing well, thanks to Matteo's training during the day. The girl who couldn't keep her clothes at strip poker is now holding her own amongst the demons of the city.

If they aren't on the play, Enzo has his eyes glued to his phone, and it's irrationally pissing me off. It's rude to ignore company at *your* event, but it doesn't seem to bother anyone else.

The Politician has been super chatty tonight, asking me broad questions and bragging about a variety of things that I don't give a shit about, but I feign interest, using the polite manners that were beaten into me throughout childhood.

After an hour of intense play and another two drinks, I excuse myself from the table for the bathroom. Thankfully, I don't sway as I cross to Peter, who's standing by a door in our section, his eyes dropping to my chest as he opens the door.

"You look good, Siren," he murmurs as I walk past.

I turn to tell him to piss off, but I see Enzo watching the exchange. He's not close enough to hear, so I give Peter a suggestive smile as I thank him and then slip into the private bathroom.

I wrestle with the garter clips and my underwear, then sit on the toilet, fighting the dizziness and white noise in my ears. I can't drink anymore or I'll end up passed out at the poker table. I hear the door open and heels clicking on the tiles as I finish my business, fix up my clothes and leave the stall.

A stunning brunette powders her face at one of the basins. She's tall, slim and her long hair falls in perfect waves down her naked back. The dress she's wearing is silvery blue silk and drapes around her body to the floor like water.

"Wow," I muse, watching the tiny diamond straps sparkle under the vanity lights. Knowing this crowd, they're probably *actual* diamonds.

Her dark eyes meet mine in the mirror and her plush lips curve in a demure smile. "This dress is crazy, right?"

"You look incredible," I say as I wash my hands, trying not to stare at her flawless bronze skin.

"I love your dress too," she says with a genuine lilt in her honey tone. "Is that a Bastille original?"

A laugh erupts out of me as I dry my hands. "Yeah, how did you know?"

Her smile deepens. "He's a good friend of mine." She turns to me as she puts her compact in her silver clutch. "Which table are you on?"

"The Platinum table. What about you?"

Her eyes light up. "Same. Well, kind of. The person I'm here with is on that table."

"Who are you with?" The Politician was saying something about a new girlfriend which I wasn't paying attention to.

"He said his code name was the Executive."

Fuck. Is this Sienna? Does she *know*?

Despite the potential that this is his wife, hot, ugly, petty possession still courses through my veins. I keep my smile tight. "We'll be sitting next to each other, then."

"Oh, amazing," she chirps.

"Are you his wife?" I ask before I can stop myself.

Her eyes widen slightly as she shakes her head. "Oh, no. I'm Clara."

I breathe a sigh of relief. At least I won't have to defend myself to this woman. "I'm Del."

"Crap, they told me to use the code name at the reception. I'm Star."

"Siren." My throat is tight. Can this person not be so... lovely?

"That's so sexy," she muses, winking at me. "See you out there, Siren."

I nod and give her a small smile as she floats out of the bathroom. I breathe in and out slowly, trying to get a grip on the rage pressing against my skin. He didn't take very long to move on. And he's still cheating on his wife. Where is she, anyway?

I pull my phone out of my pocket with a shaky hand. I turned off my notifications at Raph's house, so there's a string of messages from earlier today.

SCAR

Why did you leave? Tell me you're okay.

UNKNOWN

It's Matteo. Your pasta was the best thing I've ever eaten. Where did you go? Scar is worried about you.

How he got my number, I don't even want to know.

SCAR

I'm about to send a search party.

ENZO

Tell me why...

I open the full message.

> Tell me why you keep running. I thought you'd have a better handle on your emotions, but I guess not.

Fury fills my body. He's accusing me of not handling *my* emotions better? Has he looked in a mirror?

I scroll his other messages, the time stamps indicating that they were sent when I arrived at the poker table.

ENZO

> You ran to him. Really?

> Have you been fucking him the whole time?

> Does he make you come when he fucks you, Delphine? Do you scream his name?

> Do you think of me when he's inside you?

> Do you love him?

> Too bad if you do, because I'm going to kill him. Maybe I'll do it tonight.

> You're still mine, Delphine. You know what happens when someone touches what's mine.

Is he drunk? He's definitely fucking delusional. My phone buzzes with a new message.

SCAR

> I'm warning you so you don't come out here swinging, but there is some fucking skank on Enzo's lap.

I snort and type a reply.

> Yes, Star. I met her in the bathroom.

SCAR

> Her vibe is off. Enzo is acting so weird.

I frown.

> Is it weird, or do we not know him at all?

SCAR

> My gut says weird.

I sigh.

> He's just a dog, Scar. Let it go.

I put my phone in my pocket, check my make-up in the mirror, and pull my shoulders back.

Fuck Enzo, fuck Clara, and fuck all this Herrington bullshit. None of this is my business anymore.

I walk out of the bathroom, embracing the fury, encasing myself in the hard armour I built over years of abuse as I open the door to the poker table. I ignore Clara in Enzo's lap, turning my gaze up to Peter.

"What are you doing later?" I ask softly, giving a soft smile.

Peter's tongue swipes over his teeth, his eyes darkening. "Aren't you with the boss?"

I tilt my head toward the table. "Obviously not anymore."

His eyes flick in Enzo's direction, and then back to me, leaning forward slightly. "I can be free later."

"Good," I croon, smoothing down Peter's tie, "because I'll need a... ride home."

Peter's lips twist into a smug grin, understanding my suggestion. I wink at him as I turn back to the table and slip back into my seat with a satisfied smirk. I ignore the giggling and hushed words next to me and catch Scar's wide eyes.

She taps on her phone, so I pull mine out and read her message.

SCAR

> You are playing with the fucking Devil, Del. Enzo has murder in his eyes.

I scramble out a response.

> He doesn't give a shit about me. He has a new toy, and I'm not his wife.

I watch Scarlett read my response from across the table and frown at her screen. Her eyes lift to mine and she shakes her head, slipping her phone onto her lap.

"Let's get serious friends, and play some poker," I say to the table.

I'm playing dirty and recklessly, and out of pure luck, I'm doing very well.

I've almost wiped out the Politician, and I'm pissing off the Barrister. Raph excused himself about an hour ago and hasn't come back. Creed, Scar, and Matteo are playing a safe game, and keep the mood light at the table, but they all throw cautious glances between me and the couple next to me.

Clara doesn't move from Enzo's lap the whole time he plays, whispering into his ear and running her hand down his chest. I'm drunk on fury and gin, brimming with dark, feral energy, waiting for something to tip me over the edge.

I have the strongest urge to fight someone.

Not just *someone.* I want to fight Clara and mess up her stupid perfection. And I *definitely* want to fight Enzo for being such a fucking asshole.

Instead of my fists, I throw caution to the wind and play the Devil's game. I send Peter suggestive looks and soft smiles.

At first he was hesitant, but he quickly grew bolder and started reciprocating with cocky smiles, even coming up a couple times and whispering about the filthy things he wants to do with me later. Too bad I'm going to leave him high and dry.

We play a few more rounds, and I demolish the Politician, resulting in him giving up and leaving the table. I'm a hundred grand up from the buy-in.

"You're on the warpath today, Siren," Creed muses.

I smile. "Do you need a private lesson, Mechanic?"

His eyes go to Enzo immediately and then he chuckles, his hands flying up in front of him. "I have enough game."

"How disappointing," I breathe, playing with a stack of chips.

Raphael decides to make an appearance again and sits down with a hard expression on his face. "We need to talk business."

"That's our cue," Scar mutters, grabbing Creed's hand and pulling him away from the table.

I shove my chips at the dealer. "I'd like to cash in."

He nods and writes me a slip to take to the cashier, and I get up from the table.

"I'll come with you," Clara announces, standing from Enzo's lap. "Let's go to the bar."

I nod and then turn to Peter. "I require an extra set of hands for all the cash I've won tonight. Are you available?"

"Absolutely," he says immediately, following Clara and me as we walk past Lucas.

I don't miss the disapproving look from him, but I don't fucking care anymore. Clara chatters away about something as we cross to the cashier and I hand him the slip. He congratulates me on my winnings, puts all the cash in a small case, and hands it to me.

I pass it to Peter, my hand brushing over his in the process, and then lead our small party over to the bar. Clara orders a vodka and soda, and I order us a tequila shot each, and decide on a gin and orange juice chaser.

"I can't believe you're making me do a tequila shot," Clara giggles, her nose wrinkling as she sniffs the glass.

"Bottoms up," I say, clinking my shot with hers and drink. It burns across my tongue and I take a mouthful of my other drink to ease the peppery taste.

Clara shakes her head, her face screwed up as she sips on her drink. "Gosh, that's awful."

"But it gets the job done," I muse. "So, how did you meet the Executive?"

"Lorenzo?" Clara sighs. "I've known him for a long time."

"And his wife?" I can't help myself. I need to know.

Clara's face falls as she takes a sip of her drink. "Sienna and I were friends."

"Were?"

Clara gives me a tight smile. "It's complicated."

God, I hate vague answers, but I don't push her. "How long have you been dating Lorenzo?"

"We aren't dating exactly," she says with a small frown. "He doesn't date. The most you would get from him is an intense affair and then a cordial farewell. I'm surprised he sent this invite at the last minute. I honestly thought he'd forgotten about me."

"How could someone forget about you?" I genuinely ask. "You're so beautiful."

"You're too sweet," she muses, her eyes drifting over in his direction. "He's notorious for being reclusive and keeps his affairs private." Probably because he has a wife stashed away somewhere that everyone knows about except me.

"It feels like a display of some sort," Clara continues. "There's a lot of his business connections here, so he's probably using me to show he isn't as intimidating as he probably is in the boardroom."

I don't think Clara knows about his *other* profession. "And you're okay with that? Being used for his own agenda?"

She lifts one shoulder. "I don't expect much from him. If it's a little fun I get out of this, then I'll take it."

Clara starts talking about her work in fashion as Lucas appears and murmurs something low to Peter. He nods, gives my cash case to Lucas before flashing me a smile and heading in the direction of our poker table.

That pent up aggressive energy is slowly seeping out of me.

I'm done with this tense competition with Enzo, and I hope he doesn't ruin Clara, because she's kind of nice. I nod and smile along with Clara as I plan on how I'm going to slip out of here without anyone noticing. Lucas has Enzo's money, so at least I won't have to find a way to return it back to him.

Lucas takes a phone call and I'm about to excuse myself to go to the bathroom and get out of here, but Lucas steps toward us, ending his call.

"Star, The Executive sends his apologies. An emergency has come up with work. One of our men is in the foyer waiting to take you home."

Clara sighs, nods to Lucas and then turns to me. "It was a pleasure to meet you, Del."

She pulls me into a tight hug, her floral scent tickling my nose before she releases me and walks away.

"You're needed in the penthouse," Lucas says, sweeping his hand toward the exit.

"I'm going home," I say before finishing my entire drink and pulling out my phone to order a car service. "Please give Enzo back all his money."

"Del." Lucas' tone makes me look up at him. His eyes almost plead with me.

"No, Lucas," I whisper.

"You're the only one he'll... You need to come with me."

I sigh, dropping my shoulders. At least if I go up there, I can make a clean break.

I cross to the exit with Lucas on my tail and call the elevator. Lucas swipes a card and hits the penthouse button. My stomach dips as we rise and I close my eyes. I am definitely drunk. That last tequila shot really got me to that point.

I need to remember to think before I speak or I might end up saying some really stupid shit to a dangerous man.

Lucas leads me to the door and opens it. He's avoiding my gaze as I walk past. It must be that...

The smell of iron sours the air. The penthouse is dark except for the city lights filtering in. I walk further into the apartment hesitantly. That's blood in the air.

I realise the dining table isn't in the right place. And there's fallen chairs across the floor. What the hell?

Oh god, did Enzo *actually* murder Raphael?

The living room comes into view, and I gape. There's blood streaked across the floor. I don't want to follow the trail that leads past the fireplace, but what if it's Raph? Mario's going to start a war over this.

It looks like someone was dragged down the hall. I step around the blood and follow it to Enzo's office. The door is slightly ajar. I push it open slowly with the toe of my boot and my stomach twists at the scene.

I want to puke and run for my fucking life.

A body lies on the floor in a growing pool of blood. The black suit is torn, and the shirt shredded. Knife slashes and bruises litter the guy's chest. Blood seeps out around the knife lodged in his neck. His hands are mangled beyond repair.

His face is unrecognisable; the beating he got was brutal. His blonde hair has...

Blonde.

"Peter," I whisper.

Heavy footsteps stomp toward me, and the office door is wrenched open.

I freeze. The knuckles on the hand holding the door open are split. Enzo's once white shirt is soaked in blood. The blood splattered over his face accentuates the feral cerulean flames of his eyes.

His filthy hand strikes out and clutches a fistful of hair as he pulls me into the office and shoves me closer to Peter's body. The force of his touch sends me stumbling, but he pulls me against his chest.

"See what you made me do," he sneers, his hot breath in my ear. "His death is on *your* hands."

"*My* fault?" I rasp. "How is this my fault?"

"I fucking warned you about what would happen." His grip moves from my hair to my throat.

Fuck no. I start clawing at Enzo's grip, and when it doesn't make him let go, I drive my elbow into Enzo's side hard.

The move probably hurts me more than him, but it stuns Enzo enough that he releases me and I stumble away, putting Peter's body between us.

"Touch me again, and it will be the last time you breathe," I grit out, trying to wipe the blood off my throat, but making it smear worse.

"You're threatening me?" I turn to Enzo and he's livid. "I own this fucking city. There's nothing you can do."

I start to laugh, the hysteria seeping into my bones. How did I honestly get here?

"Is this a joke to you?" Enzo hisses.

"This death is on you," I pant.

Enzo starts walking around Peter's body, and I do the same. If I can get to the door, I can run. I'll probably need to change my name again, but I'm sure Claudine will point me to the right people.

"Is this what you wanted?" Enzo accuses. "You made open passes at one of my men for what, my attention?"

I balk. "I was vying for *your* attention? You basically fucked Clara at the poker table like the beast you are."

"Watch your mouth."

Feral energy exploding through my veins. "I'll say and do whatever the *fuck* I want, Lorenzo. I'm not your *wife*."

That stops Enzo in his tracks. "Excuse me?"

"*Sienna.*"

Enzo laughs, the sound terrifying. "Jesus, Delphine, I thought you were smarter than to believe gossip."

"It's not gossip when your brother and your new plaything confirm it."

Enzo starts stalking around Peter again as darkness seeps into every part of him. "You want to know about Sienna?"

"No, not really." I'm almost at the door, almost free of this nightmare.

"Sienna was some socialite my father pushed me to marry seventeen years ago for some political alliance he wanted with her father."

I roll my eyes. "Just because you were forced to marry her doesn't justify the fact that you lied to me about being married."

"She's been dead for ten years."

Dead?

His revelation makes me stop momentarily and Enzo takes the advantage to close the distance between us and grab my forearm. I struggle against his hold as he backs into the wall next to the door.

"I never lied to you," he states firmly.

I look up into his eyes. "You killed her, didn't you?"

"No."

"Was she just another person who you convinced yourself was trying to *fix* you?"

He narrows his eyes. "She fucked half the men in the organisation and then died in a car accident with her boyfriend's cock in her mouth."

"Is that why you decided you'd fuck one of her friends? A bit late for revenge, is it not?"

Enzo frowns. "I'm not fucking Clara."

"You don't have to hide it. I know I mean nothing."

Enzo presses me further into the wall, and one of his hands sinks into the hair at the nape of my neck. "You have no fucking idea what you're doing to me."

"Do you know what you're doing to *me*, Enzo?" The filter I promised to use has gone out the window. "You made me trust you, and I don't trust anyone, *especially* men. You feel like *home* to me, and I've never had one of those."

"Del—"

"You can't even trust *me*. I never wanted to change you. I just wanted to understand you. I wanted you to understand me and accept all the broken pieces I had left. But clearly you can't, so I'm done playing this game with you."

The world goes silent—the only sound is the heartbeat pounding in my ears. Enzo's face is blank, but those eyes, those beautiful eyes *burn*.

"No," is all he says.

"You can't just say 'no' and expect me to heel."

"Sweetheart—"

"Do you know how exhausting it is to fight for everything? I'm so tired of fighting you, and myself when I'm around you."

Enzo sighs, dropping his forehead to mine and closing his eyes. "I'm sorry."

The Devil himself is... apologising. He's probably never said those words to anyone. The armour around my heart cracks.

"I never lied to you," he says, pulling back and opening his eyes to me. "You are my *only* choice."

"That's not enough."

"Not enough?" Enzo's grip in my hair tightens, forcing my head to tilt up towards him. "What would be enough, sweetheart? Would it be hunting every person who has ever touched you? Hunting who *hurt* you? Because I will fucking do it. You will have bodies piled at your feet, if that's what it takes."

"I..." Fuck it. I don't know why I'm fighting this. I grab the front of Enzo's ruined shirt and tug hard. "I want you. Just *you*. No changes."

"I want your shattered soul the way it is."

"If you touch another woman ever again, you will find a knife in your chest."

Enzo's head jerks up, fury blazing in his eyes again. "You shouldn't threaten me, Delphine."

I slam his mouth to mine, and pour the hot possession heating my body into the kiss, biting down on his bottom lip hard, then pushing him back, staring into his furious eyes. "You shouldn't fuck with me, Lorenzo."

Enzo smiles, the harsh twist of his mouth predatory. "You think I'm scared of you, sweetheart?"

"You should be."

He tucks a stray strand of hair behind my ear, brushing my cheek with rough, sticky hands. "The world is going to burn at our feet."

I can't look away from the feral predator in front of me.

My predator.

THIRTY THREE

ENZO

*M*INE.

I crush my lips to hers, our kiss bruising, as I lean down and lift Del from the back of her thighs. She winds her legs around my waist and wraps her arms around my neck as I carry her around Peter's body.

I sit her on my desk and she tears at my ruined shirt, buttons popping in all directions. I pull back, watching the feral gleam in Del's clear green eyes as her hands roam my chest. Her touch is like wildfire over my skin, igniting feelings I can't quite explain.

Something burning, bright, and almost overwhelming.

Her fingers travel over the scars scattered across my skin almost reverently. I fight the urge to roll my eyes back—her touch is fucking addictive.

I slide my hands up each thigh, grunting in approval as I skim the lace tops of her stockings.

"No more running," I murmur, gripping her thighs tighter, probably leaving marks. I hope I'm leaving marks.

"No more," Del breathes, running her hands over my shoulders, pushing my shirt down my arms.

"How much do you like this dress?" I ask.

"Do not harm this masterpiece," she warns.

I smirk, grabbing her jaw gently tilting her head. My eyes drop to the dried blood flaking on her neck and chest, where she tried to clean it.

Church. That word has been echoing in my head since she said it, and it's fucking killed me ever since. My finger skims the column of her throat softly. "Tell me."

"No neck grabs," she whispers. "Too many memories."

My jaw tightens. "I'm sorry, sweetheart."

"We'll work on it," she says, her hands dropping to my belt.

She gets it undone, but I stop her hands from going for the button, placing both of them flat on the desk. Her skin is streaked in Peter's blood everywhere I've touched.

"Don't you dare move," I warn as I head for the office bathroom and scrub at my hands. I return with a damp towel to see she hasn't moved.

She sees the towel and tilts her chin back, bearing her neck. The fact she's letting me clean her up after causing the mess makes my chest *burn*.

I clean her neck and chest gently, before tossing the towel in the direction of the bathroom, and placing my palm flat against her chest, guiding her to lie flat on the desk.

I settle between her legs, and reach across her body and pick up my switchblade from where I left it on the desk.

The *snick* of the blade makes Del smirk. "Your obsession with knives is a little concerning."

I slide the cool flat of the blade down her thigh, pushing up her dress as I go, making sure I don't snag it on the blade. I hook it into her panties and slice them off at the hip. I do the same on the other side and then pull the ruined fabric away from her body.

My eyes devour the unmarked pale skin of her thighs as my thumb presses against her clit. She jerks at the contact as I trail a finger through her arousal and sink into her.

"Already so wet," I murmur, adding another finger, her body already clenching around me.

I lay the switchblade flat between her breasts and cover it with my hand as I stroke in and out of her lazily, curling my fingers up, revelling in her heavy breathing and her eyes rolling closed. Working her into a frenzy is my favourite part of my existence, and I'll do it every day until I die.

"You know," she pants, "you're the only one to... to taste me."

My hands still, and she looks up at me, her cheeks flushed. The only...

"Say it again," I growl.

"You're the only one," she breathes.

The sick, primal, possessive demon inside me gloats with satisfaction as I pull my fingers out and press my body into Del, smearing her arousal across her bottom lip. She moans as I suck her lip into my mouth, her fingers curling into my hair and swiping her tongue across mine.

I press my forehead onto hers. "From now on, it's just me, sweetheart."

"Only you, Enzo. All of me is yours," she breathes, her finger trailing across my facial hair.

I rear back slightly, searching her face, seeing the sincerity, the vulnerability—seeing *her*.

I cup her cheek. "I'll *never* let you go."

"Please don't," she whispers, unshed tears shining in her eyes.

I capture her mouth with a softness I've never expressed, and those bright, overwhelming *things* burn in my chest again.

Del's hand slips down my chest to my pants, unbuttoning it and sliding into the waistband. I hiss as her fingers brush down my cock, my hips jerking forward.

"Devious hands," I growl, nipping at her lower lip.

"Fuck me, Enzo," she pants, squeezing her hand around me.

"As you wish, love."

I grab the knife and clutch her hip with that hand; the tip piercing the flesh at her waist. My other hand lines up my cock and then I thrust all the way to the hilt.

Christ. I steady myself by grabbing both hips in a bruising grip, watching her eyes roll back and feel her body tighten around me.

I fuck her hard enough to imprint myself into her tainted, broken soul—she's mine, now, always.

She whimpers as she loses herself to my punishing pace, her body quivering around me with an impending orgasm.

I move my knife-free hand to her clit, my thumb applying pressure and circling. I feel Del's body relax, surrender to my touch, her body convulsing as she comes.

My mind goes hazy, my movements frantic as I press the knife into the flesh of her upper thigh, and Del rides the ecstasy over the edge, screaming my name when she comes again.

Still buried deep inside her, I drop the knife on the table and lean over Del, pushing myself deeper, enticing out a gasp.

Her clear, perfect green eyes open, swimming with so many *things*.

"Tell me again," I pant.

"Yours, Enzo," Del whispers, "I'm yours."

"*Mine*," I growl through clenched teeth.

Del cups the back of my neck. "This ownership goes both ways."

"Good." I press a hard kiss into her mouth, and she greedily swallows my moan as I slam into her once more, coming hard.

I collapse forward, tucking my arms into Del's side and bury my face into her chest as she strokes her fingers through my hair, trying to catch her breath under me.

My breathing slows, and I shiver as her fingers travel down my back, feeling my heated skin.

"Soft," she says, the word slipping out in a low murmur.

I lift my head, giving her a lazy smile. "Let's go to bed. I'm not done with you just yet."

She smiles and winces as I pull out. I help her sit up and she pulls up the skirt of her dress and almost chokes.

"*Lorenzo,*" she whispers in horror. "Tell me that's not what I think it is."

Her thighs are covered in patches of blood and there's a small 'E' sliced into the top of her right thigh, still dribbling blood.

"No need for stitches," I say, my fingers tracing around the wound.

"But it'll scar, you dick," she complains, slapping my hand away.

"Oh, I know," I chuckle, placing both palms flat on the table on either side of Del and lowering my face level with hers.

She frowns, but heat burns in her eyes. "Possessive bastard."

I cup the side of her jaw gently, my thumb brushing over her bottom lip. "Of you, definitely."

"Can I do the same to you?" she asks, arching a brow. "It's only fair."

I smile, picking up the switchblade and offering it to her. "Carve your whole name into me, love."

She wraps her fingers around mine, holding the knife. "Don't tempt me."

The smile drops from my face as I angle the blade to my chest; the tip pressing into the skin over my heart. "Do it."

She shakes her head. "No, I—"

My other hand closes over hers before she can pull away, and I slice a 'D' into my skin, the sting barely registering. Blood oozes out of the wound and she slaps her free hand over it to staunch the bleeding.

"*Fuck*, Enzo, what are you doing?"

"Like you said, this ownership goes both ways," I state matter-of-factly.

I put the knife down on the desk as Del slides off and leads me out of the office, keeping her hand over my chest.

"You must pay your cleaning staff some big bucks for all the blood they clean out of your floors," she comments as we cross the penthouse, bloody footprints marking the timber.

I laugh. "I pay them very well."

We make it to my room and cross straight to the bathroom. She pulls my hand away from the mess of my chest, quickly strips me out of my pants, then discards her dress. I'll send her dress to the dry cleaner on my payroll who doesn't ask questions.

We get into the huge shower, taking turns tending to each other's wounds, and cleaning each other from head to toe.

Neither of our wounds are deep enough for stitches, but will more than likely scar. Excellent.

After we get out, dry off, Del in nothing but my t-shirt, we both fall into bed tangled together and pass out.

"Del," someone whispers in the darkness. My body goes on alert, but the soft voice calls Del's name again, and I recognise it as Scarlett.

Del groans, her head leaning back further into my chest, and I tighten my arm around her, burying my face into my hair, trying to will myself back to sleep.

"What's wrong, Scar?" Del whispers hoarsely, settling further back into me.

"I need to talk to you," she whispers. Her words are slightly slurred. I crack an eye open to see Scarlett in Matteo's t-shirt, in our bed, sharing Del's pillows.

"What happened?" Del asks as she tucks a stray hair behind Scarlett's ear.

"Nothing happened, I just," she sighs, "Matteo's gone."

"What?" Del says a little louder, making me tense my arms again.

"I don't know what I did," Scarlett says, her bottom lip trembling slightly, "but he just... stormed out."

"Was he drunk?" I rumble.

Scarlett's eyes flick to me and then back to Del. "He... we did some stuff with Creed. And then he just left."

"You mean..." Del trails off, and Scarlett nods at the assumption.

I sigh softly, pushing a leg between Del's. "He'll be back when he's worked out his shit."

"Are you sure he's okay?" Scarlett asks.

"Lucas is probably watching him," I murmur, planting a soft kiss below Del's ear. Anytime Matteo indulges too much, he gets in this headspace that none of us can get him out of, so all we can do is make sure he doesn't start a bloodbath or get himself killed.

Scarlett nods, but hesitation is still clouding her eyes. "Can I... can I sleep here?"

Del nods, and Scarlett crawls under the blankets, turning herself away from us. Del wraps an arm around her middle and then we drift off.

THIRTY FOUR

DEL

I WAKE UP ALONE, bathed in the early morning sunshine.

I pull myself out of the bed, use the bathroom, brush my teeth with a packaged hotel dental kit I find, and pull on a pair of Enzo's tracksuit pants.

When I enter the kitchen, Enzo is sitting at the island bench in a full suit, a coffee in front of him as his thumb scrolls across his phone.

"Morning," I call as I head straight for the pot full of coffee, pulling out a mug from the overhead cupboard. "Where's Scar?"

"She left not long ago to pick up breakfast with Matteo," Enzo says absently.

His eyes are still glued to his phone when I turn around with a full cup of coffee. "When did Matteo get back?"

"When he announced he was taking Scarlett to get breakfast."

"Mm," I hum as I sip on my coffee, walking around and resting my chin on Enzo's shoulder. "Is everything alright?"

He doesn't look up from his phone, but he curls an arm around my waist, pressing me closer to him. "Not really. With the last shipment of product stolen from us, my dealers are running low and customers are getting frustrated. Dragone's new man seems decent enough, but there were cops at the meeting, which means they're either watching him or Raphael."

I can only assume the worst for those cops. "You can't get your product from another source?"

Enzo sighs and puts his phone down, picking up his coffee. "I can, but the Herringtons and the Dragones have an unwritten exclusivity deal which would be painful to get around."

"If it's not a contracted deal, and it's hurting your business, why not look at other suppliers?"

"Because this business is all about reputation, more than it is about money," he says, facing me. "If I'm not loyal to my supplier, it doesn't look good for future business transactions."

I shrug, taking a sip of my coffee. "Just do a sneaky deal on the side. Surely, being reliable to your customers is better for business."

Enzo chuckles softly and plants a soft kiss on my lips. "Devious woman."

I kiss him again, swiping my tongue over his lips. "You taste like coffee and risky decisions."

"You taste like my own personal sin," Enzo rumbles against my lips before turning on his stool and pulling me between his legs, claiming my lips in a bruising kiss.

Before I can pull him back to bed and taste other parts of his body, the front door opens, followed by laughter.

"One day we're going to walk in here and find those two naked on the kitchen counter," Scar comments.

I pull back and look at her and Matteo shaking their heads with a smile, each carrying a pastry box. I give Enzo one last hard kiss before pulling away. He swats my ass as he follows me around the island, grabbing the coffee pot and more mugs, then heading for the dining table.

I grab plates and cross to the table where Matteo and Scar have pulled out an excessive amount of baked pastries of all sorts.

"Did you buy out an entire bakery?" I say, handing out plates.

"Teo didn't know what he wanted," Scar comments, eyes flicking to him next to her, before back to me, "so we got a bit of everything."

My eyes land on Matteo. He's still in the suit he was in last night, the fabric crinkled and disheveled. His dark blue eyes are glassy, the skin around them pinched, and his hair is a bit of a mess. The smile he's sporting looks forced. I keep my comments to myself as I slide my hand onto Enzo's lap and talk to Scar about school assignments.

Matteo smiles and talks with us, but there's something empty about him today, and I don't like it. After cleaning up breakfast, and sending the spare pastries down to the front desk staff via Lucas, Matteo announces he's going to go crash for a while and Enzo retreats to his office to work.

I find my phone in Enzo's bedroom charging on the side table and scroll through all my notifications. I laugh at the garbled messages from Scarlett in her inebriated state talking about Creed, Matteo, and nonsensical things.

There's a slew of missed phone calls and messages from Raph, and a conversation thread *I* apparently had with him early this morning.

RAPH

Del, where the hell are you?

This is Herrington, she's fine.

RAPH

Where is she?

She won't be leaving with you.

RAPH

You need to leave her alone, Matteo, she's not one of your playthings.

Who said this was Matteo?

Jesus Christ. Before I can launch off the bed and go chew Enzo's ear off, an incoming call vibrates my hand, with Raph's name flashing on the screen.

"Hey," I say lightly as I answer the call.

"I thought you were fucking *dead*," he grinds out, probably clenching his jaw like he does when he's pissed.

"I'm fine, Raph, what's up?"

"*Really*, Del?"

"I don't know wh—"

"*Enzo?* Do you have a death wish?"

I sigh, rubbing my forehead. "It's really none of your—"

"*Bullshit*," he barks, "I've been here all this time, protecting you from this side of the world, and you decide you want the attention of evil fucking incarnate? Are you that fucking stupid?"

"Are you just mad because I'm not with *you*?" I bite out. "Because you're no safer than him, Raphael."

"You think he cares for you?" he asks, contention seeping through the phone. "He cares for nothing but himself. He'll take everything from you and then throw you away like garbage."

"And you wouldn't do the same? Seems like you do it every other bitch you decide to bed."

"I would never—"

"Just tell me if I still have a job so I can start looking for another one if you're firing me."

He sighs. "Of course you still have a job."

"Then we're done talking about this. As I've told you before, I can look after myself. I'll send someone to pick up my car." I hang up before he can answer, pocketing the phone and heading for Enzo's office.

I knock on the door softly before walking in, not bothering to wait for an answer. The floor is spotless, like no one was murdered here just last night. Enzo is behind his desk on the phone and typing away on his laptop, with Lucas sitting on the other side reading some sort of paperwork.

"Lucas," I whisper, not wanting to disturb Enzo's heated conversation about stocks.

The burly man puts his papers down and raises out of his chair, heading toward me.

"Can you do me a favour?" I ask softly. He nods and I ask him to send someone to grab my car from Raph's place.

"I'll go myself," Lucas rumbles low and slips out of the office before I can stop him.

Enzo hangs up his phone and tosses it on the table, tilting his head back.

"Where is Lucas going?" he asks, his eyes closed.

"To get my car from Raph's house," I respond, as I cross to stand behind him, running my hands through his hair. "Sorry I pulled him away—I thought he'd send another henchman."

"It's fine," Enzo breathes, taking my hands from his head and pulling them down his chest, angling my face closer to his.

I plant a soft kiss on his upside down lips and then straighten, and perch on his desk.

"I see you had a few words with Raph," I say, waving my phone at him.

Enzo shrugs slightly, a satisfied little smile playing across his lips. "Now he knows who you belong to."

"Yes, he does," I mutter.

"Did he say something?" Enzo asks, his eyes flashing.

"Nothing I can't handle."

"I know it's pointless to ask you to stop working there," Enzo surmises as his hand slides up from my knee, "but I'd like you to consider Lucas taking you to and from work."

"Okay," I say. My breath hitches, all my attention on his touch travelling up my inner thigh.

His hands still. "What?"

My eyes flick up to his surprised gaze, and I smile. "I'm not unreasonable. If it gives you peace of mind that Lucas does that, then that's fine. I appreciate you trying not to lock me up like a fragile flower that most people think I am."

"You're anything but fragile, sweetheart," Enzo says, his hand remaining where they are as he stands, looming over me slightly, his lips hovering over mine. "I would have broken you by now if you were."

"Care to take a work break?" I ask, one hand sliding up his chest to his neck, careful of where his wound is from last night.

"I've been working for less than an hour," he comments, both of his hands grabbing my ass and pulling me flush against him, his erection pressing into my stomach.

"Qualifies for a quick break," I say, grabbing his hand and pulling him from his desk.

"Incorrigible," Enzo chuckles as he lets me lead him across the penthouse.

"You love it," I quip, as I open the bedroom door and nudge him in, closing the door behind us.

He turns to say something, but I'm on him, throwing myself into his arms and swallowing his laughter as he stumbles a step back. Teeth knock together and our mouths consume each other as I wrestle Enzo's suit jacket off, and hastily unbutton his shirt, yanking the ends out of his pants. His hands grab for the hem of my t-shirt, but I bat them away.

"Nope, not yet," I say against his lips, going for his belt.

"I don't appreciate you holding out," Enzo grumbles into between kisses, kicking off his shoes as I manage to get his pants off.

I pull back, both of us panting, as I take in all his naked glory. The man is so fucking *huge;* it astounds me every time.

I trace my hand around the healing 'D' in his chest, skimming down to the edge of the tattoo across his ribs. The black and grey piece is a massive dragon made from smoke, starting from his hip and wraps around to his back.

"Lay on the bed," I order huskily, my fingers refusing to leave his skin.

"Sweetheart—"

"*Bed*, Enzo," I repeat, staring into those amused eyes.

He steps back without a word until his legs hit the bed and then he sinks into the middle of the bed. I crawl up onto the bed and straddle him fully clothed, his erection pressing into my clit deliciously.

He frowns slightly. "What are you up to, little siren?"

"Do you trust me?"

"With that wicked glint in your eye? Definitely not."

I laugh, pressing my chest to his, gazing up into his handsome face. "I won't hurt you too badly."

Before he has time to protest more, I slip my hand under my pillow and grab the cuff. At the same time, I take his wrist and secure the leather strap firmly around it.

"Delphine," Enzo barks as I wrangle the other cuff, using my body to hold his arm down as he struggles, but I manage to secure his wrist in the cuff.

"The benefits of my size is being able to hold strong men like you down so I can secure you for a ritual sacrifice."

"Let me go Del, before you regret your decisions," Enzo threatens, his face hard as he pulls at the restraints.

"Relax," I chuckle, "I'm not going to murder you." I pull off my t-shirt, revealing my lack of bra as I roll up the shirt into a long strip.

"Don't you dare blindfold me," Enzo warns, as I do just that.

I lean down, peppering Enzo with kisses across his mouth and jaw, reveling in the feel of his facial hair on my lips and the demands from his lips for me to release him. I work my way down his neck and chest, kissing, nipping and licking all the way down his body until I'm kneeling between his legs.

I bite the inside of his thigh hard, earning a hiss and a jerk of his restraints and then run my tongue over the teeth marks. I do the same on the other side, getting more pulling on the restraints and a grunt.

The thrill of the power I have over his body sings through my veins as I slip off the bed and strip out of my pants.

There's so many possibilities I can play out right now, it's almost overwhelming. Should I get the riding crop out, or maybe the flogger?

No, what I really want to do is have my mouth all over him.

I don't put any weight on the bed, or breathe too loud, knowing the sensory deprivation would be fucking with his head. He's anticipating my touch, but not knowing where it's coming from is all part of the game.

The air is thick with tension as I bring down my palm hard on Enzo's thigh, making his whole body jerk up and his wrist jerk hard on the restraints.

I chuckle, stroking over the red mark. "A bit too much for you, baby?"

"You better be ready to run when I get out of these restraints."

"I'm so scared," I mock as I bring my palm down on his other thigh, the slap reverberating through the room mingled with Enzo's frustrated growl.

"I see the fascination with marking skin," I croon tracing over the welted hand prints. "Maybe I *should* get out the cane."

"Unless you don't want to sit for a week, I advise against it."

"You're such a baby," I pout, slapping his outer thigh on both sides.

As much as he's struggling, his cock jerks with every slap, the tip glistening with arousal. I lick my lips as I grab both of his thighs tight over the pink flesh and run my tongue from base to tip in one long motion. I'm obsessed with the way it curves. I wrap my lips around the tip and suck his cock into my mouth until it hits the back of my throat.

The groan that's pulled out of Enzo makes my thighs clench as I drag my mouth all the way up and then back down, relaxing my throat, pushing more in, gagging a little.

"*Christ*," Enzo pants, his thighs flexing under my hands, as I start a slow, heady rhythm, bobbing up and down with a hard suction, reveling in the curses and groans that I drag out of Enzo.

His cock pulses on my tongue, and my body clenches at the thought of him being buried inside of me. I drag my mouth up his cock, releasing it with a *pop*, and then crawl up to straddle Enzo's hips.

I drag my core along his shaft, coating him with my wetness. His efforts to break away from the restraints amplify as I reach between us and line him up, sinking so very slowly down until I'm the one whimpering. At this angle, seated to the base, I feel overwhelmingly *full*, and it's the most intense feeling I've ever felt, just like at the church the first time.

"Fuck," I sob as I roll my hips, the stretch mixed with friction on my clit sending shocks down my spine.

I lift myself up only slightly and sink back down, my ass hitting his thighs. I'm dizzy with the pleasure drowning me. My fingers find my clit, leaning my body forward to change the angle as I drop my head forward, rolling and lifting my hips in a frantic rhythm, chasing a devastating orgasm which breaks me down to my soul.

I'm riding the last winds of my orgasm when I hear a clang and then a hand grips a handful of hair. I open my eyes to a cerulean inferno.

"Free my other wrist." That tone shakes me to my core and almost tips me into another orgasm. I remove my hands from my body and fumble with the cuff with shaky hands.

Once he's free, Enzo flips us over, still buried in me. "You should be *very* scared, sweetheart."

THIRTY FIVE

DEL

THE NEXT FEW MONTHS go by in a whirlwind of technicolour. Enzo and Matteo moved all of their things back to their mansion, and forced Vivienne to move into the penthouse of *Luxuria*.

Scar and I are at the Herrington house so often that we both half considered moving in, but Claudine was not having it. She didn't particularly take the news of my relationship with Enzo well, or her daughter's close friendship with Matteo, but she's getting better about it.

I've gotten into a routine of school, work, and Enzo's crazy social calendar, in which he has made me his permanent plus one. No matter how many times I've rubbed elbows with the city's high society, I still feel like I need to scrape off the layer of fake left over from the interactions.

Enzo is an absolute master at playing the game of high society business man and hiding the Demon King underneath. I *much* prefer the Demon King.

Dressed in another of the designer dresses Enzo insists on continuously buying for me, my black and purple hair pinned up and my make-up glittering under the ornate chandeliers, Enzo and I weave through the ballroom towards our seats.

He's dragged me to another fancy auction with the proceeds going to a charity that his company openly supports. We find the Herrington Global table and I immediately want to leave when I see my mother and William.

"I didn't know they were going to be here," Enzo murmurs into my ear before we get to the table and he pulls out my chair.

"Delphine, darling," my mother drawls, her eyes blazing with questions, "I didn't expect to see you here."

I know for a *fact* that she would have seen photos of Enzo and me somewhere, and knows we're together. I give her a tight smile. "Eleanor, William."

William nods once to me and shakes hands with Enzo. My mother picks up her champagne with perfect poise.

"I haven't heard from you for a while, darling," my mum croons, her eyes tracking Enzo's arm draping over my chair and my hand sliding into Enzo's lap. "How have you been?"

"Fine," I state, thanking the waiter for pouring me a glass of champagne. "Where's Bridgette?"

"Your brother is watching her," my mum announces, taking another sip of her drink. "Those two are quite fond of each other."

"Sure," I drawl, flexing my fingers on Enzo's lap. I can tell this conversation is being set up for a fight.

"Mrs. Anderson," Enzo almost purrs, drawing her attention away from me. "Have you looked through those personnel files Matteo sent through for a new Chief Financial Officer?" Thank god the man can read situations to complete accuracy.

My mother launches into a professional monologue about selecting the right people for the Anderson Technologies company, giving me time to prepare for her bullshit that's bound to come my way. Her little rant is cut off by the lights dimming and the hosts of the event starting up the bidding.

I press myself a little closer to Enzo and whisper, "Thank you."

"Anything for you, love," he murmurs back, his fingers tracing along my jaw.

Enzo ends up buying some overly expensive piece of abstract art, and my mother, via William, purchases a pair of hideous but ridiculously expensive earrings. After the auction concludes, both men stand to go sign for their items. Enzo plants a soft kiss on my lips before he leaves.

"Do you have to showcase in public that you're having pre-marital sex with someone old enough to be your father?" my mother spits across the table when they're out of earshot.

I bark a short laugh, meeting her disapproving glare. "You think I give a shit what you think?"

"I am your *mother*," she emphasises. "You cannot speak to me like that."

"There's a big difference between a person who gave birth to another human, and a mother, Eleanor."

"Who took care of you when you were ill?" she demands. "Who gave you an education and made sure you had food on the table?"

I sigh. "Do we have to do this every time we see each other? Why can't you disown me like you promised you would?"

"Because I love you, Delphine," she says in a way that would seem genuine to the outside world, but they're empty words from this woman.

"Lying is a sin, Eleanor," I point out, taking a sip of my drink. "I thought you were a righteous woman."

"Don't you dare question my dedication to my faith. You don't even go to church anymore."

I scoff. "What did you always say? If I pray to the guy in the sky, I will always be safe and cared for?" I breathe an empty laugh. "That's another lie you told me."

"It wasn't a—"

"I prayed every night *he* was around," I seethe, pinning my mother with a hard glare. "I prayed to that asshole in the sky to save me, for *anyone* to save me, and my prayers were never answered."

"He didn't deem you worthy to save," my mother states with cold indifference.

I narrow my eyes, biting down on the fury pulsing through my veins. "I really hope you're happy, *Mother*." I stand slowly from my seat, keeping my eyes on the hateful woman. "I hope you're *deliriously* happy, because when someone rips that happiness away, your pain is going to give me so much fucking pleasure."

"You make me so sad, darling," she pouts, sitting back in her chair, looking defeated. "It hurts me to know you can't be saved from an eternity in hellfire."

"It's okay, Eleanor," I say, pulling the strap of my bag over my shoulder. "I'm fucking the Devil. There's a throne waiting for me in Hell."

Enzo and I leave the charity event after I leave my mother at the table, picking up Greek food on the way home as we didn't even make it to that part of the evening.

Enzo doesn't ask any questions, even though I can see them rolling around in his eyes. We get to the Herrington house to find Scar and Matteo on the couch, with a board game in front of them on the coffee table.

"You're home early," Matteo calls, his eyes trained on the game in front of him.

"We brought dinner," I say as Enzo and I head straight to the kitchen. We pull out food containers and plates as the other two filter in, sitting on the island stools.

"Did you decide that buying useless items for charity was pretentious and boring?" Scar asks, a sly grin on her face.

"My mother was there," I grumble, handing everyone a plate.

"Shit," Scar breathes, "what did she say?"

"Oh, you know, the usual."

"Which is?" Matteo asks.

I sigh. "Only that I was disgusting for dating someone old enough to be my father, God hates me, but *she* loves me, and I wasn't worthy of being saved."

"What a bitch," Matteo breathes, serving out the shaved gyros meat on our plates.

"She's the worst person I've ever met," Scar declares as she deals out the pita bread.

"She's good at playing the doting wife and mother," Enzo muses, pulling out vodka from the freezer and some cranberry juice from the fridge. "If you didn't know what you were looking for, you'd almost believe her."

"The only person she cares about is herself," I say as we all dive into the rest of the food.

We all eat our fill and have a couple of drinks, the vodka heating my skin as the mundane conversations around me soothes the tension my mother likes to ignite. Scar and Matteo clean up after dinner as Enzo and I head upstairs to shower and change into comfy clothes.

When we get back, Scar and Matteo are sitting on top of the island bench with a tub of ice cream between them.

"Del," Scar says with a mouth full of ice cream, "I forgot to ask you about—"

"No, I told you a hundred times, no." The bitch keeps asking me what I want to for—

"We have to do *something* for your birthday," she whines.

"Did you forget to tell me something?" Enzo asks next to me.

I cringe as I look up at him. "She's drunk—she has no idea what she's talking about. I don't actually have a birthday."

"You dirty liar," Scar accuses, pointing a spoon at me, "her birthday is Halloween."

"Snitch," I grumble, crossing over and stealing her ice cream and spoon. "We aren't doing anything to mark the day I spawned into this world."

"That's where you're wrong," Matteo declares, hopping down from the bench and draping an arm across my shoulders. "We will definitely be partying. And besides," Matteo says with a shit-eating grin, "Enzo's birthday is the day after."

My head whips to Enzo and I tilt my head. "Did *you* forget to mention something?"

Enzo rolls his eyes, crossing to the small bar area along the other wall and grabbing a bottle of what looks like whiskey or bourbon.

"We aren't celebrating," I say, pulling away from Matteo and heading to the lounge with my stolen ice cream, "and *no* gifts."

"Too late!" Scar calls after me.

My phone starts buzzing in my pocket, and I ignore it, not wanting to ruin this peaceful afternoon. Scar and I have finished all our assignments and we've decided that no one is going to disturb our movie marathon today.

The phone finally stops buzzing, but then starts again almost instantly. I groan, pulling it out and answer without looking at the number.

"Hello?"

"Del?" Isaac asks on the other end.

I shoot straight up. "How did you get my number?"

"I asked Mum."

Time for a new number. "What do you want?"

"What are you doing today? I thought we could catch up."

"I already told you that I don't want to talk to you." Scar sits up next to me, concern across her face. *Isaac*, I mouth and she rolls her eyes.

"Please, Del," Isaac pleads, "I just want to talk to you."

"Then talk. I probably won't listen."

"Meet me somewhere. I want to do it in person."

He's probably never going to stop bothering me if I don't meet with him. I sigh, running my hands through my hair. "Fine."

"Thank you," he breathes.

"I'm near the city—how far are you?" I ask.

"I'm at the office."

"I'll send you an address. Meet you there in fifteen minutes." I hang up the phone, save his number, and send him the address for a cafe I saw around the corner.

"Do you want me to go with you?" Scar asks.

"No, I won't be long." I kiss the top of her head and head for Enzo's room, swap tracksuit pants for my jeans, slip on a bra, keep Enzo's t-shirt, and pull on sneakers. I head to the office and knock on the door softly.

"Come in," his deep voice says through the door. I open the door and step inside. Matteo sits in one of the armchairs by a bookshelf on his phone as Enzo sits behind the desk, typing furiously on his laptop.

He looks up and takes in my outfit. "Where are you going?"

"I have to meet my brother," I say, crossing over and perching on the desk.

"Your cop brother?" Matteo asks, peering over his phone.

"This has nothing to do with you or any of your activities," I say, pulling my hair into a haphazard bun.

"Then what is it about?" Enzo asks, drawing my attention. His jaw is tight, his brow furrowed.

"He wants to hash out some family drama," I sigh. "Trust me, I would rather not go, but he won't stop bothering me until I hear him out."

"Give us the room," Enzo says to his brother. Matteo leaves without another word. Enzo closes his laptop and sits back in his chair. "Is he the one from your dreams?"

"God, no," I say, trying not to shudder, "but he knows about it."

"What does he want, then?"

"He thinks he can fix our relationship, even though I've told him that it's too late for that."

"Don't go then."

I smile. "It's fine. I'll give him fifteen minutes of my time and then I'll be back naked in your bed."

A devilish smile heats Enzo's face. "Insatiable."

I stand. "For you, I'll never have enough."

"Where are you meeting?" Enzo asks, also standing and walking me to the front door.

"The cafe near the park," I say, pulling my phone out of my back pocket. "I'll call if I need a rescue."

Enzo wraps an arm around my waist, pressing a possessive kiss onto my lips. "Fifteen minutes and then my bed."

"See you soon."

THIRTY SIX

DEL

I SPOT ISAAC SITTING in the back at a small table, looking at his phone as I enter the cafe. I take a grounding breath before crossing over and taking the seat opposite him, pulling off my jacket and draping it over the back of my chair.

Isaac's brown eyes soften. "You came."

"You have fifteen minutes," I say, sitting back and crossing my arms.

"Del, please, I—"

"That's all you get, so make it count."

Isaac sighs, scraping his hand through his hair. The movement lifts his t-shirt, revealing the bottom of the leather gun holster. I force my gaze back to his face as he leans his elbows on the table.

"Where are you staying these days?" he asks.

I shrug. "Around."

"If you need a place to stay—"

"I don't."

A flicker of frustration crosses his face before it goes blank again. "Are you working?"

"Yes."

"Do you like it?"

"You could have messaged all of this to me so I could ignore it." I turn to grab my jacket, but Isaac reaches out and grabs my wrist. I pull my arm roughly out of his touch, my skin crawling at the contact.

"I'm sorry," he whispers, sitting back in his chair with his arms flat on the table. "That's what I wanted to say. I'm sorry."

"Sorry for *what*, exactly?" I want him to say the words.

"I'm sorry that I left." His eyes plead with me.

I frown, sitting back in my chair again. "That's it? You're sorry you left?"

"I should have stayed, and—"

"Did you know what was happening?" I ask.

"I..." Isaac clears his throat and shuffles in his seat. "I didn't know all of it."

"What *did* you know?"

"Del, we don't—"

"Yes, we do. What did you know, Isaac?"

He looks physically uncomfortable. "At the time, I had my suspicions that it was more than..."

"More than the beatings?" I laugh, the sound bitter. "You had your *suspicions*, and you still thought leaving me there was the best option?"

"I got the shit kicked out of me," Isaac growls low, leaning forward, keeping our conversation hushed. "For far longer. I was one more hit away from doing something I'd regret."

"Would you really have regretted killing that monster?" I ask.

Isaac blinks incredulously. "Murder is against the law, and a sin."

I laugh a little louder than I should. "So you *still* believe in all that shit?"

"Of course I do."

"So what he did to me, or Mum, or *you*, was good with God? Really, Isaac?"

"What he did was abhorrent," Isaac huffs. "And he's been punished for that."

"Punished?" I scoff. "Do you actually know what he is?"

"I do, yes."

"Say the words, *brother*," I challenge.

"We don't need to—"

"The words you're looking for are pedophile and rapist," I state louder than necessary, but I don't give a shit if anyone overhears.

Isaac looks around, then lowers his head toward me again. "We shouldn't talk about this here."

"When did you find out the rest?" I ask.

He lets out a breath, his eyes closing. "About a year after I left."

My heart stammers. He knew all that time, and he still—"I'm done with this conversation."

I grab the jacket, and storm out of the cafe, Isaac close on my heels.

"Del, where are you going?" he asks, trying to reach for me again.

I take two big steps back. "You knew what was happening, and you did fucking *nothing.*"

"I didn't know what to do at the time," Isaac argues, "and when I could do something, I did. I helped get him sent to prison. The worst one in the country."

"It was too late at that point! He had broken me beyond repair."

"There was nothing—"

"You could have taken me with you," I yell, my whole body radiating with fury. "You promised me you would."

"I... I couldn't, Del," Isaac murmurs. "I was barely eighteen. I didn't know how to look after myself, let alone a kid."

"I was nine, Isaac, *nine*," I say, backing away, my whole body shaking, unshed tears burning my eyes. "You should have gotten me away from that place—you should have *tried*. That's what my brother would have done."

"You're five minutes late," Enzo calls as I open the door to the house.

I'm clenching my jaw so hard against the torrent of rage ready to unleash.

Enzo appears from the direction of his office, a smirk on his face, but he freezes, his face dropping as he sees me. "What's wrong?"

Scar appears next to him and steps toward me, with Matteo stopping next to Enzo. She slows her approach, her eyes soft, understanding.

"We should go home," she calls behind her, eyes still on me. "Del needs to be in her—"

"That stupid piece of shit," I yell, throwing my jacket at the stairs and pacing in front of the door.

I feel like a caged animal, desperate for escape. But I can't escape my past, I never have. Heartbreak and fury drown me, my mind fracturing as Isaac's words play over and over in my head.

"He knew," I pant heavily, "he fucking *knew*!"

"That fucking..." the rest of Scar's words fade out as my heart pounds in my ears. Memories that I'd kept locked up start pouring out, making me choke on a sob.

"Isaac knew about all the disgusting things that man did to me, and he just *left* me there." I don't know if I'm screaming. Tears track down my face and neck. "He let that man touch me for all those years and he didn't help me. And then he has the fucking nerve to think I would want *anything* to do with him?"

White and grey spots play over my eyesight, sending me half blind. Rage erupts through my entire body as my fist slams into the wall by the front door, the wall cracking. I don't feel the impact.

My knees give out and I collapse to the floor. I start sobbing uncontrollably, struggling to breathe.

I can feel his hot, panting breath in my ear. His hands groping my body. The bruises and broken body parts he left behind.

I'm stuck in a loop of memories, pulling me to those places, trapping me in a nightmare.

"These were mother's," he says, draping the rosary beads over my head. "I want you to have them, so I'm always with you."

I claw at my neck. I don't want them. I choke as they tighten—why can't I get them off?

Muffled sounds mix with my strangled sobs in my head as a large body looms over me. The air shifts and hands take mine, pulling them away from my neck, and then a large hand covers my throat gently. The beads are gone. I can breathe again.

"Del," the deep voice rumbles softly. I know that voice. It's not *his* voice. I blink through the tear haze blinding me.

Bright, cerulean blue eyes surrounded by black lashes. Such soft looking lashes.

"Sweetheart," he says in that soft but deep tone again, drawing my attention to his mouth. It's a sharp mouth, all hard, defined lines with a larger bottom lip.

"Enzo," I croak, the recognition slowly coaxing me out of the hole of nightmares.

"Yes, baby." He's crouched down on his haunches, his elbows propped on his thighs as one hand holds both my wrists, and the other caresses my throat softly. His eyes flick to my hands in his. "How's your hand?"

I look down at my shaking hands, stretch my fingers a few times. My left knuckles are pink, but still working. "I can't feel anything."

"That's good," he croons, not moving from his spot. "Teo's getting you some ice to get ahead of any swelling."

"Why didn't he help me?" I whisper, staring at my shaking hands. I turn my head to Enzo. "He promised. He promised he'd never leave me behind."

"He doesn't deserve to be breathing," he says simply.

"You can't go around murdering people, Enzo."

A cruel smirk lifts Enzo's devious lips. "I beg to differ."

I tug my hands gently out of his grip, and Enzo removes his hand from my throat as I haul myself up off the floor on shaky legs. My heart is still shredding apart. Isaac *knew*. He—

A sob chokes up my throat, and I double over, grasping my knees. Tears stream down my face as I try to separate my nightmares and my reality, shoving those tainted memories back into the vault in the back of my head.

Warm fingers trailing down my back startle me, and I jerk up, catching a warm wrist.

"You're safe here," Enzo murmurs, not moving, giving me the time for my brain to process his words. Safe. *Safe.*

"I don't know what safe means," I whisper, stepping forward and placing Enzo's hand over my racing heart.

Enzo steps closer, his arm wrapping around me, pressing our bodies together and his hand slipping from my chest and into my hair. "Let me show you."

That statement chips away more of the walls around me, leaking bits of Enzo into my heart. My lip trembles as I crush my arms around him, burying my head in his chest. His citrus and spice scent fills my lungs as my tears soak his shirt. Grapefruit, black pepper, sandalwood, and...

I pull away from Enzo's chest, my stomach turning.

Enzo's arms tense around me, not letting me move any further away from him. "Tell me."

That haunting scent burns the back of my throat. Dark. Sweet. "Bourbon."

"What?"

I strain in Enzo's grasp. "You smell like *him*."

Matteo enters the foyer then with a bag of ice. Enzo finally lets me go, running his hand through his hair. "Get rid of all the bourbon in the house, Teo."

Matteo blinks. "What? Why—"

"All of it," Enzo seethes, snatching the ice from him. "And you don't touch a drop of it ever again."

Matteo nods once and disappears further into the house. Enzo pulls back, but I grip his shirt with my uninjured hand, not wanting him to leave. He takes my injured hand and places the ice over my knuckles, drawing out a hiss from me.

"He knew," I whisper again, resting my forehead on Enzo's chest. Tears track down my face as I close my eyes.

"Pick someone," he murmurs. I tilt my head up and meet serious cerulean eyes.

"What?" I whisper hoarsely.

"Pick someone from your list, and I'll bring you their head."

"No, I—"

"Give me a name."

"He isn't worth the effort," I whisper, tracing the buttons of his t-shirt with my good hand.

"I want the names of every person who has ever hurt you," Enzo growls.

"I—"

"Tell me how you want me to do it," he says softly, sending chills over my skin. "Or should we do it together? Should we just shoot them? Or drag it out and cut them up, watch them bleed out slowly?"

The cold reverence in his voice as he describes such brutality would send anyone else running, but my broken body quivers in need. The images of him covered in the blood of every person who's taken a piece of my soul makes my thighs clench.

"Slowly," I pant, blood rushing to my face, "I want them to suffer really fucking slowly."

"Let me make your dreams come true, love," Enzo proposes, his arm snaking around my waist.

"The name on the top of my list is in prison," I whisper.

"I have a connection in every prison in the country. One phone call and he's gone."

Tempting, but... "If it's going to be anyone, it's going to be us."

A predatory smile blooms on his face. "Done."

"Fuck me."

Enzo frowns. "Del—"

"Make me feel nothing but you."

He grabs the nape of my neck, forcing me to look up into his eyes. They have a stern glint. "You were late."

"What are you going to do about it?" I challenge.

He smirks. "Many things to you and your smart mouth."

Enzo crushes his mouth to mine, taking what's his as his tongue thrusts into my mouth. All the dark, suffocating memories slowly recede back behind the steel door they pushed past, and my body finally starts to relax.

You're safe here.

The first time in my life, I actually believe those words.

As I abandon the ice on the floor and wrap both my arms around Enzo's neck, I finally allow myself to truly feel it.

Enzo pushes me up against the front door, crushing me under his weight. His hand slides into my hair, tugging at the tie and releasing the bun. He then takes my uninjured hand and pulls me up the stairs, heading for his room.

He has me naked, pinned down on the bed, and his tongue swirling over my clit before I can ever breathe properly. The orgasm builds so quickly that my lungs can't compete with the feral lust gripping onto my whole body, onto my *soul.*

My body careens into oblivion, and I let go.

I'm restless and sated, wanting to laugh and cry and dissolve into the insanity.

My brain is screaming but quiet, completely obliterated by all these *things* coursing through me.

Enzo is a poison I never want to stop tasting, no matter how much damage he can do. He's the Devil, and I'm willingly selling my soul.

THIRTY SEVEN

ENZO

SHE'S HERE, SAFE, BREATHING deeply as she sleeps in my arms, but I can't get her words out of my head.

He knew about all the disgusting things that man did to me...

Rage heats my blood, my hands itching to kill someone. Not just someone, but the man responsible for hurting Del. The fact he laid his hands on a child is despicable. But the fact that it was her...

I take a deep breath in, inhaling her addictive scent, smothering the murderous flames plaguing me. She said he was in prison, and he better hope he never comes out.

Until she tells me his name so I can inflict my wrath on him, that will have to do for now.

I forcibly relax my body, matching my breathing to Del and willing my mind to shut down enough to let me sleep.

As I'm almost at the brink of unconsciousness, Del starts breathing heavily, and a tremor runs through her body.

"No, please," she whimpers, clawing at my arm around her waist, trying to push me away. I pull my arm away as she brings her knees closer to her chest, her arms wrapping around herself.

"Please... *please*, stop," she whines, sobbing in her sleep. "I'll be good, sir, please."

I lean closer, careful not to touch Del, in case I startle her.

"Delphine, sweetheart," I coax. "Wake up, love."

"No, sir," she mumbles, now rocking slightly. "I don't... no... don't make me again."

Her begging wraps a fist around my heart and starts the rage fire in my veins again. I place my hand gently on her clammy shoulder and roll Del onto her back.

"Del, wake up," I say a little louder, brushing a few damp curls from her face that have escaped her bun. "Come on, love, come back to me."

Her hands shoot out and wrap around my forearm, her breathing hard. Those terrified eyes turn to me, cloudy with terror.

She rolls away from me, ripping herself out of bed, and bolts toward the bathroom. I scramble out of bed and follow to find her emptying her stomach into the toilet.

I take a hand towel from under the sink and dampen it with cool water, then crouch down beside Del and place it gently on the back of her neck. She grips my hand over the towel as her retching subsides and she works to calm her laboured breathing.

My hand slips away as she lifts her head, drawing the towel around her neck, wiping her face.

"I'm sorry if I woke you," she whispers, her voice hoarse.

"You didn't," I murmur as I stand, offering my hand. "Are you okay?"

She takes my hand and stands on shaky legs, nodding. Her eyes lift to mine, the green more vibrant against the redness from her tears. The scratched welts on her neck are fading, but the sight of them still sends adrenaline pumping through my veins.

Someone needs to die.

I cup her cheek gently, running my thumb over her cheekbone, under the dark circles under her eyes.

"The bastard should pay for stealing rest from you," I say through clenched teeth. Del averts her gaze and steps out of my touch, moving toward the sink.

"And he robs me of the ability to touch you, as well."

Del says nothing in return as she rinses the towel under the tap and wrings it out.

"Has he stolen your voice, too?" I ask, crossing my arms across my chest.

"I have nothing to say," she says, folding the towel and putting it down next to the sink. She cups her hand under the running water and leans down, tipping the pooled liquid in her mouth and spitting it back out.

"Delphine—"

She stills, her eyes staring hard at the running water. "Don't fucking try me, Lorenzo."

"Talk to me," I demand.

She rinses her mouth out once more and then turns the water off, wiping her mouth with the back of her dry hand. She still won't look at me. "I don't need anything."

"Bullshit—"

She spins quickly towards me, her eyes a fiery emerald. "You can't just demand me to be okay. I'm barely surviving, and I don't need you to tip me over the edge."

"Tell me what you need."

"You can't give me what I need."

I narrow my eyes. "I have resources you—"

"You can't take these memories," she barks.

I take a step toward her without thought, making her flinch back. "One word. One word from you, and I can eliminate the source."

Del frowns. "Killing *him* won't help with this."

"But at least you'll never have to look over your shoulder."

"He'll still haunt my nightmares." Her lip trembles as she huffs a humourless laugh. "It's exactly what he wanted, to be with me forever. The pain he inflicted, the terror—it's ingrained into my very bones. I relive every single moment, almost every fucking day."

She's falling apart. I can almost feel it.

This is the side she hides from everyone, but I realise I've seen it before. Last night when she lost it after Isaac. After the incident with Peter. In the penthouse, before I pushed her away. These are the dark parts of her that she doesn't want to let into the sunlight.

I feel similar pieces in me, the ones I release under the veil of night.

We're two broken souls calling to each other with a dark siren call, trying to find one another to become whole again.

"I'm drowning, Enzo, and I don't know how long I'm going to last, so there's no point in you trying to understand any of this."

I move before Del registers, grabbing her jaw, avoiding a full neck grab, and backing her into the shower, pinning her against the glass pane with my body. I tilt her head up, forcing her to look at me.

"Do you know the fucking torture you put me through as you force me to stand by and watch you fight to keep breathing?"

"I—"

"You don't think I understand? I *understand* having a past that haunts you every day. I *understand* being in a waking nightmare with no escape."

"You can't know anything about what I've been through."

"Then fucking *tell* me—the pain, the terror, all of it. I'm a selfish prick, Del. I'm not losing you to some fleeting memories."

Anger hardens Del's eyes as she pushes against my chest. "This isn't something you can throw money or a knife at—these 'fleeting' memories eat away at anything good left in me. They're turning me into a monster."

I smirk. "What do you think I am? A saint?" I squeeze her neck a little harder. "This life made me into the sickest of all monsters, and it suffers the consequences. So feed your monster, love, let the world tremble beneath you."

Those beautiful, broken eyes bore into mine. "I... I don't..."

"Let your darkness fill the cracks that *bastard* made in your soul. Let's revel in the darkness together. Marry me."

Del's eyes flash with too many things to decipher. She inhales sharply. "No."

"*No?*"

"I've told you before, you don't own me."

I scoff, move my hand from her neck and cup her cheek lightly. "Sweetheart, I already own you. This body, your broken soul, *everything.*"

Her eyes narrow. "Then why do we have to put a contract on it?"

"Because I need every fucker on this earth to know that if they try to touch what's mine, then they'll beg me for a quick death."

"I won't be another one of your possessions."

I laugh, the sound empty. "You, a possession? Baby, the Devil is offering you a seat on his throne."

Del tries to hide her smirk behind a scowl. "And where will you be when I'm lording over your territory?"

"Preferably under you, with my cock buried deep in you."

Del rolls her eyes, but her breathing is a little shallower.

"Or maybe on my knees, with my mouth on that dripping—"

"Okay, *okay,*" Del's cheeks are a delicious shade of pink as she pushes out of my arms.

"So, you'll marry me."

"No... I mean..." She scrubs her hands over her face. "I need time. Just... time."

I press her back into the wall, resting my forehead on hers, never breaking eye contact. Her eyes flashing with so many *things* again, mainly hesitation, as she cups my cheek and she closes her eyes.

"Take all the time you need," I murmur softly, revelling in her touch. "But don't run."

"I won't," she whispers. "You're home."

My chest stills at Del's words.

Home.

I press my lips to hers lightly, savouring the way she relaxes against me. I take her hand without another word and pull her back to bed.

When we climb in, she flings an arm over me, fits her leg in between mine, and buries her face in the crook of my neck. I wrap myself around her, my hands stroking her back rhythmically as I listen to her breathing start to slow.

"You'll always be safe with me," I murmur softly, finally closing my eyes.

"Safe with the Devil," she mumbles against my neck, almost as if she's talking in her sleep. "Who knew?"

THIRTY EIGHT

DEL

*Y*OU'LL ALWAYS BE SAFE *with me.*

Those words burn bright in my chest even after a month since Enzo whispered them to me. Between checking in constantly and having Lucas basically become my personal driver, he's kept his promise.

"Thank the universe that's over," Scarlett sighs, linking her arm with mine as we head to our lockers.

"We still have exams," I remind her.

"But classes are done. We're one step closer to never having to come here again."

"Very true." I've been hesitant to think about the impending freedom, the ability to *choose* my future. It's such a foreign feeling for someone who had their choice taken from them for so long.

We collect our things and head for the car park, where Lucas is waiting to take us home. As we get to the gates, I get jolted forward and would have crashed to the ground if Scar didn't tighten her hold on my arm.

"You stupid *bitch!*" Silvia shrieks as I turn to the snivelling woman. "What did you do to him?"

I frown. "What are you talking about?"

"Isaac!" she bellows, her blue eyes shining with rage.

"She did nothing to him," Scar spits. It's my turn to tighten my hold—the tremor in Scar's arm indicates she's ready to pounce.

"He was ranting about *you* and now he's been missing for a month."

I roll my eyes. "He's the definition of flaky; that doesn't make it my problem."

"I know who you're fucking, so tell me what he did to my brother!"

Lucas appears between us, making Silvia scramble backward. "I think it's best you leave now, Miss Bennett."

Silvia scoffs, crossing her arms over her chest. "No, I want answers. What did your boss do to my brother?"

"We have no knowledge of Mr. Bennett's whereabouts," Lucas states.

Silvia looks around Lucas directly at me. "I'm going to find out what you did to him, and then I'm going to *ruin* your life."

Scar starts laughing, drawing Silvia's attention. "Try it and a few select people will find out about last summer."

Panic washes over Silvia's face and she stumbles back. "You wouldn't."

"I'll do it with *pleasure*."

Tears well up in Silvia's eyes as she bolts away further into the parking lot. Lucas turns to us, ushering us toward the car.

"Details, immediately," I demand as we buckle up in the backseat and Lucas slides into the front seat.

Scar's devilish smile radiates on her face. "Remember when I was working at my dad's clinic? Guess who showed up under a false name?"

"For what?"

"A certain someone has such a strong relationship with a cocktail of substances that Dad admitted her to rehab."

I gape. "And she's been convincing people I'm an alcoholic? Fucking hypocrite."

"As you know, the school board has a strict drug and alcohol policy, and I could still tell them since we haven't done exams yet, so..."

"And you're only telling me now?"

Scar shrugs. "I was keeping it in the arsenal in case we needed it."

I turn to Lucas. "Did Enzo do anything to Isaac?"

"No."

I sigh, settling into the seat. I guess Lucas would be the one to do those things if Enzo ordered it. But if he has been missing since we last met, where did Isaac go? Surely a federal agent can't disappear without a trace. Then again, he'd know how.

"Are you excited for tonight?" Scar asks, squeezing my hand.

I sigh. "You're forcing me to be."

"Oh please, there's booze, and music, and costumes. I'm jealous your birthday is Halloween."

"You can have it, honestly."

We pull up to Enzo's house and head inside with our bags, using the key Enzo gave me since both men are at the office for a change.

Despite my protests, Matteo organised a special event at *Decadence* for Halloween, and Scar made sure I had the whole weekend off from work, which Raph was not too happy about.

We both head straight upstairs, going our separate ways on the top floor. I drop my things off in Enzo's room and have a quick shower, changing into bike shorts and one of Enzo's t-shirts, before heading for the kitchen.

My phone rings, Claudine flashing on the screen, and I listen to her chatter about the birthday brunch she organised for Sunday as I turn on the oven and pull out the ingredients for dinner. Every year on my birthday, I feel out of place, so usually I spend the night cooking up a storm to avoid thinking about it.

It doesn't help that my mother likes to remind me how much my presence irritates her every year, but surprisingly, she hasn't even sent a message this time. Maybe she's truly cutting me out of my life?

I doubt it.

I lay the cut-up vegetables on a tray, drizzle oil over and season them before putting them in the oven, and start making the herb crust for the lamb racks. I fall into that sweet, calm headspace that cooking always puts me into as I continue to work, almost missing the murmurs of deep voices through the house.

"Did you hire a chef?" I hear Matteo ask.

"That's signature Del cooking you're smelling," Scar announces proudly as she bounds into the kitchen, followed closely by Matteo and Enzo.

Despite being here every day for the last month, the sight of Enzo still sends my heart sputtering and my body reacting in wicked ways. He loosens his tie at the collar as he stalks towards me, pulling me into his arms and kissing me like he didn't just fuck me this morning.

I pull back, breathless. "Hi."

"Marry me," he asks for the thousandth time.

I smile. "Maybe."

"Tease."

"Impatient."

He smirks, eyes dancing with humour. He places a small black bag on the counter and brushes his lips over mine softly. "Happy birthday."

I narrow my gaze, grabbing the lapel of Enzo's suit jacket. "What did I say about gifts?"

"You're beautiful when you try to assert control."

"I'm not accepting whatever it is."

Enzo's chest rumbles with laughter as he swats me on the ass and walks away, leaving the bag, with Matteo following behind him. Scar skips over and hoists herself onto the counter next to the bag, peering in.

"Open it," she says, her legs kicking out in excitement.

"No," I grit out, opening the oven and sticking a meat thermometer into the lamb.

"Come on," she whines, nudging the bag. "You know you want to."

I close the oven with a huff and set a timer before washing my hands and eyeing the offensive bag. Scar continues to swing her legs, her giddy energy pulsing off her as she waits for me to cave. I approach the bag like it's going to bite me and carefully undo the ribbon, then reach in and feel a small rectangular box.

"I swear to God if this is jewellery, I'm going to make *him* wear it," I mutter, pulling out the box and setting it on the counter. Scar pulls out a card and hands it to me. I read the handwritten note.

Think of me when you use it.
—Enzo

"I'm going to punch him straight in the face if this is a sex toy—"

The most beautiful switchblade I've ever seen sits nestled in silk. The whole thing is matte black, sleek and lethal. The handle has a deep purple stone glittering at the base and the initials *'DH'* engraved just above it.

"DH?" Scar asks, her eyes focused on the blade.

"*Herrington*," I clarify, a smile tugging at lips. "Presumptuous asshole."

Scar laughs, hopping off the bench and stretching. "You love it."

405

I roll my eyes as I close the lid of the box, putting it back into the bag and moving it to the side bench. "Go tell those two that dinner is ready."

I turn back to the task at hand as Scar disappears, collecting plates and setting them across the counter, trying my hardest to ignore the warmth spreading through my chest.

Enzo's stupid gift couldn't be more perfect.

The timer goes off, and I start serving out the food as everyone returns to the kitchen. Matteo and Enzo each collect two plates as Scar pulls two bottles of champagne from the fridge and champagne flutes from the cupboard.

I wrap the remaining plate for Lucas, putting it in the fridge before stacking the dirty trays and washing my hands before joining everyone at the table next to Enzo.

"Listen, if you don't marry Enzo, you're going to *have* to marry me," Matteo says, eyeing his food like he's never eaten in his life.

"I'll think about it," I say, biting down on a smile as Enzo stiffens next to me. It's not just Matteo who now likes to push this man's buttons.

Scar pops the champagne without taking out anyone's eye, and we fall into a comfortable conversation as we eat. Lucas finally shows up as we're clearing the table and I insist he sit down as I reheat his food and serve him before we all disappear upstairs to get ready.

I don't get more than a few steps across Enzo's room before the door is closed behind me and I'm pulled against a warm body.

"Did you like my gift?" Enzo rumbles, his lips brushing my ear.

"I think you gave me the wrong gift; the engraving was for a 'DH'."

Enzo sinks his teeth into the flesh just under my ear, the sting flooding my veins with desire. "It's definitely for you."

"Pretty sure my initials are—" Enzo spins me and grabs my chin before I can finish my remark.

Determined, lust-drunk eyes pierce through to my soul. "You *are* going to be my wife, Del."

"And if I say no?"

A feral smile curves his tempting lips. "I will keep you here until you say yes."

"Oh, really?" I arch a brow. "How exactly do you plan on doing that?"

Enzo steps forward, forcing me to step back, and continues until the back of my legs are pressed into the bed, his hand travelling down to grab my ass.

"I have some ideas," he murmurs before lifting me and dropping me in the middle of the bed—it still amazes me every time he lifts me like I weigh nothing.

Enzo kneels on the mattress, spreading my thighs wide and draping them over his, grabbing the waistband of my shorts when his phone buzzes in his pocket under my thigh.

I chuckle. "What did we say about business calls in the bedroom?"

Enzo frowns, digging out the phone, keeping one hand on my thigh. "Only Creed has this number; he knows not to call unless it's urgent." He flips the screen of the old generation flip phone, bringing it to his ear. "This better be important."

He listens for a few seconds, the hand on my thigh gripping me a little tighter.

"Fuck," he growls through clenched teeth, looking down at me. "Bring him to the church alive. We'll meet you there in a couple hours." He flips the phone closed and tosses it on the bed, running his free hand through his hair. "We have to take care of some business before we head for *Decadence*."

The fact he says 'we' does funny things to my heart. I lift onto my elbows. "Why the church?"

Enzo holds out his hands, helping into a sitting position, as he slides off the bed, heading for his wardrobe. "It's neutral ground for the bikers, plus the priest is part of my payroll and won't ask questions."

My mouth falls open. "The poor man we almost traumatised in that confessional is one of *yours*?"

Enzo chuckles, peeling his shirt off and working on his belt. "Father Michael is a family friend."

Heat blasts across my face. "Sweet fucking Jesus."

"Might want to watch that blasphemous language around the priest," Enzo calls as he disappears into the bathroom.

I don't bother looking up from my history book as the door opens.

"Are you guys fu—Delphine Evelyn Blaire, are you *studying* right now?"

"Our exam is next week," I say, immersed in the development of architecture in the Roman era.

The book suddenly disappears from in front of me on the bed and dull pain blooms across my bicep.

"Dick," I bark as I rub where she hit me with the textbook. I look up and gape at her outfit—she looks stunning in a blue fairy costume, the dress falling to her knees, fitted to perfection and small iridescent wings shimmering behind her. Her make-up matches her dress, blue and glittery, making her big, brown doe eyes appear even larger.

"You look so beautiful," I say, mesmerised by the whole look.

She tosses the book on the desk and puts both hands on her cinched waist. "Get your ass off the bed and let's get moving; it's almost nine."

I roll off the bed and adjust my dress. It's all black, tight around the bust, with a plunging neckline and long sleeves, and quite short, about mid-thigh, but I'm wearing a gauzy long skirt with two high slits over the top.

"Help me with my wings," I say, crossing to the small black feather wings and handing them to Scar. She holds them in place and passes the leather harness straps over my shoulder and around my waist. Once I've fastened all the buckles, I adjust it one more time and turn to Scar.

She smiles. "Fallen angel, indeed. Enzo is going to have a hard time letting you leave the house."

"He could try," I say as I readjust a pin in my black and emerald green curls.

Scar waits until I've tied up my combat boots before handing me my small clutch bag and phone as we leave the room. We meet the Herringtons in the foyer and I try my hardest not to gape.

Matteo is dressed in a sapphire suit, embroidered with silver threaded patterns down the lapels and a matching silver crown.

"Prince Charming," I muse as he loops Scar's arm through his, "how appropriate."

"Baby, I'm a *King*," he clarifies.

Scar rolls her eyes, patting his chest. "Yeah, yeah, big boy."

"We'll see you guys there," Matteo calls over his shoulder as he steers Scar out of the house.

I turn back to Enzo and try to remember to breathe. He's dressed in a fitted, deep crimson suit with a black shirt and tie. Two small horns jut out from his neatly style hair, and he's kept his facial hair longer than usual, giving him a ruthless edge.

"Didn't anyone tell you it's a costume party?" I ask, a little breathless. "You're not supposed to go as yourself."

He gives me a devilish smile, his cerulean eyes sparking in heat. "You look like sin."

"You should see what's underneath."

Enzo takes a step forward. "Are you tempting the Devil, sweetheart?"

"Is it working?" I ask as I turn on my heel and walk out the door.

THIRTY NINE

DEL

ST. JOHN'S CHURCH IS still as beautiful as it was the night I walked in and met the Devil at my side.

We walk in with our hands twined together, towards a small group gathered near the altar. Creed and two of his biker friends stand around a man tied to a chair, and a priest, I'm assuming Father Michael, stands on the other side.

I didn't know what to expect from the priest, but I didn't expect a tall, muscular, *very* attractive man who looks around Enzo's age. He's both intimidating and welcoming, and I really can't work out how.

"He'd look like one of your henchmen if not for the clerical collar," I murmur softly to Enzo, taking in Father Michael's impeccable black suit.

"He used to be."

I turn to Enzo. "Really?"

He nods, but something dark flashes in his eyes as he continues to stare forward. "Just don't ask him about it."

Now I'm curious. Of course, I'm more curious about a priest and not the beaten-up man tied to a chair surrounded by criminals. I should *really* call that psychiatrist.

Creed turns to us as we approach. The usual mischievous glint in his honey-brown eyes is gone, replaced with the cold glare of an outlaw. He doesn't say anything as he looks at Enzo, giving him a stiff nod before turning back to the man.

The guy has a busted lip and a cut on his cheek, blood and sweat dribbling down his face. But his eyes, so dark they look black, glare with hot fury at Enzo as he tries to pull out of his restraints and spits blood on the floor.

Something about his insolence makes me step in front of Enzo, drawing the man's surprised attention.

"Who are you?" I ask.

"Why would I tell Herrington's whore?" he spits.

I feel the air stir behind me, but I strike my arm out, stopping Enzo from murdering him immediately. Shockingly, he pauses.

"You don't know me, but you know Enzo," I say, closing the distance between us. "So you probably know that this will go quicker if you answer my questions."

He scoffs. "Why would I want to die quicker?"

I stand in front of him, our legs almost touching, and cross my arms, glaring down at him. I can hear the tremor in his breathing as he looks up at me confused. He's got a mouth on him, but he's not *that* brave. He's the one strapped to a chair with the city's predators waiting to tear him apart.

I smile. "Now, if you're a good boy, I can convince them to let you live."

Hope flashes fast in his gaze, but he quickly buries it by furrowing his brows further. "I'm not stupid. I'll be dead before sunrise."

"What's your name?" I ask again, my tone even.

He grinds his teeth, defiant as ever, but he must realise I'm not going anywhere, so he sighs, closing his eyes, his body relaxing slightly. "Ash."

"Why are you here?"

He doesn't move.

I grab his jaw, forcing him to open his eyes to me. "I asked a question, Ash."

Nothing.

I sigh and release his jaw. "Fine."

I step back, twist my body to walk away, but he jerks forward. "Wait, stop. I'll... Creed thinks I had something to do with the stolen shipment."

I turn back and raise a brow at him. "And did you?"

"No, I didn't, I wouldn't."

I tilt my head, contemplating, stepping to my right, slowly circling him. "Why should I believe you?"

"Enzo is the fucking Devil. No one who wants to keep his life would double-cross him, and I like breathing."

He's not wrong. "Why does Creed think you were involved?"

I'm behind him now, but I can hear him let out a shaky breath. "I...I don't know."

I chuckle softly, stepping back in front of him. "You're lying to me, Ash."

"No. Shit. Okay, I stole drugs. But they were for me. I'm an addict, and a thief, but I didn't tip anyone off." His pleading eyes dart from me to Creed on my right and then back to Enzo, as he breathes heavily. His fear rolls through me, igniting my adrenaline. I feel like I'm high.

I look over to Creed—he's got his hands in his pants pockets, and a shit-eating grin back on his face. Those honey-brown eyes dart to me, and he nods for me to continue.

I turn back to Ash. "Do you know who did?"

"No, but I don't think it was any of the Herrington or Savage Wings guys."

"Why do you say that?"

Ash swallows a few times, his eyes darting around the room again, before focusing back on me. "I've heard... some things."

I sigh. "You're boring me with your half-answers." I walk back to Enzo, and push my back into his front, annoyed that I have wings on that prevent me from feeling all of him pressed against me. "Maybe you need more persuasion?"

Ash flinches as Creed's men step forward. "Wait, wait, *wait*. I'll only talk to her."

Something smooth presses into my palm and I look to see my new switchblade being pushed into my hand. I look up at Enzo's face—feral, dark energy vibrates off him as he leans down and plants a possessive kiss on my lips.

"Show me what you got, little siren," he whispers against my lips before nudging me toward Ash.

The telltale *snick* draws Ash's attention to my hand, and he starts to struggle against his restraints again. Having this man's life in my hands is *exhilarating*—I've never felt so much control in my life.

I make a shushing sound as I step around Ash, and lean over his right shoulder. "If you want to live, convince me with your information."

"What if it's not enough?" he heaves out, still struggling against the restraints.

"You never know until you tell me."

"Promise me—"

Ash's pleas are cut off by my blade pressing into his neck. Despite whatever information he has, this back and forth is getting tedious. "You're ruining my birthday, so please stop begging and start talking."

I can feel a tremor run through Ash's body. "I heard Raph's guys talking about how the Navarros are trying to make a play for territory in Melbourne."

Someone's trying to disturb the balance in the city. Sharp, hot possession lances through my chest. Enzo might own this city, but he's *mine*, and no one will ever take him from me.

I look up at Enzo. He's deep in thought with his arms crossed over his chest and his eyes fixed on Ash. In his devil costume, he looks terrifying.

"You knew this at the time of the warehouse hit?" Father Michael asks.

I forgot he was here, but now he's stolen my attention again. His voice is deep, soothing even, but the focus in his eyes and the sharp tone of his question screams ex-henchman.

"I didn't want you to think I had anything to do with it," Ash rushes out, aiming his words at Enzo.

Enzo's hard stare doesn't waver as he continues to look at Ash. The anticipation must be excruciating to experience when your life is on the line. I keep my knife to Ash's throat, waiting for Enzo's final decision.

Enzo finally looks up at me and nods once—he doesn't need to say anything. Ash realises his fate and starts hyperventilating.

"Well, this was fun," Creed says in a bored tone, pulling out a gun from his waistband and stepping up to my side. "You might want to go now, Siren, this part gets a bit messy."

I lift my head and glare at Creed as I push the blade into Ash's throat. It takes little effort to sink the whole thing in to the hilt, and Ash starts making gurgling sounds as blood fills his throat.

Creed's eyes dart to my hand and then back to me, a wild energy glowing in his eyes, his mouth popping open slightly, those snake-bite piercings glinting in the warm church lights.

I pull out the blade swiftly and step back, not wanting to get blood all over me. "You're welcome."

Creed chuckles, walking across to Enzo and clapping him on the shoulder, his two biker buddies following closely behind him. "You two are fucking made for each other."

Enzo doesn't say anything as Creed leaves, his focus still on Ash. He's clearly not happy about what information he learned tonight. I let Enzo brood and turn to Father Michael.

"Who are the Navarros?" I ask softly.

"Colombian cartel," Father Michael answers as he holds out a handkerchief. "You must be Delphine."

I nod, taking the cloth and wiping my blade. "Just Del."

Father Michael's dark eyes are intense to meet—almost like they're seeing the sins that stain your soul. My cheeks warm, and my eyes drop from his, catching on the faint discolouration of scarring on his neck peeking out from his collar on his deep brown skin. I wonder what happened to him to get that scar?

I quickly finish wiping my blade and push it into my bra.

"I can have this washed and brought back to you," I offer as I hold the soiled handkerchief up, not able to look at the priest in the eye again.

His large hand covers mine—it's warm, and slightly rough. His touch draws my gaze back to his face. "No need. I'm going to dispose of it with the body."

"Do you... need help with that?"

Father Michael smiles. "We can manage."

Before I can ask, Lucas appears from somewhere and tilts the chair that Ash's dead body is still strapped down to. Father

Michael grabs two legs of the chair and they both lift, carrying the body further into the church.

"Who's going to clean the blood from the floor?" I ask, staring at the mess. I thought there would be more, but most of it was on Ash.

An arm wraps across my chest and I'm pressed into a warm body. Citrus and spice swirls around me as Enzo plants a soft kiss on the tip of my ear and I feel my soul relax.

"Did you know," I murmur, my voice distant even to my ears, "that most churches are designed in the shape of a cross?" I point to the two small wings of pews on the sides of the dais. "Those areas are called transepts."

I turn in Enzo's arms, looking up into hooded blue eyes. He doesn't say anything as he watches me.

"I... killed someone."

Enzo nods once in response.

Murder. A grave sin in the eyes of the Lord. And I did it in front of a priest. Laughter bubbles out of my chest, echoing in the silent sanctuary.

"I'm going to Hell," I whisper, more to myself than Enzo.

"We'll be going together."

His words settle the manic energy pulsing through my veins. My life might be forever tainted by the atrocities I've committed in my life, but at least I have a home in the arms of the Devil.

Home.

Emotions I never thought I'd feel for another person burns through my chest. They're a consuming fire, making it hard for me to breathe. That same fire seems to burn in Enzo's eyes as he holds my gaze, *seeing* me. Desire licks over my skin as his eyes turn molten.

He grabs my hand and pulls me towards the left transept. He sits on the last pew in the darkest corner of the church, and then pulls me into his lap, my back pressed into the pew in front of us.

"Grab the pew behind you," he instructs as he pushes my skirt all the way up over my hips, exposing my new lace panties.

"Christ, woman," Enzo growls as he admires the lace.

"Language."

His eyes burn hot as his thumb strokes over his scarred initial in my thigh before skimming down and under my panties, pressing into my clit. I gasp at the contact, a tremor running through my body.

"Now," Enzo drawls, his gaze holding mine captive as his thumb circles over my clit. "You're going to be a good girl and come for me."

"Here?" I ask, my arms starting to tremble at the effort to keep them where they are.

"Don't make me ask twice." His warning tone pours more fuel on the pleasure coursing through my veins, a devastating orgasm already building low in my stomach at his constant pressure.

I tip my head back and close my eyes, feeling *everything*, and trying to hold in the whimpers aching in my chest. I climb higher, my body growing hot and clenching hard, desperate to be filled. As if he could hear my body's plea, Enzo sinks two fingers into me, and I choke on a moan. His fingers move fast, relentlessly, and I come hard, slamming a hand over my mouth to muffle my cries.

Enzo continues to stroke in and out of me, prolonging the high, completely obliterating my comprehension of space and time. He finally gives me a reprieve as he pulls his hands away from my sensitive body and swipes them over my bottom lip.

I taste my arousal and I tilt my head forward, opening my eyes to hooded cerulean irises.

"You look so fucking beautiful when you do what you're told."

I press my lips to his, swiping my tongue into his mouth, taking what's mine. Enzo sinks his teeth into my bottom lip, taking back control.

This is how it will always be, two broken beings challenging each other but always finding home, no matter the circumstances.

I get lost in the kiss, and in Enzo's roaming hands. He's always so warm, the palms of his hands slightly rougher than you'd expect of a man who dominates the corporate world. I wish I could run my hands through the light dusting of hair on his chest and over the scars scattered across his body. Touching him is fucking addictive.

Instead, my hands slip down his chest and find his belt, pulling the tongue out of the loops. Murmurs and footsteps echo through the church, making my hands freeze.

I pull back and peer over my shoulder, seeing a small group of elderly ladies filing into the pews halfway up the main part of the church.

"Why are people always interrupting my fun?" I mutter, making Enzo chuckle.

"Who said you had to stop?"

His question draws my attention, the challenge sparking in his eyes. My hands resume the unbuckling of his belt in response. Enzo grabs both my forearms and stands.

"Turn," he commands, and this time I follow immediately. It's a narrow pathway between pews, so as I turn and try not to fall on the kneeling bench below, I have to brush my whole body against Enzo.

Now with my back to him, I see Father Michael and another young looking priest entering through the far side of the church. Father Michael goes towards the church ladies, his deep voice a soft hum in the church, and the other priest puts a bucket down near the mess of blood.

Enzo's hands hook into my panties and slide them off my hips, letting them fall to the ground. As I step out of them, Enzo grabs a fistful of hair and pushes me forward, forcing me to bend over the pew and use both hands to stabilise myself.

"Spread those legs for me, sweetheart," Enzo whispers into my ear as I hear his zip going down. I step wide, shame nonexistent as I wait for Enzo's next move.

I can feel the head of his cock slide through my arousal. Enzo makes an approving sound. "Always so wet."

"Only for you."

Enzo leans over me, nipping at my earlobe. Pleasure shoots straight through my body from the sharp pain. "I believe we're here for the nightly Rosary service."

"Okay?" I breathe, pushing back against Enzo, needing him in me. I'm not opposed to begging at this point.

"Be a faithful, *pious* woman and start the Hail Mary," he breathes in my ear as he buries himself to the hilt in one thrust.

My toes curl at the almost painful fullness. And then Enzo starts to move, and my resolve begins to disintegrate. "H-hail Mary... full of—*fuck*." This angle is intense.

Enzo chuckles in my ear. "I don't think those are the words."

I grip the pew like it's my only salvation as he continues his slow, agonizing pace, making me feel every curved inch of him.

Enzo's hand slips into my hair, gripping it firmly and pulling me back toward him, changing the angle.

"Try again," he growls.

He thrusts again, making me choke. "Oh, *God*."

"What would he think of you now?" His free hand slips under my dress and presses into my clit. "Desecrating his place of worship by getting fucked by the Devil."

"Have mercy," I whisper.

"*Mercy?*" Enzo growls, his grip on my hair tightening. "There's no mercy for sinners like you."

He starts a punishing pace, the intensely full feeling ricocheting through my being. He fucks me like he's marking me, completely *owning* me—and he does. One of my hands travels down my body, my fingers join Enzo's, both of us feeling him take what's his.

"This cunt is *mine*," he growls into my ear.

"Yes," I croak out, my head spinning.

"Come for me, love."

I maneuver Enzo's finger over my clit, careening myself into a devastating orgasm. Enzo releases my hair as I come and covers my mouth, muffling my choked screams as he slams into me once more and stills as he joins me.

We both try to catch our breath, as his hand falls away from my mouth and he pulls me with him as he sits back down.

"We're going to give Father Michael a stroke if he finds out we keep fucking in his church," I say as I shift slightly.

Enzo grunts, stilling my movement. "I guess we shouldn't get caught then."

I huff out a laugh before Enzo helps me off his lap. I gasp as our mixed arousal slides down my leg.

"If I wasn't on birth control, I would definitely be pregnant by now," I mutter, as I aimlessly look for something to clean up the mess.

Enzo's fingers track up my thigh, catching the spend and then pushes two fingers back into me. My legs tremble as the sensations and the possessiveness.

"You shouldn't be wasteful," he chastises, moving his fingers lazily in and out of me.

Pleasure warms in my gut as he continues to work me into a frenzy, taking me to the edge but stopping before I can come again.

"Asshole," I huff as he chuckles, helping me back into my panties. He fixes up his own clothing as I fix up my skirts, and then we exit the pew.

As I wrap my arm around his and we walk past the altar, I check the time on his watch. Past midnight. I pull him to a stop at the step of the dais, pressing my body into his, looking into his beautifully confused face.

"Happy birthday," I whisper as I wrap my arms around his neck and stretch up to plant a soft kiss on his lips.

"Del, if you don't take those sinful lips off me," Enzo growls between me peppering him with kisses, "I'll end up fucking you over the altar."

I pull back, chuckling softly. "The church ladies are trying to pray; let's not scar them for life."

Enzo shrugs. "They'd probably enjoy the show."

I laugh a little louder as I smack him on the arm and receive a disapproving shushing sound from Father Michael.

Looking up into those bright cerulean pools, I say the word that I've wanted to say for a long time. "Yes."

Enzo frowns. "What?"

"Ask me again."

Realisation races through his eyes, his eyes impossibly brighter. Instead of saying the words, Enzo's hand sinks into his jacket pocket and produces a ring box.

I arch a brow. "On your knees, Mr. Herrington."

Wicked heat darkens his eyes. "Demanding little siren."

"Are you frail in your old age? Afraid you'll put your back out?"

I just know my ass is going to be purple tomorrow from the glint in Enzo's eyes as he slowly sinks to the floor.

But he doesn't get on one knee; instead he wraps his arm around the back of my thighs and hoists me onto his shoulder. I let out a shriek as he storms off down the church aisle and out into the night.

"Put me down," I huff as we reach the church gates under the streetlights.

He obliges me and sets me on my feet, keeping one arm wrapped around her waist. "You're a troublemaker."

I smile, straightening his tie. "I know."

"Marry me."

"Yes," I say without hesitation.

The box appears again and Enzo takes out the ring and slides it on.

"Jesus *Christ*, Enzo." I gape at the thing. It fits perfectly, which means he must have measured my size in my sleep or something. It's a sizeable rock cut into a hexagon with so many facets that it catches the light every time I move. It's set in what I'm going to assume is platinum, since silver seems too ordinary for Enzo. I notice that it isn't a clear diamond, but a pale blue.

"It's a blue diamond," Enzo says as if he's reading my mind. It's probably ridiculously expensive.

I look up into his face. "How long have you had this?"

"Just after I carved my initial onto your thigh."

His words bloom in my chest, but I swallow the soft smile wanting to spread across my face. "You know, a little slicing into someone's skin doesn't usually lead to marriage."

He raises a brow. "What does it usually lead to?"

"For someone of sound mind, filing an assault charge."

Enzo chuckles, resting his forehead on mine. "It's a good thing my woman is a little insane."

"Only for you."

FORTY

DEL

I WALK INTO *SEDUZIONE*, my hand shoved into my pocket.

Now that exams are over, Enzo insists I wear my engagement ring at all times—every time I consider taking it off, I hear his harsh, possessive tone in my head and roll my eyes.

I say hello to everyone I pass, heading straight for the staff room. Raph sent me a message last night letting me know there was a dinner upstairs, so I came in a little earlier to change into my uniform and do my make-up.

As I rummage through my backpack, I chuckle at my switchblade sitting at the bottom—Enzo must have slipped it in here before I left.

My phone buzzes on the counter as I'm finishing my make-up.

ENZO

> Are you wearing it?

I smirk.

> **The ring or the switchblade?**

ENZO

> You know which one I'm talking about.

In response, I take a photo of myself in the mirror, flipping him off with my left hand, so the beautiful, stunning and obnoxiously opulent stone glitters in the bathroom lights.

His response comes quickly.

ENZO

> That attitude will get you punished.

Desire heats my blood.

> **How bad would my punishment be if I took off my ring?**

ENZO

> Don't even think about it.

> **I'm thinking about it a lot now.**

ENZO

> Don't make me come down there. I'm sure you don't want a scene.

I roll my eyes, pouting at the phone.

> **Can I please take it off? I don't want it to get damaged.**

Enzo doesn't answer straight away, so I finish getting ready and pack up my bag. My phone buzzes as I'm putting my things away in my locker.

> **ENZO**
> Why are you trying to hide our engagement?

I sigh.

> Do you know how many questions I'm about to get?

> **ENZO**
> You can't hide it forever.

I hate that he's right.

> I know. I miss you. Enjoy your work dinner.

> **ENZO**
> I'll pick you up when I'm done.

Knowing I'll see Enzo after work clears some of my apprehension about the onslaught of questions about to come my way. I take a deep cleansing breath and then head for the staff dining room.

I manage to sit in a seat before a squeal ricochets through the space. Stella next to me grabs my hand, examining the ring as Florentina and Queenie lean over the table and gape.

"Who's the lucky guy?" Queenie asks.

"His name is Enzo," I murmur low.

"A good Italian boy?" Florentina questions.

"Uh, no, not Italian."

"Where did you meet him?" Stella asks, her attention still transfixed by the sparkling rock.

"Church," I say.

"He must have some money," Queenie surmises. "That ring looks *expensive*."

I clear my throat. "Yeah, you could say that."

The three women start talking about a bachelorette party as Mario walks in, followed by a couple of the other chefs carrying trays of food.

"What are you girls gossiping about?" Mario asks as he sets down a tray of *cotolette* in front of us.

Stella shoves my hand into Mario's view. "Del is getting married."

Surprise flashes on Mario's face as he takes in the ring. "*Madonna*, that's some ring."

I tug my hand out of Stella's grasp gently and tuck it under the table.

"Who names their son Enzo if they aren't Italian?" Florentina muses out loud across the table.

Mario's face sharpens, his usually warm demeanour stiffening. "Enzo? Herrington?"

The room settles into a tense silence. My eyes sweep the room—everyone's faces are frozen in shock and disbelief.

My eyes land on Raph in the doorway, holding a tablet and staring at me.

He is *livid*.

"My office, now," he says and walks out.

I sigh, pulling myself away from the silent table and follow him. I enter his dark office and lean against the wall next to the open door.

"Close it," he growls, putting the tablet down on the desk.

"I'd rather not."

Raph spins on his heel quickly and marches toward me. This is mob boss Raphael—intimidating and dangerous.

He catches the door with his hand as he approaches, slamming it shut. I rein in my flinch, readying myself to fight my way out of here if I need to.

He wrenches my left hand into view, his grey-hazel eyes almost glowing in fury as he heaves in oxygen. "Tell me this is a lie."

"If I did, *I* would be lying."

He looks down and sneers, then drops my hand like it burned him, and paces away from me. "Why Del? Why are you doing this?"

I scoff. "You say that like I'm doing it just to piss you off."

He turns back to me. "Are you?"

I frown. "No."

"Then why?"

"I can do whatever I want with my own life."

"He's a *murderer.*"

I huff out a laugh. So am I. "You keep reminding me like you aren't."

He *tsks*, scraping his hand through his hair. "That's different."

"Are you delusional?" I take one step toward, anger boiling in my blood. "How is it all that different? You are both criminals. Your businesses *feed* off each other, for fuck's sake. So, tell me, Raph, *how* is it different?"

Raph steps up to me, our bodies almost touching. "He will never care for you like *I* do. He's a piece of shit just like his father."

His hand lifts to touch my face, but I take two steps back out of his reach. "I would never hurt you like he would, Del. You're too important to me."

"I'm *'important'* to you?" I cross my arms over my chest. "You've *never* showed any interest, Raph, so why am I suddenly *so* important to you now? Do you want what you now can't have? Is that it?"

He sighs, his frown deepening. "I've always cared for you, Del. But I'm not a fucking pervert. And you were so skittish until six months ago. You don't think I noticed you never liked to be touched, and never wanted the attention? I didn't want to push you away before I even got a chance."

"You want to know what changed, Raphael?" A taunting grin spreads across my face. "Enzo happened."

Raphael's jaw tenses so hard that I'm surprised I don't hear his teeth crack. A few things flash through his eyes—jealousy and disappointment the prominent emotions.

"Are we done now?" I ask as I back up towards the door. I'm over this bullshit—maybe it *is* time that I leave *Seduzione*.

"If you go through with this farce," he says, warning in his tone, "don't expect me to be there to pick up the pieces."

I stop with my hand on the handle. "Even if this doesn't work out, I won't be begging you to save me."

♠

Ty and I work in silence to prep the bar and the mezzanine for tonight's clients. It's a mysterious table of four—this time it isn't the Herringtons, so I can only assume it's another one of Raphael's corrupt associates.

We have about ten minutes before they arrive, so I pour myself a gin and tonic.

"Drinking on the job is a big no-no," Ty observes with a smirk.

"Raphael can go fuck himself," I say with a smile, deciding to add more gin than normal.

Ty chuckles and pours himself a vodka and lemonade and we clink our glasses. I hear footsteps on the stairs as I refill my drink and stash it under the bar. I smooth my dress as I cross to the host podium. My smile is easy as my body buzzes slightly with my drink.

Raphael appears first with Jace close behind him, both at ease and laughing at something their guest said.

I see his brown hair first, neat and styled back. And then those dark brown eyes, sparkling with mirth. That soft mouth curved in a smile.

No...

No.

No no *no*.

This can't be happening.

He's supposed to be in prison.

No.

He stands next to Jace. I can't hear his words. I won't.

He's *here.* Here in an expensive-looking suit, laughing and smiling like it's any other day.

I feel tears sting my eyes, threatening to fall, and my heart beating like it's trying to escape my chest.

I need to go. Scream. Cry. Run. *Hide.*

I force oxygen in and out of my body so I don't pass out, and school my expression as much as I can as they turn toward me.

His eyes recognise me. They fall down my body. He's pleased at what he sees.

I swallow the bile crawling up my throat.

"Adrian, this is Del," Raphael announces.

"Adrian Garcia," he introduces himself. The voice that haunts my nightmares. The voice whispered disgusting sweet nothings in my ear, and the voice that threatened to end my life.

He smiles at me, brow arching slightly, his eyes burning with sick delight. "Is Del short for something?"

"Delphine," I say softly, my voice breaking slightly.

My mind is careening into a dark place I never wanted to be in ever again.

Keep it together, Del.

"*Delphine,*" he says, like he's tasting it on his tongue. "Such a beautiful name."

You have such pretty skin, Delphine.

Please don't make me hurt you like that, Delphine.

You will always feel me, Delphine.

I'm drowning in terror, frozen in place. I can't do this. I can't be here. *He* can't be here. God, please save me.

I manage to sweep my hand toward the table, tucking my left hand behind me, and the small party moves as one. I don't dare move from the host podium until everyone is seated.

I approach the table between Raph and Jace, taking the table's drink order, only just registering another Hispanic man at the table when he orders a scotch.

"Bourbon," Adrian practically purrs, "neat."

Bourbon. He doesn't even tell me the brand, because I *know*.

I breathe through the nausea and nod, then cross to the bar and input the order. My head swims, my vision going hazy in my periphery, and my hands shake as I reach for my drink. I down the whole thing before taking the tray of drinks Ty prepared and head for the table.

Pretend he's someone else.

Stay out of reach.

I serve all the drinks quickly without my hands shaking, take everyone's food order and return to the bar. I make myself another drink, this time just water, as I try to get myself together. I just need to get through this dinner and then I'm *never* coming back to this restaurant ever again.

An alert flashes on the ordering screen to say the food is coming up in the dumbwaiter, so I leave my drink on the bench and cross to the back of the room.

"I heard there was another attempt on Herrington's storage facility again?" Adrian asks Raph.

"They questioned one of the men, and they claimed he was in the organisation, but he's not one of mine," Raph responds.

They're talking about the man I killed in the church. Apparently, no one outside of who was there knew I was the one that conducted that particular interrogation.

"Hmm," Adrian muses as I get to the back of the room and face the table.

His eyes bore into me, like he *knows*.

Breathe, Del, just *breathe*.

Those eyes used to drip with desire and harden with contempt. Hazy with inebriation, or stone cold sober—these are the eyes of my worst fucking nightmares.

I drop my gaze to the floor. Air in, air out.

"So there's another player in the city?" Adrian asks.

"Must be," Jace concludes as I hear the dumbwaiter click into place.

"The Navarros won't like that," Adrian comments as I take the plates, steeling my spine and marching over to deliver the food.

I'm quick and out of reach. If he touches me, I don't know what I'll do.

I escape back to the bar and grasp my drink, trying to find salvation in a simple glass of water.

A cool hand lands on my forearm, and I flinch back, pouring the drink all over myself.

"Shit, sorry, Del," Ty says, grabbing a clean cloth and passing it over.

I put the empty glass down and take the cloth, wiping at my chest and dabbing at the tank top I'm wearing under my dress.

"It's fine, I'm fine," I murmur, more to myself than to him. "I'm not feeling well, Ty. I think I should go. Can you finish on your own?"

He nods, concern in his gaze. "Yeah, go, I'll cover you."

I whisper my appreciation and walk calmly across the floor. I don't stop walking until I close the door behind me in the staff room.

I collapse onto my hands and knees, sobbing uncontrollably.

He's out. *Out*. He's out, and he's seen me.

I hyperventilate. My chest aches.

I'm dying.

I scramble off the floor and run to the bathroom, emptying my stomach into the toilet. Sweat breaks out over every part of my body.

After the heaving stops, I flush and collapse onto the floor, curling my arms around my knees. Tears stream down my face as my mind falls deeper into the darkest parts I've kept caged for so long.

The debilitating, horrifying memories dig their filthy claws into my soul—trying to tear it apart, and take the few morsels of good left in me and desecrate them.

Soft buzzing echoes in the room. It's soft and incessant. My phone.

I pull it out of my dress pocket and see 'Matteo' on the screen.

"Hey," he says as I answer, "I know you're at work, but—"

"Help me," I whisper, my voice hoarse.

He's silent for a moment, and then a sound of movement and a motorcycle rumbles in the background. "Creed is coming. Where are you?"

"Work," I choke out. "*Please*, help me."

"He'll be there before you know it."

"Why aren't you coming?"

"I would, but I'm dealing with some business shit right now. Creed will be faster, anyway."

I take a little sip of air, feeling a little better knowing someone is coming. "Okay."

"Don't move from where you are until Creed contacts you. I'll give him your number."

"Okay," I whisper again.

"I'll see you at home," he promises.

"Okay."

"I have to go. Wait for Creed."

I nod, even though he can't see me and hang up.

Shit, if he tells Enzo... I send Matteo a quick message.

> Don't tell Enzo. He'll freak out.

He answers almost immediately.

MATTEO

> He'll be pissed if I don't tell him.

I sigh.

> I don't need him arrested or dead right now.

MATTEO

What the fuck happened?

I'll tell you at home.

I pull myself off the floor and cross to the sink, putting my phone on the counter and looking in the mirror. My face is a mess—there's mascara tracking down my face, and my face is blotchy and red.

I crack open the door of the bathroom, make sure there's no one in the staff room, and dart over to my locker. I pull my backpack and go back to the bathroom, locking the door behind me.

I change into my jeans and the hooded jumper I found buried in Enzo's closet. His citrus and spice scent wraps around me, settling some of the panic running rampant in my body, and letting me take my first proper breath since *he* walked into the restaurant.

I take a makeup wipe and remove the remnants of my panic attack off my face when my phone buzzes on the counter. I pick it up and read the message.

UNKNOWN

It's Creed. I'll be out front in less than ten.

Park out the back.

I save his number.

I put everything back into my bag and go back into the main staff area. I empty my locker contents into my bag, neatly fold my uniform and leave it in there with the door open, and leave.

I say goodbye to everyone I see as I make my way to the back door. I feel bad that this will be the last time these wonderful people see me, but there's no way in hell I'm stepping foot in here again when *he* knows I work here.

I step out into the cool November night, staying in the glow of the lights so I know the cameras can see me.

It hits me—if Adrian is Raphael's import connection, the one that he and Enzo had at that first dinner, then he's been out of prison for a minimum of six months. And he mentioned the Navarros; he must work for them.

He might know about my relationship with Enzo.

"Fuck," I whisper up to the night sky.

"Such foul language, Kitty."

My heart seizes in my chest. My head whips to the left and Adrian appears from the darkness, blocking the door back into the restaurant. *Fuck*.

"Why did you leave dinner, Kitty?" he croons.

"Don't call me that," I manage to say. Why the fuck is my switchblade at the bottom of my bag right now and not easily accessible?

He takes a step forward and I retreat. He pouts. "Don't be like that, Kitty. I just wanted to see you—it's been so long."

He's known this whole time where I worked. He *knew*. Does he know where I live? Oh, God.

"H-how long have you been out?"

His hand caresses his tie, drawing my attention down to it. Those hands hurt me in so many ways. "Almost a year."

Almost a *year*? "How?"

He smiles, taking another step forward. I know what he's doing—I either retreat into the dark, away from the cameras, or he'll be close enough to touch me.

Creed is coming. He's coming *soon*. I just need to hold on for a few more minutes.

"I was a good man in prison—a model prisoner, they said." He steps closer again, and his scent wafts over to me.

His usual expensive cologne. And *bourbon*.

I try not to gag as memories of that stench all over me plagues me.

Creed is coming.

His eyes flick to my neck. "You aren't wearing your rosary beads."

"I destroyed them."

Anger flashes through his eyes. "It seems like you haven't been a very good girl while I've been gone."

His large hand wraps around my left wrist, his grip painful. He jerks me forward, closer to him, as he lifts my hand and inspects the ring.

"Herrington has very good taste," he muses, tilting my hand this way and that.

"Let me go," I say weakly. Damn it.

His eyes turn to mine. "Why? Because Lorenzo will hurt me for touching you?"

"He will kill you."

Adrian chuckles, the sound grating on my senses. "Have you not told him that you're already claimed, Kitty?"

"I-I'm not—"

He *tsks*. "You'll always belong to me, *mi niña*."

I feel a tear track down my face. "No."

He brushes the tear away with his thumb so gently. The tender touch ignites a fury in me that I've never felt.

This man broke me in so many ways. I should be dead by now, but I'm not. I'm still breathing, and I won't let him take that away from me.

"Take your hands *off* me," I say through clenched teeth and tug at my hand hard.

He releases me and chuckles. "There are the claws I've heard so much about."

"If you value your life, you will never touch me again."

He frowns in disappointment. "You should know by now not to threaten me."

"Fuck you, Adrian."

He goes still, his gaze hardening to cold nothingness. He's *angry*. "I was going to do this the nice way, but it seems like you've become a feral Kitty while I was gone."

He jolts forward, his hands out to grab my arms, as a loud rumble of a motorcycle echoes through the street. Headlights make Adrian squint and I take the distraction to get out of his reach, turning to Creed approaching at a worrying speed.

That's when I see the other Hispanic man from earlier standing against the building. He was hiding in the shadows *very* close to me. Was Adrian about to take me?

Creed stops right in front of me, pulling off his helmet. Rage practically radiates off him as he stares at Adrian. "What the *fuck* is going on here?"

I rush over to Creed's side. "Get me out of here."

He keeps his eyes on Adrian as he passes me the helmet he was wearing. I shove it on, and swing onto the back of the bike, and crush myself into Creed's back.

"I hope you were ready for war with the Herringtons, Adrian," Creed warns.

Adrian isn't fazed at all by the threat. He smiles at me. "I'll see you soon, Kitty."

FORTY ONE

— Q —
♠

DEL

CREED PULLS UP IN *Luxuria's* driveway, and I slide off his bike on shaky legs.

"Are you sure you're okay?" he asks, accepting his helmet back.

I nod, giving him a small smile. "Thank you for coming."

He frowns, concern across his face. "Will you tell me what I just saw?"

My heart stutters. "Not right now."

He nods, resigned. "You have my number. Call me if you need *anything*. At any time."

"Thanks, Creed." I walk into *Luxuria*, my heart frantic, my mind dizzy.

I approach the front desk, bypassing the line, the attendant immediately gives me a key without a word, and I make my way to the elevators, pulling out my phone.

> I'm coming up now.

ENZO

> You're here already. What happened?

> I'll tell you when I get upstairs.

ENZO

> We still have company.

Fuck, of all days to have someone follow him from the benefit to beg for something.

I make it to the top floor, swiping the key on the door and push through the heavy door. Familiar laughter filters through the apartment as I approach the living area to find Enzo with my mother and William. They all turn to me as I cross to Enzo's side.

"Delphine, darling," my mother drawls, "I didn't expect you to be here."

Before I can answer, Isaac appears from the direction of the kitchen with a bottle of wine and a handful of wine glasses. He's back from his mysterious departure. I turn my attention back to my mother.

"Why are you here?" I ask.

"The Andersons wanted to discuss business," Enzo answers, his arm slipping around my waist, daring someone to question my presence again.

I soak in his warmth, letting it ground me. He can tell something is wrong as he tightens his grip around me.

"You said at the benefit that you wanted to renegotiate our arrangement?" Enzo directs at William.

"We have appreciated the Herrington backing on Anderson Technologies when we were just a start-up, but," William hesitates, looking at his wife, my mother nodding encouragingly. "But we feel like it's time for us to part ways."

"You make millions a month globally under the Herrington Global banner and now you want to go solo?"

"We feel that it's best for the company to leave the nest, if you will," my mother says with that blinding, fake positivity. She's a poisonous viper disguised as a doting wife, covered in jewels.

"Did you know?" I blurt out, staring at my mother.

Her eyes are wide in question. "Excuse me?"

"Did you *know*?"

Her brow furrows in confusion. "Are you feeling okay, darling?"

"He's out of prison," I seethe. "He got out almost a *year* ago. So, I ask again, did you fucking *know*?"

"Mind your language, Delphine," she chastises.

"Answer the question, Eleanor."

We stare at each other for a few silent moments, neither of us backing down. She finally sighs, adjusting her thin, gold designer watch. "I did."

"What?" Isaac asks, disbelief and anger across his face as he places the wine and glasses down on the dining table.

"Maybe we should have this conversation elsewhere," William pipes in.

"Why does it even matter?" my mother asks, annoyance across her face.

I laugh, the sound wrong. "You're fucking kidding me, right?"

446

"Delphine—"

"You didn't think it was important to inform me, the person he victimised—"

"Victim?" she scoffs.

"Mum," Isaac breathes, stepping closer to me.

She frowns at him. "What? You believe what she said all those years ago?"

I look at William's confused expression. "What did she tell you about her last husband?"

"That he was violent, and she divorced him," he mutters.

"That's all?" I ask.

"Delphine," my mother huffs, "we don't need to—"

"Oh no, Eleanor, we *definitely* need to. What was the reason she told you we don't talk anymore?"

"She said you had a..."

"An abortion at fifteen? I'm sure your righteous cock got hard at her decision to shun me for that."

"No, I—"

"Did she tell you her ex-husband was in prison for putting me in that position in the first place?"

The room is eerily quiet at my revelation. Enzo is so still next to me that my survival instincts scream for me to run. The Devil is pushing to the surface, and about to unleash carnage.

I didn't want to tell him any of this, didn't want him to see me differently, but the words start to pour out of me.

"When I told her, she slapped me so hard she left a bruise, and blamed me for why he hadn't wanted to touch her for so long. She also tried to convince the police that I was lying about the abuse. Then tried to stop me from getting the abortion, by trying to get me committed to a mental ward."

I laugh again, the sound dripping with disdain. "She probably also didn't tell you when those tactics didn't work, she curled up in bed for days because she knew the only choice to save face was to divorce him. God forbid, those gossips found out your wayward daughter was pregnant out of wedlock. Or thought you were fine with your husband raping your daughter."

I should feel bad for blowing up William's life, but I really don't. His face is frozen in horror, staring blankly at me. No one seems to be breathing, but I feel like I can *truly* breathe for the first time in a long time.

"That outburst was unnecessary," my mother chastises.

"You have two hours," William says, his eyes turning to my mother, "two hours to pack your things and leave. I will have divorce papers and custody papers emailed from my lawyer."

"William, honey—"

"You will never have contact with Bridgette ever again," William's voice is cold and hollow.

"You better run and hide, Eleanor," Enzo says, that dangerous tone ringing in my ears. This was the Devil talking. "Disappear from the face of this earth because I have people everywhere, and they will be instructed to end your life."

My heart aches; a man as terrifying and as dangerous as Enzo should be the exact opposite of safe, but I've never felt this at ease in my entire life.

I lean further into him, sneering at my mother's shocked face. "Clock's ticking, Eleanor. You should go while you still can."

Tears slip down her face as she shuffles away as fast as her skirt allows and slams the door behind her. Enzo runs a soothing touch down my arm as I start to tremble.

"Del," Isaac murmurs, stepping closer again. "I had no idea. About any of that."

I shrink back as he reaches out, my eyes dropping to his shoes. "Get out."

"Del—"

"Go, please."

He sighs, then his shoes disappear from sight. William murmurs something about setting up a meeting with Enzo another day, and then the penthouse is quiet.

I move to step away from Enzo, but he doesn't let go. All the adrenaline drains from me, my mind spinning, the edges of my vision blurring. I turn in Enzo's arms and bury my face in his chest, gripping on the lapels of his tuxedo jacket to stop myself from falling to the floor.

I drown in Enzo's spiced grapefruit and sandalwood scent as anger and anguish pours through my veins. I can feel a scream or a sob choke me as tears threaten to spill. If I cry again, I don't think I'll ever stop.

"Sweetheart—"

"I can't," I cut in before he says something that will set me off.

Enzo leans back, grabbing my chin gently and tilting my face up, forcing me to look at him.

So many things cross those cerulean blue eyes.

So many things said and unsaid between us.

"Give me a name," he demands, his voice so, *so* low.

My lip trembles, but I hold it together. "Don't make me say it."

His jaw clenches. "Do I know him?"

I nod.

Enzo frowns. "How?"

"Import," I choke.

Realisation flares in Enzo's eyes. "Adrian?"

I nod again, his name turning my stomach.

Fury hardens Enzo's face. "He's dead."

He moves to step away from me, but I cling to his jacket, stopping him. "Don't."

"He doesn't deserve to breathe."

"He's willing to do anything to get what he wants."

Enzo's hand moves from chin into my hair, gripping a handful firmly but not painfully. "And I'll do anything for you."

I frown. "I'm not willing to lose you."

"You won't."

"I *will*."

Enzo smirks. "Did you forget you're marrying the Devil? I own this city."

I blow out a breath, untangling myself from Enzo's hold, and start to pace. "He's not one of your little demons you can command. He's a bomb ready to detonate. And this time he has the cartel as back-up."

"I can—"

"Do not tell me you will start a bloodbath for me. I won't have it."

Enzo's hand wraps around my wrist and tugs me into him again, halting my pacing. "If I want to start a fucking war to eradicate the despicable human that put his hands on a child, especially because that child was *you*, then I fucking will."

"Why?"

"Because you're the only thing that matters."

He means every word, he always does.

I sigh, resting my forehead against his chest. "I fucking hate him."

"We'll get rid of him together, like I promised."

"Slowly," I murmur, "and painfully."

"That's my girl."

I take another lungful of his scent and then step out of his reach. "We have to play this smart."

"Does Raphael know your history with the dead man?"

I shrug. "I don't know. Adrian approached me outside."

Enzo's eye narrow. "He did *what*?"

Commotion in the hallway halts my explanation and snags both of our attention as the door slams open.

Creed stumbles in, basically carrying Matteo. His hands grips his left side, dark red blooming across his white shirt from where his hand tries to staunch a wound.

I run towards him, not able to catch him before both he and Creed collapse to the floor. The blood is hot and sticky as I press both of my hands hard against Matteo's.

He winces and then his eyes roll back.

"Teo? Teo!"

Enzo sinks down next to me, tapping his brother's face. "What the fuck happened?"

Matteo's eyes open, his gaze hazy on his brother. "A-Ambush."

"Full shoot-out at the warehouse," Creed pants. I can see in my periphery that he's gripping his shoulder as it bleeds.

Blood gurgles out of Matteo's mouth and his breathing shutters under me. *No.*

"Matteo, don't you dare fucking die," I mutter, pressing further into his wound. "You can't go. I won't let you."

The sound of Enzo shouting on the phone for an ambulance fizzles to the background when Matteo grips my hand tight.

I look into his beautiful dark blue eyes, so similar to his brother's. The ghost of his signature cocky smile softens his face.

"Look after him for me," he whispers before he stops breathing.

ACKNOWLEDGEMENTS

It has been an absolute journey. Thank you for coming along for the ride.

Readers: I thank every single one of you who takes a chance on an independently published book. You have no idea how much it means to those of us who are following their dreams.

Callista: We're soul family separated halfway across the world. I can't even thank you enough for the encouragement you have given me from the beginning. The amount of times you pushed me to forget the noise and write what I want, it's a debt I will forever repay. I'm so grateful we're doing this crazy thing side by side.

Lyra: The little devil always in my brain. Thank you for understanding that fun part of my brain that not many do.

Em: My best friend, my always number one fan. Thank you for doing life with me, so we have crazy stories I can write about. You and me, forever and always.

Hive—Car, Murs, Sarah & Tay: My chaotic weird stars. You all keep my life interesting. Thank you for normalising the fact we all have figments of our imaginations living in our brains that we're trying to make pay rent. It's an absolute joy being a part of this little constellation.

Mum: Thank you for dealing with this whole chaos demon that is your child. I know I can be a pain. And thank you for promoting my books to every random person you have the opportunity to, despite them being "a little bit raunchy".

Little bro: You always know when to give me caffeine and fill up my water bottle. Thanks for keeping me functioning, and I'm sorry for scarring your ears when you hear me talk about the contents of this book.

My betas: Thank you for taking a snippet out of your life to taste test this debauchery and bring hype to an exhausted author.

The Heathens & Seventh Circle: You are the best group of people I have ever met. We have created the most encouraging, open community, and you all have kept me on my dream path. I enjoy every moment with all of you.

Also By Cassandra B. Andreucci

OTHER SIDE SERIES

Betrayer of Blood

VICIOUS GAMES SERIES

Dark Siren

WANT MORE?

ENTER THE WORLD OF CHAOS
SCAN THE QR CODE BELOW

Made in United States
North Haven, CT
25 March 2025

67242510R00276